TATTERED LACE

✹✹✹

SUZANNE GRANT

Published in the United States

Author: Suzanne Grant

ISBN-13: 978-0-984015429

Version 1.0

This is a work of fiction. All characters and events in this novel were created by the author and are purely fictitious. If you think you are portrayed on these pages, please be assured that you are not.

suzannegrant.com

For my amazing sons—Jeremy and Ian—
who have truly blessed my life.
And for my wonderful parents—Bill and Shirley—
who gifted me a rich childhood amidst the
wonder and beauty of
Central Oregon's High Desert.

✳ ✳ ✳

My grandfather Mason Grant was born, lived, and died on Oregon's High Desert. Before his death, he recorded a tape on which he documented his growing-up years there. One of his memories was of the Sheepshooters' War—a bloody, unlawful scuffle between the cattle ranchers and those who raised sheep. His reminiscences piqued my interest. Thanks to his tape, materials provided by Tim and Marcia Clark-McKitrick, and the wonders of the internet, I learned about a life-altering event in Central Oregon history. I'm passing my learning on in the pages of *Tattered Lace*. I hope you enjoy learning about it, too.

CHAPTER 1

She blew in with the wind, an icy, cutting north wind that pierced to the bone. Frigid gusts of dry air blasted across the barren fields, sliced through her, and moved on, their passing but an annoyance. Standing still and silent in a lightweight jacket and faded jeans, Lizzy stared south into the sagebrush and juniper covered hills.

If not for the rolling turmoil of gray clouds, life would have appeared frozen. For long minutes she stood there, arms stiff at her sides, head held high, baring her soul to the vast open space. In her own way, Lizzy communed with those silent hills, a plea for understanding and relief. A plea for answers.

Finally, she blinked and shook away the ghosts, then rubbed at the chill on her arms. She turned and glanced at a red SUV. A furry face peeked out through the window. Lizzy's lips curved into a smile as she opened the door and scooped the small cat into her arms. It cowered into her, and she wrapped her arms around it to comfort it and protect it from the biting wind.

Her gaze trailed to the clapboard farmhouse that stood silent and desolate apart from a few skeletal trees whose branches writhed in the winter wind. A whimper escaped her lips to join the wind's mournful wailing.

Stiffening her back, Lizzy gulped and stepped resolutely toward the weathered dwelling. At the front porch, she paused, her eyes gliding over the faded remains of something that was once charged with emotion and energy. Now it was but a shell of its former self—old, dead, and lifeless except for the memories that swirled around the loose boards and grimy windows.

Age-old wood creaked and complained as she climbed the steps and approached the front door. Lizzy adjusted the cat in her arms, grasped the battered doorknob, and tried to turn it. It resisted. Her hand slid into her pocket to retrieve a key, then halted when it brushed against aged paper.

Emotions engulfed her, heavy, pummeling her with their power, tearing at her heart. She jerked the key from her jacket pocket and jabbed it into the rust-encrusted keyhole. A forceful flick of her wrist and the door popped open to a wave of cold, musty air. Her stomach heaved. Pain blossomed between her brows. Inhaling deeply, she entered the room and closed the door.

Dead air pressed in on her as she stood in the spacious kitchen that was once alive with inviting sounds and smells, voices and laughter. Light filtering in through the windows left the room dark and dank. Lace curtains hung dingy and listless in a world encased in layers of russet dust.

With the cat clutched to her chest, Lizzy touched those curtains, fingering the grimy, tattered threads and seeing the flash of a silver shuttle and the battered hands that had woven those fragile threads into once lovely lace.

She swallowed at the burning in her throat and stepped into the next room. The ancient oak table still dominated the dining area, supported by its claw feet, a sentinel of chairs standing neatly around it. A plastic-shrouded couch sagged against the west wall, and two rocking chairs sat forlorn and empty in front of a cold red rock fireplace flanked by a cuckoo clock strewn with spider webs.

Lizzy eyed the silent clock, willing it to speak—a tick, a twitter—anything to bring life back into the death surrounding her. She sighed and touched a rocker, running her fingers over its well-worn smoothness, entranced by the appearance of the lovely dark wood that had survived beneath the layers of dirt.

Tears welled in her eyes to leak down her cheeks, and she sank into the dusty comfort of the chair. One hand slid over the cat's soft fur. The other trailed into her pocket to caress the familiar folds of a letter. It had brought her back here, a search for answers now veiled by years of neglect and decay.

She thought of those lost years—her heart heavy with their loss—as she rocked back and forth, back and forth, wallowing in the knowledge that she was twenty plus years too late.

Time passed, and a cache of tears coursed down her cheeks onto the now sleeping cat, the mesmerizing beat of the rocking chair having lulled them both with its soothing rhythm. At one time the tiny wooden bird would have popped out of its home on the wall to warn them that afternoon was fading fast, and it would soon be dark outside. Now all was silent except for the creaking cadence of the rocker and the howling of the wind.

Soon, Lizzy promised herself as she gazed at the tattered remnants surrounding her. *Soon she'd have her answers.*

❀ ❀ ❀

If Sam had known what lay ahead, chances are he would've listened to that nagging inner voice, the one that was telling him to leave it be. The premonitions were certainly there, tiny warnings pulsing through his body, prodding his heart and making his nerves twitch—familiar messages that he'd lost touch with long ago. To him, they were only annoyances, ones that he chose to ignore.

More pressing was the irritation that churned in his gut. It started as a tiny seed, but as he sat in his truck contemplating his next move, he felt it take root and blossom into a potent anger, his head pounding with its force. It was more than this current incident; its roots were long and stretched back a quarter century. He chose to ignore that, too.

Instead, Sam focused on what he needed to do right now. The fact that he didn't want to deal with it didn't matter. For him, it all came down to the issue of responsibility. In this case, it was his.

So he tugged his hat down over his ears and his collar up around his neck, then reached beneath the seat to retrieve the box of shells he kept there. Next he unzipped the gun from its case, loaded two shells into its barrel, and slammed it shut, the harsh click punctuating the silence.

Finally, he stepped from the warm cab and marched off into the frosty night, a multitude of memories held at bay and a loaded shotgun clutched in his gloved hand.

❀ ❀ ❀

A sudden sound awakened Lizzy. She jerked forward in the rocker, searching the darkness for its source. Movement in her lap made her clutch her cat Sid tightly. Blood surged through her veins as she struggled to clear the haze from her brain. Though barely discernible, the sound continued—the muffled tread of footsteps from outside.

As she shook at the mental fog, her memory slipped in. Apprehension followed, then fear. She hadn't told anyone where she'd be, so why would someone be outside this empty and long forgotten farmhouse, a house that sat beside an old muddy, rutted road in the middle of nowhere?

Unless, of course, that someone's goal had been to lure her here.

Ever so slowly, she rose. Her trembling legs, stiff from sitting in the frigid dampness, complained. She flexed them to get the blood flowing and struggled to orient herself in the utter darkness. The noise moved to the kitchen door; had she remembered to lock it?

Her answer was the click of the doorknob and the squeak of rusty hinges. Vacillating rays of light infused themselves into her world to provide a muted view of the room. Her heart pounding in her throat, she searched for a hiding place. The slow, soft whisper of someone moving cautiously and quietly taunted her.

At last, she broke free from her frozen state and flew to a far corner of the room. With Sid clasped to her chest, she crouched down between the couch and the wall and became one with the shadows.

The footsteps grew nearer, then stopped. A beam of light hesitantly circled the room, passed over her hiding place, and moved on to the fireplace and the silent cuckoo clock before it settled. Sid was restless, wiggling and fighting the tight hold Lizzy had on his lithe body.

Several more footsteps were followed by the creaking of a rocker. Her breath hitched. Would he notice the disturbed dust? She watched in horror as the beam of light trailed along the floor to her corner.

Unable to hold onto the squirming cat any longer, Lizzy released her grip, and Sid leaped away from her. A startled oath followed, deep and terse. Without the cat's comfort, Lizzy's limbs shook harder than the Quaking Aspens that had once dotted the backyard.

When he spoke, irritation crackled in his voice. "I know you're back there. If I have to come over there and pull you out, you're not gonna like it."

Lizzy sucked air, struggling to steady her frazzled nerves. Who was standing there? She tugged her mind back from a world of frightening possibilities. Instead, she clamped her chattering teeth together and prayed that the man behind the threat was as unfamiliar to her as was his alarmingly gruff voice.

"This is your last chance," he growled.

Out of options, Lizzy forced a mask of confident defiance onto her face, then grabbed onto the edge of the couch and pulled herself out of her hiding place. Her legs were mush—useless—so she balanced on the couch's armrest, her head held high, glaring defiantly into the beam of light. Seconds passed while she battled the blinding rays.

He broke the silence. "What are *you* doing here?"

Prickles danced up her spine. He knew who she was. She grappled for a familiar face to put with the hostile voice. None came.

"A more appropriate question might be what are *you* doing here? This house and the land surrounding it belong to me. You can't say that, can you?" Though tethered by fear, her voice was clear and forceful.

"Depends on how you look at it. Most likely, it's more mine than yours now since I'm the one's been taking care of it and chasing away trespassers before they cart off *your* belongings." Resentment clung to his assertion.

"Who are you?" Lizzy demanded, squinting into the shaft of light, her curiosity overtaking her fear.

The beam lifted to the ceiling. Lizzy's stomach lurched. She grabbed it and fought to still it as she stared at a man whose features were all too familiar—a man whose dangling shotgun was aimed directly at her!

He was Sam Craig, a man she'd never forget, though God knows she'd tried. More than twenty years had passed since she'd seen him, yet he still emitted that same aura of self-confidence and aloofness that he had so many years before. Only now there was something different about him, something that slithered across the room to wrap itself around her body and zap her strength.

Though his face was partially shadowed by the cowboy hat he wore low on his forehead, she could discern eyes that had once glowed with the promise of life were now, barring a few errant sparks of anger, listless. The lean, angular lines of early adulthood were replaced by the weathered creases of middle age.

Lizzy studied this man who she had once called friend and wondered what had transpired during those years. Had guilt eaten away at him and eventually claimed his soul? He appeared to be as agitated by her presence as she by his.

"Well, what are you doing here?" he uttered.

Lizzy had come to this remote Oregon oasis for solitude and resolution. Yes, she was seeking a place to escape from the fiasco her life had become. But she was also here to sort through the shambles she'd raced from years ago, to see if some minute piece of it could be salvaged. It was too little, too late, but at least she was now making the effort to deal with it.

And here he was—the man who held much of the blame for the whole destructive mess—intruding into her world and demanding answers she had no intention to share with anyone, especially him.

"Since this house belongs to me, I don't have to explain to you or anyone else why I'm here. Though I never asked you to, I appreciate you keeping an eye on it. But I'm here now, so you can wash your hands of it and forget you even saw me." She glared at him, hoping he saw the fury reeling through her. "Leave . . . and take your gun with you!"

The gun barrel dropped, but still he studied her, as if struggling with what to do next. Several tense moments later, he spoke, his voice gruff, little more than a whisper. "If I leave, it'll be dark in here. You have some wood? I'll start a fire."

Yes, Lizzy wanted to say. But her trust in him had been shattered in another lifetime. "Just go," she demanded.

He set his jaw, and she recognized it for what it was: he'd always needed to be the one in control.

"Please," she added, her own control fading fast. She disliked pleading, but she wanted him gone.

Without another word, he huffed and stomped from the room, leaving her alone and trembling in the frigid darkness.

The slamming of the kitchen door jarred her. He was right, of course. If she stayed, she needed heat. The rest of it could wait. But thinking through the furor of questions swirling inside her head was difficult. She breathed deeply and swallowed the rampant emotions begging to burst from her chest, then retrieved the keys from her pocket and stepped cautiously toward the door, arms out to feel her way through the suffocating blackness.

Familiarity soon led her to the front door. There she froze, a frightened bunny, staring into the dark. The roughness of peeling paint scratched her fingertips as they inched down to the doorknob.

What if Sam was still out there, and if not him, then someone else? This house was supposed to be her safe haven, at least for now. She needed time to settle in before she could move forward in her search for answers. Not now. Please, not now.

"Buck up," she quietly stormed. "You're not gonna sit here in the dark and freeze to death."

Lizzy turned the knob, cracked the door, and peered into a sea of black. If someone was out there, he was as blinded by the lack of light as she. She pushed the door open and vigilantly made her way to her Explorer, her heart beating loud enough to silence any mysterious noises.

Headlight beams soon flooded the deserted farmyard. The wind had died, but a bitter cold had settled in, and a shiny layer of frost now dusted this outside world. Lizzy examined the smudgy fringes that faded into darkness, then expelled the breath she'd been holding.

"See, no boogie men tonight," she muttered as she stepped to the rear of the vehicle. She reached inside and drew out a bulging cardboard box. Alert to the slightest noise or movement, she lifted it, hurried up the steps, and deposited it in the kitchen. Several trips later, she and her possessions were safely stowed inside the locked house, and she set purposefully to work.

She lit candles and spread them around the two rooms. After opening the chimney vent, she stacked two pressed logs neatly in the fireplace and lit them. The logs caught fire quickly, and soon heat reached out to provide a warm haven in the area surrounding the leaping flames. Sid crept from the shadows to meow and rub against Lizzy's legs. Seeking comfort and reassurance, she stroked his silky fur before she searched for provisions for herself and her steadfast friend.

Fortunately, she unearthed two chipped saucers to hold Sid's food and water and a half-eaten Subway sandwich for herself. She pulled a dust-mottled chair close to the fire, settled into it, and gazed into the mesmerizing flames, halfheartedly nibbling on the stale sandwich and wondering what in the world she'd gotten herself into.

Things were not as they should be—at least, not as she'd imagined they'd be. Sam shouldn't be here. He'd betrayed them all before he turned his arrogant back on them and flew away. The mere sight of him after all of these years brought it all rushing back, all that she'd once held so dear, now lost forever. And here she sat, consumed with anger, hurt, and a paralyzing fear.

If she'd allowed her thoughts to tread that path, she'd have suspected he'd have returned to manage the family ranch—someone had to. But she didn't let herself think about Sam Craig, hadn't for twenty-five years. As far as she was concerned, he was dead, too.

"So why didn't you stay dead," she whispered into the stillness.

Lizzy reached into her pocket, pulled out the letter, and cradled it in her hands, running her thumbs over the smooth, yellowed paper, seeking comfort and the courage to remain here—the courage to make things right.

John had written it, a call for help that she'd ignored far too long. She should've been here to support him through his bad times, to stand beside him when he'd felt threatened. As his friend, she'd failed miserably. If she allowed it, the angst would eat a hole through what was left of her heart. Her return to the farm was a last ditch effort to prevent that from happening. She clung to the hope it offered. She *would* discover what had happened to John.

An hour passed and still she sat, the untouched sandwich in her lap. Sid lay stretched out next to the fire, surely dreaming of tasty mice scampering nearby.

Rather abruptly, he rose, stretched, and yawned. The sudden movement startled Lizzy. Her eyes darted to the dark periphery, then slowly scanned it, finally settling on the cat. As if to chastise her for being so silly, Sid meowed.

"Yeah? Well, if you knew the whole story, you'd be jumping at shadows, too. I think we're in way over our heads here, Sid," Lizzy mumbled as she stuffed the letter back into her pocket and rose to trail after her cat out the front door.

This time her feet slipped on the frost-slickened boards. She zipped her jacket against the biting cold and stretched her arms out to keep from falling, then shuffled to the steps.

Sid continued on into the yard—a quest for soft dirt—while Lizzy gazed up in wonder at a sky sprinkled liberally with twinkling stars. In the black High Desert sky, they surrounded her, enticing her to touch them. Her hand reached up to trace a familiar constellation, connecting each tiny sparkle to form the Big Dipper.

She'd just reached the North Star when she felt it—that vague, but all too familiar, feeling. He was out there watching her!

She froze, her eyes searching into the darkness before they were drawn to the road that led into town. Try as she might, she couldn't see him, but she knew he was there. The knowledge of it left her weak. A burning shudder sliced through her, breaking the spell. After a final frantic search, she hurried back into the house, Sid at her feet.

Anxiety and fatigue battled within Lizzy. She stifled an overwhelming urge to crawl back into her Explorer and escape. "Not this time," she vowed. She owed it to John, and this time she would be here for him, even if she endangered her own life in the process.

Lizzy's sigh turned to a yawn; exhaustion was overtaking trepidation. She grabbed a sleeping bag from the heap in the middle of the kitchen floor, carried it to the couch, and pulled the plastic shroud aside. The sleeping bag unrolled into a makeshift bed on the musty, threadbare fabric.

Before she settled in for the night, she stacked two more logs on the fire, blew out the candles, and slipped out of her boots. Fully clothed, she cocooned herself inside the bag and rolled onto her side to watch the undulating flames.

Sid curled himself into the nest at her belly and hummed a soft purr, an antidote to Lizzy's pent-up emotions. Ever so slowly, Lizzy's muscles loosened. Her eyes drifted shut.

Suddenly, the purring ceased. Sid's head shot up, and his luminous eyes fastened on the window facing them. Lizzy tensed, too. She forced herself to lie still, to close her lids and keep them shut, as she listened to the scratching on the window.

She knew who was out there, felt his presence in every pore of her body. Yes, he was angry. But he was also curious. He'd waited until he was certain she'd be asleep. Then he'd crept down here like the sneak that he was to have another look, to make sure it was really her.

Well, look all you want, her mind screamed as she strained to keep her breathing steady, her body still, *because it is me, in the flesh. And I'm gonna find out what really happened to your little brother. So just take that and deal with it, Sam Craig. Then get your deceitful ass off my property, and don't ever come near me again.*

❋ ❋ ❋

After Sam slammed the farmhouse door shut, he stood still as a startled deer in the frozen silence. His heart rammed against his chest as though it might burst right through his skin and the layers of clothing he wore and shoot off into the darkness that stretched out before him—an endless void. He took several deep breaths, feeling their warmth fan his face, then flicked off the flashlight, shifted the gun to his right hand, and stepped cautiously down the porch steps and into the darkness.

Night's icy covering closed in around him, wrapping him in obscurity. Sam welcomed it. He reeled from his encounter with Lizzy, some debilitating form of shock that had invaded his mind and body the moment she'd slid from the shadows. His brain was a muddled mess. He needed an even darker corner to think this thing through. To regain control

He didn't want her here. No doubt about it, Lizzy Stewart meant trouble. He knew it, a bug in his gut that gnawed at his innards, sounding alarms. What in the hell was she doing here after all of these years? He had to know. He had to protect himself . . . and all that he'd worked his butt off to accomplish during the past ten years—and his father before him, and his father.

Behind him, the farmhouse door clicked. Sam froze in his tracks. He turned to search through the murkiness, to listen for the sound of a car engine—a signal that Lizzy's departure would be as sudden as her arrival. There was none.

Instead, bright beams suddenly spotlighted the isolated farmyard and filtered towards him. He shifted into the shadows to watch Lizzy haul load after load from her SUV into the house, the trepidation in his gut growing stronger with each load. Lizzy had the look of someone who aimed to stay awhile.

Then darkness engulfed him. An intense chill shivered through his body and settled into the deep ache of loss. It didn't sit well. He shook away the discomfort and turned to make his way back to the solace of his truck—not an easy task. At one time, the muddy, rutted road had been a thoroughfare, humming with motors from cars and trucks that carried people in and out of the rolling hills and to and from the small towns that lay beyond. Now it was pushing it to call it a road.

Sam had been on his way home to the neighboring ranch when he'd noticed the vehicle parked in the driveway of the old farmhouse. Intent on surprising the trespasser before he ousted him, he'd parked quite a stretch down the battered road. Now he navigated that distance in the darkness on foot, barely aware of his stumbling feet. He was too busy waging a losing battle with his normally well-checked emotions. He was irritated, and now that he was past the initial shock, he was working up a first-class anger, one aimed at Lizzy.

What right did she have to waltz back in here and expect to take up where she'd left off, as if a shit load of living hadn't transpired while she was off doing her thing. Life here, as she'd known it, had vanished, and in Sam's mind, she shouldered a whole lot of the responsibility for that.

By the time he reached his truck, Sam was fuming. He

jammed the shotgun into its case—shells and all—and hauled himself into the cab to glare at the farmhouse. Flickering light softened several windows, and smoke puffed into the clear night air from the chimney, which only added to his irritation; she'd started her own damn fire.

He turned the key in the ignition, and the engine purred to life. Whether he did it to warm up the frigid air in the cab to a tolerable temperature or because his instincts told him to get out of there while he could, he wasn't sure. Whatever the case, he continued to sit, his gloved fingers drumming on the steering wheel and his mind besieged by too many memories.

He pictured the Lizzy of thirty-some years before, dark from the sun's rays and all arms and legs. She must've been about eight years old the first time he saw her. It was as if he were watching it happen—the two of them sitting on the front porch on that sweltering June day. A frosty glass of lemonade is in his hand, and he's doing his utmost to focus on his conversation with Con and Dottie Stewart, Lizzy's grandparents. Lizzy's in a rocking chair, shelling a pile of peas and staring at him with those unnerving dark eyes of hers, her hands opening pods and scooping out peas, sometimes flicking over to stroke the cat that shares her chair. Her unsettling eyes never once drift from Sam's face.

Sam squelched the unsettling vision, then rubbed at the hunger in his gut. There was something mesmerizing about Lizzy, something that drew him towards her. It had always been so. *This time it will be different,* he told himself. This time he would tread cautiously and be on guard. This time he would keep his distance.

Movement in the yard below caught his attention. Lizzy stood in the wisps of light that filtered onto the porch, her face turned up to the sky and its endless carpet of stars. She reached up as if to catch one in the palm of her hand, then turned towards him, and he felt her unsettling presence as if she were sitting in the seat next to him. It infuriated him that she had this effect on him.

In truth, it didn't make sense. She'd been joined at the hip to his younger brother John, not to him. Sam had always felt like an outsider around the two of them—their knowing looks and unspoken language.

Sam shook the images from his head. His hands gripped the steering wheel tightly, palms pressed into its leather cover as if it might absorb some of the energy buzzing inside him. He tried to wet his dry lips with his tongue, but worry had sucked his mouth dry and left it feeling like parchment. And still he sat there.

Eventually, the suffocating stream of hot air pouring from the vents penetrated his ponderings, and he switched the motor off. Lizzy was back inside the house, and the light from inside had dimmed, an indication that she was settling in for the night.

Sam sat in the gloomy silence, his eyes glued to the farmhouse. He felt its pull. It was a feeling from times long past, one that he had no wish to explore. Yet, against his better judgment, he finally succumbed to the overwhelming urge to climb out of his warm truck and into the frozen night to walk that rutted road to the decaying farmhouse.

The window was so encrusted with dirt that he had to wipe it off with his handkerchief before he could see through it. There she was, curled up in a sleeping bag on the drooping couch with the cat, facing the flames that glowed in the fireplace. Though parts of her were shadowed, he could see that her eyes were closed, and her face held the peace of deep sleep.

For several minutes he stood and watched her as she slept— watched the sleeping bag rise and fall in rhythm to her breathing, mesmerized by the lights and shadows as they danced across the contours of her face.

He wasn't sure why he was hesitant to leave her, but finally, he did. He walked back to his truck and drove off into the night, wondering what he was going to do about her.

He'd given up his career and a whole lot more these past ten years. He wouldn't give that up without a fight. Yes, in the end, he knew he'd do whatever it took to protect the life he'd worked so hard to establish.

"So stay the hell out of my way, Lizzy Stewart," he uttered defiantly.

CHAPTER 2

Sam slumped in his saddle, hunched into the turned-up collar of his down jacket. He'd slept fitfully, tossing and turning and dreaming of times that were best forgotten. Usually, he could dump things onto the back forty and deal with them when it was convenient—or not deal with them. He had Lizzy to thank for this upheaval. Her presence opened doors he'd shut and locked a long time ago, doors he didn't ever want to reopen. Like a pestering tune, Lizzy was stuck in his head—wouldn't get out. This morning he was taking a giant step toward getting her out; he was going to the farm to have a friendly chat with Lizzy, one that would hopefully ease his mind.

Shaking at that dreamlike state somewhere between sleep and wakefulness, he'd ridden from the ranch and into the icy, predawn on the back of his favorite horse Ranger. The lack of light didn't worry him. He knew his ranch like he knew each ache and pain in his forty-nine-years-old body, and a few stars had still twinkled to provide a hint of light. A thick layer of frost formed a slick mantle over the land, so Sam had set a slow pace. Ranger's steady, rhythmic gait and the familiarity of it all had been calming, slowly unwinding the tangle in his brain. By the time a fiery glow stretched across the eastern horizon and the hill overlooking the farmhouse came into view, he was well on his way to convincing himself that his problems would soon be only an unpleasant memory—one he'd tear into tiny pieces and toss in with the trash.

Sensing sudden movement to his left, Sam's body stiffened; his eyes searched the murky dawn. A rider on a chestnut quarter horse trotted towards him. The set of his shoulders, the easy rocking in the saddle, the beat-up Stetson worn low on his forehead were all too familiar.

The relaxing effects of Sam's morning ride faded. "Shit!" he muttered. What was Chet doing out here at this time of the morning?

Though Sam and Chet had grown up together on the Craig ranch, Sam wasn't above avoiding Chet's company, especially when his patience was stretched as thin as it was this morning. Chet was a talker, and Sam was in no mood to listen.

It was typical of Chet that he took his own sweet time. Sam

reined in Ranger and waited, chewing on the inside of his jaw and telling himself to calm down; tearing into Chet wouldn't help matters. By the time Chet pulled up beside him, Sam had gained a slight edge over his frustration.

"Mornin'," Chet muttered from the side of his mouth, tipping his head in Sam's direction. A stream of chewing tobacco spewed out the other side.

"Mornin'," Sam muttered, fearful that if he said much more it would be to order Chet to hightail his lazy butt back to the ranch and to stay away from the farm.

For several long moments, the two men eyed each other warily. Chet finally spit a plug of chew onto the frosty ground at Ranger's feet and broke the silence. "You're out here early."

"I was thinking the same about you," Sam prodded, narrowing his eyes to study what he could see of Chet's face. Fact was, Chet wasn't one to climb out of bed before he had to. "Why're you here?"

Chet shrugged. "I was drivin' home. Saw the car at the farm down there and got to wonderin' about it. Decided to ride over and have a look. Check things out myself. That why you're here?"

Sam nodded curtly. "More or less. So . . . you were out all night then?"

"More or less." Chet drawled. "Why? You gonna play daddy and ground me for takin' a night off to have some fun?" A scornful snort punctuated his remark.

Sam swallowed a retort and let it slide. He squeezed Ranger forward toward the crest of the hill. Chet followed. The sun peeked over the tops of the junipers in the distance, but the temperature hadn't risen with it. Snow-capped peaks to the west blushed in the early morning rays. A shiver sliced across Sam's shoulders and slithered down into the layers of clothing he wore.

The two men sat in silence, eyes glued to the scene below. Except for the red SUV in the driveway, the farm looked as desolate and deserted as it had during the last two decades. No smoke puffed from the chimney, no light shown through the windows, and there was no evidence that someone had been in the yard.

"You know who it is?" Chet finally asked, his eyes still on the farmyard.

"Yep," Sam replied, hopeful Chet would leave it at that. Truth be told, he suspected that Chet already knew who was down there, a thought that only fueled his irritation.

Chet eyed Sam as if he expected him to elaborate. When that didn't happen, he nudged: "So, you gonna make me go down there and find out?"

Sam thought it might be worth seeing, but he'd probably take the brunt of it himself. "It's Lizzy," he muttered, careful to keep his voice neutral.

"Lizzy? Damn! Are you shittin' me?" Chet stared at Sam, eyes popping, mouth gaping.

A trickle of relief eased the mounting pressure throbbing in Sam's head; so Chet hadn't known Lizzy was back. He really had spent the night out carousing. "Nope," Sam confirmed.

"You know what she's doin' here?" Chet probed.

"Nope." Sam was ready to drop the subject and move on to Chet heading back to the ranch, so he could work on solving his problems.

But Chet wouldn't let it go. "So you got to thinkin' about what she's gonna do when she notices you've taken over her land, huh? That what's got you worried?"

Hell yes, he was worried. Sam worked his jaw, struggling to keep his tongue in check. He studied the neglected fields surrounding him. Each spring they sprouted into a sea of green that, with midsummer's intense heat, ripened to a golden yellow and filled with seed. Though it fell far short of Con Stewart's handiwork, it was still prime grazing land, and Sam relied on it to feed his growing herd throughout the summer and early fall.

And that wasn't the worst of it: his cattle needed Lizzy's water. Con had been a wizard when he'd gone out to hunt water with his witching stick. He could witch a spring out of a slab of basalt and tell you exactly how far you had to drill to find it. Thanks to Con's supernatural talent, the Stewart farm was riddled with springs and wells, enough to service Sam's cattle and a whole lot more. If only he could make that claim about his ranch. Many of his springs were going dry. If he didn't have access to Lizzy's water, he'd need to make some changes—expensive ones.

He rubbed at the pounding between his brows. At the moment a sizeable number of his cattle were settled comfortably on Lizzy's land, and he had every intention to keep them there. Only now there was an obstacle sitting smack dab in his path—Lizzy.

Sam knew she had inherited the farm. But what the hell, she wasn't here. He was the one who took care of the place. Frustrated by Lizzy's absence and apathy, her attorney, old Gus Woolridge, had pretty much turned the farm over to Sam.

Chet didn't need Sam to tell him all that; he knew. Of course, Chet wouldn't be above rubbing it in. "I'm planning to talk with her about it," Sam finally confirmed.

"I'll just bet you are," Chet snorted. "You might want to do it soon. There's a small herd that likes to hang out in that farmyard down there. If she wakes up and finds a bunch of cows gettin' cozy in her front yard, she's gonna be spittin' venom. And for once, it ain't gonna be aimed at me."

Thank God that wasn't the case this morning. Sam ignored Chet and instead turned his attention to the surrounding countryside to inspect each slope and gully for any sign of movement. The cups of coffee he'd chugged before setting out on this foolhardy venture churned in his gut. His current dilemma had his insides wiggling and twisting like an irritated rattler. There was no way around it; he had to hammer it out face to face with Lizzy. But he'd need an opportune moment. Otherwise, it could blow up in his face.

"Hot damn! I thought she was gone for good," Chet exclaimed.

"Guess not," Sam muttered, focused more on where his cattle might be wandering than on Chet's small talk.

"She sure as hell was a looker. I know she was John's, but she was well worth lookin' at. Course, I ain't tellin' you nothin' you don't already know, am I?"

Heat flooded Sam's face. He set his jaw and shifted uncomfortably in his saddle, refusing to be drawn into Chet's machinations. It left a bitter taste in his mouth.

Chet wouldn't let it rest. "You seen her?"

"Yep," Sam growled, wondering if there was a stray piece of duct tape stuffed inside one of his pockets to slap over Chet's wayward mouth.

"She still worth lookin' at?"

Sam's heart pounded in his chest. "Didn't notice," he hissed through clenched teeth.

"Hmmm . . . might be I should mosey on down there and take a look."

Sam knew Chet was bluffing. Still, he turned to study him. In truth, he was tempted to wander on down himself, to peek through the window and see how she'd fared through the night—to see if she was preparing to pack those boxes back inside her car and vanish again. But she'd be furious if she caught him snooping around.

"Only if you're interested in losing a couple of teeth," he warned Chet.

"That don't worry me none." Chet harrumphed. "Her tongue's her weapon of choice, that and those weird eyes. Damn, she had a smart mouth on her. So cool and composed, but what came out of that mouth. . . . Never think it from lookin' at her."

Chet was right about that. Lizzy did have a way with words. She didn't get upset or throw a tizzy fit or yell like a normal woman. No, she just stared right into you with those unnerving eyes.

Sam surveyed the frigid landscape one last time, then exhaled, satisfied that his cattle were well away from the farmhouse. Relief relaxed him into his saddle. With luck, he'd get rid of Chet and have that chat with Lizzy this morning, before she discovered that he'd helped himself to her land. He eyed Chet. "Don't you have something you should be doing back at the ranch?"

Chet shot him a sardonic smile and chuckled. "Not if you're plannin' to talk with Lizzy. I ain't gonna miss that."

Frustration eating at him, Sam shifted his gaze to the scene below. Experience had taught him that the more he pushed up against Chet, the more determined Chet became. So he conceded and settled in to wait with Chet at the top of the hill in the frozen stillness of early morning, staring at the deserted farmyard and wishing Lizzy would make her appearance, so he could get this ordeal over and get on with his day. With luck, Chet would keep his big mouth shut until then.

"You know, seein' that barn down there reminds me of when John fell off Old Dozer, remember that?" Chet pestered.

Sam ignored him. He wanted to leave the past right where it was and not dredge up a slew of memories that didn't do a whole lot of good to anyone.

As usual, Chet didn't need an answer. "We were on the porch with old Con Stewart that afternoon. It was hot as hell, and Dottie brought us some iced tea and homemade snicker doodles. Con was goin' on about how the Democrats were takin' over the country and how we all had to stick together and keep Republicans in office. We told John to stay with us, but he never did do what we told him to. No. He wandered off down the road to that barn down there. You remember?"

Sam remembered all right. John was about ten at the time, old enough that he should've been able to stay out of trouble. But John was always into mischief. On that particular day, he'd ended up at the maze of livestock pens that flowed from the barn's back doors. Con housed his prized bull in one of those pens. As a general rule, Old Dozer didn't put much effort into anything other than tail-swatting flies. John had come face-to-face with the snoozing bull, eyeballing him through a rickety split-rail fence that had withstood several generations of Stewart livestock.

Chet spit a wad of crud and continued to rehash the past. "I would've paid good money to see John ride Old Dozer. He must've thought he was one hell of a bull rider when he crawled on that bony back. Kind of hard to believe Old Dozer had it in him, but John swore the second his butt hit that bull's back, Old Dozer came to life, twistin' and turnin' and kickin'. Must've been a sight to see, especially when he plowed through that fence and took off." Chet ended with an appreciative chuckle.

"Yep, that must've been a sight, especially when he brushed John off and cracked his leg in two places," Sam barked, hoping it would shut Chet up. Thank goodness Lizzy had been in the barn. She'd heard John's screams and rushed to help him.

Chet glanced his way and rambled on. "And to think we didn't have a clue what was goin' on down there. Not until Lizzy came racin' up from the barn howlin' like a calf that's lost its mama."

Sam pictured Lizzy tearing up the road towards the farmhouse, her arms pumping and her skinny legs whipping out in front of her, screaming loud enough that Dottie rushed from the house to see what was going on.

"Then John spent that whole summer with a cast on his leg—pretty harsh punishment for a kid who couldn't sit still for even a five-minute stretch. I always wondered how he got through that." Chet's expression turned pensive. He seemed to mull something over before he added, "You know, sometimes I wonder if things would've turned out a whole lot different if John hadn't climbed on that old bull's back that day."

Even more curious to Sam was the unique bond cemented between John and Lizzy on that scorching summer afternoon. Sam had never understood it, and he didn't want to ponder it now.

But once Chet hooked a trout, he worked it until it was plum exhausted. "Old Dozer sure made his mark that day. That old geezer romped his way through a good portion of the heifers in the lower pasture before Con and I got him corralled." Chet paused to have himself a hearty laugh. "Got himself a new nickname, too—Old Casanova."

Even in his current state—his body bundled taut with nervous energy—Sam let himself smile at the memory of that lazy old bull having his way with a herd of willing young heifers.

"Remember when you and John and me used to play in that yard down there? Damn, we got ourselves into some trouble—chasin' Dottie's chickens until they made that awful squawkin' racket and gave us away. Buildin' forts in her flower gardens. My mom'd stop by the farm on the way to town. Then she'd get to talkin' with Dottie and forget about us."

Sam did remember. He didn't know if it was the number of years accumulating under his belt or what, but life sure seemed a whole lot sweeter back then. Ever so slowly, his thought meandered back to a time when shimmering fields of wheat surrounded the farmhouse and the yard was alive with a flock of scavenging chickens, a couple of mangy mutts, and the cloying scent of sweet peas. Of course, that stretched way back before Lizzy when he must've been about ten years old or so, when his mother was still a part of their lives. For the first time in years, he perused that past. It left an ache deep down inside him, one he couldn't stifle.

Rather abruptly, movement in the yard below silenced Sam's ruminations.

"Why do you think she's here?" Chet's voice was a splash of

ice water.

Sam shook his head to erase a heavy, lethargic haze. He stared down at the woman who appeared to be searching the ground for something. Like a summer hailstorm on a golden, ripe wheat field, she'd returned to wreak havoc to the comfortable routine to which he'd become accustomed. The last thing he'd expected was for her to show up at the farm to reclaim it—or God forbid, to sell it to some stranger! Bile lodged in his throat at the thought, bitter and burning.

To him Lizzy Stewart was history—dead. So why was she here? Until he had an answer to that nagging question, Sam's life would be an intolerable mess.

With those disquieting thoughts, Sam glared at the woman whose eyes now held his. He felt her presence—the pain, the anger, the fear—and for a moment, he understood. Then he shuddered, ousting the disturbing trance, while Chet continued his one-sided conversation.

"If you're thinkin' about ridin' down there, you might want to rethink that plan. She looks to be in a mighty foul mood this mornin', and Lizzy in a foul mood'll be something' to reckon with."

Should he ride down the hill and confront her? The prospect of it being over and done with—of knowing the outcome—appealed to him. But Sam's instincts told him to cut his losses and let it go for now. To come up with another plan.

Lost in a mental debate on the pros and cons, his eyes caught a flash of russet stirring down by the old barn. His breath hitched; his stomach heaved.

Chet whistled, long and slow. "Hot damn! That could spell trouble."

As Sam watched helplessly, about twenty head of his cattle wandered from behind the barn. They appeared to be regrouping for an amble down the road to the farmhouse.

"Looks like it's out of your hands now," Chet jabbed.

CHAPTER 3

A cold, moist nose nudged Lizzy. She struggled through the disorienting haze to identify the annoying wetness. For the first time in months, she'd enjoyed the sleep of the dead, free of disturbing dreams and anxious deliberation. She lolled in the alluring pull of that blessed relief—numbing sleep.

The persistent stream of plaintive "meows" prodded Lizzy's eyes open. Hers met those of her perturbed friend, and she reached out to calm the cat, speaking words of reassurance. "Come on, Sid. I need you to hold it together. You fall apart on me, and we'll never find out what happened to John."

A vision of John flashed before her—blue eyes filled with pain. It ignited a familiar hollow feeling. "I *will* hold it together," she muttered, wanting to remember John's eyes as they had once been: filled with life's promises. The possibility that he hadn't taken his own life now dangled before her. No way would she let it sneak away.

"I *will* know the truth," she added so emphatically that Sid flinched. Lizzy stroked a finger along the soft underside of his neck. "Don't worry; I'm not going to drag you into this. Your job is to hold down the fort."

The fort—such as it was. Her eyes trailed to the cold fireplace and on around the dismal room, and her heart sank. With resolve, she shrugged the misgivings aside. "Well, let's get to it," she announced to the watchful cat. "We don't have time to loll here in bed all day."

The sleeping bag was thrown aside, and she reached for her boots. Clouds puffed from her mouth with each breath, proof that the room was as frigid as it felt. Quickly, she stuffed her feet into the boots and stood to stretch the stiffness from her body, then grabbed her jacket as she passed by the mountain of boxes. Before she stepped past the kitchen door, she stuck her head out to inspect the countryside. Sid darted down the steps. Nothing appeared to be amiss, so Lizzy followed, shuffling gingerly on the slick boards.

A blanket of frost spread out as far as the eye could see, a clean white disguise that sparkled like diamonds in the early morning sun. Lizzy paused to marvel at its brilliance, then wondered if it might be later than she'd thought.

Scanning the overgrown yard, she stepped into it but was waylaid by numerous mounds scattered at her feet. Intrigued, she scraped the frost from one with the toe of her boot and bent to examine it. Sure enough, freshly frozen cow patties littered her yard.

Was someone housing their cattle on her land? If so, they wouldn't be thrilled when they discovered she now resided here and didn't intend to share her home with interlopers, even the four-legged kind.

Tiny prickles on her neck turned to shivers. She glanced furtively around at the surrounding fields and sagebrush-covered slopes while her hand trailed into her pocket to caress John's letter.

Two riders on horseback sat at the top of the hill, silhouettes against the vivid blue sky. One was Sam—she knew it like she'd always known when he was nearby—but who was the other person? The unexpected intrusion erased the serene beauty of the frosty morning.

Though she couldn't discern his face, she knew Sam was staring at her, studying her every movement, plotting his next move. He didn't want her here. Didn't want her standing on her own land. Didn't want to face the many repercussions from his past. Lizzy refused to be intimidated. She shuttered the pangs of paralyzing fear and glared at him until the two of them reined their horses around and galloped off in the direction of the Craig ranch.

Why were they here . . . on *her* property? Would this be Sam's strategy: to subject her to a "cat and mouse" game until he wore her down to the point that she felt too frightened and vulnerable to remain here? Was he hoping to chase her away again?

"Not this time!" she yelled at his retreating back. "I can play this game, too." With that, she huffed and said a silent plea that she spoke the truth.

Lizzy fought the desire to dash back into the house. Instead, she met Sid at the steps, and they entered their new home together, leisurely, as though they hadn't a care in the world. Once inside, she locked the door securely against the outside world, her racing heart testament to the fear sitting heavy in her gut.

She resolutely stepped to the sink and turned the faucet. No water gushed out, no gurgling sound—nothing. Reality smothered her with its honesty. She had envisioned the house as it once was, clean and homey and full of enticing smells. The truth was that no one had lived in this house during the twenty-five years she'd been gone. Neglect had taken its toll and left very little. This real world was one of dirt, grime, and cobwebs. They were everywhere, concealing whatever might have survived of that past life.

With that thought, Lizzy froze, erratic word snippets churning through her caffeine-deprived brain. Her eyes darted around the room in speculation. What if something from the past was left here for her, concealed in a secret hiding place? One of John's many diversions was to leave notes scattered around for her to discover. Had he left something behind to explain his death, or maybe something that would explain the words in his letter?

Lizzy slipped the letter from her pocket and studied the familiar script—sloppily printed mismatched letters. John had never put the necessary effort into learning cursive. It was something she'd always chided him about—that his writing was beautiful to the ear but not the eye. She ran an index finger over the faded lines, seeking clarification. Clearly, the letter hadn't been written recently. But if he'd written it twenty-five years ago, why had she just received it? Was someone trying to lure her back here?

With angst settling into her like a bout of stomach flu, Lizzy returned the letter to her pocket and strode into the living room. Her gaze cautiously circled the room. It was a disheartening orbit; the room was a cracked and crumbling shell of its former self.

Beside the round oak table were the empty china hutch and sideboard, once home to her grandmother's many treasures—the crystal, china, and silver that had survived several generations. Another responsibility she'd walked away from, Lizzy reflected as, for the first time, she questioned the fate of her grandparents' many possessions.

Her grandfather's oak desk stood against the side wall, its top rolled neatly into place just as it always had been when she was a child. Curiosity drew her to it. Did John leave something here, knowing, should Lizzy take his summons to heart, she'd return to the farm first? Nervous flutters unsettled her as she rolled the top back to expose a series of empty compartments. She slowly ran her fingers along the back of each of them, her heart leaping when she felt a piece of paper. Carefully, she wriggled two fingertips around it and eased it out, inch by inch, from its hiding place.

Trembling with anticipation, she carried it to the window. It appeared to be a page ripped from a diary, only a date and a couple of sentences to record their origin: *April 24, 1964; It's done. Now I will live my dream.* It was penned in indigo ink, flowery letters that spoke of a woman's painstaking hand. Was it a page from a diary her grandmother had kept? No, Grandma hadn't had time to record her mundane life. When she wrote, it was with the intent to get it done as quickly as possible. Deciphering Grandma's scribbled script had always been a challenge.

But who then? John's mother? Prickly goose-bumps peppered her arms. When had John's mother died? Though Lizzy had never met her, as a child she'd invented an image of her that portrayed her as an elegant, sophisticated lady who loved beautiful things. Lizzy pictured her sitting at her spinet desk, forming meticulous letters with graceful, flowing lines.

The image faded. Why would one page from John's mother's diary be cloistered in Granddad's desk? John wouldn't leave a meaningless piece of paper for her to find, would he? But then, maybe John hadn't left it there.

Lizzy stuffed the paper back into the desk and closed the lid. There had to be something here. Her perusal of the room continued and landed on the bookcase that stood in the corner, its thick glass protecting several of her grandfather's precious books. Those books and the few chipped dishes and dented pots she'd uncovered in the kitchen the previous evening appeared to be the only personal items that had survived her absence.

Wasn't it odd, though, that only a few books remained in the bookcase? She walked to the leaded glass doors, opened them, and removed the books one at a time to flip through their pages. As she opened the last book, something dropped from it to land on the floor at her feet. It appeared to be a small photograph. Lizzy retrieved it and squinted at the image.

Again, she made her way to the light filtering in through the grimy window. Sure enough, it was an old black-and-white photo of a young boy. He looked to be about ten years old, dark hair clipped short and a crooked smile highlighting his impish face. Lizzy studied it, fascinated by its familiarity. Who was he? The hair and smile were John's. But the eyes, they reminded her of someone else. Who? The answer tickled at the back of her mind, refusing to crystallize.

She turned the photo over and read *Summer of '41* in what was clearly her grandmother's scrawl. Obviously, it wasn't John; he wasn't even born in 1941. Perhaps it was a picture of his father as a young boy.

His father—J.D. Craig! The mere thought of that evil man prompted a tight knot to coil in the pit of her stomach, along with an overwhelming urge to lash out at him—with a bullwhip. She heaved a frustrated sigh and turned her thoughts back to the matter at hand.

Three doors stood against the back wall. Lizzy slid the photo into her jacket pocket, then walked to the first door and opened it. Her grandparents had slept in this room. A wrought iron bed frame hogged space, its mattress encased in a sheet of plastic.

Sadness engulfed her, but she pressed on. John had left something here for her—an explanation for his actions. She knew it in the same way that she could sense a thunderstorm long before it struck. Even if he had taken his own life, he would've left a message for her, rationale for an act that was so inconceivable.

An oak wardrobe, her grandmother's dressing table, and an intricately carved chest of drawers took up the rest of the space, leaving little room to maneuver. Lizzy cautiously opened a drawer and then another until she had inspected them all. Empty.

Her mounting frustration gave way to determination, a need to find something—anything—that would provide answers. With renewed resolve, she stalked out of the gloomy room and opened the next door to glance through it into what would've been considered by today's standards a miniscule bathroom. She paused, drew a deep breath, and stared at the third door briefly before she backed away. If there was an illuminating tidbit in that room, it could wait.

The tiny strand of hope she'd managed to hold onto gradually slipped away. Determined to keep a firm grip on her resolve, she strode purposefully to the kitchen, grabbed several pressed logs, and carried them to the fireplace where she stacked two of the logs neatly in place and lit them with a match. Flames leapt up to entice her. She surrendered to the invitation and dropped onto the floor, crossing her legs in front of her, so she could lean into the heat.

Soon Sid appeared to rub his sleek, striped body against Lizzy's thigh. She stroked the curve of the cat's velvety neck, seeking reassurance from Sid as she voiced her frustration. "He did leave something here; I know it. This is the only place he could be sure I'd come."

A cold thought suddenly chilled her. What if someone had already searched the farmhouse, someone who had access to it, someone who was familiar with John's habits? Perhaps the letter in her pocket had been secreted away in this very house.

She'd give her diamond earrings for a cup of strong black coffee—even a couple of sips to take the edge off—but it was a lost cause, just like her search.

Her hopes shattered by her fruitless rummaging, Lizzy was now forced to initiate a new plan of action. But first she needed to take a trip into town, a dreaded task that loomed before her like a den of unpredictable and often lethal rattlesnakes. She didn't know how those who lived in the area felt about her return, but she suspected they hadn't spoken kindly of her departure. She wished she could say it didn't matter what they thought, but she knew it did.

Of more concern to her though were John's words. They claimed that Lizzy's life was in danger, too. She didn't want to believe that someone would hold enough of a grudge that they'd try to harm her, especially after a twenty-five year lapse. However, she'd learned in her forty-three years of living that one couldn't truly count on anything.

If what John had written was the actual, honest-to-God truth—the jury was still out on that—then her mere presence in the community might also make her a target. Perhaps that would be her new action plan: she'd be the bait to draw the truth out into the open.

It was only a matter of time before she'd know for sure, but time was something she didn't have much of—two months to be exact.

A faint bawling sound from outside interrupted Lizzy's ruminations. Irritation sprouted in her chest and pulsed in her forehead as she strode to the window and glared at the commotion taking place down the road near the rickety barn. A hefty herd of cows milled around, obviously congregating for a stroll down the road to her front door.

If she were closer, she knew she'd see the Craigs' *Diamond C* brand emblazoned on the rump of every single one of them. The Craigs had never let the fact that they didn't own it stop them from helping themselves to prime acreage.

"Things are gonna change around here, Sam Craig!" she growled as she stormed out the kitchen door.

CHAPTER 4

Sam's insides were tangled into a lead knot, one that reached up to lodge in his throat. He tried to swallow, but that knot was in the way. Beneath him, Ranger's muscular legs churned, kicking up clods of frozen mud as he galloped through the blinding rays of early dawn.

Sam pictured his chance of reconciliation with Lizzy spiral down the drain with each passing second. Cows were such irrational creatures. Out of the hundreds of acres on the farm, his had to pick the farmyard and appear while Lizzy was standing in their hangout. A few more minutes, and they'd be rubbing butt cheeks with her.

Maybe not, Sam tried to reassure himself. Maybe Lizzy couldn't see them from the farmyard. His mind shot back to the day he and Chet had sat on that front porch, the day John fell off Old Dozer. As he remembered it, they hadn't been able to see to that side of the barn from the house on that day. And he was sure they hadn't heard the ruckus going on down there. If his cows kept their big mouths shut, he just might be able to divert them before they paid Lizzy a visit.

Encouraged, Sam leaned lower over Ranger's neck, spurring him on. The beating of horse hooves from the rear told him Chet was on his heels. Though a thick layer of frost coated the ground and it was a rough ride, Ranger was sure-footed and kept his footing on the rugged terrain. Sam rode along the slope behind the farmhouse, his heart pounding along with the horse's four hooves.

When he reached the edge of the once intact fence line, he reined in Ranger. Chet slid to a stop beside him. "You wait here," he ordered. "I'll drive them up here on that stretch of pasture behind the barn."

"Sure you don't want some help?" Chet offered, obviously chomping at the bit to join Sam in his foolhardy venture.

Sam's eyes flicked to his cattle. A couple of eager leaders meandered away from the rest of the herd. "No, I don't want them to get so excited that they start bellowing."

That said, Sam leaned forward and squeezed Ranger into a mad race across the long pasture that led to the back of the barn. In front of him, his cattle filtered down the road toward the farmhouse.

Fearful that he would only speed up their progress if he came from behind them, he veered to cut in front of the plodding animals. He didn't let his eyes wander to the farmhouse in search of Lizzy or halt to contemplate the ramifications of being caught with *his* cattle in *her* yard. When he reached the road, he pulled Ranger to a walk and made his way to the front of the line, his pace slow and steady, his aim to turn the cows back towards the barn.

Ranger took over, head down, attention riveted on the vexing animals. Sam sat deep in the saddle, his body one with the horse's movements, fearing he'd hear an irate female voice from somewhere behind him.

To his consternation, the beasts refused to turn, and cattle tended to be mighty obstinate creatures when they set their minds to do something. The loud bawling of a determined cow shattered the silence. Sam's heart rate skyrocketed. Others joined her, and soon an incessant caterwauling that could most likely be heard back at the ranch filled the air.

Frustrated, Sam uttered a string of expletives that would've offended even his father and quickly revised his plan. He reined Ranger to the side of the herd and made his way to the back of the line. There he surveyed the bunchgrass-riddled soil on each side of the rugged road. Lizzy owned that land; she didn't own the road.

Sam mumbled himself into a relaxed stance, an effort to appear nonchalant and at ease. He loosened the reins to let Ranger do his work and fought the urge to glance at the farmhouse. Once the herd reached the driveway into the yard, he nudged Ranger forward to discourage a few mulish leaders from taking a left turn.

That's when he noticed Lizzy. She stood on the porch, hands embedded on her hips, her lethal eyes shooting bullets at him. "Damn, Ranger, that's one angry woman. We sure aren't earning any gold stars here," he mumbled while he wrangled with his own anger. He had an overwhelming urge to ride over there and have it out with her—to get it over with, so he'd know the outcome.

Then he sighed. "Nope. Won't work, will it. We can't afford to take chances here." No matter how he looked at it, a confrontation with Lizzy this morning wasn't gonna happen.

Sam tipped his hat to her in greeting and turned his eyes—if not his attention—back to his cattle. Somehow he managed to get through the next few minutes without even a fleeting glance back at the imposing figure on the porch.

He drove the beasts past the farmyard and up to the top of the hill where Chet lounged in his saddle, a sardonic smile twisting his face. Another clump of chew bulged inside his lower lip.

Chet spit and swiped his mouth. "That was some show, boss. Amazin' how quiet a bunch of cows are when they want to be, ain't it?"

Sam paused to catch his breath and settle his pulse. His patience had run out long ago. Frustration blazing inside him, he turned in his saddle to glare at Chet. "I'm in one hell of a mood right now, and your smart ass wisecracks aren't helping matters. The outcome of this affects you, too, you know. So if you can't say something helpful, keep your mouth shut or hightail it back to the ranch. I've got these cattle this far; the drive to the ranch will be a cake walk."

"Just wonderin' how you're feelin' about all this." Chet drawled, his hazel eyes studying Sam. "Guess I know now." A stream of muddy juice spewed from his lips before he reined his horse towards the far side of the herd.

Sam watched him, ire burning in his craw. "How I'm feeling? Well, so far nothing's been settled with that very pissed off woman down there. In fact, seems to me, I've just dug this hole a whole lot deeper, and from where I stand, the climb out of it's looking insurmountable. That's how I'm feeling," Sam muttered, more to himself than to Chet's retreating back.

❀ ❀ ❀

By the time he walked Ranger into the barn, frustration had Sam kicking himself. If anything, his predawn jaunt had exacerbated his worries. Though he and Chet had managed to drive the small herd back onto the ranch, he still had at least a hundred head wandering around on the farm, and there'd be a lot more come spring.

He brushed the horse's wooly winter coat until it was nearly dry, then threw a blanket across his back. Finished, he tossed the brush onto a shelf, cinched the blanket straps snugly into place, and lead Ranger into his stall. After he removed the harness, he gave the gelding some fresh water and a scoop of oats. Ranger was so anxious to get to his breakfast that the oats nearly ended up on the floor.

As Sam strode toward the ranch house, he wondered if there was even half a chance that his absence had gone unnoticed. He had no desire to be bombarded with more probing questions—this time from Eb—even if it might provide some answers to a few of his own. And he sure as hell wasn't going to discuss his morning joy ride with Eb.

When he opened the mudroom door, the smells of bacon frying and coffee brewing welcomed him. His stomach responded with a serious growl. Discarding the layers of warm clothing took nearly as long as it had taken to put them on, but soon he joined Eb in the inviting warmth of the kitchen.

Eb had arrived at the Craig Ranch when Sam was a young boy

and had soon become a permanent fixture. Back then, he'd lived in a small house on the ranch with his sister Rose and her son—Chet. Eb had been his father's right-hand man and close friend. Now he was Sam's.

Though Eb was getting along in years, Sam couldn't imagine life on the ranch without him. For one thing, even with the ranch hands Sam hired, the ranch was too large for Sam to manage on his own. After Sam's mother had died, Eb had moved into a bedroom in the main house, a move which Sam suspected was an attempt on Eb's part to put some distance between him and his rebellious nephew— Chet. At one time, Rose had done the cooking and cleaning in the main house, but after her death, Eb had taken over most of the household duties, a routine that had continued when Sam returned to the ranch ten years ago.

Eb, up to his elbows in bacon, glanced Sam's way. Sam nodded. "Mornin'."

Eb muttered, "Mornin'," and continued to fork sizzling strips of bacon from the frying pan onto a stack of paper towels. "You were out early. Is there a problem?"

Sam sighed, seeing the prospect of a peaceful breakfast fizzle. The aroma of freshly brewed coffee enticed him. He grabbed a mug, poured himself a hearty cup, and took a cautious sip. As usual, its taste wasn't quite as satisfying as its smell, but the warmth of it felt good on his frozen fingers and sliding down his throat.

Considering how to answer Eb's question, he indulged in a few more warming gulps. "I couldn't sleep. Finally gave up trying. Chet and I spent some time checking on the cattle." Sam eyed Eb, hoping he'd move on to another topic.

But Eb wasn't easily deterred. He raised his bushy eyebrows, probably at the thought of Chet climbing out of bed at such an ungodly hour. "Mighty cold mornin' for a ride before the sun's even thinkin' about risin'," he observed, spreading butter on steaming toast. "How'd you rope Chet into goin' with you?"

Sam watched butter melt into the toast and considered Eb's question. Was Lizzy's return going to ruin his breakfast, too? He slid into a chair and rested his forearms on the well-worn oak of the kitchen table, the heat from the mug cupped in his hands doing nothing to warm the cold anger that coursed through his veins at the thought of her.

"Guess he was in the mood for an early morning ride," he finally muttered.

Though Eb appeared to be merely initiating idle conversation, Sam didn't buy it; Eb's radar was on high alert. When Sam had stomped in and sullenly downed a couple of shots of scotch the previous evening, Eb was in the living room, his nose in a novel. The two of them hadn't said more than "goodnight" to each other before they'd retired to their respective bedrooms. Now Sam had detoured from his regimented routine, yet again. Eb knew something was up.

While Sam mentally argued the pros and cons of spilling the news of Lizzy's reappearance, Eb loaded a couple of plates with bacon, scrambled eggs, and toast. Sam understood Ranger's impatience to get to his oats. He wished Eb would quit fiddling around and got breakfast on the table. He was starving.

Eb set a steaming plate of food in front of Sam and paused to study him closely. "You seem a bit on edge."

Sam's eyes dropped to his grub. He plucked a strip of crisp bacon and broke off a bite, savoring the smoky flavor as he chewed it. Eb refilled their coffee mugs and sat down across from Sam. Sam could feel Eb's probing gaze, but he remained silent. He listened to the crunching, chewing, swallowing, and slurping of Eb devouring his breakfast, refusing to meet that gaze and get caught up in a conversation he didn't want to have. Instead, he engrossed himself in the food's comfort.

Finally, Sam swallowed the last bite of bacon. He pushed at his empty plate, grabbed his coffee, and scooted back his chair to stretch his long legs out in front of him before he glanced at Eb. Just as he'd thought, Eb was still eyeballing him, a hint of concern in his aging eyes.

"Lizzy's back," Sam muttered disgustedly.

Worry turned to shock on Eb's craggy face. "Lizzy? Johnny's Lizzy?"

"Yeah," Sam confirmed as he watched the color drain from Eb's ruddy complexion.

"You see her?" Eb asked, clearly struggling to come to grips with Sam's news.

Sam nodded. "She's at the farm. I saw her last night and again this morning."

Eb seemed to be rolling Sam's news around in his mind, probably trying to make sense of it. "Was she alone?"

"Appeared to be."

Air spewed from Eb's mouth—a long whistle—and he visibly relaxed before he continued his inquisition. "Did you talk to her?"

"Not much. She wasn't any too thrilled to see me. Pretty much ordered me to leave."

"Well, did she give you any indication of what she's doin' here?" A touch of irritation had crept into Eb's voice.

"Nope. Just told me to leave."

Eb chewed on this information a bit. Obviously, Lizzy's return caused him some stress, which surprised Sam. Eb and Lizzy had seemed to have a mutual respect and admiration for each other. Sam had thought that if anyone had kept in touch with Lizzy, it would be

Eb. Now here Eb was, clearly troubled by Sam's news and no more knowledgeable than Sam concerning the specifics surrounding Lizzy's return.

"You think she'll stay?" Eb finally asked.

"Your guess is as good as mine. She has a lot of work cut out for her if she does. After spending the night in that dump, maybe she'll leave."

"I seriously doubt Lizzy would give up that easily if she has plans to stay there," Eb argued.

Eb was probably right. Lizzy was too strong-willed to give up without a fight. He added his two cents worth: "Lizzy always did pretty much whatever she wanted, and only she and God know what she's up to now." *But soon I'll know, too*, he promised himself.

"Be good to see that place take shape in the next year, all decked out to greet the new century. Makes me want to shut my eyes every time I drive by that farm and see what a mess it is. Con and Dottie poured their hearts into it. Be good to see Lizzy again, too." Eb paused and shook his head, his eyes troubled. "Maybe she will stay."

That last remark sparked a firestorm inside Sam. "Yes, and maybe she'll demand that we get our cattle off her land. Maybe she's here because she sold the farm. Maybe she's here to wreak havoc with what we've worked so hard to accrue. There are a few too many 'maybes' floating around here for my comfort."

His face flushed, Eb gaped at Sam and spluttered, "That don't sound like Lizzy."

"This is a very different Lizzy." Sam barked, anger burning inside him. "She's older. And she's damned mad about something."

Sam watched Eb's complexion shift from crimson to pasty white. "Well, maybe I should wander on over there and find out what's goin' on?" he mumbled. "Make sure she's okay."

Be my guest, Sam wanted to say. But he couldn't chance Eb messing things up worse than they already were. No. If Sam were to find out what Lizzy was up to and confront her about his cattle, he needed to take it on himself.

"I suppose I should face her wrath and drop off some firewood. She'll freeze to death if she doesn't keep some heat going in that house. It's the least I can do for Con and Dottie," Sam rationalized, knowing full well he was doing it more for himself than for Lizzy's grandparents. "I have to go into town this afternoon and pick up some parts for that broken faucet in the barn. Maybe I'll drop a load of wood off on my way in."

Sam wondered what he'd said to elicit the even closer scrutiny he was getting from Eb. In fact, now that he thought about it. Eb's response to this whole situation seemed off. Perhaps he should do some probing of his own. "You know, I wasn't here when Lizzy left," he began. "To be quite truthful, I don't know much about it except that it happened after Con and Dottie's deaths."

Sam had been caught up in starting a career in a law firm in Chicago when life as he'd known it back at the ranch had been blown to hell and gone. At the time, he'd accepted what he was told and continued on with his new life. What was done was done, and there hadn't been anything he could do about it except take note of those responsible—that being Lizzy and harbor a few resentments. Now he realized that for the first time in twenty-five years, he was questioning something that had completely altered the path his life had taken.

"It seems odd that she'd just walk away from everything and never come back—not like Lizzy at all," he murmured, more to himself than to Eb.

Eb was quick to defend her. "She did come back the one time—at the cemetery."

"As if you could count that. She didn't even get out of her car, most likely feeling too guilty," Sam groused.

Sam watched Eb's weather-beaten features vacillate between frustration and sadness. He appeared to be waging some inner battle, unsuccessfully attempting to control whatever emotions consumed him. With a huff, Eb pried himself up out of his chair, grabbed the plates from the table, and strode to the sink.

The hell with it. Sam decided that now was as good a time as any to get some answers. "So when *did* Lizzy leave?" he demanded.

Eb filled the sink with hot water and started scouring dishes. Sam almost gave up on getting a response when Eb finally spoke, his hands busy in the soapy water. "Lizzy left the evenin' of Con and Dottie's funeral. The way I heard it, she packed a suitcase, climbed into Dottie's old blue Buick, and drove off. She signed over control of everything here to Gus Woolridge. Then, except for a couple of letters to Johnny and showin' up to see him buried, she pretty much disappeared. Gus was fit to be tied. Luckily, Con and Dottie's life insurance policy covered the expenses that came up. Otherwise, Lizzy wouldn't have a farm to come back to.

"When it became evident that Lizzy wasn't gonna be returnin', Johnny and I went over to the farm and packed up everything of value and brought it back here. Gus asked your dad to keep an eye on the farm, and he did—fixed what needed to be fixed and made sure that it was locked up tight. Course, just like you, J.D. couldn't let that land sit idle." Eb stilled, then snorted disgustedly. "No Craig ever could."

He sighed deeply. "If she plans on stayin', I suppose Lizzy'll be wantin' her stuff back. I think it's still stored in one of those sheds out by the barn."

That was news to Sam. Of course, when one considered the

generations of junk stored in numerous buildings scattered around the ranch, he supposed his ignorance was warranted. He pushed on. "Where did she go?"

"That I don't know. I think Johnny knew, but he didn't say one word about Lizzy after she left."

"So you haven't heard from her during the last twenty-five years?"

"Nope."

Well, Sam guessed that was that. Back then, he'd figured John and Lizzy would end up married—they'd been inseparable—and the Stewart farm would become part of the ranch, with John running it, of course. That's the way it was meant to be. And it would've been if Lizzy hadn't packed up and left, abandoning both John and the farm and leaving both to deteriorate.

Sam decided he'd pumped Eb's mind dry on this subject, so he left Eb to finish the dishes and headed to the barn to make sure Chet had a handle on what the day's chores entailed. Once he did that, he was thinking he might have a look inside that shed out next to the barn. The back half of it was packed with boxes, maybe Lizzy's.

But the conversation he'd had with Eb didn't sit well. He stopped in mid-stride to glance back and noted that Eb had halted his scrubbing to stare out the kitchen window, a faraway look to his eyes and deep worry lines furrowing his face.

As he continued on his way, Sam rubbed the prickly stubble on his chin, unable to let go of Eb's uncharacteristic reaction to Lizzy's return. Sam's instincts were hollering that something was afoot.

CHAPTER 5

Lizzy bounced her way down the heavily rutted dirt road. Though the Explorer was in four-wheel-drive, it was still a bone-rattling ride.

She dreaded this venture into town—her stomach churning, head thumping— but if she was going to stay at the farm, she had no recourse. Hopefully, no one would recognize her, and she'd be able to take care of business and return to the seclusion of the farm in no time. As a precaution, she'd pulled her dark, shoulder-length hair into a ponytail and tugged a baseball cap down over her forehead. The heavy down-filled jacket and a pair of sunglasses were added insurance that she'd get in and out of town incognito.

At last, she pulled onto the highway and relaxed back into the seat to enjoy a reprieve from the jarring ride. No longer focused on staying on the road, her mind wandered to a place she didn't want it to go: Sam Craig.

Years ago he'd cut a swath through life in this little corner of the world. Then he'd walked away from it without a backward glance. He should be gone from the ranch—busy being J.D.'s puppet—a successful attorney in some prestigious law firm or immersed in shady politics back east somewhere. What had brought him back to the ranch?

Sam's presence brought with it a rush of feelings that Lizzy had no desire to revive, nor scrutinize. She'd been working her way through a rough time in her life when John's letter had arrived. The prospect of being here surrounded by endless acres of empty land and no people to intrude into her solitude had drawn her. That and the fact that John had needed her. Painful memories were tied to the farm, but good memories were, too. Besides, it was the only childhood home she'd known.

Lizzy clenched her jaw. She wouldn't let Sam interfere with what she'd come here to do. She wanted to be left alone, and by God, he, of all people, had better do just that.

If that morning's spectacle was any indication of what was to come, she had her work cut out for her. Her blood boiled with the memory of Craig cows traipsing around her house and the offensive manner in which he'd tipped his hat to her, as if she didn't know what was really going on. He'd brushed her aside like she was a filthy, annoying cobweb, just like his daddy had.

"Well, guess what, you pack of lying thieves? No Craig is ever gonna steal Stewart land, that's what," she seethed aloud.

By the time Lizzy drove down Main Street, she'd cooled off enough to note how little the town had changed. Although she noticed a video store and a gourmet coffee and wine shop, no mini-malls or fast food chain drive-thrus littered the landscape. In fact, it appeared to be one of the few communities to escape a string of stoplights dotting its streets. So far, Lizzy had only noticed a couple.

Standing guard along each side of the narrow street were what looked to be the original parking meters. Lizzy spotted the building she sought and sent a brief prayer of thanks that she didn't have to parallel park before she slid into a marked space. She sat for several minutes, a bundle of twitching nerves, her heart thudding in her chest. Every cell in her body begged to retreat to the safety of the farm. To calm herself, she mentally chanted *I can do this*.

At last her head cleared, and her thoughts turned to the imposing red brick building in front of her. It had been built some time in the late 1800's, a warning to local folks that law and order would reign, even way out here in this obscure land of sagebrush, rocks, and tumbleweeds.

Too bad it hadn't worked. Granddad had warned her: the law turned a blind eye, and mayhem reigned too often in these parts. That didn't surprise Lizzy; J.D. Craig and Sheriff Mulkins—he was the sleazy county sheriff during her growing-up years—were drinking buddies. It was rare that they didn't have their hands in the same pot, no matter what was brewing in it.

Lizzy took a deep breath to fortify herself, then grabbed her purse and slid from the SUV. Though the sun shone brightly, the outside air was crisp and cold against her cheeks and turned her breath into puffy clouds. Frost clung like powdered sugar sprinkles to everything. Lizzy inserted a couple of nickels into the meter and turned the red knob. She'd have twenty minutes, more than enough time to set up a post office box.

Focused on the slick cement, she walked down the sidewalk and carefully climbed the foot-worn steps that adorned the courthouse entrance. Her eyes were drawn down the long hall to the back of the building where Sheriff Mulkin's office had been housed. She shuddered and, instead, turned to the double doors on her right. As she remembered it, the post office was through those doors. She pushed them open and stepped inside.

It was a step back in time. The odor of old wood, the elevated ceiling, the rows of tiny brass doors, and the echo of footsteps on the aged hardwood floor assaulted her senses. Memories that had lain dormant for many years emerged to besiege her.

She saw a young girl expectantly open a mailbox, hoping there would be a letter inside from her father. And she saw an older, but no less hopeful, girl open that same box, anticipation beaming on her face at the prospect of a letter from the man she loved. She watched them each pull out a bundle of letters and leaf painstakingly through the stack, certain that the next letter would be the right one.

Of course, there had been no letter, and Lizzy felt their pain once again. Sorrow consumed her, and she reached for a wall, fearing that without something stable to hold onto, she'd melt into an unremarkable puddle on the aged, scuff-marked floor.

For long moments, she remained caught in that inanimate state. Then gradually she became aware of people milling about, staring at her. She forced herself to breathe slowly and deeply and concentrate on reclaiming control. When she was confident she could manage it, she shuffled shakily to the counter at the far end of the room. There, she came face-to-face with an older gentleman who looked vaguely familiar. He peered at her, concern etched on his otherwise friendly face.

"You okay?" he inquired.

Lizzy smiled weakly and nodded, feeling foolish and shaken. If merely walking into this post office sparked such an intense response, was coming back here a serious mistake? She had to get her business taken care of quickly and get back to the farm. Perhaps she could arrange it so she wouldn't have to leave the farm again, at least not until she was ready to move forward with her investigation.

Fearful the man might recognize her, she tugged the brim of her cap lower. "I'm interested in getting a mailbox," she informed him.

The man became all business. His bushy gray eyebrows furrowed as he settled a pair of thick, horn-rimmed eyeglasses into place and pulled a card from under the counter to set it in front of her. "You'll need to fill out this form," he stated. "Regular boxes are twenty dollars a year, to be paid in advance. You want a larger one, you'll have to wait; don't have any of those open right now."

"A regular one will be fine," Lizzy murmured as she selected a pen from the cup on the counter and began writing.

The form was brief and only took a couple of minutes to complete. Soon she slid it back across the counter to him, and he drew it close to examine what she'd written. His eyes shifted to study her with as much scrutiny as they had the form.

Lizzy struggled to maintain a neutral expression. "I'm in kind of a hurry," she muttered.

He pursed his lips and huffed, then turned and tottered off towards the back of the mailroom, leaving Lizzy to wonder what she should do. She needed the mailbox, and she didn't want to return to town to get it. Muted noises filtered out from somewhere back there, so he must still be here. Hopeful that he would return, she pulled a thick envelope from her purse, extracted a twenty dollar bill from it, and placed the money on the counter.

Just as she was about to yell to him, he reappeared, clutching a wrinkled brown paper bag with the word *Stewart* penned on it in large black letters. Lizzy's heart rate soared. The man had recognized her name, if not her. There were certainly advantages to holding onto a dirt-bag ex-husband's surname; in this instance, it was unfortunate that she hadn't.

"These have been sitting around here collecting dust for years. Wasn't sure what to do with them, so I just held onto them. Figured as long they owned land here, someone from the family would show up someday. Guess that someone's you," he said and handed her the bag.

Lizzy took it and glanced inside. It was nearly half full of what appeared to be mail—letters and bills, magazines and ads, who knew what else. Her stomach heaved. What if the letter she'd longed for so many years ago had actually been written and mailed? What if it was in this bag? She swallowed at the burning ache in her throat. Drawn to the comfort of her Explorer, she turned to make a mad dash from the room

"You want the box?" the man asked.

She gazed back at him, her mind jumbled by emotion. "The box?" Surely he wasn't holding a package back there for her, too?

He frowned, studying her, a slip of paper in his outstretched hand. "The post office box, you want it?"

"Oh . . . yes. Yes, I do want it," she whispered as she reached out to grab the paper. And then it hit her. "You didn't forward this mail to me. Does that mean you don't have access to my current address?"

He shook his head. "Nope. No address. Not ever. Just stuffed it all into that bag there. Like I said, figured someone would pick it up someday."

"Then you didn't post a letter to me recently?"

"Nope. Not me." His furry brows lifted. "Course, I did get a phone call not too long ago. Some guy wanting to know if we had your address on file. Told him I didn't, and that was that."

Her heart pounded against her ribs. Thinking was like swimming through a sea of mud. "A man?" she rasped.

"Yeah, it was a man all right. Didn't recognize his voice, though. And he didn't give a name."

"Did he say anything else?"

"Nope. Just asked for your address. When I told him we didn't have it, he hung up."

A man, huh? He had to be the person who'd mailed John's letter to her. It was odd, though, since it had been posted from here. Who was he? And where had he gotten her address?

"Thank you," she muttered before she turned away and made a hasty retreat.

Overwhelmed by the need for sanctuary, she strode briskly towards her car and threw the bag into the back. With luck, it would vanish before she got back to the farm. She had no desire to take that trip down memory lane—no desire to relive the pain and loss. No. Those memories were locked away, and that's where they'd stay. While she struggled to regain her composure, she promised herself that after three more stops, she'd return to her safe haven.

Traffic had picked up when Lizzy pulled back onto Main Street. She glanced at the clock on the dashboard—almost noon. Although she hadn't eaten enough to keep a flea alive in the past few days, the thought of food was nauseating.

"Well, you won't waste valuable time eating then, will you? Right now, we need to find a hardware store," she mumbled to herself as she rolled down the street, her eyes searching business signs for a store that might carry cleaning and building supplies.

At one time, Milt Hawkins had run a thriving hardware business on the northern edge of town. Milt Jr. was two years older than Lizzy and had been more John's friend than hers, which was fine and dandy with her. The prospect of coming face-to-face with him was motivation enough to cruise several side streets before she finally gave in to her fruitless search and forged on north.

Sure enough, there sat Hawkins Hardware, decked out in a fresh coat of barn red paint, looking much the same as it had when she'd last seen it. She half expected to walk inside and see Milt Sr. sitting behind the counter, wire rims perched on the end of his hawk-like nose and pencil stub in hand, eyes glued to a folded newspaper. Every so often he'd look up to answer a customer's question or inquire if anyone knew a three-letter word for a river in India or some other obscure term. There were even a few rare moments when he'd stand up to assist a customer. Lizzy had often wondered how he maintained a thriving business from the top of a four-foot stool, but the fact that she was now gazing at the store's vivid exterior was proof that it could be done.

There was a small parking lot next to the building. Lizzy parked, then eyed the other cars in the lot, tallying how many customers might be inside the store. That jittery feeling was back, and she fought to subdue it, telling herself that the odds of Milt Sr., or anyone else who might recognize her, being inside were—well, she didn't know exactly what they were, but they were surely way down there. Most likely, Junior had become a casualty of his wild, reckless ways long ago.

Lizzy skimmed the shopping list she'd composed back at the farm, categorizing the items in her head. She'd slip down the necessary aisles, grab what she needed, pay, and get out of there pronto. Steeling herself, she yanked the bill of her cap down, grabbed her purse, and climbed out of the Explorer. Resolutely, she strode toward the front door.

Bells chimed as she swung the door open, but there were no Milt Sr. or ogling customers to greet her, only a display of faux paint techniques and several vintage shopping carts. Like a cool mist on a hot day, relief flowed through her. She grabbed a cart and plowed down the first aisle, filling it with cleaning supplies as she went.

At the corner, she made a sharp right turn and scanned the remaining aisles. All she needed were a few tools and some nails. Then she could pay and be on her way. Only one aisle left; it had to be the one she was seeking. She rounded the corner and uprooted a man who was bent over. Fortunately, he didn't appear to be hurt. He also didn't mask his displeasure when he stood up and glared at her.

Lizzy froze. Her thoughts fled. All she could do was ogle him—him being Milt Sr. Only, it couldn't be Milt Sr., because he'd be an elderly man by now. This man was closer to her age.

"Well, well. If it ain't Lizzy Stewart," the man smirked, his face twisted in disgust. "I didn't think you'd ever show your face around here again. And here you are in broad daylight. You think I wouldn't recognize you in that getup?"

It felt like a steel basketball landed in Lizzy's stomach. She grabbed it, wishing she could shrink into her clothing, just disappear.

Instead she did what she'd learned to do long ago—as a young child: she yanked off her sunglasses, looked Junior squarely in the eye, smiled sweetly, and chimed, "Well, well. If it isn't Milt Jr. It's nice to see you, too, Junior. When I have more time, you'll have to fill me in on the last twenty-five years of your life—or not. Sorry, but right now I don't have time to visit. I need to get one of those axes, and a hammer and nails, and then I need to scoot on out of here."

With that, she rammed her cart on past him and his reproachful eyes and grabbed what she needed from the shelves as she raced down the aisle, her heart beating frantically along with the spiraling wheels. And just when she thought it couldn't get any worse, she spotted the check-out counter and the woman behind it. Thoughts of abandoning the cart where it was and slinking out the door crossed her mind just as the woman looked up.

Lizzy observed the play of expressions on the woman's face— from a puzzled frown to a glint of comprehension and finally, startled surprise. "Lizzy, is it really you?" she asked hesitantly.

Lizzy nodded. "It's really me, Franny."

Then something wonderful happened. A smile lit up Franny's

face, the kind of smile that left no doubt; Franny was genuinely happy to see her. "Oh, my gosh. It's so nice to see you," Franny's warm voice confirmed.

Tears stung Lizzy's eyes. She pushed the cart to the counter, and the first really true smile she'd felt in months stretched her lips. "It's good to see you, too, Franny. It's been a long time," she said to the woman who'd once been her very dear friend.

When Franny walked around the counter and enfolded Lizzy in a welcoming hug, a tiny, cold lump of something inside Lizzy melted. Tears pooled in her eyes and streamed down her cheeks.

Franny handed Lizzy several tissues and looked her over from the top of her head to the soles of her leather boots. She shook her head and smiled. "Lizzy Stewart, you haven't changed a bit. You're just as pretty as you were in high school. What in the world have you been up to that's kept you so young . . . and thin?"

Lizzy smiled through her tears. Franny might've put on a couple of pounds here and there and she hadn't masked the gray threads that blended nicely with her thick auburn hair, but she'd changed very little. She was the same friend Lizzy had run around with in her younger years, a friend who always found the good in everything and everyone.

"You're the same, too, Franny. And it really is nice to see you," Lizzy blubbered. "I'm back at the farm, and I'm planning to live there awhile, so I imagine we'll have a lot of time to catch up. Today I'm in kind of a hurry, though. The old house is a mess, so I came to town to get a few things I need to make it livable. I have to get back there right away and get started." With that, she blew her nose and sniffled.

"Of course, you do. I'll just get this stuff rang up, so you can be on your way. But the next time you're in town, we're having coffee and a nice, long chat. I can't wait to hear all about your life. It has to be more exciting than mine," Franny said as she pulled things from the shopping cart and set them on the counter.

"I think we know enough about Lizzy, Fran. I don't imagine there's anything else we need to know," a deep voice snarled from behind Lizzy.

Both women turned to face Junior. When Lizzy saw the accusation in his eyes, blood drained from her head and left her nauseas. Why was he so hateful? She stiffened her back and turned away to help Franny.

"Don't mind Junior," Franny said rather pointedly, glaring a warning at him. "He's just being his grumpy old self."

With that, Junior huffed and stomped off through a door behind the counter, slamming it shut behind him.

Junior's rude behavior didn't appear to faze Franny. She

rolled her eyes as she began to scan the items on the counter. "I swear, if that man gets much more moody, I'm gonna come join you on the farm and leave married life behind. Who would've guessed that the Junior we both avoided in high school because he had too much fun would become a crotchety old man before he even reached fifty." She paused and shook her head. "Remember how wild and crazy he was back then? Well, after John died, he changed. Just like that, he turned into one of the most decent guys around here. Now I'd give up chocolate for good to see even a glimmer of that old fun-loving Junior we avoided more than those showers in gym class— remember those? Yuck!"

Franny rambled on about her life—or lack of it—with Junior as she packed items into plastic bags and accepted the stack of twenty-dollar bills Lizzy handed her. Lizzy remained mum, reeling with the preposterous news that Junior and Franny were husband and wife, definitely an example of opposites attracting each other. She bit her lip to avoid a prying comment and accepted the change Franny handed her.

Lizzy grabbed several bags; Franny snatched the rest, and they headed for the front door. It was while they were stowing them into the back of the vehicle that Franny stepped back, a quizzical expression on her face, and asked, "Did you get the letter then? Is that why you're here?"

Lizzy froze, bag in hand. "The letter?" she spluttered.

"John's letter; did you get it?"

Franny had sent her the letter? Lizzy closed her eyes, trying to make sense of it. She dropped the bag and faced Franny. "Uh . . . yes, I got it. You sent it to me?" Why would Franny have John's twenty-five-year-old letter?

"Well, not exactly. I didn't know where to send it, but I knew Gus Woolridge used to be your grandparents' attorney, and I figured he might have your address. Gus died last year, but his office is still open, so I took the letter over there, and sure enough, they found your address in some files. Only they wouldn't give it to me—you know, privacy laws and all. They said they'd send the letter to you, so I left it with them."

With that, her face scrunched up into a puzzled look. "I'm surprised you didn't know it was from me. My address was on the envelope, and I wrote a little note to you and stuck it inside with John's letter."

Franny shook her head as if to shake her concern aside, then rambled on as if she didn't notice Lizzy's ramped up emotional state—confused. "Hmmm. . . . Well, anyway, I'm sure glad you got it. I just feel so awful; I really do. John gave it to me all those years ago and made me promise to put it in the mail as soon I got back to town. He said it was real important, that you had to get it right away. And honest, Lizzy, I don't know what happened. I guess I must've forgot all about it 'cause I was cleaning out some old boxes in the attic a couple of months ago, and there it was, boxed up with a bunch of my old high school photos."

Lizzy searched for words. "You put a note inside? Franny, there was no return address on the envelope, and the only thing that was sealed inside was John's letter in its original envelope."

"Well, I put the note in it; I know I did. I wonder why they put it in a different envelope, and if they did, wouldn't they use one with their own return address on it?"

"You'd sure think so," Lizzy muttered, still struggling to decipher the puzzle. She'd been so stunned when she'd received the letter that she'd ripped it open impulsively and hadn't thought to check the envelope for signs that someone else had already opened it to read its contents. "So John gave it to you? When?"

"Oh, gosh. It must've been a couple of days before—well, you know—'cause of course, I didn't see him again after that. He seemed upset about something and asked me to put the letter in the mail here in town. For some reason, he didn't want it in the mail out at the ranch." She sighed dejectedly. "I guess I forgot. I'm really sorry. I hope I didn't mess up."

Lizzy wasn't sure how to respond. Although Franny might have messed up royally, rubbing it in wouldn't help. "It's okay. It probably wouldn't have made any difference," she finally said. "Did anyone else know about the letter?"

Franny's face brightened. "Well, Junior did, of course. And then Sam Craig was in the store one day, and I asked him if he had your address. He just got real silent and gave me that look—you know, the brooding one, the one that makes you want to jump into his arms and let him know that he can have his way with you right there and then. Only, what he said was, 'I don't know where the hell she is.' Could be the two of you need to get together and mend some fences if you're gonna be neighbors again, huh?"

Not in this lifetime, Lizzy wanted to say. What she said was, "Anyone else?"

"Well, I suppose Sam might've asked Eb about the address. I don't remember for sure, but Chet or one of the hired hands might've been with Sam that day, so I suppose they could've heard me talking with him."

With the mention of Eb, a warm glow settled somewhere near Lizzy's heart. But Chet: actually, she was surprised that he was still at the ranch. He'd raised his share of hell when he was younger and quite frankly, his licentious stares and suggestive language had caused her to go out of her way to steer clear of him.

"So Chet and Eb are still at the ranch then? How about

Rose?" she asked

"Oh yeah, Eb still lives in the ranch house and does the cooking and upkeep there. I guess you could say that Chet helps Sam with the ranching—you know Chet. He finally settled down some once he was married, although the marriage didn't last long. Rose died quite a while back. Had a stroke and didn't last long after that."

And life went on, even without me here to be a part of it, Lizzy reflected. She'd reached today's quota of blasts from her past. It was time to retreat to the farm.

"Well, if I'm gonna get any work done today, I'd better get going. Thanks a lot, Franny. And thank you for your efforts to get John's letter to me," she said. Then she gave Franny an affectionate hug and assured her that she'd look her up the next time she came to town. She was surprised at how much she looked forward to the prospect of spending more time with her old friend.

Prickles of uneasiness continued to poke at Lizzy as she pulled out onto Main Street. She now knew where the letter had originated and who had mailed it to her. Surely Franny had no ulterior motive to lure her back to the farm and harm her, so she could kiss goodbye to that disquieting notion and, for now, concentrate on making the farmhouse fit for human habitation.

Then she'd find out what had driven John to write the letter. Thanks to Franny, she knew where to commence that search: Gus Woolridge's law office. Why had they switched envelopes and removed Franny's note before mailing the letter to Lizzy?

Of course, someone—a man, according to the guy at the post office—had searched for her address. Perhaps it was just Sam or Eb seeking the address to pass on to Franny. Lizzy couldn't imagine either of them feeling threatened enough to hurt her, unless, of course, their goal was to erase a past mistake. She shuddered with the knowledge that some mistakes can't be erased and didn't let her mind wander there.

Instead, she turned her thoughts to Junior. Franny was right. Junior had been unpredictable and was usually in some kind of trouble when he was younger. He was one of John's closest friends. The two of them together was like mixing gasoline and fire; some big blowup was inevitable.

The fact that Franny had hooked up with Junior was something Lizzy would need to think about. John's death must've had a real impact on Junior if it had caused the changes Franny claimed it had. Was that why he was so rude to Lizzy, because he blamed *her* for John's death? If so, he was probably only one of many, Lizzy acknowledged.

Her disposition lightened somewhat by her visit with Franny, Lizzy stopped at a gas station on the way out of town. She'd noticed that a small convenience store was attached to the station. While a greasy, whiskered kid in coveralls filled her gas tank, Lizzy walked into the store and searched for a pay phone—out here in the sticks, her cell was as dead as the pump on the farmhouse well. Spying a phone in the corner, she headed towards it.

A few minutes later, she was well on her way to having electricity at the farm. In fact, the young woman she'd spoken with had assured her that she'd have power in less than an hour. Elated, Lizzy purchased a few grocery items and said a silent prayer that her grandmother's old Montgomery Ward refrigerator still had some oomph left in it. With food stowed in the back seat and a tank full of gas, Lizzy headed home.

As she drove south, Lizzy's thoughts were bombarded with recollections she'd refused to think about for many years: How had she forgotten about Franny's friendship? And how had she let Eb slip from her life—Eb who had always been there with a warm hug when she needed one? She couldn't help but wonder how many other memories she'd lost because they were attached to things too painful to remember.

It was not yet two o'clock when Lizzy rattled down the ruts on her final stretch of road to the Stewart farm. As she came over the last hill, she noticed a mammoth steel-gray pickup truck barreling towards her—Sam's, for sure.

Expecting the truck to zoom right on past, Lizzy slowed and edged over to the far right side of the road. Instead, she watched in dismay as the truck slowed, then made a sharp turn into the farmyard. Her stomach heaved, and blood throbbed in her temples. Of all the people she didn't want hanging around her farm, Sam Craig was number one on her list.

She muttered something she knew would've raised Grandma's hackles and landed Lizzy in her bedroom. Then she stiffened her back and ground her back teeth together, readying herself for the confrontation.

CHAPTER 6

Sam's day so far had been something on the far side of tolerable. Since their breakfast chat, Eb treated Sam like he was carrying a deadly bug around with him. If their paths crossed, Eb hustled off to tend to something he claimed needed immediate attention. That was fine with Sam since he was in a foul mood himself. Still, a little conversation might've occupied his mind and kept it from roaming where he didn't want it to go.

One minute he remembered the many good qualities Lizzy once possessed: her spirit, her kindness, her intelligence, her humor, the care she'd given John. Thirty minutes of angry reflecting on the ruinous results of her selfishness would follow that.

To top it off, he was being dogged by a relentless need to know what she was up to. It ground away at his peace of mind. He needed resolution now. Truth be told, he should probably be out rounding up the rest of his cattle off of Lizzy's land. But he was a determined man, one with no plans to relinquish that land—not without a fight.

Try as he might to forget it all and concentrate on the mundane tasks of running the ranch, his day had become one long string of mood fluctuations. He was jittery and on edge, and if someone had been around to take it out on, he'd have made that person's life miserable, too. Maybe it was best that Eb was avoiding him.

Around noon, Sam decided to run into town to purchase the parts for the broken faucet. Rather than chance a replay of his breakfast conversation, he decided to grab a sandwich at Mel's Diner. But first he'd stop by the farm and resolve the future status of a good number of his cattle.

No doubt, Lizzy needed a load of firewood to keep that old place heated, so he tossed some into the back of his truck and checked to make sure his toolbox was well stocked. Although he didn't owe Lizzy a thing, he still felt an allegiance to Con and Dottie, and his mother had firmly ingrained in him the importance of loving one's neighbor as himself. If only Lizzy would take that edict to heart, too, it would make his mission a whole lot easier.

Sam parked the truck in front of the ranch house and stepped inside to let Eb know he'd get a bite to eat in town. Evidently, Eb was still hiding, so Sam jotted a quick note and secured it to the refrigerator door with a silver horseshoe magnet.

A quick glance in the bathroom mirror reminded him that he hadn't showered or shaved that morning. A fatigue-streaked face with day-old beard and bloodshot eyes stared back at him, and the acrid aftertaste from too much coffee and stress was bitter in his mouth. Still, when he considered taking the time to brush his teeth and shave, his only thought was that town folk had seen him looking a whole lot worse. So he hopped back into his truck and headed north.

Since there was little traffic on the dirt road to the ranch, it was pretty much left to do its own thing. Consequently, over the years it had become a bone-jarring series of ruts and holes and particularly in winter, it could be a real bitch to navigate. Today Sam didn't let its dilapidated condition slow him down. He cruised along over potholes, washboards, and furrows, averaging about fifty miles-per-hour and splattering globs of frozen mud in his wake.

The truck's twisting and bouncing put him in mind of the bronc riding he'd done when he was a kid, the trick being to stay on the seat and move with the truck's bucking motion in this instance. Heat poured from the vents, the sun shone down through a cloudless sky, and Sam let himself meld with the warmth and focus on the Dodge's movements, his mission taking backseat to the challenge of staying on the road.

As he bounded over the ridge above the farmhouse, his gaze landed on a red SUV headed towards him. It had to be Lizzy, but something had sure slowed her down. There was a time when he would've pushed to keep up with her, no matter the condition of the road. At the rate she was now moving, the wood would be unloaded and stacked in a neat pile before she arrived.

Sam slammed on his brakes, ground the steering wheel to the right, and stopped in front of the desolate house. Even clear air and radiant sunshine didn't brighten the downtrodden condition of the farmyard. It was downright depressing. When Lizzy finally pulled up behind him, he stepped out of his truck and shivered at the change in temperature. Yep, the old place was as cold and foreboding as it looked.

He steeled himself, then turned to watch Lizzy, figuring it might be wise to let her make the first move. Only it took her an eternity to get her door open. When he finally heard it click and saw her slip out onto the frost-covered ground, his patience had worn down to a fine thread. She was so bundled up that all he could see was her firm mouth and the determined set to her chin. She unclenched one fist to snatch her sunglasses from her eyes.

Sam's heart slammed up against his chest. No doubt about it, she was gearing up for a tussle. Deciding the offensive stance might be the wiser one, he played his trump card, the peace offering: "Thought you might need some firewood," he offered, watching her face closely for signs of what might be going on beneath the unflattering baseball cap she wore.

She stood there and glared at him, and he could hear the struggle going on inside her head: she needed the wood, but she didn't want his help.

Without uttering a word, she stomped to the truck—swerving clear of him—and climbed up to gaze into the bed. "Well?" she challenged in a voice laced with irritation.

"Well?" he mimicked, wishing he hadn't.

"*Well*, are you going to put the tailgate down, so I can get it out of here?"

"*Well*, why don't you tell me where you want it, so I can do it," Sam countered, his body charged with irritation . . . and something else that he didn't want to contemplate—Lizzy was too close for comfort.

"I can stack my own firewood. And I'm gonna pay for it, so while I'm hauling wood, you figure out how much I owe you."

The woman was too much. Sam, who prided himself on his discipline and self-control, lost it. "Dammit, Lizzy. I don't know what the hell your problem is. What I do know is that you're Con and Dottie's granddaughter, and because of my respect and affection for them, I'm here to offer you some assistance.

"You're also currently my closest neighbor, and as such, I'm here to offer you some firewood so you don't freeze to death tonight, something I really don't want on my conscience. And just in case you've forgotten, in this neighborhood it's an insult to offer to pay for a gift." Sam paused when he noticed he was venting his anger and frustration on a now teary-eyed Lizzy.

"Okay," she whispered. With that, she stepped down and hastened towards the house, where she unlocked the door and disappeared inside without a backwards glance.

Sam stared after her, dumbfounded. What the hell had just happened? Lizzy didn't cry, not ever. Levelheaded, independent, stubborn, practical, and reliable were all words to describe Lizzy Stewart. That Lizzy he could accept and even admire at times. This new Lizzy was an enigma—unpredictable and emotional. And those were two qualities he couldn't tolerate in any woman.

Well, if she thought he felt lousy because of what he'd said, she was dead wrong. And if she thought he'd apologize for pointing out her rude behavior, she'd better not hold her breath. No! She needed a good lesson in eating what she dished out.

As he stacked the firewood in a sheltered corner against the porch, Sam continued to chew on Lizzy's response. With the rhythm of the task and the physical exertion involved, his anger slowly dissipated, replaced by a concern he couldn't ignore. Why hadn't she laid into him about his cattle? Then at least he'd have some answers instead of this queasy disquiet that kept nagging at him. Once he had closure, he *would* stay away from her.

Finally, he placed the last chunk of wood on top of the pile and covered it with a canvas tarp he'd stashed in the back of his truck. That done, Sam glanced at the door of the old house and considered his options. He hadn't heard a single sound from behind that door since Lizzy had closed it. He knew he should just hop into his truck, hightail it on out of there, and consider it lucky that he'd only tangled with her the one time. In truth, he couldn't afford to tussle with Lizzy.

However, the altercation left a bitter taste in his mouth. His sense of decency was waging a battle with his will to escape, and the former was winning. Perhaps he should make sure she was okay. And if she was, well, maybe he'd mention his dilemma—the land he needed for his cattle—before she sent him on his way.

A puffy-eyed Lizzy answered the door, the bill of her cap pulled low to try to hide them. Those red-rimmed eyes weren't as lethal as during their previous encounters. Even so, she only stared at him—a distant look to her—and left him standing on the frosty porch.

"Do you suppose I could come in?" he asked, careful to keep a neutral tone in his voice. "I don't want to let out what little heat you have in there."

She frowned, eyeballing him long and hard, before she stepped back to let him inside. To his surprise, the damp, musty room was lit by several glowing light bulbs. Stacks of cardboard boxes and an ice chest cluttered the grimy floor, and it appeared that she was stocking the ancient refrigerator—now home to a variety of vegetables, meats, and small containers.

"You might want to close that," he said, nodding toward the fridge.

Lizzy stepped around the ice chest, carefully pushed the refrigerator door shut, and pressed an ear to it as if to make certain it was humming away on its way to preserving her perishables. Then she stood still and silent, like a frosty ice sculpture, cold eyes on him.

Evidently, she had no plans to apologize. In fact, he doubted that she'd even speak to him. She didn't appear to be angry anymore; she seemed more resigned to him being there—merely enduring his presence.

Shivers slithered across his shoulders, whether from Lizzy or the temperature in the room, he wasn't sure. Lizzy still wore her down jacket. He wondered how she would've kept warm if he hadn't brought her the wood. The obsolete furnace, used to heat the house in its prime, had most likely conked out long ago.

"I'm gonna bring some of that wood in and start a fire; get it warmed up in here," Sam told her. Before she could formulate a rejoinder, he turned and strode out the door.

He loaded his arms with several hefty chunks and carried them into the house, eyeing Lizzy when he passed by her. She still stood by the fridge, her gaze tracking him as he crossed to the living room.

"You have a hatchet?" he yelled. Hopefully, he wouldn't be whittling a pile of kindling with his pocket knife.

His answer was a muffled sound followed by the closing of the kitchen door. Sam huffed, then searched the gloomy rooms for some paper. He found part of a yellowed newspaper lining a kitchen cabinet and had just wadded it into a ball when Lizzy reappeared with a shiny hatchet clutched in her hand. She looked as if she might be planning to hack off his head or some other major body part. Instead, she handed it to him without a word, then disappeared out the kitchen door with a resounding slam.

The striped cat materialized from the shadows and sat nonchalantly, eyes glued on Sam while he chopped small sticks from a hunk of wood and layered them around the newspaper. He dug a battered butane lighter out of his pocket and lit the pile, then, once bright flames licked up around it, carefully positioned a couple of pieces of firewood over the blaze. Smoke filtered around him, masking the fetid odor of mildew. He could hear Lizzy shuffling in and out of the kitchen.

When the fire was burning well, he hauled in several more logs and stacked them next to the hearth. The cat had stretched out on its side, its four paws reaching toward the heat, clearly appreciative of Sam's efforts even if Lizzy wasn't.

Warmth radiated from the leaping flames, enticing Sam to pull up one of the rocking chairs and settle into it to thaw his chilled middle-age body. It felt right to be sitting in the familiar, old rocker, so Sam leaned back, his feet joining the cat's in a search for heat and his fingers stroking the well-worn smoothness of the chair's arms.

If he closed his eyes just so, he could almost picture Con Stewart in the chair beside him, his deep, melodic voice in cadence with the rhythmic rocking and his eyes twinkling as he recounted some tale of rural farm life. Con had always found humor in even the most mundane situations. A warm glow flowed through Sam as he mused over a few of Con's more colorful stories.

What the hell was going on? Sam wondered, his body shooting upright. He was getting downright morbid, sitting here conjuring ghosts of people who were long gone. And this, too, was because of Lizzy.

Speaking of Lizzy, where was she? He needed to corner her, discuss his use of her land, and be on his way. He hadn't heard a peep from her for—well, actually, he wasn't sure how long he'd sat there lost in "la-la-land." Sam pushed himself out of the chair and coached his protesting body towards the kitchen. The sleeping cat didn't even peek up at him.

Except for the addition of a few more bags to the mountain of boxes, the kitchen was empty, which meant that Lizzy must be outside. Sam tugged up his coat collar against the chill and headed out the door. The sun was well into the west—time for him to get a move on if he wanted to arrive in town before the hardware store closed. There was no sign of Lizzy, but her Explorer still sat in the driveway, so she had to be nearby.

Hammering sounds were coming from somewhere—Lizzy? Sam surveyed the rest of the farmyard. It looked dilapidated and undisturbed. Several weather-worn sheds dotted the landscape, their gray exteriors and sagging roofs testament to years of neglect. His eyes landed on one of the smaller shacks, one nestled down into the cold soil, its doors thrown open. He walked toward it, and as he got nearer, the harsh clanking of metal against metal grew louder.

It took a few seconds for his eyes to adjust when he peeked in through the door. A weak flashlight beam and hazy rays filtering in through the open doorway provided meager light in the tiny cavern. Lizzy kneeled in the dank shadows, but he couldn't quite make out what she was doing. With a wrench clenched in her pounding fist, she appeared to be demolishing a piece of equipment.

When Sam stepped through the doorway, her head jerked up, a wary expression evident even in the dim light. The baseball cap was pushed back, and strands of dark hair floated around her dirt-streaked face. Noting her bright red nose and ears, Sam figured she must be half frozen. He'd been in here less than a minute, and a deep chill had already settled into his bones. The smell of dirt permeated the place, the taste of it thick on his tongue.

"You really think you're gonna get that thing going?" he asked, nodding at the rust-encrusted motor.

Eyes wary, she slowly nodded.

"It looks older than this farm. You might need to haul your water in while you're here," Sam advised, hoping she'd take the hint and give up on something so hopeless.

"Granddad put this one in new that last summer. It's hardly been used. If I can knock off some of this rust and get it started, it'll work fine," she argued before she turned back to her wrench and the abused hunk of corroded iron she pounded on.

Sam had serious doubts. Still, if what she said was true, the pump might provide her with enough water to get by for the short stretch she'd be here—the shorter, the better as far as he was concerned.

"Why don't you let me have a look?" he prodded, bracing himself.

She didn't even glance up. "Thank you, but I'll manage." There was determination and a "don't mess with me" tone to her voice.

Sam knew he should walk away and let her beat the old pump to death, but something was stopping him. Maybe it was a vision of Lizzy—grimy, frozen, and indomitable—hammering away for several hours in this icy tomb. Or maybe it was the spirits of Con and Dottie urging him on.

"Dammit, Lizzy. Do we have to go through this again? You keep banging on that, and no one is gonna be able to fix it. Now will you just leave it the hell alone and let me see what I can do with it?"

Her head shot up. "Why won't you just leave *me* the hell alone? I don't want you here."

She reminded Sam of a mare he'd once had who'd spent more than thirty hours struggling to deliver her foal, only to have it die shortly afterward. Lizzy and that mare had the same look about them—beaten.

"We've already covered that," he told her, a serious edge to his voice though he fought to appear calm.

Her look said she just might use the wrench on him, but with a huff, she rose, tossed the wrench onto the dirt floor, and stomped out of the pump house.

Sam shook his head and breathed a deep sigh, exasperated. Then he picked up the flashlight and took inventory of the situation before he headed to his truck to get his toolbox and a more powerful light. Lizzy was nowhere in sight. Sam steered his mind from an image of her sitting in that bleak house sobbing and forced himself to concentrate on the matter at hand.

He needed to get that pump sucking water and get out of here before he got any more mixed up in restoring life to something that was better off dead.

❀ ❀ ❀

As it turned out, Lizzy was right. Underneath the dirt and grime and layers of rust, the pump still had some life in it. Sam double-checked the fittings, gauges, and switches, then collected his tools before he lugged them to the front porch. He slid the idea of a productive conversation with Lizzy into the "to do" pile and didn't bother to knock.

Lizzy, a filthy rag clutched in her hand, stopped her scrubbing to eyeball him as he walked through the door. Sam ignored her and stepped to the sink. He turned the cold water knob as far as it would go. There were some gurgling, belching sounds, and at last, a brown-tainted spurt of water gushed from the nozzle.

He turned the knob off and faced Lizzy. "You'd better let that run awhile before you use it," he said matter-of-factly.

Lizzy nodded, eyes glazed. Though she still wore her jacket, the air inside the house felt warmer. He walked into the living room and threw a couple more logs onto the fire, disturbing the slumbering cat, which promptly rose, stretched, and sauntered off.

When Sam returned to the kitchen, Lizzy held the purring cat, her slender fingers stroking its sleek dark fur. Sam's mind flashed back to another time, to a younger Lizzy, her hands slowly caressing an adoring feline while her dark eyes probed his as if they knew his every thought and a whole lot more. He shook the ghosts aside and studied her. It seemed she always had a cat attached to her—almost spooky. Of course, he'd always found Lizzy a bit unnerving. Today was no exception.

"The house shouldn't give you much trouble. We made the repairs that needed to be made—replaced some windows and the roof and any boards that needed it. You've got water, electricity, and enough wood to last awhile, so you should be fine." With that, Sam was ready to get out of there. Though he had no resolution about his cattle, things were looking up: Lizzy hadn't hounded him about her mooing morning visitors.

"Thank you," Lizzy murmured, her eyes still probing his.

This time Sam just nodded, surprised that she'd thanked him since she was clearly pissed off about his interference. "If you need anything else, you know where the ranch is."

Now it's on her shoulders, Sam promised himself as he mentally wiped his hands of all responsibilities relating to Lizzy and the farm and turned to leave.

"Keep your cows away from my house," came a quiet voice from behind him.

It stopped him in his tracks. Warmth flooded his cheeks. "Beg your pardon?" he probed, turning to face her.

She was pulling strength from somewhere—he could see it—bracing herself for a quarrel. "I said, 'Keep your cows away from my house.'" It was definitely a demand, not a request.

Sam's blood simmered. He locked his jaw to prevent something from slipping out that he'd regret later. For several long moments, their eyes remained locked.

There was something else in Lizzy's eyes, something that spoke of times Sam didn't want to revisit, something that set his heart to hammering in his chest. He fought to control a deluge of emotions and finally broke free.

Now was definitely not the time to ask her if his cows *could* be on her property as long as they stayed away from her house, so with a brief nod, he made a hasty exit, grabbed his toolbox, and strode to his truck. He was desperate to put some distance between himself and Lizzy.

But as he headed down the road, he gave in to the urge to glance in the rearview mirror. Lizzy stood on the porch with the cat cradled in her arms, eyes riveted on him.

"Lord, help me," Sam whispered into the silence. He gunned the motor and felt the wheels slide, then stick as he sped over the hill towards town.

CHAPTER 7

Sam knew he was pushing it on the way into town, but he was running late and that last encounter with Lizzy had left his insides twisted into tight knots. He'd rather focus on keeping his truck on the road than on Lizzy and her erratic behaviors. Right now, he had a serious hankering for a little peace and quiet, and he was determined to get it.

It had been hours since his prickly breakfast with Eb, and his stomach was grumbling its protest. The sun now stretched out to the mountain range, shrouding the sagebrush-covered hills with a vivid tangerine veil and the promise of more frost. Though heat streamed from the vents, Sam still shivered from the hour he'd spent in the icy pump house.

When he pulled into the parking lot at the hardware store, Sam figured he'd probably set some kind of record, matched only by his recklessness in adolescence. He perused the lot, hoping to see Franny's red Toyota, not Junior's Silverado. He was in no mood to tolerate Junior's haranguing and complaining today. The man had an opinion about everything and no qualms about sharing them with everyone within earshot. Though it was general knowledge that folks went to extreme measures to avoid crossing paths with Junior and his tetchy attitude, Hawkins Hardware seemed to prosper, owing much to the fact that it was the only hardware store in the area and to Junior's good fortune in convincing Franny to be his wife.

There was no sign of the Silverado, so Sam figured he'd pick up the faucet, chitchat with Franny a few moments, and be on his way. The store bordered on empty with a couple of women roaming the aisles. Sam found what he needed to get the faucet back in working order, then made his way to the checkout counter and a scowling Junior.

"Afternoon, Junior," Sam greeted him, struggling to mask his displeasure.

"Sam," Junior grumbled. "Kind of late in the day for you to be in town, ain't it?"

"Got a late start. Just needed to pick up this faucet."

"You the one that needs it?"

Sam wasn't sure what Junior was getting at. He seemed even more surly than usual. Surely, Junior wasn't going to provoke an argument over a fixture?

"Can't think of anyone else I'd be buying it for." He confirmed, setting the faucet on the counter and hoping to escape before Junior subjected him to a lengthy diatribe.

"Lizzy Stewart was in here today. Thought you might be buying it for her," Junior challenged, his voice and general attitude conveying a contempt that Sam was sure he'd hear all about if he let himself be drawn into this conversation.

"Nope," Sam uttered through clenched teeth. He slid his debit card from his wallet and handed it to Junior.

Junior eyed the card, then grabbed it out of Sam's hands. "Hiding behind a hat and some fancy sunglasses, she was, but I'd recognize her anywhere. She's got her nerve, coming back here after what she done." He snorted disgustedly, processed the transaction, and stuffed the faucet into a paper bag.

Sam bit his tongue, determined to not feed Junior's tirade. Sam might not like it, but the farm was Lizzy's, and she had every right to be there, no matter what she had or hadn't done. He seriously doubted that she'd be around for long, but he chose not to share that thought with Junior.

"J.D. just might pop up out of his grave with her out there livin' right next to the ranch, as if she belongs there and has any right to that farm after walkin' away and leavin' it for—must be more than twenty years. Can't think Con and Dottie would be any too thrilled with her either. After all the hard work they put into that farm, she takes off without a backward glance. Lets it become the rundown place it is today. Probably didn't have a second thought about what she did to Con and Dottie either. Most likely, glad to be rid of them, so they didn't tie her down.

"J.D. told me all about it, you know. Still riles me that Lizzy got away free and clear. Slipped away in the middle of the night like a sneaky, flea-ridden coyote."

Similar thoughts had passed through Sam's mind, but hearing them uttered by Junior irritated him. He signed the debit slip, stuffed his copy into his pocket, and picked up the bag. "Nice chatting with you, Junior," he murmured as he turned to leave.

Being Junior, he couldn't leave it at that. "John bein' your brother and all, I'd think you'd have somethin' to say on the subject. You know, don't you, if she'd stayed, he'd still be alive."

Sam hesitated for only an instant, then expelled the air he'd held and continued on towards the doors, slamming through them.

Of course, walking out of there without having it out with Junior took its toll on him. By the time he reached his truck, he swore sparks were shooting from his body. If he had it to do over, he'd deck Junior and let the consequences be what they were. The message Junior had thrown at him was a blatant insult, one meant to challenge Sam to do the honorable thing, whatever Junior, in his warped and deviant mind, conceived that to be.

Truth be told, it was none of Junior's business what Sam did—or Lizzy, for that matter. The past was over and done with, and it was long past time for Junior to move on and let go of his caustic obsession with something that couldn't be redone. Sam was tired of hearing about it from him.

Still fuming, Sam pointed his truck back down Main Street. Daylight was fading; lights flickered on up and down the street. Sam parked across the street from Mel's Diner and sat in the cab, determined to get a grip on his anger. He filled his mind with pleasant thoughts, like the thick, juicy t-bone he planned to order when he felt calm enough to do so and the baked potato he'd slather with sour cream and butter. And even though he knew he shouldn't, he'd reward himself for surviving this day from hell with a warm slice of Mel's apple pie. He might even have a couple of beers. They should help take the edge off.

Unable to waylay his rumbling stomach any longer, Sam crossed the street and entered the diner. The dinner crowd hadn't settled in yet, but a few teenagers lounged in booths, sipping pop and nibbling fries, and a couple of blue-haired women conversed conspiringly over mugs of coffee. The mouth-watering smell of roasting beef permeated the air, prompting Sam's stomach to growl loudly. Noises filtering from the bar indicated that a lively happy hour was in progress. Sam was in no mood to spend an hour pretending to be happy or, for that matter, to indulge in idle conversation.

He spotted a corner booth and climbed in, his back towards the door. Though he had memorized the menu forty years ago, he was engrossed in reading each and every word on it when Mel arrived to take his order. She gave him a questioning look, raised one perfectly painted eyebrow, and nodded towards the menu.

"Hmmm. Memory problems already, huh? And here you are, a man still in your prime. If it weren't for the whiskers and the bloodshot eyes and the fact that your hair looks like it hasn't seen a comb since winter set in, the temptation might even be too much for me. Is this a new rugged look you're going for, or is there a reason you're sitting here in the corner hiding behind a menu you know full well I'll never change?"

Once again, Mel and her tart tongue didn't mince words. Nothing got by her. She always sensed when something was bothering him and was there to confront, listen, and offer her own brand of advice, which was usually pretty sound since Mel had done a lot more living than most people.

Though she must be well into her seventies, Mel still did a lot more living than most people, himself included. Through the years, her red hair had acquired a brassier luster, and a network of deep wrinkles now lurked under the layers of makeup. But Mel was still as full of spit and fire as the alluring younger woman who had frequented Sam's earlier years.

"You're right, as usual, Mel." He left it at that. "I'll have a t-bone—rare—a baked potato, and a salad with ranch dressing. And . . . a Heineken." Sam evaded Mel's probing eyes. Hopefully, she'd take his not-so-subtle hint and leave him alone.

She did, then returned a couple of minutes later with a cold beer and a basket of warm bread. Without comment, she walked off. Sam swigged beer and dug into the bread, slathering it with honey-butter. He was so engrossed in easing his hunger that he didn't recognize the pungent perfume wafting his way until it was too late.

"Hi, Sam. I saw your truck across the street. It's a good thing I was passing by, or we would've missed each other. How's about I join you? You're looking kind of lonely. I'll cheer you up."

Caught off guard, Sam just gawked at the beautiful young blonde who blabbered while she slid into *his* booth. Before she quite sat down, an older, more mature woman maneuvered into the space across from him and plopped a dinner salad down in front of him.

"I'm sorry, dear. Sam and I made arrangements for dinner. Guess you'll have to take a rain check," Mel informed Gina with a "don't even think about it" attitude.

Gina, a determined set to her mouth, glowered at Mel. The standoff was short-lived with the more experienced woman winning, of course.

Recovering quickly, Gina blinked fitfully, then flashed a syrupy smile at Sam. "I'll just hang out in the bar until you're through with your dinner. Join me when you're done. I'll keep a seat nice and warm for you, right next to me." She flashed him a suggestive smile and wiggled off in a pair of jeans Sam thought must wreak havoc with her circulatory system.

Sam watched her, shaking his head with frustration. Hopefully, she'd become attached to some unsuspecting younger man and forget she'd ever known Sam.

"You owe me big time for this one," Mel informed him. "I should be back there getting ready for the dinner hour, and now I'm stuck here with you. And it's just my luck that you're in one of the foulest moods I've ever seen you in."

Sam forked lettuce into his mouth. He chewed and swallowed while he considered Mel's words. She was probably right. Usually, he was amiable and even-tempered and tolerated the company of others—well, most others. Something was poking away beneath his skin. He knew what that something was, but he sure couldn't figure out how to handle her.

"Thanks, Mel," he muttered. "Actually, you probably saved us both from a heap of trouble. I don't think I could've put up with Gina tonight. Probably would've strangled her right here in this booth to shut her up."

"She seems to think she's tagged you," Mel said, studying him closely.

Sam shrugged. "All I did was take her out a couple of times—in hindsight, two times too many."

He'd made a mistake: he hadn't taken Gina seriously when she'd come on to him. Usually he was spot-on when it came to women. He knew what worked for him and what to avoid, and he stuck to it.

He didn't know if he'd just been out of the circuit too long and was desperate for female company or what, but the impression he'd formed of Gina was that she liked to play the field and had no interest in a serious relationship. He'd blindly taken the bait and had quickly discovered that he couldn't have been more wrong. Gina was out to land a husband, and he'd become her primary target. As luck would have it, she now refused to get the blatant message he was sending her: he was *not* interested.

Sam munched on salad while Mel contemplated fuchsia fingernails sharp enough to classify as weapons. Finally, she spoke. "She'll come to terms with that, eventually. She's nearing thirty. She probably sees that perfect body of hers starting to sag a bit here and there, and she panics. Most of the men around here are either married or younger than her, so the pickings are getting pretty slim—no offense meant. Lately, Gina seems desperate to find herself a husband with money while she's still got the looks to attract one.

"I know she can be a pain in the butt, but I feel kind of sorry for her. Since her grandmother died, she's been alone. She's always flitted from one man to the next. Never stuck with any of them. Then she latches onto you, and now you're gonna dump her. Might've been that you shouldn't have taken her up on her offer in the first place."

Mel's disapproval stung. Still, Sam couldn't work up much sympathy towards Gina. She really was a pain in the butt. He noted the sadness that had settled into Mel's usually bright eyes and took a long chug of beer, letting the rebuke slide.

She gave him a stern look, her eyebrows raised, eyes firm. "Don't be too hard on her, Sam. You weren't here to see it, but she's been through some tough times. When Jean Riley—Gina's mom—got that brain tumor, she needed some special treatment and had to go to Seattle to get it. J.D. loaned Pete the money. Pete wanted to be near his wife, so Gina was shipped off to stay with friends and relatives. By the time Jean passed away, Pete owed J.D. a bundle. I can't fault J.D. for taking the Riley farm in payment; it was the only way he'd get his money back.

"But Pete didn't take it well. It seems that back during the sheep and cattle scuffles, J.D.'s granddaddy fenced Riley sheep off of open grazing land. Claimed it was his, not the government's. The Rileys being a bunch of hotheads, they tore down the fence, which only infuriated your great-granddaddy. He slaughtered close to a hundred Riley sheep—with the Sheepshooters' support, no doubt. You know how it went back then. The local law didn't step in, and the Rileys lost a big chunk of their land, which ended up in your great-granddaddy's hands."

Mel sighed deeply. "Well, Pete still harbored some ill-will over that whole mess, especially after the rest of his family land was handed over to J.D. When he and Gina moved into town . . . well, things fell apart for both of them. Gina was pretty much left in the care of her grandmother. Now she's gone, too."

A wave of remorse unsettled Sam. Although he knew J.D. had managed to get his hands on Pete's land—land that J.D. had always had his covetous eyes on—he hadn't known the specifics. "Dad was involved in a lot of sleazy deals, but that pretty much takes the cake," he muttered.

Mel nodded. "Pete was never the same after that. He took to drinking and ended up dead in a pile of fresh snow behind the Corral. Sheriff Mulkins figured he came out of there drunk and passed out in the alley. I suppose that's why Gina's always chasing after some man—looking for what she lost. A father."

While guilt nagged at Sam with news of another of his father's shenanigans, his steak arrived, sizzling hot, bathing his face in a mouth-watering haze. Sam thanked the young man who delivered it.

"Well, gotta go help out. I'll be back with another beer," Mel said as she scooted out of the booth.

Sam, determined to enjoy the few moments of peace and quiet, devoured his dinner in solitude. He'd swallowed the last bite when Mel returned, dew-dripping Heineken in one hand and a steaming mug of coffee in the other. It appeared she was settling in, and coffee only meant one thing—conversation. Satiated and somewhat mellowed by his full stomach and the beer, Sam pushed his empty plate aside and relaxed back against the padded seat, bottle in hand.

The two of them sat in silence, her sipping, him swilling. Sam knew she'd wait until he was ready. "Lizzy Stewart's back," he finally said, watching for her reaction. She didn't even bat an eye.

"That poor girl. So she finally returned, did she?" Mel was eyeing him closely, too.

"Yep. Only I wouldn't call her a girl. She looks pretty much the same, but she's definitely a woman." It didn't come out sounding like he'd meant it to. Not that Lizzy had aged badly—she was still attractive. He could see that even with most of her body bundled inside several layers of heavy clothing and half of her face covered.

Mel smile knowingly. "She always was a pretty little thing, especially after she grew into her arms and legs," she observed. "I liked Lizzy. She was odd in some ways, but who wouldn't be after all she went through? That father of hers was a real piece of work. I'll bet her life wasn't all that great before she got dropped off at Con and Dottie's." Mel paused to sip some coffee, then sighed. "So, you've seen her then?"

Sam nodded. "Yeah, a couple of times. Stopped by there last night when I noticed a car parked outside the house and again this afternoon to drop off some firewood." He chose not to mention his early morning fiasco.

"And how does she seem?"

Fighting mad Sam almost growled. Instead, he breathed deeply and spilled his guts. "I can't figure it out. Last night she seemed like Lizzy, more or less, all headstrong and independent and 'I can take care of myself, so don't get too close.' Same thing this afternoon, at first. But then, just like that, she cracked and turned . . . well, fragile, like she was barely holding it together. She definitely wants to be left alone. And she's made it perfectly clear that she can barely tolerate the sight of me."

Mel appeared to be lost in her own thoughts, searching the depths of her coffee, fingers stroking the sides of the mug. Several long moments passed before she spoke. "Is she alone?"

Sam thought it odd that Eb and Mel had both asked if Lizzy was alone. "Appears to be," he replied.

She looked up, more relaxed. "Did she say why she's here?"

"Nope. But I have a case of Glenfarclas Single Malt Scotch stashed in my basement that I'd be willing to trade for the answer to that question," Sam informed her.

He paused, something tickling at the back of his mind. It took several seconds of silent searching before he captured it. "You know, a couple of months ago, Franny Hawkins asked me if I had Lizzy's address. Said she'd found one of John's letters, and she wanted to send it to Lizzy. Maybe Franny asked her to come back. Wouldn't make sense, though, since Junior's gone beyond what is even tolerable to let Franny and everyone else in town know his feelings for Lizzy. I was just at the hardware store and had to listen to Junior rant about Lizzy being back."

Mel's gaze turned oddly intense. "So . . . Franny found John's letter, huh? And she was gonna send it to Lizzy?"

Sam shrugged. "That's what she said. Course, I don't know if she ever got the address. Like I said, I can't see Junior tolerating it if Franny gets chummy with Lizzy again."

"Hmmm." Mel focus seemed to drift. "So is that why you came in here in such a foul mood, because of Lizzy? Or was it because you had to deal with Junior?" she finally asked.

"It's her. Well, not just her. It's all that shit that comes with her—you know, all of those things that happened. With Lizzy gone, it was all dead and buried. It's been years since I've even thought about it. Now here she is, and it's being dredged up again."

Once Sam started talking, he couldn't stop. Putting his thoughts into words felt good, like discarding a fifty-pound pack after a twenty-mile hike.

"I'm starting to think it affected me more than I thought it did. I'm angry, and I'm on edge. I can't seem to settle down. I've got a bunch of cattle on her land, and I need to keep them there. I'd sure like to know if she's gonna kick them off. If she does, it'll cost me more than I want to think about.

"There's something else, too, something that keeps pestering me. I can't put my finger on it, but it's damn disturbing, and I know it's connected to Lizzy."

He gulped beer and rubbed his bristly chin before he added, "There's always been something about her that throws me off balance. And I'm feeling a hell of a lot of animosity towards her. She shouldn't have left John. She knew he needed her. No matter what she did, she should've stayed to face the consequences and marry John instead of running away."

Mel looked as troubled as Sam. "You know, Sam, sometimes things aren't what they appear to be. J.D. or Eb didn't talk with you about Lizzy's leaving?" She seemed surprised.

Sam shook his head. "I never asked," Sam confessed. "I wasn't here when it happened, and I never bothered to question it. I suppose I really didn't want to know. Maybe I was in denial, but it didn't seem important, probably because none of it affected me at the time. If I had my druthers, I'd rather just leave it in the past where it belongs now, too. I wish I wouldn't think about it, and I wish I could figure out what it is that I don't want to think about. Maybe then I could lay it to rest.

"And I wish Lizzy would go back to wherever the hell she came from and stay out of our lives." He shook his head, an effort to shake her from his life. "Any words of wisdom for me?"

Mel was visibly upset, her mouth working, eyes not quite meeting his. "You need to discuss this with Eb, or Lizzy," she informed him matter-of-factly. "Right now, I have customers I need to see to."

Sam glanced around the corner of the booth. Three more

tables were occupied, not enough to put Mel into a lather. He turned back to her. Yes, she was clearly troubled. "Thanks for listening, Mel," Sam said as he handed her his debit card. "I hope I didn't upset you with my ramblings?"

She sighed and managed a half smile. "I'm fine. How can I be upset when I can still lure a good-looking guy from a beautiful woman and enjoy his company for a short while?" She paused to pat his hand reassuringly. "You be sure to have that chat with Eb or Lizzy now. Maybe one of them can answer your questions."

Sam grabbed his coat and hat and followed Mel to the cash register. While she completed the transaction, he slipped the coat on and nodded a greeting to a couple at a nearby table.

As Mel handed him the slip to sign, she murmured, "You know, I'm always here for you when you need someone to talk to." A sad, faraway look settled into her eyes. "You're so much like your daddy. He used to come in here, and we'd sit and visit just like you and I did tonight." With a deep sigh, she wandered off and left Sam to sign the slip and to wonder what that comment about J.D. was all about. It wasn't like Mel to wander off in the middle of a business transaction.

When Sam stepped outside, a wall of icy air blasted him, sneaking down his neck, into his jacket and across his shoulders. He tugged at his collar before he jogged across the street, climbed into his truck, and started the engine to get the heat flowing. While he worked sheepskin-lined gloves onto his fingers, he happened to glance across the street. Gina stood outside the diner, her intense stare riveted on him, pleading.

"Shit!" he hissed. Why did J.D. have to take her home from her in such a heartless manner? Telling himself that it was J.D. that did it, not him, he pulled away from the curb and drove off without a backward glance. It was time he made a clean break from Gina. The whole lousy mess left a sour taste in his mouth.

Sam took his time on the drive home. The roads shimmered in the glow from his headlights, slick from frost that had settled onto them. Thanks to Mel's listening ear, he felt better. Still, he had reservations about confronting Eb with any more questions. Eb's actions earlier today clearly indicated that he didn't want to relive the past either. And Sam sure as hell wouldn't be conducting any lengthy conversations with Lizzy.

He'd missed something—something important. He knew that even if he didn't know what it was. Still, he didn't want to pursue the issue. A portentous feeling deep in his gut kept warning him that it was a dead-end road—over and done with—and stirring up the ashes might not be worth the firestorm.

By the time Sam passed by Lizzy's farm, he'd decided to avoid

Lizzy as much as it was humanly possible to avoid your nearest neighbor. If he steered clear of her for a couple of days, they both might calm down enough to have a civilized conversation concerning his use of her land. Then he'd reclaim his mundane—but oh so comfortable—life and move on. They would both get what they wanted: Lizzy would get him out of her life, and he'd get her out of his.

He barely noticed the smoke billowing from the chimney or the soft glow through the now clean and bare windows. As he drove past, he only allowed himself a fleeting thought concerning Lizzy and what she might be doing inside that house.

In fact, he was so focused on barring thoughts of Lizzy from his mind that he didn't pause to question it when the automobile lights that had been annoyingly bright in his rearview mirror during the last ten minutes suddenly darkened.

CHAPTER 8

Lizzy's eyes shot open. She laid stick still, orienting herself, her heart pounding. Glowing coals provided a nest of amber light near the fireplace, fading to black as it filtered out into the room. She pushed the sleeping bag to her waist, shivers snaking across her shoulders, and sat up to search the dark spaces. Something had awakened her. What?

Her gaze dropped—no Sid. Was it him she'd heard, prowling the house in the middle of the night, hopefully annihilating a few pesky rodents?

Air spewed from her mouth as she settled back down onto the sagging couch and tugged the sleeping bag up against the biting chill. Her mind slid back to the previous day—to Sam—and she shivered again, not from the cold this time. His presence had brought disturbing feelings gushing to the surface, feelings she'd kept hidden in some dark cavern deep within herself.

She'd watched him drive off before she stepped into the house to crumple into a heap on the kitchen floor, trembling and sobbing with hurt and anger, and with self-disgust because she hadn't stood up to him. Lately, she was too often devastated by the realization that she was only a remnant of the person she'd once been.

"And I have you to thank for that, Sam Craig," she hissed. "You and your daddy. I. . . ."

A thumping sound from outside halted her ranting. She froze, straining to hear what was going on in her yard, but the pounding in her head drowned any outside noises. "Kitty. Kitty," she squeaked. No Sid. She swallowed over the painful lump lodged in her throat and sat up.

Were those blasted cows back? Or Sam—she'd watched his truck fly by earlier on his way back to the ranch—had he returned to snoop again? Maybe there was a reason he wouldn't stay away. Maybe there was something here that he wanted.

With that thought, Lizzy slipped out of the sleeping bag and pushed herself onto her stocking-covered feet. She took a stiff breath to fortify herself and shuffled to the east window, clinging to the dark shadows. Thanks to hot water and a lot of elbow grease, she could now see out that window. Unfortunately, even with a sea of stars sparkling in the sky, it was as black as J.D. Craig's heart out there. Hoping her eyes would adjust, she searched the darkness for any signs of movement. There were none.

Still, she swore she heard soft wisps of sound. It had to be Sam's cows. He'd probably driven them back here to torment her.

She slid across to the west window and trailed her eyes towards where the barn would be. Surely noise wouldn't reach her from way down there?

Contemplating her options, she rubbed her trembling arms against the piercing chill. Should she turn on a light or shine one out into the blackened yard? No, if someone was out there, that might endanger her life. And she certainly couldn't step outside to take a look in the middle of the night, alone and weaponless. Her eyes grazed the three doors on the back wall, and she shuddered. The sounds were from this end of the house, thank goodness.

It has to be those pesky cows she assured herself. Still, she felt her way to the kitchen door, checked the lock to make sure it was secure, and as an added precaution, slid a couple of heavy cardboard boxes against the door. Then she hustled back to the relative warmth of the sleeping bag and crawled inside to cocoon herself against the chill from both the air and those persistent outside noises.

Sid hopped up to curl in next to her belly. She stroked him and told herself to get some sleep. Tomorrow would be a busy day. If she was ever going to get off this musty couch and into one of the bedrooms, she'd either have to confront the old furnace and breathe some life into it or have a new one installed. And that was only half of it. The ancient monster water heater that occupied more than its share of the laundry room called to her, too. Once she tackled it, she had a house to clean, a grimy, filthy, badly-in-need-of-a-coat-of-fresh-paint house. And a body to bathe—hers.

She continued to map and plan—anything to keep her mind off Sam and the rustling noises—until her body relaxed into the warmth of the bag and her eyes grew heavy. Her last thought was that once she'd accomplished all of that, she'd find out what happened to John.

❀ ❀ ❀

Goosebumps sprouted on Lizzy's arms and torso, painful pricks that made her shiver. Grabbing her coat and tugging it on, she followed in Sid's paw prints to the kitchen door. The boxes shoved against it were a silent reminder of her nearly sleepless night. She yawned and lugged them aside before she opened the door a crack to let Sid squeeze through to the outside and to peek out into the yard.

All was quiet this morning, just a couple of turkey buzzards soaring overhead, dive-bombing, their wings dark against the blue sky. No cows wandering about. And no Sam.

Still groggy, she closed and locked the door, then eyeballed the mess in front of her. *One step at a time* she assured herself as she grabbed some matches and several paper towels and plodded to the fireplace.

Soon the fire was restored, oozing tendrils of heat into the frigid room, mingling with the aroma of freshly brewed coffee and the steam that billowed from a pot of water heating on the stove.

Lizzy pulled a chipped "Elect Dick" mug from the cabinet and rinsed it well before filling it with a shot of caffeine—her first in nearly forty-eight hours. Even the thought of holding Richard Nixon's tarnished image in her hands didn't deter her from savoring that first sip. With a breakfast bar and a notepad and pen, she settled into a rocker to put her in-the-wee-hours planning session to paper.

Though she'd spent the previous evening cleaning and polishing, she'd barely touched the surface. The work necessary to make the farmhouse habitable was overwhelming, a good thing from Lizzy's perspective. If she kept her mind and body occupied with the numerous menial tasks, she might get some reprieve from the mind-numbing pain and nagging questions. And if she worked to the point of exhaustion, she'd fall into a deep sleep tonight—dream free.

So she set to work. First, she attacked the old water heater in the washroom with a hefty wrench. She detached the pipes from it and cleaned them all, just as she'd watched her grandfather do so many years before. Luckily, she was able to get it all put back together, and when she cautiously turned some knobs and switches, it began to fill with water and make a humming noise. She stood back a ways and held her breath, half expecting it to blow up, then breathed out and decided not to push her luck; the furnace could wait for another day.

When she walked into the kitchen, her eyes landed on the front door, and she paused. Sid! He was still out in the cold, surely anxious to get inside to his morning chow. She hurried to the door and drew it open, her eyes dropping to apologize to the poor cat. Only Sid wasn't there. Where was he?

She searched the frost-dusted yard. "Kitty! Kitty! Kitty!" she cried. Three black vultures shot up from behind her Explorer and soared high into the sky over the farmyard, their massive wings fanned out.

Lizzy flinched, her pulse skyrocketing. Vultures could only mean one thing—not Sid; please, not Sid. She raced down the steps and around to the far side of the vehicle, then slid to a stop, trying to get her brain and eyes to agree on what lay at her feet. Her hand automatically reached for her stomach to still it.

Lying next to her Explorer was a bloody mass of bones, flesh, guts, and ginger hide. A cow's head with blank, glassy eyes clung to the disgusting carnage. Two turkey vultures tore at the carcass, their hooked beaks and black feathers dripping blood.

Bile rose in Lizzy's throat, bitter and burning. She swallowed hard and searched for signs that Sid might be a part of the bloodbath, then sighed deeply. Sid must be hiding somewhere, too frightened to sneak back to the house.

Lizzy shrieked, waving her arms madly at the ugly birds. They made a deep hissing sound, flapped their wings, and rose to join the three buzzards circling overhead. But they wouldn't stay away for long—experience had taught Lizzy that. She didn't want them near the house, but as long as their food was here, they would be, too.

Shaking her head with frustration, she eyed the dead cow. Something had killed it during the night, right here in her front yard while she was inside, too frightened to step outside and save its life. "Stop it," she muttered. "You're feeling guilty over the death of a cow—Sam's cow. Coyotes probably killed it, and you have no business messing with them."

Still, she hadn't heard any coyotes howling or cows bawling last night, just some bumping and rustling sounds. Maybe she'd slept through the slaughter, or maybe it's what had awakened her. Or maybe the cow died from natural causes. She wouldn't contemplate any other scenarios. After all, why would someone kill one of Sam's cows in her front yard?

Whatever the case, she'd have to let Sam know about it. That meant a trip to the ranch. She rubbed at the pressure building in her forehead, pushing thoughts of his reaction to the death of one of his precious cows aside. It could wait. Right now, she needed to move this carcass away from the farmhouse, and it was a given that she couldn't carry it out of here.

She studied the mangled mess, then dug in her jacket pocket for her keys and unlocked the car with the click of a button. After a quick rummage, she unearthed a nylon rope. Telling herself she'd touched much worse than this when she'd helped Granddad on the farm, she held her breath while she slipped the rope under the dead body, the fur scratchy against her frozen fingers. She secured the rope beneath a front leg with a square knot. With luck, it would hold long enough to get the carcass out of the yard. Then she climbed into the Explorer and backed it around to tie the other end of the rope to the trailer hitch.

She eyed the vultures circling overhead. Hopefully, they would follow her to gorge on the body and not swoop down to nibble on the tasty tidbits left behind. Sid would stay hidden until danger was gone, but Lizzy wouldn't be able to relax and get some work done until Sid was safely tucked inside the house.

"Well, get to it then," she muttered. With that, she climbed into her car, turned the key, and more slowly than a lazy porcupine, she dragged Sam's disgusting, dead cow down the bumpy, rutted road to the barn, the whole time picturing the gory trail being dribbled along the way.

She didn't even bother to gather her rope. She loosened it from the hitch and headed back to the house. In the front yard, a couple of buzzards were gnawing on the bloody leftovers. She honked her horn several times, the sharp blasts jarring in the silence, and jettisoned the nasty birds. Then she pulled the vehicle over the remains and switched off the ignition.

"Try and get to it now, you filthy scavengers," she murmured as she slid to the ground.

A quick perusal of the yard didn't disclose anything significant. The only footprints marring the morning frost were hers, and she couldn't tell if the cow pies and hoof prints were new or not. When she rounded the corner from the side yard, no vultures circled the farmyard. Sid waited patiently at the front door.

"We're gonna have to get used to this country living, huh, Sid," she murmured, reaching down to stroke his head. "Night noises. Dead cows. Scary birds. Sam Craig. What's next?" She shook her head. Hopefully, this would be the end of it.

Before she stepped inside, she grabbed an armful of firewood to add to the pile beside the hearth. She stacked a dry log onto the hot coals and held her numb hands out to the heat, wiggling the fingers to get blood flowing through them. Sid contentedly nibbled on his morning chow, then stretched out in front of the fire.

Wishing she could join Sid, Lizzy stifled a yawn and walked to the kitchen sink. "Please let there be hot water," she begged as she turned the handle. She dangled a finger in the stream of cold water, praying it would turn warm. Ever so slowly, it did—not hot yet, but warm. It was truly a blessing, a blessing that she scoured her dead-cow-infested hands in.

Impelled by the vision of a long, luxuriant soak in a tub of steaming hot water at the end of the day, she hauled her cleaning supplies into the bathroom and spent the next two hours scouring and scrubbing. By the time it was clean, if not sparkling, her stomach was grumbling annoyingly. She grabbed a cluster of grapes from the fridge and nibbled on them while she took stock of the clutter in the kitchen and considered her options: to attack this mess or drive to the ranch?

Her eyes drifted north to where the barn stood. That cow wasn't going anywhere—other than into those buzzards' bellies—and neither would the filth in this kitchen if she didn't get it out of here.

She sighed, knowing that eventually she'd have to make that drive south and chance another meeting with Sam.

❀ ❀ ❀

As the day progressed, Lizzy found it increasingly difficult to hold the memories at bay. They were a part of the aura surrounding her, intertwined with all that she saw and touched and heard and the very air she breathed. The crackling of the fire and its smoky tang, the tiny cracks in her grandmother's well-used dishes, the minute speckled dust mites floating in the rays of sunlight streaming through the luminous windows, and the encompassing stillness of it all were laced with warm memories. In this place, time was a ruse, changing and shifting and always lingering to relish the mundane.

Lizzy simply became a part of it all. She traveled to a time when the kitchen was full of the hustle and bustle of farm life. Her grandmother was there, stuffing cucumbers into canning jars at the sink and pulling a bubbling huckleberry pie from the oven. The enticing fragrance of freshly baked bread permeated the air, and Grandma's soothing alto voice humming the "Tennessee Waltz" echoed through the rooms.

And there they were—she and John—sitting across from each other at the battered kitchen table, seriously contemplating the cards they held in their hands, a plate of John's favorite chocolate chip cookies sitting within arm's reach. John's dark hair was a tousled mess, his gangly legs sprawled, feet encased in a pair of scuffed cowboy boots. In her denim cutoffs, Lizzy resembled a young sapling, her willowy legs curled beneath her, a couple of bare feet sticking out here and there.

"I'll see ya and raise ya five browns," John informed her, his face a blank slate as he pushed ten brown M&Ms to add to the growing pile in the center of the table.

Lizzy studied his blue eyes, searching for the tiniest shift. There was none. Of course, that meant nothing. Playing cards was one of their favorite pastimes, and they were both darn good at it. It was also one of the few times John stayed put. While life went on around them, they sat for hours, shuffling, dealing, and trying to outmaneuver each other.

Lizzy contemplated her cards, then glanced quickly up at John to catch him off guard. The two stared at each other over their fanned cards.

Few bluffers could match the two of them. Sam had been their teacher—Sam, whose legal career would provide him with ample opportunities to convince others to believe the unbelievable. Sam, it turned out, was the best bluffer of all. Ultimately, he deceived both her and John.

"Clock's tickin', Lizzy," John would prod her. "What's it gonna be?"

Lizzy contemplated her pile of candy. Finally, she selected three of the favored yellow M&Ms. "Raise ya ten," she declared and pushed them into the pot.

John flicked one yellow and five browns into the growing pile and laid down his cards: three jacks and a couple of threes. He gazed at Lizzy, his face lit in a dazzling smile. "Got ya," he declared.

Lizzy flashed him that special smile she saved only for him. "Not this time," she teased as she fanned her cards out on the table.

Of course, the joy wasn't so much in winning as it was in making the more astute move. Perhaps that was why in the end, they'd both lost.

The notes of the "Tennessee Waltz" hummed in the background, Grandma's voice lamenting betrayal on the dance floor. Lizzy didn't want to go there. She pulled her thoughts back to the present. It had been a long time since she'd allowed her heart to open up to John. The cherished memories were still laced with pain. Could the John of her childhood have taken his own life?

That was a different John, her mind whispered.

"But it was still John," she argued.

Lizzy thought back to the day she'd first met John, a day clouded in odd coincidence. On that particular day, Chet, Sam, and Granddad sat on the porch chatting. Lizzy had slipped out of the house while her grandmother served iced tea and cookies to the men.

The discomfort she'd felt around others on that day was with her again. She followed in recollection's footsteps out the kitchen door to stand on the porch, warmed by memories of the intense heat on that long ago day. Her gaze traveled to the old ramshackle barn, its grandeur but a memory. On that day, no ravaging vultures had lunched in the barnyard. No, the barn's welcoming comfort enticed her to settle into a cool nest of fragrant hay with Trixie Beldon's latest adventure tucked in her lap and a Tupperware tumbler of lemonade clutched in her hand.

Lizzy heard the shrieks as they reached out to her from the past. She saw herself—the book and lemonade in the hay at her feet—shoot to her feet to race to the back of the barn, only to stop dead in her tracks. Flat on his back on the ground under a jumbled pile of poles lay what appeared to be a boy not much older than she. Screams and sobs poured from his mouth. His eyes were squeezed shut, his face scrunched up with pain.

Breaking from her frozen state, Lizzy had hauled the heavier pieces of wood off of him. Then she'd knelt beside him and cradled his hand in her own. He opened his tear-filled eyes and looked into hers, and in those few moments, something remarkable happened:

their eyes locked in an uncanny understanding. For the first time in her young life, Lizzy knew what it meant to be needed. Struck silent, Lizzy's heart went out to him.

"And there it stayed," Lizzy whispered into the lonely afternoon as she turned to take in the empty porch. Now there were no men's voices to fill the void with their lofty opinions and humorous ramblings. No Grandma with her comforting hugs and laughter. And no John. The knowledge of it swelled into a deep ache in her chest.

Certain that John was counting on her, the next day she'd convinced her grandmother to drive her to the Craig ranch. A deck of cards, her book, and a dozen of Grandma's chocolate chip cookies were stuffed into a canvas bag she'd found in the laundry room. Grandma eyed the bag and nodded knowingly.

Rose had answered the door. Lizzy could picture her now, stunningly beautiful with her blonde hair flowing around her face and her green feline eyes. Those eyes turned to scary slits when she saw Lizzy, but Lizzy didn't back down. She couldn't; she was stranded at the ranch. Grandma had driven off.

"I'm here to see John," she'd announced with as much aplomb as she could muster.

"And you are. . . ?" the woman asked, her eyes gliding over Lizzy, disdain apparent in the curl of her lip.

Lizzy had stood tall and looked the strange lady in the eye. "I'm Lizzy Stewart, Con and Dottie's granddaughter. Grandma brought me over to watch after John."

And she had watched after John, that day and for too many days to count after that. She'd found him lying in his bed, floating in a sea of blue pillows, his right leg propped high in the air. Pleasure lit up his face when she entered the room. It was as she knew it would be, as if they'd been friends forever. They talked. They played cards. When John drifted off to sleep, Lizzy picked up her book and read until he awoke. Then towards evening, Granddad arrived in his old battered pickup to take her home.

For ten-year-old Lizzy, it was the best day of her young life and the first of many days filled with cards and cookies and John. When he could negotiate well on crutches, he'd convince someone from the ranch to drop him off at the farm on their way into town. Then he and Lizzy would sit on the porch, sip grape Kool-Aid, and shell peas or string beans while life buzzed on around them. It was while they chatted over a never-ending box of bush beans that John convinced Lizzy she had to learn to ride a horse.

Lizzy's lips twitched at the bittersweet memory. His reasoning had made sense: if Lizzy could ride a horse, their opportunities to get together would no longer be contingent on the adults in their lives. The problem lay with Lizzy. She went out of her way to avoid the larger animals on the farm. It wasn't that she feared them. It was more that they were overwhelmingly large, living, breathing things that she didn't understand, things that were unpredictable and unreliable.

Her faith in John got her through it. She still remembered how she'd felt that first time she stood beneath the four-hoofed beast and gazed up to where she would soon be sitting—engulfed. With her grandparents' permission, John saddled Tonka, an old bay gelding that had been put out to pasture a couple of years before. His belly bulged like a giant blow-up toy from too much grain and too little exercise, and all Lizzy could see from below him was the stirrup.

"How do I get up there?" Lizzy asked, doubtful that there was a way to reach the top.

John tugged the horse over next to a fence. "Okay, Lizzy. It's showtime," he'd announced. "You can do this. I'll be here for you if you fall."

How many times had John told her he'd be there for her? Too many to count, she was sure.

Lizzy had eyed John dubiously before she climbed to the top rail of the fence. With her heart beating so hard she feared it would burst from her chest and a determined set to her mouth, she stretched a leg out over Tonka's broad back and slid into the saddle.

Something wonderful happened when she settled into that saddle. With each waddling step the horse took, a little more of her anxiety withered away. Now she was the one on top. She was the one in control. She had a whole new perspective from the top of Tonka's tired old sway back.

Lizzy's gaze traveled to the land that stretched out beyond the derelict farmyard, and her heart swelled with longing, her thoughts on that first summer and those leisurely rides to the ranch and back. At first, the going was slow, as just a few minutes of trotting or galloping would wind the aged horse. Lizzy didn't mind; she was slowly melding with her new home. It was becoming a part of her, and she of it.

The long rides gave her time to soak it all up and to reflect on the changes she was feeling inside. She grew to love the feel of the sun's rays on her bare skin, their warmth seeping clear to her bones, and the whisper of the breeze that blew across the open spaces, its breath caressing and soothing. In this stagnant world of sagebrush, juniper trees, bunchgrass, and tumbleweeds, each minute change took on such wonder: the vibrant violet and yellow swatches of blooming wildflowers, the pungent odor of pollinating junipers, and the sudden scampering of ground squirrels and jackrabbits. And enfolding it all was a peaceful silence, one that gradually found its way into her heart to melt away some of the icicles she'd collected during her eight years of living.

Thoughts of those piercing icicles and the realization that her heart was once again a frozen mass of pain brought Lizzy abruptly back to the present. Somewhere along the way, she'd mislaid that wonderful peace that had come with the knowledge that she was loved and needed and that she had a place in the world that was meant only for her.

An all-encompassing sickness settled inside her. It tore at her soul and weakened her limbs. Lizzy gaped at her austere surroundings, stunned that she was standing on a frosty porch in the middle of winter without a coat on to keep her warm. She tucked her chilled fingers into the warmth of her armpits and shuffled back into the house. Slipping into a kitchen chair, she dropped her face into her hands and fought the waves of nausea coursing through her body as her mind traveled to a place she'd avoided for a very long time.

Lizzy never let herself think about the day her father dropped her off at the farm. It was just something that had happened, something over which she had no control. Her life up to that point had consisted of an endless series of new homes and new faces, a life full of unspoken words. Wandering in and out of that life, her mother and father often left her for long periods of time but had always returned to assure her that they would always be there for her.

Then her mother died. The following morning Lizzy's father roused her from a deep sleep and told her to get dressed. He'd hustled her downstairs to a car, and as soon as the suitcases he'd stuffed with clothing were stashed into the trunk and she'd settled into the back seat with a blanket and a pillow, they drove off.

Lizzy had laid awake, worry twisting inside her, too frightened to ask any questions. When the car stopped, she sat up and found herself in an unfamiliar world, one inhabited by a white house with a big front porch and two massive dogs with scary teeth and eyes.

Her father had opened the car door to stare down at her—a sad look on his face—and to whisper. "Watch out for each other."

"As if that could explain what you did," Lizzy now challenged her fickle, long gone father, her voice startling Sid, who had been napping in the chair next to her. Lizzy's heart beat wildly, just as it had on that day, a day that had altered the course of her life. She'd gazed into her father's eyes for the last time. Then he'd driven off and up and over the hill without saying another word to her.

After the initial shock, she became determined not to let those two new wonderful people know how fragile she felt. Though she grew to love her grandparents in a way in which she'd never loved her parents, she'd always held onto a secret hope that one day her father would return to tell her that he loved her. He didn't.

Now, Lizzy again felt that overwhelming sense of loss. Her

eyes scanned the kitchen. It looked much as it had that day so many years before when she'd first seen it. Missing were the spirit and the love that her grandparents had bestowed upon her from the very first moment she'd stepped into their lives. Her heart yearned for what she could never reclaim. Perhaps one day she'd have her own grandchildren to love in that same unconditional manner.

On that one tiny uplifting note, Lizzy rose and searched through the stack of boxes until she found what she wanted. She pulled out five framed photographs and carried them into the living room to kiss each of them as she positioned them lovingly on the mantel. Though her mouth automatically crinkled into a smile, her heart was heavy with the deep ache of loss. They were her reminder that she had until the first of April to take care of business.

Aware of the minutes ticking away, Lizzy glanced at the cuckoo clock. Its silence was troubling. How often had she stood in front of it, waiting patiently for the cheerful little bird to appear? She'd needed assurance that he'd always be there. Now she couldn't even count on the chirping of that tiny wooden bird.

Lizzy sighed deeply, then returned to the kitchen. Before her unsettling ruminations, her hands had stayed busy. Cupboards had been cleaned and restocked, and everything had been scrubbed with Pine Sol and water. A new coat of paint would definitely help, but for now, things didn't look all that bad, did they?

She glanced at the lace curtains she'd salvaged from the windows—Grandma had spent her evenings tatting them in front of the TV—and she pictured the tiny threads that held them together. Would she be able to mend those broken threads and return them to their former beauty? She sighed. It was certainly worth a try.

While a few dented pots and pans and some chipped and cracked dishes were left in the house, most of her grandparents' belongings had disappeared. Hopefully, since the Craigs had taken it upon themselves to keep the farmhouse repaired, they'd also packed up everything of value at the farm and stored it somewhere.

Though she'd rather endure a five-day migraine, she had no choice; she had to visit the ranch. If she played her cards right, she'd get to chat with Eb—tell him about the dead cow and ask about her grandparents' belongings. Eb, who must be well into his seventies, surely spent most of his time around the ranch house. With luck, he'd be alone, and she'd be able to ask him about John, too.

The key was timing. She didn't want to arrive too late and chance running into Sam. If she came face-to-face with him and had to look into those icy blue eyes again, God only knew what might pop out of her mouth. Yes, she had to stay well away from Sam Craig.

CHAPTER 9

When the bright rays from outside began to fade to dull shadows, Lizzy called a halt to the day's cleaning. She glanced out the west window and froze. A silver truck sat in the middle of the road, its hood facing south. It was difficult to tell its exact color in the late afternoon haziness, but it looked to be a shade or two lighter than Sam's truck. Her heart pummeling her chest, she clung to the shadows as she inched toward the window to get a closer look. Perhaps someone had been outside her house last night. Perhaps Sam wasn't the only person snooping around the farm.

Suddenly, the truck shot off up the hill. By the time she reached the window, it was a barely discernable blob. She watched it until it disappeared, her mind fabricating worrisome possibilities. They rolled around in her head for several minutes before she pulled the plug on them.

"It's just someone curious about what's going on here," she told Sid, who'd hopped up on the window ledge to have a look. Still, she checked to make sure the door lock was secure when she put her cleaning supplies away.

A glance at her watch revealed that time had slipped away from her. It was closing in on five o'clock. To avoid Sam, she needed to get a move on.

It was a luxury to step into a clean bathroom and scrub her face and hands with soap and hot water. She dug clean clothes from her travel bag, then tugged a black sweater over her head and faded Lee Riders over her feet.

Pulling several strands of hair to the top of her head, she wove a french braid down to the nape of her neck and secured it with a sterling barrette John had given her on her sixteenth birthday.

For a brief moment, she considered dabbing on makeup to put some color to her pale face and hide the dark smudges under her eyes. Instead, she spread plum lipstick over her lips. The effect was like looking at one of those photos done all in black and white and shades of gray except for the one vibrantly-colored orchid or lily or whatever, her lips being the one vividly-noticeable feature in an otherwise drab face. Satisfied, Lizzy grabbed her coat and purse as she hurried out the door.

The road to the ranch was more weather-beaten than the one into town. There was a time when she could've driven it blindfolded, but today she had to concentrate to keep the SUV from bouncing off the road or landing in a deep pothole. When Lizzy did chance a glimpse at the countryside, she discovered that it had changed very little. Much of the land was still open and in its natural state, protected by cattle guards where the few fence lines met the road.

Lizzy spotted a couple of small herds of cattle in the muted light and wondered how many head the Craigs now owned. As a child, she'd been in awe of the vastness of the Craig ranch and of the great herds of cattle that wandered around on the hills, in the gullies, and across the long open stretches that made up the ranch. She and John could spend a day in their saddles and not leave its borders.

As she approached the final hill before she reached the ranch, Lizzy's heart rate accelerated. Nausea and dizziness threatened to undo her. She focused on the road ahead, struggling to block out the images—relentless rain, mangled metal, and death—lurking in the corners of her mind, images that belonged to another era.

Rounding the crest was a journey back in time. The sun left behind enough straggling rays to illuminate the scene below. Floating in a ginger sea, the impressive two-storied ranch house was as she remembered it, the stone path to its wide front porch an open invitation to visitors. Beyond it were the many buildings she recalled: the massive red barn, the stables, a sprinkling of smaller sheds, and the row of modest houses where the ranch hands lived.

Sam's truck and a red jeep were the only vehicles in sight. Lizzy pulled in next to the steel gray truck, hoping that the presence of Sam's truck didn't mean that he was in the house. She touched the hood of his truck to see if the engine was warm; it wasn't.

In the past, she'd entered the house through the mudroom, but today she trudged down the path to the front door. There, she took a deep breath, rang the doorbell, and waited. When no one answered, she rang it again, then turned to try her luck in the barn.

The door opened, and it was her bad luck that Sam stood there, a towel in one hand and a scowl on his flushed face. His hair was wet, his sleeves rolled up. Clearly, he wasn't any happier to see her than she was to see him. If only she'd left the house a half hour earlier, he would've been outside working.

"Evenin', Lizzy," he muttered with a slight nod, eyes flinty.

Since she was on his doorstep now, manners and civility were musts, so she curbed her tongue and the urge to escape to her Explorer and mentally braced herself. No matter what, she had to control her turbulent emotions.

"Hello," she replied evenly. "I was hoping to talk with Eb. Is he here?"

"Nope," he said, shaking his head, water droplets trickling.

Lizzy waited for him to elaborate. He just glared. She supposed she deserved it after the way she'd treated him. Still, she was heating up inside. She gulped to keep it there. "Do you know where he is?" she prodded in what she hoped was a pleasant voice.

Sam took his own sweet time to think that one through. "Nope." He hesitated a few seconds too long before he acknowledged the fact that Lizzy wasn't going anywhere, then added. "I suppose you want to come in and wait for him?"

Not with you Lizzy's inner voice screamed. She swallowed the words, but it made her throat burn. She had business here that she needed to take care of, so she forced herself to say a gracious, "Yes, thank you." Then she sidled through the door Sam begrudgingly held open, thinking there was absolutely no way that brooding look of his was even remotely sexy—what was Franny thinking?

The interior of the house had changed. The huge red rock fireplace still dominated one end of the room, but the furniture and general décor screamed "contemporary bachelor household." Gone were the aqua and rose she remembered so vividly, and in their place were muted neutral tones and leather—lots of it. Flowers, candles, knick-knacks, and floral fabric had been banned. At least, the valuable antiques that had been scattered around the many spacious rooms in the house still remained. John would have been pleased with the new look.

Sam didn't comment on her perusal. He walked straight to a taupe recliner and dropped into it, then indicated that she was to sit in an over-stuffed beige chair that faced him.

Panic threatened to undo her. She pressed a hand to her stomach to settle the empty, queasy feeling. After what he and J.D. had done to her—admittedly, it was ages ago, but it still counted for something—etiquette surely didn't demand that she sit here and carry on a civil conversation with him?

"You don't have to wait here with me. Go ahead and do whatever you were doing. I'm sure Eb will be here soon. I'll just wait right here for him . . . alone." And yes, her voice did sound as frantic as she felt.

Sam flashed her an annoyingly perceptive look. "Have a seat, Lizzy. You must have it in you to tolerate my company for a few minutes."

Lizzy dropped into the chair. She crossed her arms and legs and glared at him. "I found one of your cows dead in my front yard this morning," she muttered.

He shot forward. "What do you mean, dead?"

She guiltily relished the incredulous look on his face. "Dead as in not breathing, bloody, being devoured by a flock of turkey buzzards. That kind of dead."

His shock turned to a nasty scowl. "How long had it been there?"

"I heard noises in the middle of the night. That's probably when it happened?"

"Noises?"

She huffed, already annoyed with the interrogation. "Just some rustling, bumping sounds. It was too dark to see what was going on out there, and I didn't want to attract attention if there was someone out there snooping around—thought it might be you, *again*—so I didn't turn on any lights. I found it this morning."

He turned as red as those turkey buzzard's heads and shrank back a notch, but then pressed on. "Could you tell what caused it?"

"There was a lot of blood, and the buzzards were chewing on the guts." She paused, shrugged, and threw out, "Maybe a pack of coyotes?"

"Did you hear them howling?"

She shook her head. "Could be, it just died, and the scavengers opened it up. I dragged it down to the barn to get the mess away from the house. You can take your own look."

He studied her intently—probably thought she'd killed his precious cow to show him she wasn't bluffing when she'd told him to keep his cattle out of her yard. Well, she wasn't bluffing, but she wouldn't hurt an innocent animal to prove a point.

"I'll do just that," he finally uttered, "first thing tomorrow." He sank back into his chair, still eyeing her like she was plotting to sneak that cow carcass away before he collected his evidence.

She tried to relax into the chair, or at least look relaxed—not an easy thing with an irritated man glaring at you. Finally, he grabbed an *Outdoor Life* and leafed through it fitfully, his jaw muscles clenching.

The minutes dragged on. Sam ignored her, lost in his thoughts, pretending to read his magazine. That was fine with Lizzy. Gradually, her twitching nerves and racing heart settled. It had been a long day full of surprises and hard, physical labor, and her complaining muscles were zapped of energy. Though she would've liked to deny it, there was something familiar and comforting about this place that had once been her second home.

Sitting in the warm room enfolded in the plush fabric, Lizzy's eyes grew heavy, rock heavy. She fought the desire to let them close. Each time she drifted off, her eyes snapped open to eye Sam, still flipping magazine pages. At last she gave in to the pull of her exhausted body, and her eyes drifted shut.

❀ ❀ ❀

Lizzy awoke to the sound of male voices. She lifted her eyelids. Muted light from a lamp in the corner bathed the room in an amber glow. Though the lure of sleep was strong, she fought through the haze to remember where she was. She sat up. Someone had thrown a heavy afghan over her. Sam no longer sat in the chair across from her, so one of the voices must be his.

She pushed herself up out of the chair, rubbing sleep from her eyes and slicking back tickling strands of hair that had worked loose from the braid. They popped free when she tried to tuck them into place. Her stiff, aching muscles groused, and it took her a few seconds to get her balance. Grabbing the afghan, she folded it into a neat bundle and set it in the chair, then followed the deep muffled sounds to the kitchen.

If she closed her eyes, Lizzy knew she'd be in another time, a time when John's voice mingled with Sam's and Eb's as they all sat around the kitchen table discussing the day's events and filling their empty stomachs. In her groggy state, she struggled to sort her own longings from reality. She watched and listened for a few seconds, grappling to follow the discussion and focus the blur that swathed the whole scene.

Sam sat at the table, facing away from her. Leaning on his forearms, he sipped on a steaming mug of coffee and listened to something Eb was saying. Eb stood at the counter, his back to her, talking, his hands busy at something. He turned around, a berry pie-filled plate in each hand, and stopped in mid-sentence when he saw Lizzy.

Nervous energy pulsed through Lizzy. How would Eb respond to her showing up here after twenty-five years? His face broke into a beaming smile, and he set the plates on the table and held his arms out to her. "Lizzy," he murmured huskily.

With tears burning in her eyes, Lizzy stepped to him and took his hands. "Hi, Eb," she whispered, her voice quivery.

She couldn't help it; she threw her arms around him and gave him a lengthy hug. His arms circled her and held her close. By the time the hug ended, tears overflowed to stream down her cheeks. She swiped at them with her jacket sleeve, so Sam wouldn't see her crying again. "It's so good to see you," Lizzy blubbered, gazing into Eb's now watery eyes.

"You, too. I put some food on a plate for you. Figured you'd be hungry. You looked so done in that I didn't want to wake you. Sit down and I'll get it."

Lizzy stared at Eb, speechless. What was he thinking? The two of them at a table with Sam was begging for trouble. What if she or Eb slipped and said the wrong thing? All hell would break loose.

That couldn't happen. Confused, she dug for an excuse that would sound plausible. "I . . . really need to get back to the farm. Thank you, but I . . . do need to get back." It sounded lame.

Eb looked intently into her eyes. "Have somethin' to eat first," he stated emphatically. "Then you can head home. Sam said you wanted to talk with me."

Still not convinced, Lizzy eyed the berry pie, suddenly so hungry she nearly grabbed it off the table to devour it. She nodded reluctantly and looked at Sam. A puzzled expression marred his features. He glanced from her face to Eb's. Lizzy turned away. She hadn't spoken with Eb in twenty-five years, and by God, Sam was not going to ruin their little reunion. After discarding her coat, she slid into a chair.

Eb pulled aluminum wrap off of a plate and set it in front of Lizzy. The aromas drifting off it set her stomach to rumbling. Two slabs of well-done roast beef competed for space with a large dollop of potatoes slathered in rich brown gravy and an ample pile of buttery peas.

"What would you like to drink?" Eb asked.

"A glass of water would be great." Lizzy turned to Sam and said pointedly, "Eat your pie. You don't need to wait for me." Once the pie was gone, surely he'd leave, so she and Eb could *really* talk.

The glass of water appeared, and Eb dropped into the chair next to her, a half-smile tugging on his lips. "I hope you're not one of those vegetarians?"

Lizzy rarely ate red meat, but she supposed that would change now that she was back in cow country. In answer, she cut a bite of beef and forked it into her mouth, chewed it, and gave him a look of pure delight. "M-m-m, yummy," she murmured.

Eb turned several shades of pink and dug into his pie while Lizzy tasted the potatoes and peas. "When did you learn to cook like this?" she asked him. "Last time I sat here, your fried eggs could pass for rubber."

Eb chuckled. "After Rose died, I was the one who took care of J.D. Somehow, I ended up doin' the cookin', too. It came down to chancin' an early death or learnin' to cook. Didn't take many bellyaches and sleepless nights to put me on the road to improvin' my culinary skills."

Lizzy smiled, silently thanking Eb for learning to cook as she forked potatoes into her mouth. Her eyes flicked to Sam, who was ogling her, the oddest expression on his face. Why didn't he finish his pie and skedaddle? She needed to discuss a few things with Eb in private.

"Well, it worked. This is absolutely delicious," Lizzy praised, turning her attention back to Eb. "I'm sorry about Rose. You and

Chet must miss her very much."

Sorrow filled Eb's eyes, but he merely nodded. Clearly, he was still struggling with the loss of his beloved sister. Plus, he now had to deal with his nephew—Chet—on his own. Chet might be older, but no doubt, he was still a handful.

Protocol demanded that Lizzy mention another death, too, one she personally had celebrated. She dropped her fork, braced herself, and plodded on. "I read about J.D.'s death in the newspaper. It sounded like he was ill for quite some time."

"Yeah, it was cancer. Once he got it, it was all ups and downs. Luckily, more ups than downs, and it went fast at the end."

"I'm sorry for you," she murmured sincerely, though she wasn't sorry J.D. was dead. "I know how much you must miss him." She was also sorry she hadn't sent a sympathy card. Eb had been her dear friend and a dedicated friend and companion to J.D. She should've offered him support with written words, if not spoken, no matter what her feelings were for J.D.

Eb nodded, his eyes misty. "Thank you. I appreciate that."

A lump burned in her throat, too. She forked a bite of beef into her mouth and tried not to think about what she'd walked away from so many years before.

With a sigh, Eb pushed his empty plate away. He seemed to mull something over before he spoke. "Sam said you wanted to talk with me about somethin'?"

Lizzy's heart hitched. She glanced at Sam. He'd finished his pie but still sat there like a barb on wire, irritating her. She'd told him about the dead cow. He'd surely mentioned it to Eb, so there was no need to bring it up again. And she didn't want to quiz Eb about John's death with Sam sitting here. Then she remembered the other reason for her trip to the ranch.

"Yes, I was hoping you might know where all of my grandparents' belongings are. I thought someone from here might've cleaned out the house or know who did. I know I have no right to hope their things weren't sold or given away."

A smile played on Eb's lips. "Nope. Once it looked like you weren't comin' back, Johnny and I packed up pretty much everything in the house and brought it back here to the ranch. It's stored in one of those sheds out back. I'm not sure which one it's in, but as far as I know, no one did anything with it. You know where it is, Sam?"

Sam shook his head and uttered what Lizzy was starting to think must be his favorite word: "Nope." He hesitated before adding, "But I have an idea where it might be."

Eb and Lizzy stared at him, waiting for him to elaborate. Getting no response, Eb prodded, "Well, do you suppose you could share that idea with us?"

Finally, Sam huffed and said, "I'm thinking it's in that shed next to the barn. The back portion of it is stuffed to the rafters with boxes. We'll have to pull out a hundred years accumulation of discarded furniture to get to it."

"It's too late to do it tonight, but we'll get out there first thing in the mornin' and have a look," Eb promised Lizzy. "Someone'll bring it over to the farm as soon as we find it."

"You don't have to do that," Lizzy interjected. "I'll pick it up."

"If that's your vehicle I saw out front, it'd take you into spring," Eb advised. "And with the roads in the condition they're in right now, a lot of it'd end up broken. It'll only be one or two truck loads and won't jar so much if we bring it over."

Yes, and it was a given that Sam would bring it since he had to come to the farm to check on his dead cow. She didn't want to be around him, and quite frankly, she had to keep him away from her house. "I really don't mind, and I'll drive slowly so nothing gets broken. I don't have a phone yet, and my cell phone doesn't have service out here, so just have someone stop by the house when you've found it. I'll come right over and get it."

"I'll bring it over tomorrow," Sam decreed in a tone that defied any further argument. As if that wasn't enough, he added, "It seems that in her time away from us, Lizzy's forgotten what it means to be *neighborly*."

Eb watched the two of them intently. Feeling heat in her cheeks, Lizzy set her jaw and refused to acknowledge Sam's rude remark. Obviously, he was enjoying himself at her expense, yet again. If he wasn't going to leave so she and Eb could have their private conversation, then she'd leave.

She patted her mouth with her napkin and placed it and the silverware on her nearly empty plate. Before making her exit, she graciously addressed her parting remarks to Eb. "Thank you for dinner. It really was delicious. And I do appreciate *your* offer to drop my grandparents' things off at the farm. Thank you."

Lizzy stood and carried her dishes to the sink. Eb was on her tail. She kissed him on his whiskered cheek and whispered in a shaky voice, "I've missed you." Then she grabbed her jacket and hustled toward the familiar mudroom door.

Just as she reached it, she paused to turn back to the two men. "Did either of you call the post office recently and ask for my address?"

Clearly puzzled, Eb shook his head, then turned to look at Sam, concern furrowing his brows. Seconds ticked by, the two men's eyes locked in some kind of nonverbal communiqué. Lizzy watched in silence, willing Sam to nod.

When she'd nearly given up on it, Sam glanced her way and uttered, "Nope."

Wondering what had just transpired between the two men, Lizzy studied Sam.

"Why the hell would I want to know your address?" he added gruffly.

"Maybe because Franny asked you if you knew it," Lizzy retorted, making no attempt to mask her irritation.

"And I told her I didn't."

"You didn't ask anyone?"

He took a deep, perturbed breath before he answered. "Lizzy, I've had enough to keep myself busy without wandering around trying to find out where the hell you were. If you'd wanted to be found, you obviously wouldn't have snuck out of here in the middle of the night without saying goodbye to anyone and leaving your mess for someone else to take care of."

Lizzy stared at him as the room closed in around her. She needed fresh air—now. From the corner of her eye, she saw Eb reach out to her, but she twirled and fled through the mudroom door, fighting to control her skyrocketing emotions until she was well away from Sam. "It was your mess, too," she spit as she fled into the yard.

She halted in mid stride when it hit her. She was fleeing to the once familiar comfort of the barn where she and John had often gone to lick their wounds and commiserate. This time John wouldn't be there.

"Why aren't you here?" Lizzy whispered into the frigid, empty darkness. "I need you."

First thing in the morning, she promised herself as she turned towards her Explorer.

❈ ❈ ❈

Sam watched Lizzy's retreat through the mudroom door and squelched the guilt that battled with anger and annoyance for prominence in his emotional pool. He closed his eyes to still the turbulence. Finally, he shook himself free and turned his focus on Eb, whose eyes were throwing daggers at him. The will to escape the whirlwind of feelings whipping through the kitchen was strong, but Sam forced himself to stay right where he was until he got some answers.

"That wasn't necessary," Eb admonished, reproof darkening his watery eyes. He turned away towards the sink.

Eb's hands messed with the dishes in the sink, but the window's reflection told another story: his eyes stared out the window, a sad, faraway look to them. Eb was right, of course. That last jab had been immature and hurtful, an unchecked response to a frustrating evening. He knew better.

But he'd given in to irritation. He'd been so close to ending a full, uneventful, and relatively mundane day when Lizzy and her surly attitude showed up on his front doorstep to shatter it all to hell. What gave her the right to dismiss him from his own living room, as if she couldn't stand to sit in the same room with him? And she'd loved telling him about the dead cow—gloated in his loss. Hell, she might've even killed it, just to prove a point.

At first, he thought she was pissed off at the whole world, but he was witness to her loving reunion with Eb. And she'd mentioned a friendly conversation with Franny. It confirmed what Sam had suspected: all of her animosity was aimed directly at him. He'd sure like to know why.

Except for a brief glimpse at John's funeral, he hadn't seen Lizzy since the summer after his law school graduation. Later that same summer Lizzy had driven off in the dead of night. She was just fine that summer—well, actually more than fine—so what had happened between then and now to account for this acrimony. He'd put a lot of thought into it and hadn't come up with one thing he'd ever done to Lizzy to elicit her anger and loathing—well, there was that one little thing, but it hardly warranted her snippy attitude.

Sam shook himself free from that prickly memory and eyeballed Eb's reflection. "So what was that all about?" he demanded.

In the window, Eb's eyes refocused, then closed again. Finally, Eb turned to face Sam. "What was what all about?" he inquired innocently.

"That little scene between you and Lizzy, that's what."

"Don't know what you're talkin' about." With that, Eb returned to his dishwater swishing.

Get out of here, screamed Sam's mind, but he couldn't let it go. "Well, there was Lizzy's panicked look and you gushing reassurances. Not one word was about what she's been up to for twenty-five years or why she's decided to invade our nice, quiet life or why she deserted John when he needed her most. No, it was all about your cooking and a bunch of other crap that had absolutely nothing to do with what was going on here."

Sam was on a roll; he kept on rolling. "And her address; what was going on there? You could slice the air with a knife the way the two of you were glaring at me.

"Because of Lizzy, my life's been shot to hell. I was willing to do the neighborly thing and put it aside and be civil, but evidently, she has some bee in her bonnet and has formed the erroneous opinion that I put it there. You know anything about that, Eb? If you do, maybe you could enlighten me 'cause I've got some business I need to discuss with her, and it ain't gonna happen until I figure out what the hell's going on."

Eb's eyes were down, focused on whatever he was allegedly

scrubbing. Sam figured his chance of getting a response was pretty much nil, but he waited it out.

When Eb finally spoke, he didn't face Sam. "Seems to me you're makin' a mountain out of a molehill. Lizzy ate; we talked. Anything else is what you've made it out to be. If you're so put out by her, why'd you invite her in . . . and cover her up? Why didn't you just send her on her way?"

Eb had him there. Though he hated to admit it, some part of Lizzy appealed to what he assumed must be his more masochistic elements. He'd wanted to reach out and touch her while she slept in the chair, to wipe away the worry lines on her forehead and replace the loose strands of hair that streaked her cheeks. To rub off that awful purple stuff she'd caked on her lips.

Instead, he'd sat and stared at her, wondering where those feelings came from and trying to convince himself that it was only because she was an attractive woman. But deep down, he knew he'd always had a soft spot in his heart for Lizzy.

He'd finally concluded that the past was to blame for those spontaneous feelings that kept cropping up; they were remnants from a life he'd lived long ago, a life in which a very different Lizzy was an interwoven and pleasant element. *A life that's long gone*, he reminded himself.

In deference to what had once been, Sam had gently slipped an afghan over Lizzy's sleeping body before leaving the room to join Eb, who had returned to the house and was banging pots and pans in the kitchen.

Eb was again banging pots and pans as he organized them in the dishwasher. Sam watched him. He was in no mood to share his reasons for not shooing Lizzy away. Eb seemed content to let it slide, so Sam pushed himself to his feet and carried his dishes to the counter.

"I'm heading outside to check that shed. Come morning, I have to go to the farm to check on that dead cow. I'll take a load of Lizzy's boxes with me," Sam offered in reconciliation.

Eb glanced his way and nodded knowingly. Their eyes caught and held briefly. Sam would've willingly given his new pair of Tony Lamas to know what was going on behind the fretful eyes he was staring into.

Instead, Eb returned to his dishes and Sam trekked out into the freezing darkness in search of a way out of this living hell and a return to his once quiet, uncomplicated life.

CHAPTER 10

Sam inhaled a deep, chilling breath through clenched teeth as he hefted the bulky cardboard box. He adjusted it in his gloved hands and checked its balance before he lugged it to the truck and packed it into place with the numerous boxes he'd already loaded.

Although the temperature hovered in the upper teens, perspiration dampened the inner layers of clothing he'd donned well before dawn that morning. He ran a sleeve across his face to wipe the rivulets of sweat trickling annoyingly down his forehead and trudged back into the musty shed.

The pace he'd set was brutal, and he knew he'd suffer for it. He'd deal with that later. Right now, it felt good to work off the nervous energy simmering inside him. It felt good to take action. He'd told himself that he was going to get his life back on track and get Lizzy out of it, and that's exactly what he was doing. The sooner he got these boxes off of his property and onto hers, the closer he was to making that happen.

He shoved a hefty box into place and stepped back to survey the tower he'd erected on the truck bed. Determined to deliver all of Lizzy's belongings in one trip, he'd packed the boxes like he packed bales of hay. Unlike bales of hay, the boxes were varying sizes and shapes, and the result was a somewhat unstable pile. With the addition of this last box, the load leaned precariously to the right.

If he left it as it was, there was a good chance he'd lose a few boxes on the bumpy drive to the Stewart farm. On the one hand, Lizzy probably wouldn't miss them, and he would be able to finally have his chat with her and then dust off his gloves and be rid of her. But on the other hand, one of those boxes might be filled with Dottie's beautiful dishes or Con's treasured books.

Sam emitted a series of colorful expletives as he pulled the top layer of boxes off the truck. There was no avoiding it; he'd have to make two trips. But he didn't have to make them both in one day.

He pulled another box from the pile and replayed his sleepless night of tossing and turning and trying to get comfortable in a bed that had never before given him any trouble. He'd spent those restless hours trying to figure out what was behind Eb's uncharacteristic behavior and how to work the future of his cattle into what was sure to be a meager morning conversation with Lizzy.

Thoughts of yet another confrontation with an unpredictable and perplexing Lizzy, spurred him on to get the job done. Then he'd saddle up Ranger and ride out to check on his cattle. The familiar rocking of the horse's gait and their solitary companionship would be the perfect antidote to his inner turmoil. He might even put on a clean shirt and drive into town this evening. There was always something kicking around there on a Saturday night. A little female company was probably what he needed to get Lizzy off his mind—assuming he steered clear of Gina, that is.

By the time he made the adjustments to Lizzy's boxes and secured them with a tarp and several nylon ropes, Sam's stomach was rumbling and he was craving his morning caffeine. He glanced at the ranch house. Should he abandon breakfast and another uncomfortable tête-à-tête with Eb in favor of getting this dreaded delivery out of the way? His empty stomach growled in alarm, so he headed towards the house.

He'd only taken a few steps when Chet stepped from the shadows, a shifty look to his eyes as he peeked from beneath the wide brim of his Stetson. He spit a stream of chewing tobacco from the bulge in his lower lip and swiped his gloved hand across his mouth.

"You think next time you could give me some warning?" Sam grumbled, unbalanced by the rush of adrenalin.

As usual, Sam was struck by the contrast between Chet and Eb. That two such opposite personalities could descend from the same gene pool was an enigma. When they were younger, Chet's entertainment had usually been at the expense of those around him, and Sam suspected that he still derived pleasure from annoying others, especially Sam. Though Chet's short-lived marriage had settled him down some, he could still try one's patience. This morning was no exception.

Chet gave him a well-honed look of innocence that would've been more effective on a man half his age and replied, "Sorry. You seem a mite jumpy this mornin'. Somethin' up?"

"Just heading into the kitchen to get some breakfast," Sam muttered, sideswiping a discussion about his forthcoming trip to the farm.

Chet studied him way too closely. "I saw you loadin' the truck. You goin' someplace?"

Sam was in no mood to spar with Chet. "Lizzy found a dead cow in her yard yesterday. I'm driving over to have a look at it, so I loaded up some of Con and Dottie's things to take to her."

Sam moved toward the house, but Chet stepped in front of him to block his path. "Why would ya want to do that? Lizzy stays, and you lose your grazin' rights."

Blood pounded in Sam's temples. He fought the urge to push Chet aside. At his age, he had no business getting into a fistfight, even if it was warranted, and he was determined not to let Chet know how much Chet's shenanigans aggravated him. "It's her stuff. She wants it back," he replied.

Chet curled his upper lip and chuckled, his eyes full of contempt. "It's Lizzy, ain't it? That stuck-up bitch is back and look at you. You're at her beck and call already. Horse whipped by a piece of ass you'll never get your hands on. Feels like old times, don't it? Truth is, if there's a dead cow in her yard, she probably did the killin'."

Sam saw red, but he refused to take part in Chet's adolescent games. He shoved his way past a still sniggering Chet and hustled toward the mudroom. Three strides into it, he stopped, hesitated, and finally turned back to Chet. "Stay away from her," he advised Chet, his eyes narrowed in forewarning.

"Why's that? I've always been welcome to your leftovers before. In fact, I'm seeing one of them now—Gina." Chet grinned, clearly waiting for Sam to take the bait. When he didn't get a response, he added, "So what makes Lizzy different?"

Sam's hands curled into fists that ached to take the smirk off Chet's face. "I mean it."

A puzzled frown creased Chet's eyes. "Ah!" he finally drawled knowingly. "That why you're takin' her stuff back to her, thinkin' maybe she'll forget all about your little cattle drive through her front yard? Or maybe, in true Craig fashion, you're gonna get hold of her land any way you can. If that's what's on your mind, I'd be happy to help out any way I can. This time, she might take to me more than you. Don't worry; you can have Gina back."

"You heard me. Stay away from her," Sam snarled through clenched teeth.

Chet chuckled. "Me? You're orderin' *me* to stay clear of her? Kind of like the wolf warnin' the fox to stay clear of the henhouse, ain't it?"

"Consider yourself warned," Sam uttered before he strode towards the house, his limbs shaking from the pent-up energy vibrating through them.

When he stepped into the kitchen, Eb was rinsing off dishes and strategically loading them into what appeared to be a fully loaded dishwasher. The aroma of coffee and breakfast grub misted the air, but the table was empty and no food was in sight. Eb glanced his way, mumbled a perfunctory, "Mornin'," then returned to loading dishes.

Sam mumbled, "Mornin'," back at him, grabbed a travel mug from the cupboard, and filled it to the brim with black coffee. Before he screwed the lid on, he took a long, satisfying gulp, burning the roof of his mouth. He winced just as Eb shoved the dishwasher door into place and glanced his way. Eb gave him a long, probing look.

"Coffee's hot," Sam muttered.

"Your breakfast is in the warmin' drawer. I figured you'd want to get those boxes loaded, so I didn't call you in. I went ahead and ate. You want me to go to the farm with you?"

The prospect of Eb keeping Lizzy occupied while Sam unloaded boxes was tempting, but Sam wasn't in a mood to play mind games with Eb on the snail-paced drive to the farm. "No. Thanks for the offer, but I can manage it myself. No reason for you to freeze your butt off if you don't have to."

Eb looked relieved. "Well, if you're sure you can handle it, I do have some things I need to get done here. I stuck some breakfast in that bag there for you to take to Lizzy. She looks like she could use a few square meals."

Sam nodded to let Eb know he'd make the food delivery, too. "Don't worry about cooking supper for me. I'm gonna head into town a little later. If I get hungry, I'll eat at Mel's," he informed Eb.

It elicited a pair of raised eyebrows from Eb. "On a Saturday night? You haven't done that in quite some time. You feelin' okay?"

Feeling okay? Sam stared at Eb, who stared right back. He felt as good as he could feel with ghosts and murky, half-formed memories assaulting him at every turn. How could he feel okay when he was forced to deal with something he didn't understand?

Even good old, steadfast Eb was acting peculiar. Not calling him in when breakfast was ready, when had Eb ever done that before? Come hell or high water, Eb had always insisted on the earth itself stopping to partake of a healthy, hearty, and hot breakfast.

"I'm fine," Sam retorted. He pulled his dehydrated breakfast out of the warming drawer and contemplated the possibilities. Laying half of the limp English muffin on the counter, he mounded the rubbery fried eggs on it, then pulled the greasy bacon strips in half and added them to the heap. Lastly, he topped it with the other half of the muffin. The unappealing mess was quickly wrapped inside a paper towel and shoved into his jacket pocket.

Then, grasping Lizzy's bag in one hand and his coffee in the other, he headed back out into the frosty morning. There, he studied the formation on the back of his truck, did a quick mental calculation, and swore under his breath. If his math was correct, he had one hell of a long, slow drive in front of him.

With any luck, he'd be back at the ranch by noon, one step closer to being rid of Lizzy Stewart. Of course, luck appeared to be mighty scarce around these parts lately.

CHAPTER 11

Lizzy had sat in the Explorer for nigh on thirty minutes, staring at the rusty, wrought iron gate, building up enough courage to open it and open herself to the possibilities that lay inside.

Sorrow dragged her down—a lead weight. It raged a silent battle against the tiny, relentless spark of hope that kept her moving forward. She knew that if that spark was ever going to grow into something of power and significance, into something she could bask in and not just tenuously cling to, she needed to dig deep inside herself and find the guts to open that gate.

She glanced at the silk flowers on the seat beside her: purple pansies for Grandma, yellow roses for Granddad, and lilacs for John. John had always loved lilacs, perhaps because of the huge lilac bushes outside his bedroom window, the ones he and his mother had planted when he was a small boy. Lizzy had thought it odd that a guy would be that attached to such a fragrant, lovely, and undeniably feminine flower.

If only she had the real thing instead of these sterile facsimiles, but these would have to do for now. Once spring was here, she'd plant a garden of smiling purple and yellow pansies on her grandmother's grave, a sweet-smelling yellow rose to twine on her grandfather's headstone, and a lilac bush to protect John's grave from the scorching sun and biting winds. She'd have to haul water out here every day mid summer. It wouldn't make up for the years in which she'd deserted, neglected, and, yes, even forgotten them, but it would be a start.

Determined to get on with it, she tugged her wool cap snugly into place and zipped her jacket to her chin before she gathered the fake flowers and eased out of the SUV onto the frozen ground. The air was still and sharp with the sting of ice, each breath a reminder of how cold it was.

Lizzy walked to the gate, unlatched it, and pushed. The frozen rust protested. She wedged a shoulder against it and put her weight into the next push until it budged open far enough to squeeze through. Before her stood a hodgepodge of gravestones, an amalgamation of variations of opulence and neglect.

To some, the setting would be stark and bleak. To Lizzy, it was beautiful in its imperfection. Worn white limestone formations of varying shapes and sizes leaned with age and mingled with newer and more solid gray and coral granite towers. Tall blades of bunchgrass reached up and threatened to obscure those whose identity was but a flat slab on the ground. Juniper and sagebrush seedlings questioned the rights of this speck of development to survive in this massive, silent land. Over it all, the early morning sun sparkled radiantly from the frost-encrusted stones as Lizzy looked beyond, to the rolling hills where she and John had spent much of their free time exploring and talking and just being kids.

Above her, a flat-topped butte stood watch over the desolate cemetery. Lizzy's eyes traced their way to the top, to the spot John had called Eagles' Nest, a place where she and John had spent countless hours lazing in the sun and daydreaming their futures.

Yes, she thought, *they are happy here.* And when her time came, she would join them because it was becoming clear to her that her heart resided in this land of veiled riches.

Lizzy ambled down the dirt path toward the plot where her grandparents had been laid to rest that fateful day so many years ago when summer had been turning into fall, the end of one season and the beginning of another. It had been a time of intense daytime heat and nippy nights, a time when familiar routines were adjusting to fit new schedules, a time of uncertainty and change. For eighteen-year-old Lizzy, it had been the end of one life and the beginning of another.

The massive chunk of rock towering over her grandparents' graves wasn't something she would have chosen. In truth, she hadn't chosen it. She'd requested its requisition in a letter to her grandparents' attorney and had included a check to cover the costs. This monstrosity screamed of J.D. Lizzy apologized for the offensive slab and promised as soon as the weather permitted, they would be resting beneath a more suitable memorial.

Kneeling, Lizzy placed the pansies on the grave to her left and the roses on the one to her right. It looked wrong, so she gathered them both into a bundle and pushed them into the hard soil where the two graves touched.

To be here with her grandparents so many years after their passing permeated her with a warm, mellow glow. She sat and crossed her legs in front of her, surrendering to the powerful urge to pour her heart's contents into the surrounding silence. If only some of it would reach the souls of those she loved.

"I'm so sorry for what happened and for how I handled it. Sorry that because of me, you were taken from a life that you loved so much. Sorry I failed you and everyone else who counted on me. But most of all, I'm sorry that I didn't wake up every morning and tell you how much I love you and how thankful I am that you're my grandparents," she whispered. "You took me into your home, loved me, and made me so happy. And I didn't tell you any of this."

Lizzy wallowed in the weighty feelings. Tears streamed down her cheeks to speckle the silk lilacs she clutched in her gloved hands. John wouldn't care.

She stood and said her goodbyes to her grandparents, promising she'd be back to visit them soon. Then she continued on down the path in search of John. He'd taken her to visit his mother's grave many times. She hoped that in death, he laid near her.

The Craigs had their own family burial plot within the cemetery with an imposing iron fence surrounding it and a gate with the family name artistically welded into it. Lizzy opened the gate and stepped into the well-cared-for plot. The gravestones were impressive. She knew J.D.'s would be the biggest and the best. She was right.

An imposing black block stood at the head of J.D.'s final resting place, a testament to the man he once was. A short distance from it, John's mother's gravestone stood just as she remembered it, carved out of a beautiful coral marble with dark veins webbing through it and graceful floral carvings framing her epitaph.

At one time, Lizzy had loved to run her fingers over the smooth surface and trace the hollowed paths of the letters and numbers. Sighing, she tugged off a glove and touched the stone, guiding her fingers to follow the flowing letters of her own name through the frost that clung to them. She'd thought it providence that she shared a name with John's mother. Her eyes lingered on the spray of rose blossoms that edged the stone, and she ran her fingertips over their smooth petals. John had said that his mother hated roses.

Lost in thought, Lizzy watched her fingers continue their once familiar journey. Her breath caught. She moved closer to study the date on the stone: *April 24, 1964.* It was a familiar date, not only because it was the day John's mother died. Her heart did a wild dance while her mind reeled back to her first morning back at the farm. The date on Elizabeth Craig's headstone was the same date as the one on the diary entry in Granddad's desk.

Was it only an unusual coincidence, or was it significant? Lizzy replayed the message: *It's done. Now I will live my dream.* Had John's mother written it before she took her life, her parting message in a secreted diary later discovered by a loved one, perhaps John.

Or had someone else written the entry and then secreted it away from prying eyes, her intention being that it would never be seen. Perhaps that someone had harmed another to realize her own dream. Lizzy shuddered and pushed the thought from her mind. She was here to visit John, not to frighten herself with outlandish suppositions. Still, it was curious.

She turned to the next gravestone, a mixture of feelings flooding her when she read the name on it: relief that J.D. had buried John here beside his mother and pain because his death was now a harsh reality. She touched the beautiful ivory stone and knew that Eb had done this for his Johnny.

"Oh, John," she managed to choke before pain-filled sobs overtook her. She sank down onto the frozen ground, clinging to the one remaining affirmation that John had once walked on this earth, laughing and hurting and always there for her. Her deluge of emotions poured out onto the lovely stone.

Ever so slowly, a wonderful tranquility saturated her entire being. She glanced around. Nothing seemed amiss; it was the same frost-covered world of muted grays, greens, and browns. Not a sign of life anywhere.

Relaxing onto the base of the gravestone, Lizzy settled in to have a conversation with her best friend. "I brought you lilacs. They're not real and actually, they got squished, but I thought you might like them. Come spring, I'll bring you real ones. I'm sorry I teased you about the lilacs. I didn't understand then, but I do now." Lizzy pushed the bunch of lavender flowers into the hard ground and fluffed them.

What happened, John, she implored? All of the things they'd planned to do. All of their hopes and dreams. Nothing had worked out like it was supposed to. Nothing! Why? It wasn't as if they were seeking wealth or fame. They'd just wanted to be normal, everyday people. To be with the people they loved. To live here on this land.

"At least you got to stay on the land and be near someone you love. I guess that's something," she whispered.

Lizzy reached down and scraped some icy dirt into her hand. She sniffed its earthy scent, wondering what it felt like to be encased in it. "I'm sorry, so sorry, I left you. It wasn't because I blamed you." She'd never, ever thought John was responsible for what happened. After J.D. had come to the farm and had that little talk with her, she'd thought her only choice was to leave.

"But I did have another choice: I could've stood up to J. D. and stayed here to face the consequences. I could've helped you. With you and me working together, we both would've gotten through it. I know that now." For Lizzy, that was the worst part; had she been here, she might have been able to save John.

"I was so afraid and confused, and J.D. wouldn't let me talk with you. At the time, the only acceptable solution I saw was to just walk away." Then of course, she couldn't come back. That would've only made the whole mess worse.

Lizzy remembered those days well. The urge to return to her home had consumed her, but it was also impossible. She and John had exchanged a few letters, but news from the only home she'd ever known was a bittersweet reminder of all that she'd lost. She had to move on. She had to cut the cord.

In truth, it hadn't all been bad. There were parts of the last twenty-five years that she wouldn't ever give up. If only she could have brought it back here. Too often it hadn't felt real, not like it did when she'd lived here with her grandparents. *I don't understand it, but someday I will,* Lizzy promised herself.

She reached into her pocket to pull out John's letter and felt a familiar closeness to her long ago friend. "I got your letter. This time I won't leave. I'm going to find out the truth. I promise," she whispered.

Lizzy unfolded the letter and silently begged John to speak to her as her eyes scanned the lines:

Lizzy,

I wish you were here. I go to Eagles' Nest a lot to think and write and try to piece things together, but still it makes no sense. Things are so different now. Sometimes, I'm not sure what's real and what's not.

I know I shouldn't write to you, but there's no one else I trust. Besides, you and I are both in danger. I've made a terrible discovery. I'm afraid someone might get hold of this letter, so I can't write about it here. All I can say is that things aren't what they appear to be. It's as if we're all acting in a play, and there's a whole other scene going on backstage.

I need you to come home, so we can talk about this and figure out what to do. Don't write to me! Just phone me when you get this letter. Make sure it's after midnight, and hang up if anyone else answers the phone.

Remember that day when I fell off Old Dozer? I've always wondered about that day. Now I understand. And the roses and lilacs—I understand that, too.

I'll be waiting for your call. I miss you. Love, John

Lizzy studied the firm lines on the aged paper, straining to see beyond them to the person who had written them. What was John's state of mind at the time? It was all too hazy and too full of possibilities.

"What are you telling me, John? I've read this so many times, and still I can't figure it out," she murmured, her voice a scream in the pristine silence. "I need your help here."

For several agonizing moments, Lizzy waited, praying for answers from beyond the grave. When none materialized, she sighed and added, "I'm living at the farm now, so I'm not far away. It looks awful, rundown and falling apart—rotting away. I can feel Grandma and Granddad tossing and turning in their graves at the sight of it."

Maybe it would look better when their belongings came home. With that thought, Sam's brooding face popped into Lizzy's mind. He said he'd deliver the goods that morning. She eyed the sun, which had crept higher into the sky.

"I need to get back to the farm before Sam gets there, or I'll never hear the end of it from his Royal Highness," she muttered as she grabbed the top of the gravestone and pulled herself up.

She gently refolded the letter and slid it into her pocket, then slipped the glove back onto her frozen hand and brushed at the seat of her jeans. As she locked the gate, she glanced at the three headstones. It was as it should be. Even in death, John was isolated from his father, separated by a woman they both had loved, and so near the fence that he was nearly straddling it—J.D.'s means of finally dealing with John, Lizzy supposed.

She wondered where Sam would fit into this family plot. Most likely, lying solidly next to J.D.—patting each other on their backs—with a monument twice as large and commanding as his father's erected at his head. No doubt, J.D. would smile up at that from down below—way down below.

And maybe, just maybe, when she did her spring planting, she'd plant something appropriate for the two of them: a thorny thistle or a prickly wild blackberry bramble to grow and spread, choking out everything in its path, preventing anyone from getting near. Of course, something that lethal would wipe out the beauty surrounding it, gradually eating away at its existence day after day until eventually nothing was left. She gazed at John's grave. Perhaps she needed to rethink that plan.

Lizzy sighed. Her eyes grazed the small enclosure one last time and came to rest on a lovely rose-colored stone that she hadn't noticed before. Curiosity peaked her interest, and she stepped along the outside of the iron fence until she could make out the inscription: *Rosalee Alma Duncan.*

It was certainly a day for intriguing discoveries. John had always ridiculed his family plot and the lengths to which people would go in an effort to be buried within its confines. Fact was, you had to either be a Craig or marry one to gain admittance. J.D. had been adamant about that.

So what in the world was Rose doing here surrounded by several generations of Craigs?

CHAPTER 12

The farmyard looked deserted when Sam pulled to a stop in front of the ramshackle house. Lizzy's red Explorer wasn't in the driveway, which meant that she must be gone, too. He'd just spent the slowest trip on record on his drive from the ranch, and the fact that she was missing did little to improve his foul mood.

For a fleeting second, he thought that maybe she'd packed up and gone back to where she'd come from—disappeared again into the night. That sent his mood meter up a couple of notches. He'd tolerate another marathon drive back to the ranch if he could keep his cattle right where they were and restore peace to his life.

He killed the engine, and his eyes traveled down the road to the weather-beaten barn where Lizzy said she'd dragged the carcass. After a day of feeding off of it, the scavengers would've picked it to pieces. Hopefully, they'd left enough that he'd be able to figure out why the cow had died.

A persistent little brain cell hidden deep in his skull kept him wondering if it might be Lizzy's handiwork, a message to him that she meant what she said. He didn't want to believe Lizzy would commit an act like that, but quite truthfully, this new Lizzy seemed totally irrational. He had no idea what she was capable of doing, but he sure hoped it didn't include slaughtering his cattle.

Those cattle were on the line here. He'd put it off long enough; it was time to resolve the future of his livelihood.

"Well, best get to it," he muttered as he stepped out of the cozy cab of his Dodge Ram into the chilly morning. Painful tendrils slithered across his shoulders. He shivered and tugged at his collar, surveying the ground in front of him.

Though frost clung to it, he detected drag marks in the soil beneath. He followed them to where the cow had died. Blood saturated the dirt in places, dark against the sandy soil and a vivid red in frosty patches. Scavengers had picked the ground clean. Slight imprints spoke of a lot of foot traffic—both human and bovine. Several black feathers littered the ground, but there were no signs of coyotes.

Sam eyed the front porch. Lizzy had said she'd heard bumping and rustling noises, nothing that sounded violent. Exasperated with the whole situation, he huffed and stepped into the side yard and circled the house, examining the house and ground as he walked. Nothing looked amiss.

The farmhouse had definitely seen better days. It was badly in need of a fresh coat of paint, but thanks to his efforts, the roof and windows were sound and weather tight, and the siding was nailed securely into place.

Bunchgrass and sagebrush had laid claim to Dottie's beautiful yard, fertilized by the abundance of cow manure that Lizzy had surely noticed. Sam shook his head resignedly at the sight of it, his mind flitting to spring when the survivors of Dottie's many shrubs and flowers would transform the yard into a Monet painting—wisps of brilliant color floating amidst a sea of drab.

After the cold, dreary winter months, Sam sometimes concocted a reason to drive to town just so he could stop at the farm to enjoy Dottie's handiwork. Of course, once summer hit full force, the lovely garden slowly withered back into the soil to gather strength for its next unveiling.

Actually, Lizzy should thank him. Because of his cattle, this spring's garden was sure to be an eye-opener.

Sam had stopped to check the last window when he heard the crunch of tires in the driveway. He finished inspecting the seams and rounded the corner of the house, meeting Lizzy face-to-face.

Startled, they stared at each other for long seconds. Sam caught a whiff of her fragrance, and his body tightened in response. In the morning light, he noticed tiny lines at the corners of her eyes and mouth, lines that added character to an attractive, intriguing, and all-too-familiar face. There was something else about her this morning, too, something softer, less troubled. He didn't have the feeling she'd go for his throat just because he was alive and within striking distance.

Trickles of alarm prickled his spine. An angry Lizzy he could handle; not this one.

Lizzy eyed him, too, and no doubt found his appearance lacking. As a rule, he was clean and neat, sometimes to a fault, but lately he hadn't been inspired to spruce himself up. So now here he stood, a foot from Lizzy with two-days-growth of beard and a greasy mop of hair that was, thankfully, hidden beneath his hat. And if he were a gambling man, he'd bet that he didn't smell that nice either.

Lizzy retreated a couple of paces and broke the silence. "I'm sorry I wasn't here when you arrived. I didn't think you'd be here this early."

Poised for battle, Sam struggled to reorient himself. At last, he found words. "I took advantage of the time to snoop around and check the outside of the house. Everything looks sound." *Let's see you pass up snapping at that little tidbit,* he silently added.

To his consternation, she did. "Yes, thanks to you and J.D. I do appreciate all you did to take care of the place and to look after my grandparents' possessions."

The woman really was a brainteaser. Was she doing it intentionally, to bait him? Well, he wasn't gonna bite. If Lizzy was in a mood to be civil, it would only play to his advantage. Transfixed by her dark, disturbing eyes, Sam wondered if he might need to rethink that assumption. Lizzy's antagonistic side was definitely not so disconcerting.

"Why don't you show me where you want the boxes," he demanded as he broke free and abruptly walked away.

She met him at the front door but gave no indication that she intended to open it. Instead, she stood there, her unsettling eyes probing his.

"I was at the cemetery talking with John," she murmured. "I wanted to be there when the sun came up. He loved that time of day, you know. 'Dusk and dawn,' he'd say. 'Time to wipe out the old and begin anew.' Just think of it, two opportunities each day when we can forget all the bad things we've gone through and focus on the good."

Sam stared at her, stunned. She'd been talking with John? Was the woman crazy? "John's dead, Lizzy. You can't talk *with* dead people."

"To me, death is a relative term," she informed him before she unlocked the door and stepped into the kitchen ahead of him. "The boxes can go against the back wall in there as long as I can still reach the bathroom door," she added, pointing into the living area. "After I put some wood on the fire and get some coffee started, I'll help you."

Sam was befuddled, yet again. One minute Lizzy was discussing her conversations with the dead, and the next moment she was lucidly pointing out where she wanted boxes stacked. What did she mean, anyway—death, a relative term? Relative to what?

Though he knew he should let it go, he didn't. "So what did John have to say?" he asked pointedly.

She eyeballed him as if he now had the loose screw, a frown furling her dark eyebrows, the corner of her mouth curled derisively.

"You did say you were talking *with* him, didn't you?" he probed, hell bent on annoying her though he knew it would only work against him.

The frown deepened; her jaw line tightened. "I was thinking out loud, that's all. Forget it."

He wished he could, but words slipped out. "You were thinking about the sun coming up?"

Her mouth worked back and forth, and a slow simmer settled into her eyes, but when she spoke, her voice was more resigned than angry. "I was thinking that it doesn't make sense that someone who considers every single sunrise and sunset an opportunity to wipe the slate clean and begin anew would suddenly decide to wipe himself completely off the slate."

Her words caught Sam by surprise, and he blurted, "What are you saying?"

When she replied, it was hesitantly, her eyes searching his. "Have you ever thought that he might've not taken his own life? That something else might've happened to him?"

Sam's stomach roiled. Had she gone completely off the deep end? He'd never once questioned the awful fact that John had taken his own life. The John he'd seen that last summer had been a catastrophe waiting to happen. "Like what?" he finally uttered.

"Maybe someone wanted to get rid of him." Her voice was still tentative.

"That's bullshit! Who would want to get rid of John? He was like a puppy; everyone liked him."

He didn't realize he'd spoken his thoughts aloud until she answered them. "I know, but what if someone *didn't* like him? What if that someone didn't want him around? What then? You've got to admit it's a possibility. Was that ever considered?" The words poured from her mouth, as if they might convince him of their truth.

As much as he wanted to accept her suppositions, they were ludicrous. "Sounds like wishful thinking, Lizzy. John killed himself. You've got to face that fact." He watched the sadness creep back into her eyes and added, "It'd make all of us feel better if it weren't the truth . . . but it is."

Desolation settled onto her features. "Just forget it," she mumbled as she turned away from him to fill the coffee decanter with water.

This time he did forget it—at least, he tried—but that old familiar ache settled in his chest with a heaviness that wouldn't go away. He rubbed at it, trying to relieve the pressure building in his throat, then walked into the living area and stopped, surprised at what he saw. Lizzy had certainly worked hard to get the place cleaned up. Though the room looked bare and dilapidated, years of accumulated dirt and grime had disappeared. The place even smelled better, the tang of Pine Sol overpowering the repugnant odor of mildew. With a few gallons of paint and new curtains, the house might even be habitable.

Sam shook his head, struggling to clear it and slough the heavy feeling hanging onto him. He promised himself that future conversations with Lizzy would be limited, especially those that dealt with the past. He didn't want to think about John's death, let alone talk about it.

That done, he turned back to a more pressing promise he'd made himself: do what needed to be done as quickly as possible and hightail it away from the farm and Lizzy.

"What about the bedrooms? Don't you want to get into them?" he yelled into the kitchen

Lizzy appeared at his side and frowned at the rooms in question. That beaten look was back on her face. "I haven't been able to get the furnace working, so it's too cold to sleep in there. The rooms aren't even cleaned yet," she murmured.

To Sam, the living room was too cold for comfort, too. Lizzy looked so down that guilt prodded him to make an offer he knew he'd regret. "When I finish unloading the truck, I'll take a look at the furnace."

Alarm flashed in her eyes. "You don't need to do that. I'll probably have to buy a new one. This one's ancient."

"Can't hurt to take a look," he reasoned. Maybe a warm house would lift her spirits and make her amenable to the request he planned to put on the table before he took off.

To his surprise, instead of arguing, she selected several chunks of wood from a corner pile and placed them on the hot embers in the fireplace. He watched her crumple a piece of newspaper and push it under the logs. Flames leapt up and consumed the paper. It would take her awhile to get the fire burning, so he headed out the door to begin his work.

By the time he'd backed the truck up to the porch and divested it of the tarp and straps, Lizzy had joined him. "There's a bag on the seat for you," he said, nodding towards the cab of the truck. He noted her sudden wariness and added, "Eb sent you some breakfast. He thinks you're going to shrivel away if he doesn't feed you."

A smile touched her lips as she descended the steps to retrieve her gift. Sam patted the untouched breakfast in his pocket and wondered if Lizzy would offer to share hers with him. No doubt, hers was the better of the two. Evidently, her stomach wasn't complaining like his; she put the bag inside the house and returned to help him.

The two of them developed an unspoken rhythm as they transported the boxes into the house. In truth, Sam thought, they each appeared to be totally oblivious to the other's presence. If he hadn't caught a hint of her unsettling perfume as he passed by her every few minutes, he would've sworn he was working alone.

As the pile in the truck dwindled, the one inside the house spread until it consumed a good half of the living room. Finally, he dropped the last box onto the stack and turned to Lizzy. Noting the dazed look on her face, he said, "You still have a few more boxes at the ranch. I'll drop them off tomorrow morning."

"Thank you," she said, fixated on the accumulation in front of her.

"I'll take a look at the furnace now," Sam reminded her.

Lizzy glanced his way, a subdued air still glazing her features. "Oh, uh . . . yeah. It's in the laundry room," she mumbled before she headed towards the kitchen.

Sam turned to follow her when he noticed the cuckoo clock on the wall beside the fireplace. He stepped closer to check the time and was waylaid by the row of pictures displayed on the mantel. Curiosity drew him nearer. His chilled hands automatically reached out to the warmth radiating from the leaping flames as he studied the photos.

Con and Dottie smiled at him from the confines of a beautiful antique frame, his eyes twinkling mischievously and hers alight with warmth and humor. Maybe it was because he was standing in their house with their newly returned possessions, or maybe it was because of Lizzy's presence, but the two of them seemed to reach out of the photo and touch him in some odd, unexplained way. An intense surge coursed through him—a weak, empty feeling that he couldn't shake. He swallowed at the lump in his throat as he gazed at the remaining four photographs.

Three were of teenage boys, professionally done and characteristic of high school graduation photos. They were nice-looking boys, brimming with health and the promise of success, dark hair combed neat and straight white teeth brightening what were already compelling smiles. Who were they? Something about them nagged at Sam's memory and sent unsettling twitters through him.

The other photo was one that had been snapped on a beach—three little boys in colorful bathing trunks, full of life and laughter. Their bodies dripped with water from large waves rolling in behind them, and seagulls dove down to catch the chunks of bread they tossed into the air.

Sam pulled off his hat and leaned forward to examine the picture more closely. Then he sensed Lizzy's presence. Their eyes met, and he was struck by her panicked look. Two steaming mugs of coffee shook precariously in her trembling hands. He watched her eyelids drop and deep breaths lift her shoulders and wondered what was going on inside that unpredictable head of hers.

At last, she opened her eyes to study him long and hard before she walked forward to hand him one of the mugs. Sam took it and returned his focus to the photos.

"You had the picture of Con and Dottie."

He'd meant it more as a statement than a question, but Lizzy answered. "Yes."

"They're just as I remember them. I thought I'd forgotten . . .

but I guess I didn't." Sam was talking more to himself than to Lizzy, trying to get a handle on the feelings laying siege to his carefully maintained emotions. In defense, he took a sip of the scalding coffee, winced, and shifted his scrutiny to the other four framed photographs. "Who are they?" he finally asked.

Lizzy frowned and hesitantly shifted her gaze to the photos of the three boys. "My sons," she murmured, her voice barely discernible.

Sam's stomach heaved. His heart did erratic things. He swallowed hard and muttered, "You're married?"

She shook her head. "I was."

Relief took the edge off. What the hell was the matter with him? "Not anymore?" he prodded, overwhelmed with a need for confirmation.

She shook her head again.

Sam had to probe deeper. He knew it was none of his business, but what the hell; he had to know.

She spared him the deliberation. "I'm divorced."

Lizzy's discomfort appeared to increase with Sam's scrutiny of her. "I'm sorry," he mumbled—protocol demanded it—and his gaze returned to the pictures. "They look like you. Where are they now?"

"School; they're in college."

With those words, she disappeared into the kitchen. He wasn't far behind, clutching his hat in one hand and the mug of coffee in the other. Lizzy grabbed a dishrag and swiped at the already clean counter.

Sam couldn't let it go. "You don't want to talk about it?"

She didn't respond, just scrubbed on the worn Formica until Sam feared she'd wear through the faded color.

"How long were you married?" he persisted.

She lifted her face to glare at him. "Too long. And you're right, I don't want to talk about it, so let's just leave it at that." Desperation laced her voice.

Sam warned himself to back off. Pushing her to talk about something that was so obviously upsetting her would do little to further his cause. He'd give her some time to get herself together while he checked the furnace. Then he'd sit down and discuss his cattle with her before he headed to the barn to take a look at what was left of that dead cow.

Swallowing a lengthy list of questions, he turned away from her and walked into the laundry room to confront what had certainly been a relic even twenty years ago. To his way of thinking, it was a hopeless cause, but there was no harm in looking, especially if it would put a few gold stars next to his name. "I'll get my tools," he said as he set his coffee mug on the counter and passed by Lizzy to head out the door to his truck.

When he returned, Lizzy was fiddling in the kitchen sink. He'd just pulled off the furnace cover when she set a fresh mug of coffee on the washing machine. He glimpsed her retreat through the door and wondered why she was being so nice. Well, not exactly nice, but pleasant. Actually, it wasn't even pleasant; more like polite. Whatever it was, it made him uneasy. The coffee smelled good though. The first sip confirmed that it tasted good, too.

After adjusting and probing for a half hour or so, Sam had a tighter rein on his errant emotions. His sleepless night and eventful morning had left him feeling all of his forty-nine years—well used and worn thin, rather like the tired, old furnace. He was fairly certain that he needed to replace a couple of parts, and then, just possibly, it might decide to answer the call to duty one last time before it expired. He replaced the cover and placed his tools in his toolbox.

He found Lizzy sitting at the kitchen table, a mug of coffee and a half dozen blueberry muffins within easy reach. She was scribbling on a notepad. The pen stopped, and she glanced up, her eyes questioning.

"With luck, it might just need a couple of parts. It's worth a try, anyway, before you spend the money on a new one. I'll check in town Monday morning, see if I can find them." He didn't want to get her hopes up. He also didn't want to spend any more time than he had to hanging around this house and her; there was no need to press his luck.

She pushed the plate of muffins toward him. "Would you like one? They were in the bag Eb sent."

Would he like one? Hell, he was so hungry he could eat all of them with a dozen eggs and a slab of bacon on the side. He gulped down the lukewarm dregs in the coffee mug and set it on the table, cringing at the image of Richard Nixon printed on it.

Never one to pass up an opportune moment, Sam slid a chair out and plopped down into it. He slipped a muffin off of the plate, crammed a good portion of it into his mouth, and proceeded to chew and watch Lizzy as she watched him.

"Would you like more coffee?" she offered, reaching out to touch Nixon's deceitful smile.

"Yes, thank you," he managed to say once he'd swallowed.

Lizzy wandered off with the mug in her hand. The fact that she was thinking about buying a furnace caused Sam to wonder how long she planned to stay at the farm. He'd hoped she was just checking things out or was on some kind of vacation, a return to her roots, whatever.

His mind reeled with the need to get things settled, and now was as good a time as any to broach the subject. He stiffened his spine and dove in. "It appears you might be planning to be here awhile?"

She set the steaming mug in front of him, sank back into her chair, and slowly nodded.

"You're planning to live here . . . permanently?"

She still nodded. "I hope to."

Sam's mouth went dry. Without thinking, he grabbed the mug and took a hefty gulp. Pain exploded across his tongue. He closed his eyes and swallowed the scalding liquid. The word "permanent" had an ominous ring to it. If she were here to stay, how in the world would he avoid her? Could he handle being around her, even if only on occasion? From now on, his life would be one living hell. This was something he was going to need to chew on—soon.

Right now, he had something else to discuss with her, something that could be a source of contention. He dreaded it.

Sam didn't know how long he'd sat there pondering, but it must've been awhile, and he must've appeared to be upset because when Lizzy finally spoke, she was clearly irritated.

"You know, my being here doesn't have to change your life. Once I get my grandparents' possessions, there'll be no reason for you to come to the farm. I plan to just blend into the landscape and stay out of everyone's way, including yours."

Well, yes, he thought. *That would be nice.* But his immediate concerns were running in another direction. "I'm just wondering what to do with the cattle I have on your land. I figured it'd be okay to use it since you weren't. It helps keep the tumbleweeds and bunchgrass under control, and it allowed me to build up my herd. If you're not planning to farm the land, I was hoping I could leave my cattle on it." Sam watched her intently, prepared to argue his case if it became necessary.

She seemed to relax a bit. "I don't plan to do any farming right away. Your cattle can stay where they are for now." She paused as if to consider something, then added pointedly, "As long as they don't get near the house."

Relief oozed through Sam like warm honey. "Thank you," he murmured sincerely.

"Just being neighborly," she rejoined, the trace of a smile lurking at the corners of her mouth.

Bravo, thought Sam. *This is more like the Lizzy I once knew.* "Well, I'll be neighborly back at ya then. If you ever want to look around your land, you're welcome to saddle up a horse over at the ranch. We've got several hanging around there that need to be ridden." *Why the hell did I say that,* Sam wondered as soon as the words left his mouth.

Surprise flickered in her eyes, turning quickly to distrust. She appeared to think it through before she responded. "Maybe I'll take you up on that . . . sometime."

He couldn't take back the offer, so he pushed himself out of the chair and added, "Just hunt up Eb or one of the ranch hands. They'll point you in the right direction, get you set up with a horse and some tack. I'll let them know you might be coming around."

"Thank you," she mumbled distractedly before offering him the plate of muffins.

"I'll stop by with the rest of the boxes tomorrow morning. Right now I'm gonna take a look at that carcass," he informed her as he pushed his hat onto his head. Then he grabbed another muffin and headed for the kitchen door, feeling as if he'd just conquered the world.

"Sam," she called after him.

He stopped and turned to face her, heart fluttering, alarms blaring.

"You can leave your cows here for now, but they'll need to be gone by the first of April." She said it quietly, as if she didn't know the havoc her words would cause.

The fluttering in Sam's chest became an all out hammering. Anger surged through his veins. He set his jaw to keep his thoughts from spewing out through his mouth and made a hasty exit, already planning what his next move would be.

A couple of minutes later, he stared down at the mutilated remains of a once healthy cow, rubbed at his scruffy chin, and struggled with his fury. The scavengers had pretty much picked the carcass clean and left bones and hide, but it wouldn't take a coroner to figure out that the animal's throat and belly had been slit with what must've been one very sharp knife. Someone had wanted to make a mess, a mess with a message—for him or Lizzy?

That pesky brain cell returned to plant a niggling suspicion that Lizzy might be the one sending the message. He didn't want to believe it—he couldn't picture her slaughtering an innocent animal with a butcher knife, a gory bloodbath—but he had to admit that he didn't know the Lizzy who'd returned to the farm after twenty-five years of doing whatever the hell she'd been doing.

But why would she butcher one of his cows and then calmly tell him he could keep his cattle on her farm for a couple of months, as if it didn't matter to her? Lizzy was smart, too. If she'd slit that cow's throat, she'd know that Sam would take one look at the carcass and know how it had died.

It didn't make sense, unless she was certifiably crazy. Since she talked with dead people, he supposed he had to consider that possibility.

He shook his head at the visual images swimming around inside it and turned to the matter at hand. Inhaling deeply, he lifted the frozen carcass, dumped it into the back of his truck, and pulled a tarp over it. When he returned to the ranch, he'd find a safe place to bury it. He might need to dig it up to use as evidence later.

He dusted the dregs of death off his gloves, and his gaze wandered down the road to the farmhouse. Someone had killed that cow. If not Lizzy, then who? And why? Sam couldn't think of one poooible ouopoot. Of oourʊo, it oould'ʋe boon a rɑndom killing oomo drunk kids whose fun got away from them or someone foraging for free beef, fleeing when they heard Lizzy moving about inside the house.

Whatever the case, Sam decided to keep the cause of the cow's death to himself for now. He'd keep his eyes and ears open though and be on alert for anything the least bit suspicious.

With that thought, his mind flashed back a couple of nights. It was dark, the road icy, when he'd passed by the farmyard on his way home from town. And he'd been focused on keeping his thoughts off of Lizzy, so focused that he'd nearly missed it when the blinding lights in his rearview mirror suddenly went black.

Later that same night, his cow had been slaughtered in that farmyard.

CHAPTER 13

Sam slammed the truck door shut, his head pounding with an angry headache. His suicidal trip back to the ranch had done little to calm him. He had to figure out what the hell was going on around here.

First Lizzy had told him he could keep his cattle on her land; then she'd set a deadline for him to have them off her land. The first of April! A lot of good that would do him. What was going to happen on the first of April, anyway?

Next he'd learned that one of his cows was murdered right there in the farmyard on the same night that someone had tailed him from town. That someone had stopped at the farm and not followed him to the ranch—to slaughter his cow?

Sam rubbed his throbbing temples and eyed the ranch house resolutely. No doubt, Eb knew more that he was willing to share. For a man who liked to chew the fat as much as Eb did, he'd been far too conspicuously short-winded lately. What was he hiding? Sam hadn't pushed Eb, mainly because he wasn't sure he wanted to know what lay behind his actions, but after this morning's upsets, he was hell bent on prying some answers out of him.

When he walked into the kitchen, Eb sat at the kitchen table, engrossed in one of his cowboy paperbacks and nursing a half-empty mug of coffee. Sam poured himself a cup and plopped into the chair across from him. Eb glanced up, mumbled, "Back already?" and returned to his reading.

"Yep," Sam responded. He sat there several minutes, his frustration mounting, before he forced the issue. "Cold out there."

"Uh-huh." Eb didn't even look up.

"Lizzy's got her stuff back."

"That's good." Not even an eye-flick from Eb.

"Saw some pictures of her three sons."

Eb's eyes shot up, locking with Sam's, his face as white as the divinity he made Sam beat to death every holiday season. His lips were actually vibrating.

"Nice looking boys," Sam added, wondering about Eb's agitation. Had he imagined it as Sam had, that Lizzy hadn't had a life away from John and the farm? In Sam's mind, she'd stepped out of the picture and had now stepped back into it, and in between, she'd been sitting on some closet shelf somewhere. He knew that didn't make sense, but it sure felt right. His dilemma was that John was no longer in the picture, so things didn't fit together like they were supposed to.

"Lizzy has three sons?" Eb squeaked.

"Yep."

"She married?"

"Divorced." Sam continued to study Eb. It appeared that this was new information to him. But what was causing his distress?

Eb studied Sam, too, licking his lips and wringing his hands. "Where are her sons?" he finally asked.

"Seems they're all in college." Sam paused to convert his thoughts into words. "She must've been pretty busy after she left here to have three sons who are that old. You reckon that's why she left? I never noticed Lizzy with any boys other than John. Do you know anything about her having a boyfriend?"

"Lizzy didn't have no boyfriends," Eb stated emphatically. He sighed and relaxed back into his chair. Sam followed suit.

Now that he really thought about it, her leaving wasn't a match with the Lizzy Sam had known. She'd loved life here in this desolate part of Oregon as much as John had. But even more, she'd loved John. Eb had to know more than he was revealing. "You didn't know about her sons?"

Eb shook his head, then broke eye contact and rose unsteadily to shuffle to the sink with his mug.

Fearing Eb would escape again, Sam switched tactics. "You know anything about Lizzy's parents?"

Color had returned to Eb's features, and he looked less troubled when he faced Sam. He leaned his back against the counter and crossed his arms over his chest, an indication to Sam that he might finally get some answers.

"Con and Dottie had one child, a son they called Skip. If you didn't know they were a family, you'd never've put the child with the parents. From the time he was a young kid, Skip was into trouble. I've never really thought it was possible to love a kid too much, but in Skip's case, I think that might've been true. Con'd bail him out, and Dottie'd dote on him and give him pretty much anything he asked for. I suppose that didn't do Skip a whole lot of good."

Now that Eb was finally talking, Sam sat silently and let him recollect.

"There was a time when J.D. and Skip were best friends, but eventually, even your dad couldn't stomach him. Seems like they were still in high school when they had the fallin' out that ended their friendship. Not too long after that, Con seemed to have had his fill of

Skip's shenanigans and lies, too."

Eb stopped, a faraway look in his eyes. He took a deep, resigned breath and shrugged his shoulders. "I'm not sure what happened next, but one day Skip took off. He'd been kicked out of high school enough times that he wasn't gonna graduate, and he was too lazy to help Con around the farm or get himself a job. I suppose Con finally got tired of him hangin' around. I don't know if they kept track of Skip or not. It was one of those topics you didn't bring up. I'll tell you one thing though: it was a whole lot quieter around here without Skip rilin' things up all the time.

"Anyway, the next thing I heard about Skip was when he showed up on Con and Dottie's doorstep with Lizzy. He left her there and took off. As far as I know, they didn't hear from him again. Right after their deaths, he was seen around town a few times. Con and Dottie left the farm and all of their money to Lizzy. From what I heard, Skip wasn't even mentioned in their will, not that folks were any too happy about it all bein' left to Lizzy either, especially after she took off."

The lengthy recounting of what must've been a not-so-fond memory appeared to zap Eb's strength. He looked drained, his back hunched, eyes weary. A sigh escaped through his lips before he turned towards the sink to rinse out his mug.

Sam sat silently sipping his coffee, stunned that he hadn't known the story of Con and Dottie's son. Eb must be right; the subject must've been taboo. He couldn't remember his father ever talking about Skip, nor Con, nor Dottie. In fact, he'd never even heard Lizzy mention her father.

His eyes flicked to Eb and held. The man looked completely done in, lost in his own world as he removed clean dishes from the dishwasher and shoved them into cupboards. Guilt pricked Sam. Eb was such a sharp-minded, fit old man—a champion bronc rider in his day—that it was easy to forget he was getting along in years. Still, Eb was the one person who'd had a front row seat at the goings-on at the ranch during the last fifty years.

Eb suddenly turned to Sam, apprehension crinkling the deep lines on his face. "You know, Sam, you start stirrin' up the ashes, and you might not like what's buried in them."

His words caught Sam by surprise. "What's that supposed to mean?" he growled.

"It means you weren't around here back then, when Lizzy took off. You don't have a clue what was goin' on. You came back here with your mind set that things were a certain way. Well, that don't mean that's the way it was. You get nosey and go diggin' now, and you just might get more than you bargained for." Eb started out quiet, but with each word he spoke, his volume increased as did the verve in his voice. By the end of his speech, he was downright emphatic.

"Dammit, Eb. I'm nearly fifty years old," Sam retorted, unable to contain his irritation. "Whatever it is, I'm sure I can handle it."

Eb was clearly irritated, too. "Suit yourself, but don't come cryin' to me when the truth is starin' you in the face and knockin' that big head of yours down a couple of sizes. You just take it off somewhere and *handle it!*"

With that said, Eb left the dishwasher door hanging wide open and huffed out of the kitchen. Sam stared after him. What in the world was Eb talking about?

CHAPTER 14

Lizzy rocked in front of the warm fire, relishing the heat soaking into her chilled limbs. She examined the tattered lace curtain in her lap. While unpacking her grandparents' belongings the previous day, she'd uncovered Grandma's sewing box along with her tatting shuttle and spools of thread. She might not know how to tat, but if it was humanly possible, she'd patch Grandma's curtains with a needle and thread.

She squinted in concentration and pulled the needle through a coil to secure one of the numerous fine threads into place. All it took was one of those broken threads, and the delicate loops would unravel and spring other threads and loops loose. Soon, a tiny hole would appear in the beautiful lace, one that would grow and spread if it wasn't mended.

Lizzy sighed resignedly. Grandma's lace curtains were littered with those holes. It might take Lizzy the rest of her life to repair the damage.

She paused to flex her fingers and rest her eyes, then gazed at Sid while she savored a few sips of her third cup of coffee. Satiated by his morning vittles, Sid licked fastidiously at his front paws and rubbed them across his whiskered cheeks.

"Yeah, I know. That's what I should be doing, too," she murmured. Lately, she couldn't generate any interest in her appearance. She'd done the minimum—clean teeth, face, and hands—and let the rest go. The disheveled results of her negligence screamed at her every time she glanced into a mirror.

She shrugged and told herself that it didn't matter. The only person who'd see her this morning was Sam, and she wasn't going to fix herself up for him. She wanted him to leave her alone, and if he couldn't stand to look at her, maybe he'd skedaddle out of here as soon as he'd unloaded her boxes. Then she could get on with her day in peace. At the moment, she longed for a few tranquil hours and the time to get her house in order. The clock was ticking, and she was anxious to move on to uncovering the cause of John's death.

With that thought, she shuddered. Why in the world had she discussed her speculations with Sam the previous day? He'd never understood John—had never even tried. After she'd opened her big mouth, he'd looked at her like she was a raving idiot.

Actually, her reactions to Sam the previous day still puzzled her. She hadn't expected him to arrive at the farm so early in the morning. The guilt she'd felt over her absence had helped fuel her actions.

But it wasn't only that, she was healing. She felt it. The constant barrage of both cherished and pain-filled memories and her visit to the cemetery had drained her, but they'd also had a therapeutic effect, both mentally and emotionally. She felt less threatened and frightened. At times, the hurt was still with her— giant engulfing waves of it—but it was more manageable, too.

In truth, she was weary of her anger. It was a relentless force, spiraling and consuming, sucking the life from her. And the only person she seemed to be hurting was herself. A nagging desire to get on with her life had taken seed, and if being civil to Sam was a step in that direction, so be it.

The slam of a door interrupted her ruminations. "Speak of His Greatness. He must be anxious to be rid of me, too, to be here this early," she muttered, eyeing her empty coffee mug. "What do you think, Sid? Can I just warm up the leftover dregs for him?"

The cat halted his toiletries long enough to stare at Lizzy and meow a reply.

"I suppose you're right. Men like Sam don't settle for second best. I better be *neighborly* and brew a fresh pot," Lizzy conceded irreverently as she pushed herself out of the rocker and trekked to the door, setting the curtains on the oak table as she passed by it.

She jerked the door open, then just stood there, stunned and silent, her thoughts reeling. Sam had definitely improved with age. Instead of his usual grimy Wranglers and Carhartts, he wore charcoal slacks and a black wool coat, a white shirt and blue tie peeking through his open collar. The tie was a perfect match to his eyes. This time his dark hair was combed neatly into place, and his face sported a smooth shave and a subtle scent that was way too familiar and caused her insides to do funny things. Irritated because she was grubby and disheveled and it seemed to matter to her, Lizzy met his intense gaze and held it.

"We're letting your heat out. Maybe we could come inside?" Sam finally said.

Lizzy blinked, then blinked again. Heat blossomed in her cheeks, as her eyes slid to Eb, who looked as dapper as Sam in a brown tweed jacket. She clamped her teeth together to keep a retort from slipping out as she stepped back to let them pass.

Mentally pulling herself together, she closed the door. Why did Sam rattle her like this? Her eyes turned to him, and she noticed that his arm was hanging at an awkward angle, the hand flexed back. Had he hurt it when he was hauling boxes the previous day?

He huffed resignedly and the hand shot forward, a folded piece of paper clasped in it. Anxiety twisted in Lizzy's gut. She stared at the paper and then up at Sam before she reached for it.

It was a plain white sheet. She unfolded it and read the message that was written on it in large black letters: *LEAVE NOW BEFORE IT'S TOO LATE!*

Blood drained from her brain. Her limbs went numb, and she leaned against the counter for support. The room, along with Sam and Eb, spun around her as if she were a ballerina twirling on her tiptoes. She closed her eyes and took slow, deep breaths. When she lifted her lids, it took forever for Sam's face to focus.

"It was stuck to your door," Eb informed her. "Did you hear anything around here last night?"

Lizzy fought her way through the gooey haze that engulfed her. Her eyes shifted from Sam to Eb and shook her head. "No, I was unpacking boxes until the wee hours."

She thought back to the previous night, replaying it in her mind. She'd opened box after box and sorted through cherished items. The experience had been bittersweet; warm memories had deepened the pain of what was no longer, while a poignant ache filled her heart to the point that she'd thought it would burst. She'd been so caught up in her reminiscences that noises from outside would have gone unnoticed.

"I cleaned up Granddad and Grandma's bedroom, so I slept in there. I didn't hear anything outside last night, not like I did the night your cow died." She paused, a memory pestering at the back of her mind. "You know, there was a truck stopped on the road outside my window a couple of evenings ago, before I drove to the ranch. I walked to the window to get a closer look, and it took off."

"What did it look like?" Sam demanded so curtly that Lizzy twitched.

She studied his troubled features. Frown lines creased his forehead, and his eyes looked fretful. Did he know something she didn't? "It was getting dark, so I didn't get a good look. But the truck was gray, lighter than yours . . . and not as big as yours. Not old, new." She shrugged. "Other than that, just a truck."

"You haven't seen it again?"

She shook her head.

"I'll take a look around outside," Sam announced before he turned and walked back out into the icy morning.

Once Sam was gone, Eb slipped his arm around Lizzy's shoulders and led her to the warmth of the fireplace. "Don't you worry now. We'll get to the bottom of this. It's probably just someone still upset with the way you took off after Con and Dottie's funeral.

Sometimes folks can have awful long memories. It probably don't amount to nothin'.."

Lizzy wanted to believe Eb's words, but she had her doubts. John had written that she was in danger. What if he was right? The thought brought icy shivers with it. A tight ball of fear had settled in her chest.

"Sam and I are on our way to church. Why don't you join us?" Eb invited, worry furrowing his aged features.

So that was why they were spiffed up. It was Sunday. Maybe a church service would help. The prospect of peaceful meditation was appealing, but the thought of confronting all of those faces from her past, even in the relative hospitality of a church, was nearly as unnerving as that warning note.

So was the alternative: once Sam and Eb left, she'd be here alone with her fear. Standing here beside Eb, she was shaking as if she'd just sprinted a marathon. When he and Sam left, it'd be worse. Until she could make peace with the fact that John's letter might be the honest-to-God truth and someone *really* did want to harm her, she didn't want to be alone.

"I think I'd like that. Thank you for inviting me," she said feebly.

The photographs had caught Eb's attention. He picked one up to study it. Apprehension hit Lizzy like a two-ton wrecking ball, knocking the wind from her. He looked up, his weary, aged eyes oozing despair. "Why're you doin' this to Sam, Lizzy? Do you want to hurt him that much?"

❋ ❋ ❋

Sam stood outside the kitchen door, rubbing at the pressure between his brows while he sorted through options. Should he mention the cow's slit throat or keep it to himself until he figured out what was going on? He didn't want to frighten Lizzy, but he didn't want to leave her here if she was in danger either. Then again, maybe she'd slit the throat herself . . . and written the note. But why would she do that? And if she didn't do it, then who did?

Whatever the case, he'd talk it out with Eb on the drive to church. Eb might've been as mute as a Trappist monk on the way to the farm, but that was about to change. It was time for Eb to open up and let Sam in on his little cache of secrets.

Sam scanned the farmyard. He'd walked around the house and examined the driveway and road. Everything looked much the same as it had the previous morning, so the note had been tacked to the door early enough that the frost appeared undisturbed this morning.

Sam tried to rub his trepidation away, but it clung to him like a bad stench. He sighed a long stream of fog, then walked into the house and caught the tail end of what Eb was saying. It sounded like Eb was upset about something Lizzy planned to do, something that would hurt someone. He hoped that someone wasn't him. He'd already had his share of upsets lately.

When he stepped into the living room, tension crackled in the air. The room reeked of secrets, ones to which he was not privy. Eb stared at him, his face an ashen mask of fear and guilt. As an attorney, Sam had seen that look enough to recognize it. Lizzy slowly turned to Sam, that same desperate expression on her face. Her eyes flicked to Eb's, and Sam noted the barely perceptible shaking of her head.

"What're you planning to do, Lizzy?" Sam asked at last.

A quizzical look settled onto her features.

"Why did you come back here," he demanded.

Her eyes were round saucers. "I'm going to get cleaned up," she announced in a squeaky voice. Before Sam could utter a rejoinder, she disappeared through the bathroom door.

Sam turned to Eb, determined to stare him down.

Eb rallied. "Shouldn't we be haulin' those boxes in here, so we'll get to church on time?"

Seething with frustration, Sam confronted him. "Out with it. What's going on here?"

"That's between me and Lizzy and none of your business. You shouldn't have been eavesdropping." Eb informed him. He returned the photo he was holding to the mantel and shuffled towards the kitchen. "You gonna help me, or not?"

Sam's blood simmered. Once again, he'd been thwarted. On top of that, Lizzy had ordered him to get his cattle off her land and to only God knew where by the first of April. He was still seeing red over that. Then there was the slaughtered cow and this morning's warning note. He hadn't a clue what those were all about.

And all Eb seemed to do lately was grouse at him.

Thank God he was heading to church this morning. At least, he'd get an hour or so of peace and quiet, free from Lizzy and her disturbing presence. And he'd have Eb cornered in the cab of his truck during the drive in and back. He'd get his answers then.

"I'll get the boxes; you get the door for me," Sam barked as he pulled his gaze from the photo Eb had been holding and trailed him into the kitchen.

Twenty minutes later the boxes were stacked in Lizzy's living room. Eb and Sam hadn't exchanged anything other than a few glowers during the entire transaction. Sam didn't care. He was still fuming. He wanted to get out of there. Where the hell was Lizzy, anyway? He should tell her they were leaving.

He strode into the living room—Eb riding his heels—and stopped dead in his tracks, his breath caught in his throat, his heart fluttering in his chest. Damn, she was a beautiful woman—all dark shadows, rounded curves, and long limbs. That part of her had certainly not changed. But why was she gussied up like that in a kick-ass black suit that had no business being out here in the sticks?

"Shit," he hissed when it hit him that she must be accompanying them to church. His hour of church refuge died an agonizing death.

His face must have voiced his thoughts because Lizzy's eyes threw daggers at him, and a scowl furled her perfect brows. "Eb invited me to church," she informed Sam. She seemed uncomfortable with the attention her lack of dirt and denim was eliciting, her face aglow with a pink flush. "Did you see anything outside?"

Worry snaked its way back into Sam's thoughts. "Not anything out of the ordinary—footprints and tire tracks. All but ours and your cat's paw prints were covered with frost. Other than those, it's hard to tell whose is whose. Keep your doors and windows locked and your eyes peeled for anything suspicious." He scanned the room, searching. "If you don't have a phone yet, you might want to get one."

"Thank you for looking," Lizzy murmured forlornly, her worried eyes shifting nervously to Eb.

"We could take the note to Matt Grover, the county sheriff," Eb offered. "He might have some ideas about who put it there."

"No!" Lizzy practically shouted. "It's probably like you said, just someone who's holding a grudge." Her eyes dropped to the note she held in her hand, and she walked to the desk, opened it, and stuffed the note inside.

Sam hoped she was right, but he didn't have a good feeling about it. He also didn't have a good feeling about Lizzy being within arm's reach for several hours. Prickles on his arms told him goose bumps were rising at the thought of it. He turned abruptly towards the door and muttered gruffly, "Let's get going."

From behind him, he heard Eb say, "Don't worry. You're going to church with me, not him." After a short pause filled with muffled whisperings, Eb added, "We'll talk about it later."

Yeah, when I'm not around, Sam almost growled. What in the hell could Lizzy be up to that would have Eb so upset?

Sam climbed into the truck, started the motor to heat the chilly interior, and watched the two of them make their way to the Dodge Ram. Lizzy had a pair of high-heeled shoes on her feet that put her at Eb's height. Her hair was twisted up on her head in some kind of fancy knot, and a pair of sparkling earrings dangled from her earlobes. Sam faced the steering wheel and bumped his forehead against it several times in frustration. The next few hours would be pure torture. He ground his molars together and told himself to suck it up and be tough.

Eb opened the door for Lizzy. She lifted a leg up to put it into the truck, but her skirt was so snug that she couldn't make the step. Sam watched her, mesmerized. Finally, Eb circled her waist with his hands and lifted her in. She slid across the seat and bumped up against Sam. Caught off guard, he automatically shifted away from her. She glanced up, then shimmied towards Eb, who was now settled into place. The two of them eyed each other, some kind of silent communiqué.

Sam backed out onto the rutted road and started the jarring ride into town. Eb sat silent, staring straight ahead, a worried frown etching deep furrows into his wrinkled face. Beside him, Lizzy perched straight as a rod, eyes front and center. Though she had a death grip on the seat, she kept bouncing into Sam. The tension inside the cab was as thick as Eb's milk gravy.

He knew he was pushing sanity's line with his driving speed, but he wanted this agony to be gone. They hit a particularly deep rut, and Lizzy slammed up against him and braced her hand on his thigh. His breath hitched, and his muscles tightened. Adrenaline coursed through his body. When she looked up, he expected to see a pair of disturbing dark eyes, their gaze as cold as the icy peaks in the distance. Though her jaw was set defiantly, there was something else in her eyes—a warm fire that turned Sam's limbs to mush and made his stomach somersault.

"Sorry," she whispered before she scooted up next to Eb.

Alarmed, Sam slowed the truck to a speed that would keep Lizzy in her center seat. He focused on regaining control over his body—the hammering of his heart and the fluttering in his gut. There was no need to panic. He'd been here before—back when he was much younger and lacked the experience he now had. He'd gotten through it then, hadn't he?

He didn't have an answer. He glanced fleetingly at Lizzy, and his mind shot back to that morning, the morning she'd walked through the mudroom door and changed his life.

It was the summer after he'd completed law school. He'd returned to the ranch for a couple of weeks of R&R before he started work in a Chicago law firm. It was a big mistake. J.D. welcomed Sam home and then spent most of those two weeks either in town or out working the ranch, leaving Sam to deal with the goings-on back at the ranch house.

Luckily—or unluckily, depending on how you looked at it— Lizzy walked through the door, so Sam didn't have to deal with his younger brother. The problem was that the Lizzy who floated around the ranch house during those two weeks was an alarmingly different Lizzy. Gone was the young girl he'd chased and tickled into giggling fits and carted around on his shoulder. In her place, was an attractive eighteen-year-old woman. She still had the long, slender limbs, but in between she'd developed a body full of curves and breasts, and her face was no longer that of a child. Her eyes were even more mysterious, exuding allure and wisdom.

Sam's gaze sidled over to the woman beside him in the truck, a middle-aged woman who had ripened to perfection with time. Something tugged at his insides, and he wrenched his eyes back to the road, a vision of her as she'd looked on *that* morning forming before him.

His father had already made his escape. Eb and Rose had gone into town to buy groceries, and John hadn't yet made an appearance. Sam sat alone at the kitchen table, perusing the *Oregonian* and nursing a second cup of coffee. He'd glanced up to see who had walked into the kitchen and was blindsided by what stood before him. Unable to process what he was seeing, he'd gaped at her for several long seconds while their eyes locked in some kind of silent battle.

"Better shut that fly trap before something finds its way in there," she'd snapped at him as she dropped a leather bag onto the table. "John said you'd be home for a visit." The hint of a smile had touched her lips before she walked to the stove to pour herself a cup of coffee.

She'd filled the sink with soapy water and washed the dirty dishes that were piled on the counter. Every so often, she'd turn to glance at him, a troubled look on her face, clearly unnerved by his perusal. But there was something else, too, something he'd forgotten. Even then, she'd been upset with him about something. "Don't you have somewhere else you need to be?" she'd finally asked.

Sam was so spellbound that all he could do was shake his head, his mind busily coming to terms with the loss of the girl he'd known and his fascination with this new woman. The two wouldn't fit together. As a young girl, Lizzy had always been engaging, but this new Lizzy was downright intriguing.

Eventually, her snugly encased derriere had disappeared through the kitchen door. Sam had sighed in relief and sank back into the kitchen chair to mull over what had just transpired. Guilt and loathing engulfed him. After some serious reflection, he'd finally admitted to being a couple of notches below a pile of cow dung for having even one lustful thought about his brother's future wife.

Now, sitting in his truck with Lizzy a touch away, he again wrestled with those familiar feelings—the helplessness and frustration that had plagued him during that entire two weeks and had continued to haunt him for years afterward. It had been pure hell. With Sam, Lizzy emanated a magnetic presence, one to which he was drawn. The only way to escape it was to avoid her all together, so he did. Or, at least, he'd tried. It hadn't worked then, and it wasn't working now.

Lost in his thoughts, Sam automatically braked to a stop before he pulled onto the highway. From beside him, he heard Lizzy sigh and sensed that she'd relaxed into the seat.

Angry at himself for dredging up a bunch of futile memories, Sam pushed his wayward thoughts aside. Nothing had changed. Whether John was dead or alive, Lizzy still belonged to him.

CHAPTER 15

Lizzy's eyes were drawn to the familiar lines of the picturesque white church, it's steeple rising high to pierce the cloudless sky. As if on cue, a curtain of grief smothered her. The last time she'd seen that church had been the saddest day of her life. Eb's hand squeezed hers in reassurance. *At least, today you have someone to go through this with,* she consoled herself, smiling feebly at Eb.

She felt Sam's eyes on her as she slid from the truck and landed in Eb's arms. Eb tucked her hand inside his elbow, and they made their way toward the church. Noting that Sam was a few paces behind, she whispered to Eb, "We need to talk. It's not what you think it is."

"Well, I'd sure be interested in what's goin' on then," he muttered, his lips barely moving. "Cause it looks to me like you're beggin' for trouble."

"I'm not," she assured him, shaking her head slightly to emphasize the point. Trepidation curled inside her. "Please don't say anything about the photograph to Sam." They reached the front door, and Sam stepped ahead to open it. "We'll talk after the service," she quickly added.

"Great. Where do you want to meet for our little tête-à-tête?" Sam murmured near her ear.

Heat glowed in Lizzy's cheeks. She sent him a glare that certainly didn't belong in church.

Before she could compose herself, Eb escorted her down the aisle, a sea of faces fanning out on both sides of them. Plodding organ notes hummed but didn't block out the murmur of voices that increased in volume with each step they took. Lizzy stared straight ahead to where the choir sat in straight lines clothed in scarlet robes and the pastor fidgeted with his eyeglasses and the pile of papers in his lap.

A voice to her right caught her attention: "That's her, all right. I heard she was back. I can't believe she had the nerve to. . . ." Lizzy's head whipped around to locate the offensive mouth. It was attached to a gray-haired woman who had the decency to turn as red as the choir robes when Lizzy locked eyes with her.

Of course, she couldn't hunt down every stray mouth in the place; it would've taken her the whole service. As they searched for a place to sit, she heard snippets though: "Isn't that the Stewart girl, the one who. . . ?" "I thought she was in prison or something. . . ." "She think God will forgive her for. . . ?" Lizzy stretched her head high and trembled uncontrollably inside the comfort of her designer black wool suit while Eb patted the hand that had a death grip on his elbow.

Finally, they squeezed into an empty space in a pew about midway down the aisle, Lizzy sandwiched between the two men. She wiggled into her tiny spot, crossed her legs to take up less room, and leaned against Eb, seeking his comfort.

In front of her, a woman glanced back over her shoulder and gave Lizzy the once-over. It was Mildred Bramley, twenty-five years more intimidating and still sporting her trademark purple Pendleton jacket. She whispered something to her husband Rex, who then had to check Lizzy out for himself. Lizzy flashed him a killer smile and watched his eyes bug out before he jerked back around rather hastily.

Determined to get her hour of relief and solace, Lizzy swallowed her tempestuous emotions. They landed in her stomach and settled into a fiery lump. As the choir rose for the opening hymn, Lizzy switched her focus from the congregation to the service. Granddad had called Sundays a day for spiritual and physical renewal. Squeezing Eb's hand, she longed for even one tiny morsel of that renewal.

She rose for the hymn and prayer, then squished herself back in between Sam and Eb with the cue to sit, the whole time wishing she were tucked safely into a pocket between her grandparents as in years past.

Only, the last time she was here, they hadn't sat with her. They were up front, wearing their Sunday best but lying like wax figures in those awful wooden caskets. Nauseatingly fragrant flowers blossomed everywhere, their sickly scent so thick that, sitting alone in her front row seat, she'd thought she would suffocate. All she remembered of that day was the grief that had consumed her, a ravenous parasite chomping away at her heart and soul. And Eb, he was there for her on that day, too, to walk her down the aisle and make sure she got to the cemetery and then home.

Another memory sparked, then glowed, one Lizzy had completely forgotten. As the pallbearers carried her grandparents' caskets down the aisle to the entry, she'd turned to follow their progress. Just as they'd reached the doors, her eyes had caught movement in the back pew. It was a man. He wore a heavy coat and a hat pulled low over his forehead, but Lizzy had recognized him. It was her father. Their eyes had locked for a few fleeting seconds before he'd rushed out the door.

Lizzy glanced back now as if he might still be there. He wasn't. In truth, she had no idea what had become of her father.

Sounds of the congregation settling in hinted that the sermon was at hand. Lizzy watched a slight, middle-aged man rise and step to the podium. He fiddled with his notes for several uncomfortable moments before he spoke, the deep roar of his voice more than compensating for his diminutive size. *"For there is nothing covered that shall not be revealed; neither hid that shall not be known.* These are the words of Jesus as written in the book of Luke, chapter twelve, verse two. Jesus is speaking to. . . ."

With his words, a surprised jolt slammed through Lizzy. Her eyes flicked here and there to see how others were reacting, then landed on Sam. A knowing smile curled the corner of his lips when their eyes met.

In the background, the pastor charged on. *". . . whatsoever ye have spoken in darkness shall be heard in the light; and that which ye have spoken in the ear in closets shall be proclaimed upon the housetops. And I say unto. . . ."*

Good grief! Was the pastor speaking directly to her? Surely, he didn't know? Her eyes hesitantly lifted to the pulpit to meet the fierce glow in his. *"Be not afraid of them that kill the body, and after that have no more that they can do. But I will forewarn you whom ye shall fear. . . ."*

Lizzy dropped her gaze to her hands clenched in her lap as she fought to still her sprinting heart and control her ragged breathing. This was ridiculous. Whoever that pastor was, he had no idea she would be in the congregation this morning. His message was for his entire flock, a warning to them that none of their secrets were hidden from God, that they would be held accountable for every single one of them.

As would she, she felt certain.

But would she receive some recompense if she fessed up to her sins before dying? Of course, that would mean she'd have to seek forgiveness, too. She glanced up at Sam. Life could be downright daunting.

The rest of the sermon remained a blur. Lizzy was too busy tallying up her transgressions and categorizing them to process the pastor's words. When she sensed the rustling of those around her, she blinked her ruminations aside, then noticed the hymnal Eb held. He reached out to share it with her as they stood, and she grasped it and peered up at Sam. He'd ignored her throughout the rest of the sermon. Well, she hoped he'd been listening to the pastor's words. His accounting to God was sure to take up a good deal of time.

The last note hung in the air as the congregations began to mill around and filter towards the back of the church. Lizzy was poised to make a beeline for the nearest exit, but Sam stood his ground, a solid barrier in her quest to reach the aisle. Rather than squeeze past him, she surveyed the people around her as they filed by, her heart pitter-pattering in her chest. Several of them nodded to Sam and Eb but passed right over her as if they didn't notice her parked between the two of them.

Though she recognized a few faces here and there, on the whole, they were strangers. Then she spotted Franny on one of the side aisles. Junior had an arm around her shoulders, and he appeared to be steering her towards a side door. Franny glanced around, locked eyes with Lizzy, and threw her a dazzling smile. A tiny angel touched Lizzy's heart, and she returned the smile just as Junior turned, a mask of pure hate distorting his features. He said something to Franny and pushed her through the door.

Junior's actions seemed way over the top. Lizzy and he had never been close. In truth, she'd not hidden the fact that she disliked the shady influence he had over John. But where had this out-and-out hatred come from? Twenty-five years ago, they'd managed a distant, but civil, truce. Something was out of sync now.

Thoughts of Junior vanished when she noticed three women talking and eyeballing her from behind their programs. The lump in her stomach churned. She thought she remembered two of them from high school—the Bronsford sisters. Back then they favored bold fabrics, and their extracurricular activity was spreading rumors. Some things never changed.

A couple stopped in front of Sam. It was Roy and Eunice Sargent. At one time Roy owned the feed store in town, and Eunice had been in Grandma's pinochle group. Lizzy felt a smile curve her lips. Finally, someone was going to be hospitable.

"Howdy, Sam. Eb," Roy greeted them, nodding to each of the two men.

"Good morning," Eunice chimed in. "Nice you could make it to church this morning."

"Mornin'," Sam and Eb voiced together.

"You remember Lizzy, Con and Dottie's granddaughter," Sam reminded them.

"Hello," Lizzy said. "It's nice to see you again."

"Lizzy." Roy gave her a nod, his eyes fidgeting guiltily.

She only got a cursory nod from Eunice. The smile froze on Lizzy's lips.

Sam wouldn't let it go. "Lizzy's living out at the farm."

Roy was still trying to get a handle on his discomfort, so Eunice spoke up, disdain sketched on her face, her Bible clutched in her gloved hands to shield her from potential corruption. "You planning to stay there long? I can't imagine that place is very livable what with the way you've left it to rot away."

"I plan to live there," Lizzy said sweetly. "Sam has been such a big help. He's so *neighborly* that he comes over pretty much every day to help out. It's really quite livable now." She smiled up at Sam and watched his jaw tighten. Well, good. Maybe he'd quit yapping and move out of her way. Eunice's jaw dropped—rendering her silent. She studied Sam speculatively, then moved on, Roy in tow.

Lizzy had the lay of the land, and she'd had her fill of their brand of Christian love. She nudged Sam to get him moving. He glanced down, and though she tried to disguise her hurt, he must've seen it because he stepped into the aisle and let her pass in front of him. His hand on her back maneuvered her out of the church past several pious church-goers who were clearly gossiping about her.

By the time she reached the parking lot, tears pooled in Lizzy's eyes. She fought to keep them there. She understood a few people looking down their noses at her because of her sudden departure, but what was all of this animosity about? First the note, and now this; what had she gotten herself into?

"Are you okay?" Sam asked from somewhere near her left ear.

Lizzy looked up, and the tears she'd tried so hard to control rolled down her cheeks. Just like that, she was tucked into the comfort of Sam's immaculate wool coat, his strong arms wrapped around her. Panic stiffened her body.

But it felt so familiar, like the old Sam who'd been there to comfort and console her when her faithful horse, Tonka, had died. As now, he'd taken her into his arms, so she could shed her tears on his shoulder. Then he'd promised her that when she was ready, she could come over to the ranch and pick out a new horse for herself. *When did you change,* Lizzy silently implored. *One minute you were my Sam, and the next you were someone I didn't know.*

She pushed herself away from him to search his eyes for an answer. His were sad and troubled, and she thought she detected a hint of fear. No answers. "I'm sorry," she murmured as she turned away to get her emotions under control.

Her eyes landed on a silver pickup truck in the parking lot. A young man in a tan overcoat was climbing into it. The truck resembled the one that had been parked outside her window. And it would soon be driving off.

Lizzy sniffled hurriedly, inhaled a deep breath to steady her nerves, and asked, "Do you know who that is climbing into that truck over there?"

Eb's gravely voice answered. "That's Brad Thompkin. He's one of the attorneys that works out of Gus Woolridge's office. Why're you askin'?"

"Oh . . . it just looks like the truck that was outside my window the other night."

"I can't think why Brad'd be sittin' outside your window."

Lizzy faced Eb, apprehension poking at her. "Me neither. Never mind. I'm sure there are many more trucks just like that around here." What was wrong with her? She was becoming suspicious of everything?

"Let's get going," Sam ordered. "I've gotta get home and work on finding a place to put my cattle come April." As soon as the words left his mouth, his eyes met Lizzy's in what just might be a feeble attempt at an apology.

Lizzy wallowed in the guilt that had been hounding her since her discussion with Sam the previous day. As she walked towards Sam's truck, she wondered what had happened to her peaceful time of renewal. Since the day was already past saving, she made a hasty decision to make good use of the ride back to the farm. Surely, it wouldn't make what promised to be an intolerable ride any worse if she broached the subject of John's death.

She waited until they were well on their way—settled and silent in their respective seats—with a suffocating blast of hot air pouring from the vents. Lizzy shifted uncomfortably in her wool attire. Perspiration had the fabric itching and clinging to her, an irritant that helped spur her on.

"Eb, can I ask you something?" she murmured, a roar in the interminable silence.

Eb eyed her warily. "Depends on what it is."

Not sure how to phrase it, she hesitated a moment. "Are you and Rose related to the Craig family in some way?"

Curiosity furrowed his features. "Not that I know of. Why?"

Should she continue or not? Eb might not like her questioning his sister's right to be buried with the Craigs. It didn't seem right to leave it hanging either. "Well, I was at the cemetery and noticed that Rose is buried in the Craig family plot. That got me wondering if you were a relation to them."

Eb shook his head. "No, that was Rose's doin's. She wanted it, and J.D. gave the okay, so we buried her there. My dad'd disown her if he knew where she chose to lay her head, but there comes a time when you have to let bygones be bygones and move on. If she wants to spend eternity surrounded by a bunch of stubborn, arrogant, sheep-shootin', land-hoggin' Craigs, I wasn't gonna stop her."

Well, Lizzy could cross that question off her list now. Her gaze flicked to Sam to check his reaction to Eb's jabs—they were clearly aimed at him. His jaw was twitching, a sign that he hadn't appreciated it.

"Since you brought it up, seems like now's a good time to make use of some of that Craig stubbornness," Sam declared. "So what was that big 'to do' between you two all about, the one back at the farmhouse?"

Lizzy's eyes met Eb's. "We were having a *private* conversation. You had no right to listen in," she said.

"That might be, but I did hear something about you hurting someone. I sure hope that's not why you came back here—to settle a score and inflict your retribution on some unfortunate soul. People change, you know."

Anger burned in Lizzy's cheeks. Sam was lecturing her as if she were a ten-year-old child. He was probably afraid she'd wreak her revenge on him. Well, if she did, he'd deserve it. Seconds passed as she sat, eyes facing straight ahead, until she was certain he'd given up on his interrogation.

She glanced at Eb. He seemed lost in his own thoughts. "Eb?" she probed.

"Yeah," he answered vaguely.

Lizzy didn't want to upset him, but surely he'd want the truth to be known, too. She plotted her words before she spoke. "I've been thinking about John lately." She was sure she heard Sam mutter an oath under his breath. She ignored it.

Eb turned to her, his eyes brimming with sadness. "And?"

The look on Eb's face brought tears to her eyes. It was difficult to get words past the burning in her throat. She sniffed and pressed on. "How did he seem, you know . . . before he died?"

"What do you mean?" Eb asked in a husky voice.

What did she mean? How would John act if he'd uncovered a secret and was convinced his life was in danger? "Did he seem different in any way—maybe frightened of something, more nervous than normal?"

Eb's forehead wrinkled in thought. "Not that I recall."

Surely, Eb would've noticed if John was not himself. Eb had been nearly as close to John as she. "So nothing seemed to be bothering him?"

Sympathy now shone on Eb's face. "Don't spend time beatin' yourself up over somethin' that's over and done with, Lizzy. You know as well as I do that Johnny was havin' a tough time. Your goin' away wasn't what pushed him over that edge."

Lizzy didn't need sympathy; she needed information. "Then what did?"

Eb studied her as if he wished he could suck out all of her demons and replace them with peace. He shrugged and shook his head. "Johnny's the only one who can answer that, and I don't see that happenin'."

"What if he *didn't* take his own life?" Lizzy implored.

"I'm the one who found him. There wasn't a single sign that anything else happened." Eb turned away from her to gaze out the window.

"You found him?" Lizzy whispered, stunned.

Eb nodded. He sighed, then faced her. "Lilac came back to the ranch without him—saddle on, but no bridle. We all went out lookin' for him. I remembered that butte he called Eagles' Nest—the place you and Johnny used to hang out all the time—and headed out that way. He went up there to be close to his mama, you know. I guess he just got worn out with livin' and decided he'd be happier with her."

"Dammit!" Sam barked, interrupting their private conversation. "What the hell's the point in dredging all of this up again? You can't change what happened, Lizzy, just to ease your conscience."

Lizzy stared at him, her heart still racing from the shock of his explosive expletive. Caught up in her emotional exchange with Eb, she'd forgotten Sam was here with them.

"That'll be ten bucks," Eb angrily demanded as he held out his toughened old hand to Sam.

Reeling from her conversation with Eb and Sam's harsh accusation, Lizzy struggled to follow the exchange between the two men. She turned to Eb in search of an answer.

"Sam's workin' on curbin' his cursin' on the Sabbath," Eb explained.

"Well, I'm sure as hell not going to listen to this bullshit all the way back to the farm," Sam grumbled defiantly.

"Twenty bucks," Eb challenged.

Sam reached inside his coat and shifted his weight to produce a wallet. He tossed it at Eb and growled, "There's at least a hundred bucks in there. That should just about cover the rest of the drive."

✹ ✹ ✹

Lizzy shifted anxiously between Sam and Eb and eyed the empty farmhouse, tendrils of fear eradicating her confidence. They were going to drop her off and leave her here alone. *Buck up*, she told herself. *You're a big girl. You can handle this.*

"Why don't you come back to the ranch with us?" Eb invited. "I've got a ham in the oven. You can help me put the rest of the fixin's together, and we can sit down and chew the fat awhile."

It sounded wonderful. As a child, she'd helped her grandmother after the church service. Grandma would cook an extra special dinner, and Lizzy would cover the oak dining table with a lovely lace tablecloth, neatly pressed white linen napkins, and Grandma's best dishes and silver. Often there were guests, or they were invited to share Sunday dinner with another family. Even during the most chaotic periods of Lizzy's married life, she'd made Sundays a special time for her family.

The truck came to a stop in the driveway. Lizzy glanced at Sam. Frown lines creased his forehead, and his jaw was clenched so tight that it was plastered with white splotches. She had no desire to bankrupt Sam, and though she'd been quiet during the remainder of the trip from church to the farm, the chances of her being quiet throughout Sunday dinner were slim. She sighed resignedly. It would be best if she declined Eb's heartfelt offer. However, she did need to settle a few things with Eb before he sat down to chew the fat over ham and the fixin's with Sam.

"Thank you, Eb. That sounds wonderful, but I better stick around here and get those boxes unpacked. Would you mind walking me to the house and taking a quick look around, though?"

Eb's face blossomed with questions.

Lizzy lifted her brows and lowered her head to prod him. "Then I could give you that recipe . . . you know . . . the one you asked me about," she stammered.

"Oh, yeah. Sure," he finally mumbled, understanding flashing in his eyes.

"Be quick about it," Sam grumbled.

Eb slid out onto the frozen ground and turned to catch Lizzy. He wrapped his arm around her as they stepped gingerly to the front door. Thoughts of the note made Lizzy shiver. "Do you think I'm safe here?" she murmured.

"I suppose so. I wouldn't let you stay here alone if I didn't think you'd be okay. You saw how it was at church, and I'm sorry about that. It's gonna take people awhile to get used to you bein' here. They don't know what happened or why you left, and you know how folks are. They made up their own stories, most of them based on a pack of lies."

Lizzy turned to study his gnarled face. Lies—what kinds of lies? Of course, Eb wasn't privy to the contents of John's letter. Well, she wasn't ready to share it with him, not yet.

After she opened the front door, she tugged Eb into the living room to stand before the mantel. The five photos reached out to tug at her heart. Though her nerves were taut wires, she managed a weak smile. "These are my three sons, Eb."

She hesitated, not sure what to say next. Eb *had* to understand. He was silent, as if he knew how difficult this was for her.

"Because of them—and only them—I've kept on going. During the last twenty-five years, they've been my lifeline, and I miss them so much. Surely I should be able to have their pictures out where I can see them. I mean, this is my house, for God's sake." Her pulse accelerated to a pounding crescendo, throbbing in her head. "Is it that obvious?" she finally murmured.

Eb shook his head, his answer barely more than a whisper. "Couldn't miss him. I'm surprised Sam did. He's got 'Craig' written all over him. Course, Sam doesn't know what we do, does he?"

Fury surged through Lizzy. It caught her off guard, consuming her with its force. "Maybe Sam does know! How could he not see it? You did. The pictures upset him; that was obvious. I find it hard to believe that he doesn't know. J.D. wouldn't have kept his big mouth shut. He'd make sure Sam got an earful, and then Sam made his choice. He can't go back and change that now." She thought about what she'd said, then added, "You know, it's odd, but all three boys kind of remind me of John."

His face deathly pale, Eb studied her. "You put them out here . . . knowin' he'd see them."

She rubbed at the pain in her forehead, wondering if Eb was right. Did she want to see Sam's reaction? "I don't know, Eb. I'm just so tired of it all. I'm tired of the hurt and anger and loss I feel every time I look at Sam. I'm tired of all the secrets. And I'm so very tired of more than half a lifetime of wondering." Suddenly bone weary, she paused to gather strength. "Maybe all I want is resolution, no matter the outcome. I really don't know. But I don't think I can handle it all coming to a head right now."

"Well, you might be gettin' more than you bargained for 'cause I'd stake my life on the fact that Sam doesn't know anything about that boy. But Sam's not blind. If your sons shows up here, he's gonna figure it out, and it ain't gonna be a pretty sight," Eb warned.

Eb was right. She was courting danger on more than one front. When she thought about it, the possibilities overwhelmed her. "I know. That's why Sam has to have his cattle off the farm by the first of April. Those boys will be here for spring break, and I can't take the chance of him running into the wrong one." Struck by a sudden thought, she offered, "Maybe you could keep Sam busy at the ranch? They'll only be here a week."

"You don't ask for much, do you?" Eb snorted. "The only way I could keep Sam at the ranch if he didn't want to be there is to break both his legs and destroy every vehicle on the place. And then what? Are we gonna do that every time your sons decide to visit?"

He shook his head in disgust. "You know, don't you, that he's relyin' on this farm to keep his herd goin'?"

"I know," Lizzy admitted, guilt nagging at her. "After the week's up, I'll tell him I've changed my mind, and he can move his cattle back. For some reason, they like to hang out in the farmyard. Once I get the fences back up, it won't be as much of a problem."

She knew it sounded lame and would create a lot of extra work for those at the ranch, but for now, it would have to do. She couldn't take the chance of Sam being at the wrong place at the right time. Later she'd come up with a long-term solution.

Eb's sad eyes searched Lizzy's. "Do you have any idea what it will do to Sam if he finds out why you left here? One of us should've talked with him back then. Now . . . it's too late."

Though she fought it, Lizzy felt the sting of tears. "I know. But I couldn't talk with him, not after all that happened. J.D. told me Sam didn't want to see me. That he wanted me to go away and never show my face around here again. That I brought disgrace on both our families. I believed him. But now—well now, after seeing Sam again after all these years—I just don't know what to believe."

Lizzy managed to get the words out before a sob escaped. She covered her face with her hands. Eb pulled her into his shoulder, cocooning her in his frail arms, and she released twenty-five years of pent-up pain. It rolled down her cheeks to saturate Eb's scratchy wool jacket.

Gradually, she became aware that Eb's body had stiffened. She looked up into eyes that were focused behind her—Sam. Her stomach lurched. How much of their conversation had he heard?

❋ ❋ ❋

If he painted a picture of dread, Sam thought it would be a reflection of Lizzy's face. She'd hesitantly turned to face him, her eyes huge, dark pools, tears overflowing to trickle down her cheeks. Sam stood firm, his fists clenched, fighting the urge to take her into his arms and comfort her. Behind Lizzy, Eb stared at him, too, shadows lurking in his weary eyes.

Sam pinched the ridge between his brows—the niggling pain was fast becoming a full-fledged headache. For certain, Eb and Lizzy were hiding something. Twice this morning he'd caught them with guilt-ridden faces. Should he hound them until they gave in to his badgering, or should be let it go for now? The honest-to-God truth was that he'd welcome an excuse to walk out the door and leave this emotional hellhole behind. He was sick to death of the whole mess.

As if he'd read Sam's mind, Eb set his jaw and pulled Lizzy in close against him, a show of force. If Sam was to elicit their secret, he'd have to hammer away at their defenses. He studied Lizzy's defeated demeanor, his mind flicking to the treatment she'd endured at church. No, his heart wasn't into subjecting her to any more battering—at least, not today.

"If you're through in here, we need to get back to the ranch," Sam said, hoping he didn't sound as frustrated as he felt.

Relief flooded their features—two balloons deflating in unison. Even the air surrounding them seemed less charged. Irritated by the suspicion that he'd yielded during a key battle, Sam did an about face and strode briskly to the door.

"I'm coming," Eb announced from behind him.

"You might be off the hook now, Lizzy," Sam mumbled to himself. "But I'll be back tomorrow."

CHAPTER 16

Lizzy's lower back screamed. Flames shot through her knees. She flexed her fingers, trying to get feeling back into them. No doubt about it, she was reaping the painful rewards from her two days of unpacking. She eyed the three boxes that sat against the back wall and was sure she heard her weary body shriek, *No!*

"Yes," she told herself firmly. "As soon as you get this house in order, you can move on to make some sense of your chaotic life." She rubbed at her lower back, bending to flex the stiffness from it. "And once those last three boxes are unpacked, you can sit down with a well-deserved glass of wine and have a little one-on-one time with yourself."

She limped to the closest box, dug a knife from her pocket, and slit through the brittle tape that held the lid in place. When she lifted the lid, a familiar image leaped out at her. Her breath hitched; her world stopped. Weak knees buckled, and she sank to the floor, her heart dancing madly.

A quick glance at the second bedroom confirmed that its door was still closed. As yet, she'd been unable to open it and face the personal mementos of her lost life. Unbeknownst to her, they weren't behind that shut door; they were packed away in this box for safekeeping. Could she face them now?

She pushed herself up onto her throbbing knees and lifted the framed photo from the box to gaze into the perceptive eyes of her beloved friend. They were at the reservoir that day—a beautiful spring day, too cold to swim, so they'd sat on the shore. Again, she remembered the warmth of the sun's rays caressing her skin, melting away a winter of ice and snow. They had sat in silence, faces turned toward the azure sky.

That's when John told her he was leaving. That's when it all started falling apart.

Lizzy had a camera with her that day. She was supposed to use the roll of film on a photography class assignment. Instead, she'd compulsively snapped pictures of John in an attempt to preserve something she suddenly feared losing. She'd sneaked into the darkroom at school and enlarged her favorite one—John, with the breeze ruffling his dark hair and his beautiful mouth lifted on one side into a quirky smile. Horses grazed in the background, fluffy white cloud puffs dotted the sky, and the sparkling ripples in the reservoir mirrored the blue in John's eyes.

Now, with more of life under her belt, Lizzy looked at that photograph and saw what she hadn't seen then—the fear and pain in those eyes. The knowledge of it squeezed at her heart.

He didn't want to go away but didn't see that he had a choice. It was either him or Sam. J.D., as always, had expected John to do the grunt work. Lizzy cried herself to sleep that night, dreading a life without John there to help her through it, faced with the possibility that nothing would be the same again.

He left a week after his high school graduation. After hugging her tightly, he climbed on a Greyhound bus, and just like that, the boy she loved so dearly became a part of her past.

Two years later a stranger came home in his place—a bitter man—his mind and body broken by the realities of war, too soon. In too many ways, he was again that young boy she'd met behind the barn that strange day several years before. Lizzy went to him and was there for him, just as she was when he'd broken his leg. But it was never the same again.

Now she sat on the hard floor, studying John's face, sickened by her loss. She had an overwhelming urge to be near him, to tell him that she understood. She understood why he'd left her and why he'd felt it was his duty. She even understood why he'd compromised his values and ignored his beliefs and gone off to fight a war he didn't believe in—only to please his father. She hadn't understood at the time, but she did now.

A loud banging startled Lizzy. Her eyes shot to the kitchen door, her heart beating frantically. The note she'd stuffed in Granddad's desk that morning popped to the forefront of her mind. Her reminiscences vanished as she slowly rose to her feet—John's photo clutched close to her heart—and shuffled towards the door. Frightening possibilities reeled through her brain.

"Don't be ridiculous," she ordered herself. "If someone was here to kill you, they wouldn't knock on your door . . . would they?"

Lizzy took a deep breath, braced herself, and turned the lock. She crept the door open a couple of inches to peek out into the faded light of early evening. Icy air swirled around her. Shivers sliced through her as she stared into Eb's troubled face.

"I was startin' to worry," he said.

"Me, too," Lizzy squeaked, reining in her emotions. "I was worried that someone was here to follow through on their threat." She eyed the covered plate in Eb's hand. "You're taking care of me again, aren't you?"

Eb stepped inside and tugged off his hat, the outside chill

radiating off of him. "Come in by the fire. You shouldn't have come over here when it's so cold outside," she admonished him.

"You wouldn't come to Sunday dinner, so I brought it to you," he informed her as he set the plate on the counter and walked with her into the living room. "Besides, I couldn't stop frettin' about you. Had to make sure you're okay."

"Oh, Eb. How did I ever get by without you?" Overcome with a wave of gushy, warm sentiment, Lizzy leaned up to kiss him lightly on the cheek. "Thank you."

A rosy hue infused Eb's cheeks. "Well, Sam was pretty rough on you this mornin', and I knew you were worried about that note on your door."

Thorns of unease jabbed her, wiping out the warm, fuzzy feelings. "How much of our conversation do you think he heard?"

"Not much or he'd still be standin' here tryin' to wrestle the whole story out of us. He was quiet on the ride to the ranch and through dinner. Didn't push it, but he will."

Lizzy sighed and gazed at the image of John she held in her hand. She touched his features lovingly with the tips of her fingers, then set the photo on the mantel next to her other loved ones.

Eb studied it, an odd look on his face. "Sam didn't bite, so you're addin' a little more bait, huh?" He turned that look on her and shook his head. "Well, I imagine that'll do the trick."

Lizzy followed his eyes back to the photo and stared in silence, stunned at what she hadn't noticed before. The images of John and the one in the photo next to it could easily be portrayals of the same person. A giant lump burned in her throat. "I never realized," she whispered. "I saw similarities . . . but I never realized they looked so much alike."

"Well, now that you do realize it, how's about you put it somewhere safe . . . like hidden away in your bedroom. That's assumin' Sam's not gonna be in there?" Eb offered, his eyes questioning.

Warmth flooded her cheeks, growing hotter with his lengthy perusal. "Just what did bring you back here?" he finally muttered.

"Not Sam!" she snapped. "I thought he was long gone from here—like me."

She stepped to the corner, grabbed a couple of sticks of firewood, and placed them on the flames as she sorted through the tangled mess in her mind. When she stood, the words seemed to pour from her mouth.

"Oh, Eb, I'm not even sure I know what brought me back here. My life fell apart again, just like it did twenty-five years ago. My husband no longer wanted me, and my sons—who are the center of my life—took off to lead their own lives. My ex was also my employer, so that shot my job of twenty years—as Sam would put it—to hell and gone.

"I thought I had friends who would help me get through the tough times, but I found out divorce is a good way to find out who your friends really are. Turns out, mine were few and far between. Unfortunately, the woman who was always there to weather the storms with me passed away from breast cancer a couple of months ago. I lost my marriage. I lost my home. I lost my job. I lost my best friend. In so many ways, I even lost my family . . . for the third time."

Her voice cracked on those last few words, so Lizzy paused to compose herself before she continued. "I felt like I disappeared again, that my whole identity was gone. I was suddenly someone new, someone I didn't recognize. I know it's only because of my circumstances, that somewhere deep inside—in my heart and soul— the person I've always been is waiting to be rediscovered. I just want to find that person, to be me again. I think maybe I left a large part of her here . . . twenty-five years ago."

When Lizzy finished, she was trembling. Sadness etched deep grooves in Eb's gnarled face. "If you see her around, would you send her back to me," Lizzy joked, a half-hearted attempt to lift his spirits. She hadn't meant to be so morose, especially after he'd been kind enough to drive to the farm to check on her and bring her Sunday dinner.

Eb nodded, still watching her closely.

Lizzy turned to the pictures on the mantel. Eb was right; the photo of John would go into her bedroom, far from prying eyes.

"You know, there's not a day that goes by that I don't miss my sons—their endless questions, their laughter, even their arguments," she murmured. "At least, they're still a living, breathing part of my life. John and my grandparents are forever gone from our lives. I need to make peace with their ghosts. Then maybe I'll be able to let them go."

Eb had remained silent, still watching her. At long last, he spoke. "I need to show you somethin'. I was hopin' it wouldn't come to this, but. . . ." He pulled several sheets of folded paper from his jacket pocket and handed them to her.

Anxious twitters poked at Lizzy's insides. She eyed the packet, then Eb. What had him so upset? Ever so slowly, she unfolded the papers. It appeared to be a document. She leafed quickly through it— several pages of legal jargon, initialed on each page and signed on the last by J.D. Eb and Gus Woolridge had scrawled their names beneath J.D.'s. It was dated June 9, 1988. Rather than attempt to wade through the technical mumbo jumbo, she looked to Eb for an explanation.

Eb sighed, a pained look distorting his features. "J.D. had Gus write it up a few days before he died. Guess he finally realized that

Sam wasn't goin' to be marryin'. He told me to send this copy to you." Eb paused, his eyes probing. "I didn't. I figured you'd made a new life for yourself and wouldn't ever be comin' back to the farm."

A sick feeling settled in the pit of her stomach. "What is it?" she prodded, unsure if she wanted to hear his answer.

"In a nutshell, it says that your son will inherit the ranch after Sam dies. That is, as long as Sam doesn't get married and have a child. I don't see that happenin'."

Eb's news knocked the wind right out of her. It was the last thing she'd expected from J.D. There had to be a catch. "I don't understand; what's so awful about that?"

"Well, you know J.D. There was always a condition," Eb muttered. He took a deep breath and added, "To inherit the ranch, your son can't set foot on this farm or the ranch before Sam's death."

"What?" Lizzy blurted, struggling to process J.D.'s lunacy. Then it flashed as clear as the High Dessert sky, and she snarled. J.D. had reached out to control her. This was his insurance that she wouldn't return to the farm. Well, he'd made a critical error in judgment: she didn't want his precious ranch—not then and not now.

"It's not part of his will, but there's another copy, probably in Gus' office. I planned to give this one to you when it was time. I would've made sure your son got the ranch," Eb assured her.

She didn't want the ranch, but what about her son? He might feel differently about his inheritance. He was set to visit her the first week of April. But if he set foot on this farm, he wouldn't inherit the ranch. And how could she live here if he couldn't visit her?

The implications were endless—too complicated to sort through—and involved several disclosures that she wasn't sure she wanted to make. "I need some time to think about this, Eb. Can I keep the document for now?"

"It's yours," Eb murmured, shrugging as if he could push the matter aside now that it was on Lizzy's shoulders. "Should've been ten years ago. When you said your boys were comin' for a visit, I figured it was time you saw it."

Overwhelmed by this latest revelation, Lizzy nodded and rubbed the ache between her eyes. She carried the pages to the desk and added them to her stash of correspondence. Her eyes landed on John's letter and, seeking comfort, her fingers automatically reached for it.

"John sent me a letter." The words slipped out before she could stop them. She could've kicked herself, but it was too late. At least, she now had no qualms about Eb's ability to keep a secret.

"So I heard," was Eb's reply. A spark of interest glistened in his eyes. "Sam told me Franny found one of Johnny's letters. That she wanted to send it to you."

Lizzy only wavered a couple of seconds before she held the letter out to him. "You'll probably need to get close to the lamp to read it." She nodded at the softly glowing bridge lamp that flanked the desk.

Eb pulled a pair of reading glasses from inside his coat and slid them on. Then he held the letter near the light while his eyes scanned back and forth across the lines John had written. Lizzy watched, nervous flutters unsettling her stomach. When his gaze rose to meet hers, it was riddled with questions.

"Any idea what it means?" Lizzy asked.

Eb chewed his lower lip and shook his head. "Nope. After you left, he did spend a lot of time up at that place he called Eagles' Nest. But the rest of it? Your guess is as good as mine."

Hope drained from Lizzy. She felt it seep out through her pores, leaving her sad and wasted. If Eb didn't understand what John was talking about, no one would. Her hopes had been riding on him.

"You know, Lizzy, have you considered that Johnny might've been tryin' to get you to come back here? That might be what this letter's all about."

Eb was right, of course, but it just didn't ring true. "Yes, I've thought about that. I still have to follow this through, though—for John. I need to know the truth," she told him.

Lost in her own thoughts, she let Eb fold the letter, stuff it back inside the envelope, and replace it in the desk.

"Where did you get this?" he barked in a strangled voice.

She jerked and blinked him into focus. He held the page from the diary, his face ashen, stricken. "I found it in Granddad's desk. The handwriting is beautiful. Do you recognize it?" Lizzy hesitated, eyeballing Eb. He stared at the piece of paper as if it were his death sentence. "I thought it might belong to John's mother, but it's such an odd thing to write on the same day you end your own life, don't you think?"

As if it had burned his fingers, Eb released the paper. He stared at it for several seconds, then glared into Lizzy's eyes. "I have to go," he told her, his voice weak and broken.

Lizzy was bewildered. "Eb?" she called after him as he hightailed it to the kitchen door.

He stopped and turned to her. "Be careful, Lizzy," he warned.

❀ ❀ ❀

The sun rode low on the horizon, playing peek-a-boo from behind a procession of billowing clouds and painting a fiery wash over the somber landscape.

Sam sat hunched in the saddle, forearms resting on the horn, reins dangling loosely in his gloved hand. He'd sat like this for some time, fingers of icy air reaching inside his coat to distract him while he viewed the shifting panorama from the top of the butte. There was a time when he'd made his way up this hill several times a week, but as the years passed, his visits became less frequent. It'd been more than a year since the last time he'd sat here.

This was the place he usually found himself when he felt the need to cast an eye out over his land and take inventory of all that he possessed, mostly to convince himself that it really was worth it—the loss of a promising career and the blood and sweat he put into preserving his inheritance. It was also the place he came when he had something to think through. This evening it was a little of both.

As he gazed out over the gently rolling hills and off to the snow covered peaks in the distance, he felt a strong connection to this place, though not like that of his father and John, and even Con. With them, it was all about sentimental crap like being a part of the land and the land being a part of them.

With him, it was more that he was needed here, so here he was. He hadn't planned it that way, but life had its way of barging in uninvited and taking control. Then before you could think it through, the future you'd envisioned lay trampled in the dust back there somewhere, and you were struggling down some new path.

Sam was numb at the time of his father's death, just doing what he knew he had to do. Now here he sat on this cold hill with half of his life gone, wondering where it had disappeared to. Into the endless acres of High Desert dirt and sagebrush and the years of getting the job done he supposed.

The hell of it was that he was good at it. There probably wasn't anyone who could run the ranch as well as he did. With him, it was second nature. He didn't even have to put much thought into it; he just knew what to do and when to do it—that is, he did until Lizzy showed up.

But damn it all, anyway. John was supposed to be here doing it, not him. That was the plan from the very beginning.

Sam hadn't thought much about the turn of events that had put him here, and he didn't dwell on how he felt about the whole thing. To his way of thinking, what was, was, and it wouldn't do him a whole lot of good to waste his time questioning it.

Now Lizzy was here, and he was a tangled mess, fighting a losing battle with some tenacious, deep down part of him that refused to be ignored. For a man who'd become acclimated to very little change and not a lot of turmoil, his Sunday morning had been intolerable.

Sam mulled over what he'd learned in the last few days—and what he hadn't learned—and tried to fit the pieces together into something that fit comfortably, so he could ride down the hill and home to supper. He wanted to sit across from Eb and enjoy a normal conversation, free of hidden agendas and emotional roller coasters.

Mesmerized by the shifting patterns of red and orange and lost in his thoughts, a sudden movement below startled him. A vehicle wound its way towards the cemetery that was perched on the knoll below him—Lizzy's red Explorer.

The Cascade Range was swallowing the last sliver of sun, and Sam shivered with the sudden drop in temperature. He focused his attention on Lizzy's progress, his pulse quickening at the mere thought of her. She was probably on her way to John's grave. What was it she'd said about sunrise and sunset, something about it being John's favorite time of day? If it were true, why hadn't he known it, too?

The Explorer reached the gate to the cemetery, and Lizzy climbed out of it. Sam watched her push the heavy gate open and walk toward his family's plot—hurrying. She probably didn't want to get caught out here after the lingering rays disappeared and a shroud of icy darkness settled over the land, including that creepy cemetery.

Ranger was growing restless, shifting beneath Sam and pulling on the reins, anxious to get home to his warm stall and supper. "Settle down. We'll head back soon," Sam assured him as he patted his sleek neck. The horse snorted a spiraling cloud into the fading light.

Though he knew he shouldn't be snooping, Sam continued to gaze down upon Lizzy. The sun was fading fast, casting bright ribbons of blinding light and bathing the cemetery in a vibrant orange film. Lizzy sat cross-legged on the ground, facing John's grave. Sam caught snatches of her voice—a muted, distant lament— in the stillness of evening. He would give a bottle of his favorite Scotch to know what she was saying.

It annoyed him that Lizzy could have a lengthy conversation with John—a dead John, no less. Yet she barely spoke one word to him unless she was forced to—like this morning, when he'd instinctively pulled her against his shoulder. Sam clenched his jaw at the bittersweet memory. He'd played with fire, something he rarely did. Then on the drive home, Lizzy had brought up John's death again, knowing full well it would irritate him. Why couldn't she just accept the truth and be done with it.

Dusk was a fading memory when Lizzy stood. Sam sensed that her focus had turned to him. For several long moments, he felt her presence and fought the urge to ride down the hill to be near her. He could barely make out her dark form when she made her way back through the cemetery. The headlights on her car soon glowed bright in the muddy darkness. He watched the twin pools of light meander away.

Sam breathed a deep sigh of relief and huddled deeper into

his jacket, pulling his collar up around his neck to fend off the painful chill that had settled in with nighttime. Then, as he reined Ranger towards the ranch, another set of headlights came to life near the cemetery entrance. Sam's whole body twitched as he became alert and focused on this new turn of events.

Lizzy had been the only person inside the cemetery, so what was this second car? And why was it way out here in the middle of nowhere?

The image of another set of headlights popped into Sam's mind, the ones that had disappeared near the farmhouse the same night someone had slashed his cow's throat in Lizzy's front yard. And Lizzy had said she'd seen a truck parked on the road beside her house the following evening.

As he considered the note tacked to Lizzy's door that morning and observed the diffused smudge of light ever so slowly follow in her tire tracks, he rubbed his chest to ease the pounding of his heart and wrestled with the uneasiness that had settled inside him.

What the hell was going on?

There were enough people around these parts who would have plenty to say when they heard of Lizzy's return, and most of it wouldn't be flattering. He'd been witness to a sampling of that following the church service that morning. Surely, none of them would be upset enough to harm her. Would they?

CHAPTER 17

Sam cupped his hands and blew warm air into them, a feeble attempt to thaw his frozen fingers. The temperature inside the barn bordered on freezing, and after a couple of hours in there, even his bones ached from the cold.

He settled back into the soft hay and drew a wool blanket up around his shoulders, pestered by thoughts of Lizzy. That second car at the cemetery the night before nagged at him. Was it overreacting to think that someone really did intend to harm her? He'd thought long and hard about it, and he couldn't come up with anyone who disliked Lizzy that much—not even Junior. More than likely, it was just coincidence and nerves on both their parts. He shook his head as if he could shake off any such foolishness.

The little mare beside him rested. Maybe he could catch a few winks himself before the early morning rays peeked in through the east window, a signal that it was time to head into town for the parts to Lizzy's antiquated furnace.

He closed his eyes and nearly drifted off when Chet's lazy drawl shattered his lassitude. "How's she doin?"

That was followed by a weak whinny. Sam swore under his breath, then reached out a hand to stroke the mare's quivering neck. "She *was* doing okay. It's not daylight yet. What're you doing here?"

"Thought I'd take over and let you get a couple of hours of beauty sleep. Wouldn't want to disappoint all those ladies hangin' out at Mel's just hopin' to get a glimpse of you. You ain't no spring chicken anymore, you know. Your age, you need all the help you can get."

Sam wondered where Chet came up with what came out of his mouth. He swallowed at his irritation. "I don't think one night's gonna do me in," he muttered, rubbing the sleep from his tired eyes. The mare grew restless, snorting a cloud of mist into the frigid air. Sam ran a hand over her distended body, feeling for movement. He paused when he felt a bulge move across his palm. "The foal's still with her. I think it'll be awhile yet."

"That's good. It's too early for her. Every minute she can hold it will help." Chet rubbed his upper arms harshly. "Brrr. Too damn cold in here. Can't imagine what it'd be like outside for the little tike. Why don't you go up to the house and get some sleep. I'll watch her."

Sam studied Chet in the muted light cast by a single overhead bulb. What was going on with Chet lately? Once again, he was up before the sun? And he was offering to stay in this frigid barn and watch the mare, so Sam could climb into his warm bed and get some shuteye? It was like living in a sci fi thriller where some alien had moved into Chet's body—Eb's, too.

"You need your sleep," he finally said. "Come morning, you'll need to take a couple of the men over to the farm and check on the cattle—find out where they are and do a count. Chase them well away from the house. If they get in the farmyard again, there'll be hell to pay." He sighed, too tired to worry about all the strange goings-on in the last few days, and turned his focus to the fidgeting horse. "In a couple of months, we'll need to get all of them back onto the ranch."

"You ain't really gonna do that, are you?" Chet asked, scrutinizing him like he'd gone mad. "What's Lizzy gonna do if you leave 'em there? Round 'em up on foot? Hell, it's more your farm than hers, anyway. You're the one's been watchin' over it while she's off havin' herself a high time. Now she thinks she can waltz back in here and shoo you off it. Damned ungrateful if you ask me."

Busy trying to settle the mare, Sam listened to Chet run on with only half an ear. The horse struggled as if she wanted to stand. Sam rose to his feet and stood back to give her room, one hand on her neck. "It's her farm. There's not much I can do about that," he muttered through clenched teeth. But Chet was right; it was ungrateful of Lizzy to demand he get his cattle off land he'd been maintaining for ten years.

"You could buy it from her. That'd solve your problem."

Sam's breath hitched. Buy the farm. That was something he hadn't considered. His hand paused, and he turned to study Chet. For once, he just might be on to something.

Chet snickered. "That got your attention, huh? Course, you could marry her, too. That does have its appeal. Never a dull moment, if you get my drift?" he offered suggestively.

Sam's jaw tightened with Chet's words. He could just make out Chet's hard gaze beneath the shadow of his hat brim. Chet was fishing. Sam handed him an empty bucket. "The mare could use some water," he uttered.

While Chet disappeared into the shadows, Sam considered his suggestions. An offer from Sam to buy the farm might actually be a relief to Lizzy. What was she going to do with that rundown farm, anyway?

Chet returned with the water. He carried it into the stall and set it in front of the horse. "How ya doin', Angel?" he cooed, stroking the mare's long nose. Angel snorted and leaned down to slurp the water.

"You know, I've been thinkin'," Chet said. "If you're not interested in takin' on my suggestion, I might take it on myself. I've got some money saved up. Hell, on second thought, I might just hold onto the money and move on to the other option. Havin' Lizzy for a wife could be mighty interesting!"

※ ※ ※

The diner was a beehive of activity when Lizzy walked into it on Monday morning. Franny was the reason she was there; she'd insisted on it. "You can't hide out at that farm forever," she'd reasoned.

Of course, she was right. Though Lizzy dreaded it, if she was going to find out what happened to John, she had to venture out and reacquaint herself with the town and its people. Besides, a visit with Franny was a welcome reprieve from scrubbing and unpacking, and she might even have a chance to question Franny about the last few months of John's life.

Lizzy had left the farm early to get in and out of town quickly, before Sam arrived at her doorstep with the furnace part he'd promised to purchase that morning. Then at the hardware store, Junior was nowhere in sight, so she'd relaxed and let Franny help her select paint colors and gather the supplies she needed.

She'd paid and was loading the shopping cart when Franny chirped, "Let's go down the street to Mel's and continue our conversation over a cup of coffee. Junior can mix the paint while we're gone. He's in the backroom. I'll let him know where I'm going."

Franny had rushed off, and Lizzy had hurried out of the store with her packed cart before Junior peeked out from the backroom to flash her the evil eye and make a nasty remark. Franny wasn't far behind. In truth, Franny's frivolous chatter was uplifting—for sure, Lizzy could use some of that.

Now, ten minutes later, Lizzy's eyes scanned the faces in the diner. Were any of those faces attached to a veiled villain who was plotting her demise? It appeared not, as everyone seemed engrossed, either with conversation, eating, drinking coffee, or the newspaper. Unlike her religious experience the previous morning, no one even glanced her way.

Franny stepped closer to her and placed her hand around Lizzy's shoulder, then leaned close and whispered, "Over there by the window. There's an empty booth, and it's secluded enough that we can talk without it being the highlights in today's gossip mill."

With Franny's guidance, Lizzy locked her eyes on the booth and stepped towards it. Behind her, Franny tweeted morning greetings.

A familiar voice stopped Lizzy in her tracks. She turned and gazed into Sam's intense blue eyes. Evidently, a trip to town warranted a shave, a shower, and clean clothes. Even his dark hair was slicked neatly into place. He rested his forearms on the table next to a clean table setting.

Stunned, Lizzy ogled him until he spoke. "You gonna be home this morning? I was planning to stop by and work on your furnace." There was a slight edge to his voice.

Did he think she'd forgotten, or was he implying that she'd purposefully left the farmhouse to avoid him? "I'm just going to have a cup of coffee with Franny. Then I have a couple of quick stops before I head back to the farm. Looks like you haven't eaten yet, so I should be there before you," she assured him before she turned away.

When she reached the booth, Lizzy purposefully slid into the seat with her back towards the room. She tugged the wool hat off her head and slipped out of her jacket. Franny sat down across from her.

"*Mmmm.* Isn't that Sam Craig just too yummy for words? If I wasn't married . . . well, what does it matter? I am married . . . such as it is. You and him don't seem to get along too well. Did something happen? You used to be real fond of each other." Franny chattered on, obviously not expecting an answer, as she grabbed a menu and perused it.

Still a bit shaken by another surprise encounter with Sam, Lizzy bit her tongue.

Franny's eyes flicked hers over the top of her menu, and she continued. "You know, before I forget, I talked with Madge over at Gus Woolridge's old office about that letter—you know, the one John wrote."

Lizzy gaped and nodded, mentally switching gears from Sam's annoying presence to John's letter.

"Well, anyway, Madge didn't know what happened to the letter. She said it was sitting on her desk, and it just up and disappeared."

"Disappeared?" Lizzy asked, puzzled. "Did it have my address on it?"

"That's exactly what I asked Madge. She said she took the letter and my note out of the envelope I had them in because she planned to mail it in one of their envelopes—so you'd know who sent it to you. She paper clipped them together. She had someone over there look up your new address, and it was stuck to the packet on a sticky note."

Franny glanced up from the menu and rolled her eyes. "Actually, if you want to know the truth, I think Madge completely forgot about it until I asked her because she turned kind of blotchy and fretful and started rummaging through things on her desk. She's getting up there in years, you know, and has a tendency to forget things. She's always coming into the store without a list and forgetting why she's there. You remember her, don't you?"

A hazy vision formed in Lizzy's mind of a petite woman with heavy blue eye makeup and a bleached blonde beehive that more than made up for what she lacked in height. "Vaguely," Lizzy murmured.

She dug in her jacket pocket until she felt the letter she'd slipped in there that morning, then pulled it out to examine it. Perhaps she'd overlooked something. No. It looked the same—her name and address neatly printed but no return address—except that a photo clung to the envelope. Lizzy stared at the picture she'd discovered in Granddad's book. She'd forgotten she'd stuffed it into that pocket. Again, recognition nagged at her.

"Do you know who this is?" she asked as she handed the photograph to Franny.

Franny dropped her menu to study it, her brows knit in concentration. "No," she finally said. "But he does look kind of familiar. Why do you want to know?" She laid the picture on the table and returned her attention to the menu.

Lizzy shrugged. "Oh, I found it and was just curious, I guess."

"You know, I had a muffin and some fruit this morning, but I can't pass up one of Mel's cinnamon rolls. Maybe I'll just have one to tide me over until supper. Then I can skip lunch. What about you? Are you going to eat something?"

Franny had switched topics, again. Lizzy slipped the letter back into her pocket. Anxious to complete her errands quickly, she'd grabbed a cup of coffee that morning and headed out the door—no breakfast. She picked up the menu and scanned it. What she saw put a hitch in her breathing. The breakfast specials were handwritten in elegant flowing letters, much like the handwriting on the diary page in Granddad's desk.

"Lizzy!"

Startled, Lizzy gazed up into a face she'd recognize anywhere, even after it had weathered twenty-five years of hard living. Mel's hair was a shade or two brassier and her face now wore a deep network of wrinkles, but she was still the same wonderful Mel who had always been kind to her.

"I was hoping you'd stop by," Mel gushed. "It's so nice to see you. I heard you were back on the farm. Welcome home, dear."

Though her mind reeled with visions of Mel filling diary pages with flowery handwriting, a smile warmed Lizzy's face. "Mel. It's nice to see you, too. I am back on the farm. I hope to live there," she managed to murmur.

"Well, that's good, honey. Con and Dottie would be so pleased if you got that farm fixed up again. And my goodness, look at you. You haven't changed a bit. Still skinny as a pine pole. I sure do hope you'll share your beauty secrets with us, huh, Franny?"

Franny laughed good-naturedly. "I'm hopeless, Mel. I'm currently involved in a very satisfying love affair with food, and I kissed working up a good sweat and a sexy body goodbye along with my thirties. And speaking of food, Lizzy and I would like some coffee, and I'm going to have one of your famous cinnamon rolls—don't you dare tell Junior. How about you, Lizzy?"

What the heck, she'd probably be on a sugar high the rest of the morning, but sharing a tasty self-indulgence with Franny sounded like a darned good idea—a tiny step back in time. "Sounds good to me. And I'd like a glass of tomato juice," she told Mel.

"I'll have your order brought to you," Mel assured them as she reached for their menus. Her eyes landed on the photo of the young boy, and she paused. "Where did you get the picture of Skip?" she asked, an odd, faraway tone to her voice.

Lizzy struggled to breathe. Her eyes flitted to the photo. Was that why the boy looked so familiar? "That's my father?" she muttered. "I thought it might be J.D."

"No. That's skip, all right. I'd recognize that smile anywhere. And the twinkle in those eyes—just like your granddaddy's. Holy cow, your daddy was a handful, and he sure did know how to have a good time."

Lizzy was too stunned to respond. She snatched up the picture and stuffed it into her pocket. Her father might've known how to have a good time, but being a father to her was certainly at the bottom of his priority list.

"Uh . . . Mel, I noticed the handwriting on your morning specials. Is that your writing?" Lizzy asked, her brain scrambling to put words into her mouth.

"Sure is, and thanks for noticing." She glanced around, her cheeks glowing rosily. "Not a lot of people around here pay any attention to it. It's one thing I do take pride in—my penmanship. Way back when I was in eighth grade, I had a teacher who taught us how to do Calligraphy. For some reason, I took to it. Stuck with me, I guess."

Lizzy hesitated as she considered how to phrase her next question. She didn't want it to sound like she was snooping, which, of course, was exactly what she was doing. "Do you keep a diary, Mel?" she finally murmured.

Mel's eyebrows shot up; her chin dropped. "A diary? When would I find time for such foolishness? Why do you ask?"

Lizzy struggled to explain. "I just figured that . . . you must be privy to a lot of confidential conversations running a place like this and . . . you might have a need to write them down . . . somewhere, like a diary," she stammered.

Mel chuckled. "All the secrets I know wouldn't fit into a scrawny little diary, dear. Don't worry; your secrets are safe with me."

Warmth flooded Lizzy's cheeks.

"Well, I better quit standing here flappin' my jaw and go get your order turned in." Mel stepped away, then turned back to address Lizzy. "Sometime, when it's not so busy in here, stop back by for a visit. I want to hear what you've been up to. In fact, come in around four or so, and I'll buy you an early dinner—a welcome home gift."

Tears stung in Lizzy's eyes. "I'll do that. Thank you," she promised. The loving reception from Eb, Franny, and now Mel was unexpected and touched her in a place she needed to be touched. Her chest felt like it was going to burst.

"Are you okay, Lizzy? Maybe it wasn't such a good idea to come here?" Franny studied her, worry creasing her features.

Lizzy forced a weak smile. "I'm fine. It's just a bit overwhelming. You've been wonderful, and Mel was so nice to me. It feels good to be with a friend. Thank you."

Franny patted Lizzy's hand. "You know, I'll always be here for you. Remember all the things we went through together? Nothing can take that away."

Except for John, Franny had been her best friend. They'd gotten through their share of scrapes and shared too many secrets. It felt like old times to be sitting in a booth at Mel's across from Franny. "How could I forget?"

A young woman arrived with a tray. She unloaded it onto the table, setting a mug of murky coffee and a huge cinnamon roll dripping with rivulets of white icing and golden butter in front of each of the women. A cinnamon and chicory drenched haze settled in around them. Lizzy also got a jumbo glass of tomato juice, her one concession to healthy eating.

"Well, as a good friend, I can't wait to hear about your life. It has to be more exciting than mine. There's no way you fed your stress ice cream and chocolate and still have that body." Franny stopped talking to take a sip of coffee and a hefty bite from her pastry.

Lizzy gazed into the dark brew and contemplated the ramifications of opening up to Franny. In the past, Franny had been trustworthy. And what if she wasn't? It wouldn't be the end of the world if the whole town knew her life hadn't been a whirlwind of five carat diamonds and caviar. Besides, it might be good to talk about it with someone. Maybe if it wasn't locked up inside her, she could let it go. Maybe it would even stop hurting.

Franny took another gulp from her coffee and pressed on. "Or we can talk about my life, but you better get some caffeine in you first. Otherwise, you'll be falling asleep on me."

Though Franny was making light of it, her eyes told a different story. Clearly, her life with Junior was more thorns than roses. So why in the world had she married him?

"Really, my life's been normal, Franny, or at least, it was. There's not a lot to tell," Lizzy assured her.

"Ah, come on. You must've done something exciting? Traveled to fascinating places? Met some intriguing people? Surely you had some sexual liaisons you can tell me about? Junior's interest in romance is on the fritz, so I count on getting most of mine second-hand—from listening to people talk about theirs." Franny chuckled, but the look on her face said she wasn't amused.

"Sorry, no intrigues or sexual liaisons and not much travel, a snoozer," Lizzy informed her friend.

Franny studied her closely. "So, does that mean you're married . . . or not?"

"Not. But I was."

"Was?" Franny probed.

"I thought it was forever, or at least until I was old and wrinkled. It ended last year." It had actually ended three years before, but the technicalities didn't seem important. Three years, and the thought of it still sent a spear slicing through her heart. She swallowed at the hurt and anger rising in her throat and breathed deeply. Fearing that the warm coffee mug she gripped might shatter, she let go of it.

"What happened?" Franny asked cautiously.

Lizzy shook her head resignedly. "I really don't know. You're going along, and I guess you just get so caught up in your daily life and keeping up with it that you miss the signs. Somewhere along the way—way, way back there—he took off on his own path, and I didn't notice he was gone."

Lizzy paused, eyeing her trembling hands. She folded them in her lap and clenched them tightly before she continued. "I have three sons. I put a lot of time and energy into raising them and working at a full-time job. I thought he was a part of our life together, but I found out later that it was all a façade. He was a man of many lives, ones that included a lot of women. So I guess if you want to hear about sex and intrigue, he's the person to talk with."

"What a scumbag! I can't imagine any man treating you like that. The man's an idiot. I'll bet he's sorry now." She took a serious chug of coffee, shook her head disgustedly, then asked, "How'd you find out about it?"

Franny's sense of outrage warmed Lizzy's heart. "I asked him. I overlooked signs and made excuses and ignored the obvious for a long time—too long. Then one night over dinner, right out of the blue, I asked him. It even surprised me because it's not something I'd thought about. I guess at some subconscious level, my brain was putting it together all along.

"He admitted it. Turns out it was going on practically the whole time we were married—more than twenty years of lies—and there I was with my eyes closed. He'd insisted on a prenuptial agreement back before they were fashionable. That should've been my first clue."

Lizzy shook her head, sickened by the heavy ache of betrayal—a gut-wrenching, heart-stabbing hurt. "I didn't know what to do. It was such a shock. But at the same time . . . it wasn't. We tried marriage counseling. What a joke! It would be more accurate to say that I tried it. He wanted his freedom, so I gave it to him. End of story."

Lizzy huffed and sipped coffee, anything to ease the throbbing lump in her throat. She swallowed hard, then added, "Oh, except that I worked at his advertising agency, so it was the end of my job, too— plus all of the friendships I thought I'd formed there."

A waitress arrived to fill their mugs. Lizzy noticed that Franny had demolished her cinnamon roll. She forked a bite into her mouth and savored the sugary comfort.

"Well, if you ask me, you're probably a whole lot better off without the jerk. So is that why you came back here?"

Lizzy considered how much more she should share with Franny. "No. Although, I probably wouldn't have returned to the farm if it hadn't happened. It was only the beginning of a long string of things that I've been struggling with. I desperately needed to get away, and after our house sold, nothing was holding me there. I got John's letter, and the farm seemed like the right place to be. At the moment, I need some time and space to stitch my life back together."

She took another bite, hoping Franny would leave it at that. She'd already disclosed more than enough about her failed marriage, and the contents of John's letter weren't something she was ready to share with Franny, not yet.

"So that's why you seem so . . . fragile?"

"Fragile?" The word surprised Lizzy. She—who'd spent her lifetime erecting a brave front—was being called fragile? "Yes, I suppose I am a bit fragile," she admitted.

"I never thought you'd ever fall apart. You were the one who held it together—the sensible one, so level-headed and dependable. You always made the right decision. That's why I've never questioned you for leaving here. I knew you had a good reason, or you wouldn't have gone." Franny reached a hand to press Lizzy's. "You're still that person, you know. You'll get through this and be even stronger than before."

Like rays of golden sunshine, warmth spread through Lizzy. This time she squeezed her friend's hand. "Thank you, Franny. You know, if you ever need someone to talk with, I'm a pretty good listener. Used to be and still am."

"Thanks. I just might take you up on that." There was a catch in Franny's voice. She pulled her hand away, and her troubled eyes drifted off to somewhere past Lizzy's head.

Lizzy forked a bite of pastry into her mouth, then waited patiently for Franny to share her thoughts. Franny finished off her coffee in silence and was staring into her empty mug when Lizzy concluded that today was not the day Franny would be taking Lizzy up on her offer.

Aware that Franny would need to return to the store soon, Lizzy considered how to broach a new topic. "I've been thinking about John lately. I've been wondering how he was after I left?"

Franny looked up. "I'm not gonna lie to you. It was really hard for him with all that was going on and with you gone, too. I tried to help him, but I wasn't you. He spent more and more time with Junior and even some with Chet—probably not the best choices for companionship. You know how those two were back then."

Lizzy remembered all right, and they weren't pleasant memories, but since Franny was now married to one of them, she restrained from commenting on it and, instead, probed further. "Did John ever seem afraid . . . you know, fearful that something might happen to him?"

"Not that I remember," Franny answered, narrowing her eyes as if she were searching distant landscapes. "Sometimes it was hard to figure out what he was talking about, though. There was that letter. He seemed upset about something that day and insisted that I take it to town and mail it to you right away. But you know how it was; it didn't take much to upset him. Is it the letter? Is that why you're asking about John?"

"Not really," Lizzy murmured. "He did mention in it that he was concerned about some things, but he didn't say what those things were. I was hoping you might know more about it."

Franny shook her head. "Sorry. We really weren't all that close. Junior's the one you should be talking to."

The look on Lizzy's face must have spoke volumes because Franny shrugged resignedly and added, "I know. Junior probably won't speak to you. John's death really did a number on him. And then J.D. started hanging around and filling his head with lies."

Lizzy's fork halted in midair, pastry dangling. "Lies . . . about me?"

Franny seemed flustered. A rosy blush crept up her fretful features. "Oh, what the hell!" she snapped. "Yes, it was mostly lies about you. About how you were driving your granddad's pickup when your grandparents were killed. And about how you were so drunk that you shouldn't have been driving. He said you ran away in the middle of the night before they could arrest you and press charges. Said that you killed them, and you belonged in jail."

Shocked to her core, Lizzy heard the clatter of her fork hitting her plate. Her stomach heaved. She closed her eyes and breathed deeply, fighting to keep her cinnamon roll where it belonged. So that was why she'd gotten that treatment at church. People actually believed J.D.'s vile lies.

The touch of Franny's hand on her own dragged her back to the diner. She opened her eyes to meet Franny's.

She had to get away from there—*now*. Two more stops, and she'd return to the farmhouse's familiar comfort. How dare J.D. do that to her! First the document Eb had given her, and now this. Even with her gone, he couldn't let her be.

"I'm sorry, Lizzy. Anyone who knew you would know that wasn't what really happened. But you know J.D. He and Sheriff Mulkins were tighter than salt and pepper, so the truth probably never was told. I asked John about the accident, but he didn't seem to know much. Anyway, I thought you should know."

Lizzy forced a feeble smile and nodded, her heart shredded into mincemeat. "Thank you," she whispered. "For the record, I wasn't driving Granddad's truck. And now I need to get a move on."

"And I'd better get back to the store before Junior sends a posse out looking for me. Your paint's probably ready," Franny reminded her. "Are you gonna be okay?"

Lizzy nodded, grabbed her hat and jacket, and reached for the bill the waitress had set on the table. Franny beat her to it. "Oh no, you don't. This is on me—your welcome home party."

"Thank you. And next time we're going to talk about you. I can't wait to hear the saga of you and Junior. Do you have any children, Franny?"

Franny's eyes turned sad. "No, I wanted to, but it just didn't work out." She sighed. "I guess a lot of things don't work out like you expect them to, do they? It seems you've had your share of broken dreams, too. We'll talk about it next time."

"I'd like that," Lizzy said, giving Franny's hand a gentle squeeze. "I need to stop at the bank across the street. Then I'll pick up the paint." With luck, Franny would be back in place behind the counter, and Junior would be in the backroom where Lizzy wouldn't have to face his surliness and the awful lies he'd believed about her. Right now, she needed to gain control over the waves of nausea surging inside her.

As they walked towards the door, Lizzy noticed that Sam still sat at his table, his eyes focused on a dwindling pile of pancakes and bacon. Across from him, her brightly polished fingers draped around a white mug, sat a striking young blonde.

"That's Gina Riley," Franny murmured from behind her. "You remember her parents—Pete and Jean Riley? They used to own that farm out east of the Craig Ranch. Somehow, J.D. managed to get his greedy hands on it, so now it's part of Sam's ranch.

"Anyway, Gina works over in Gus Woolridge's old office with a couple of young hotshot attorneys. She'd like to be Sam's wife, but I've got news for her: it ain't gonna happen. If Sam even gets a hint of a wedding bell, he hauls ass and disappears like a big buck come fall. I've watched him escape from the best of them. Nope. She might as well give up right now. Look at him, acting like she's not even there. You'd think Gina would get the hint—poor thing."

Franny chatted on while she paid the bill. Lizzy glanced at the waitress and noted that she appeared to be entertained by the diatribe. Then her gaze drifted back to Sam and his breakfast partner, a vision of a giggling toddler with golden curls floating through her mind. Yes, little Gina Riley had certainly grown up.

Before they stepped outside, Lizzy hugged Franny. "Thank you for talking me into this. I really did enjoy it. I'll be by the store in a few minutes."

She looked up, straight into the eyes of both Sam and his stunning dining partner. Sam's eyes were unnerving, but it was Gina's that sent icy shivers streaking through her. They were downright lethal. Lizzy broke away from the unsettling gaze and made her way out the door, her mind reeling. Why in the world was Sam's girlfriend giving her such a hateful look?

❊ ❊ ❊

Sam dragged his eyes from Lizzy to Gina, who sat across from him churning out the town news. He studied her, awed by her ability to have long-winded conversations with herself. Over her right shoulder, he watched Lizzy and Franny hug. His eyes must have shifted because Gina suddenly turned to follow his gaze. Lizzy looked their way, then stepped out the door and headed across the street. Evidently encouraged by his apparent interest, Gina returned her sultry eyes to him, smiled, and continued her monologue.

He swore under his breath, unable to hide his irritation. He couldn't even buy ten minutes of peace anymore. Just as his breakfast had found its way to his table, so had Gina. Cupping a steaming mug of tea in her hands, she'd slid into the seat across from him and purred, "Good morning, Sam. Ain't we the lucky ones to start the day together like this?"

Sam had looked at her perfectly manicured nails, her

perfectly styled hair, and her perfect face and wished he hadn't bothered to clean himself up. If she'd seen him as he was after he'd birthed the filly earlier that morning, she'd have hightailed it on over to some other poor sucker's table and left him to enjoy his breakfast in peace. Chet had more than hinted that he and Gina were now an item, so why in the hell was she still hound dogging Sam? Of course, Chet had mentioned hooking up with Lizzy, too, and that would happen only over Sam's dead body.

"Mornin'," he'd muttered to Gina when she'd barged into his solitude. Niggling tendrils of guilt over J.D.'s treatment of her family had urged him to be civil.

That was all the encouragement it had taken. Gina was off, chattering about everyone and everything in town. Sam had tuned her out, his mind elsewhere—mostly over in the booth where Lizzy and Franny were engrossed in conversation.

It'd surprised him when the two of them had walked into the diner. After mulling it over a bit, he'd realized that it made perfect sense. But it also irritated him. There Lizzy was, chatting away with Franny as if they were good friends—which, admittedly, they were at one time. Well, he was her friend at one time, too, yet she'd do pretty much anything to avoid speaking to him.

Why did Lizzy despise him so much—only him?

Even Mel had mentioned something about how nice it was to have Lizzy back and how she hadn't changed a bit. But Mel didn't know the whole of it. The fate of his cattle were on the line here. Thanks to Chet's ramblings, he'd come up with a new plan, one that he planned to divulge to Lizzy when he dropped by to fix her furnace. To bring it to fruition would require an amiable conversation with Lizzy. If only Gina would leave him alone, he could work on his proposal without the distraction of her grating voice.

Sam swallowed his irritation and returned to his breakfast as he formulated his plans. If Lizzy accepted his offer, his problems were over; he'd have enough land and water to support his cattle, and Lizzy would no longer be around to stir up his life.

CHAPTER 18

Still reeling from Franny's disclosure, Lizzy waved goodbye to her and cautiously crossed the frost-slickened street to the bank. J.D.'s condemning words churned in her gut. Why would he claim *she* had been driving Granddad's truck that fateful night . . . and that she was inebriated? Anyone who knew her would know it was a blatant lie.

She paused outside the bank to pull herself together, breathing deeply, rubbing her roiling stomach. Cloudy puffs streamed from her mouth to dissipate in the dry, frigid air. Lizzy focused on them, not the occasional passerby.

The pull of the farm was strong. She wanted to climb into her Explorer and race there. But first she had to make sure some of her funds had been transferred to this bank. Although she had no idea how much of her grandparents' money remained in their bank account, it was still active under her name and had been all of these years. She'd paid the property taxes herself but had signed her grandparents' money and the care of the farm over to Gus Woolridge twenty-five years before with specific instructions that he was to get in touch with her if he needed funds to cover any costs. No one had ever contacted her. Hopefully, that meant there were no liens against the farm.

In truth, she hoped there might be some of her inheritance left. She had enough money to get by for a while, but eventually, she would need a means of support. Would anyone—other than Franny and Mel—hire her in this town? Her prospects looked downright bleak.

An elderly woman bundled up in a red parka and elaborately stitched cowboy boots stopped to stare at Lizzy. "Are you okay?" she inquired, her breath stirring the long fur that framed her face.

Lizzy blinked the woman into focus and nodded. "I'm fine," she assured her, smiling weakly. The woman turned away and shuffled off down the sidewalk. A flush warmed Lizzy's cheeks as she pushed against the double doors and entered the bank.

As a child, the bank's interior had felt like a huge, cold mausoleum. It still did. Ivory marble floors stretched out before her, leading to the row of cubbyholes that extended across one end of the room. Except for the young man who was perched behind the counter in one of the cubbies, the place looked empty. Even at this early hour, the man's face spoke of boredom. Lizzy stepped towards him, the tapping of her boot heels echoing through the silent room.

His bored look progressed to a blank stare when she parked in front of him. Lizzy tried to work up a smile. "I'd like to talk with someone about my account," she informed him.

"You have your account number?" he drawled lazily.

"Yes, I have it here somewhere." Lizzy pulled her wallet from her purse and thumbed through it until she found the slip of paper on which she'd jotted the number. She handed it to him, mentally fabricating an explanation for her lack of a checkbook or bankcard.

"It was my grandparents' account," she explained. "When they died, it became mine. Gus Woolridge's office has been handling it for me. They were supposed to turn the account over to me. I signed the paperwork, so I hope that's been done."

"You got some ID?" he asked, a spark of interest gleaming in his otherwise dead features.

She slid her drivers' license across the scarred counter. He picked it up and studied it, his eyes flicking between the document and her several times. Finally, he handed it back. Then he eyed the slip of paper she'd given him long enough to memorize the numbers ten times over. Ever so slowly, he swiveled to punch numbers into a computer.

"Yep, Madge must've taken care of it. The account's in your name," he muttered, his fingers still tapping keys.

Nervous jitters wiggled inside Lizzy. What would she do if there was no money left in her grandparents' account? Or, God forbid, what if she owed a fortune on the farm. She couldn't lose it. In hindsight, she realized that she should've made an appointment with her accountant before her hasty retreat to the farm. He was the one who'd communicated with Gus Woolridge, not her. She'd signed off on what was going on back here, wanting to put her life on the farm behind her. With Gus dead, who knew what had happened to her money?

"Holy shi. . . !" the guy yelped, his cool, laid back demeanor shattered.

Stunned, Lizzy stared at him. It must be worse than she'd thought. She tried to talk, but her mouth felt like it was stuffed with cotton balls.

"I'm sorry," he said, studying her as if she were a lab specimen. "It's just that you don't look like you're that, you know, bucks up . . . I mean, wealthy."

"Wealthy?" The guy had to be high on something. She wasn't wealthy. Granddad and Grandma didn't have that kind of money—a life insurance policy and a measly amount in savings. That was it—she'd spent her college fund. "How much is it?" she managed to choke out.

Excitement glazed his eyes. "Rounded off, it's about eight hundred thousand dollars. In my book, that counts as wealthy."

Lizzy fought for air. Eight hundred thousand dollars! That was impossible. "You must have the wrong account," she squeaked.

His eyes shot to the computer screen. "Elizabeth Stewart?"

It was her account. But where did all that money come from? "Is it possible to trace that money . . . to find out how it got there?"

He nodded and turned to his keyboard, and as he punched keys, he morphed back to cool dude with the laid back façade—probably embarrassed by his show of enthusiasm. Lizzy struggled to keep herself from crawling over the counter to do the job herself.

At last, he turned to her. "It looks like Gus has been putting money into your account for a long time." He paused and squinted at the screen. "Yep, a very long time. Years."

Whose money? Her father's? "Can you find out who gave Gus the money?" she asked, her voice shaky.

"Hold on. I might be able to if he deposited checks," he muttered, lost in the images flashing across his computer screen. Several minutes later, he glanced her way and mumbled, "I'll try the records in the backroom," before he scooted down from his stool and sauntered off.

The urge to pace was overwhelming. Instead, she chewed her lip and flexed her fingers. How could this happen without her knowing about it? In truth, she hadn't let herself think about the farm or anything related to it for such a long time. With adequate funds, she'd be able to build up the farm again. It could be like it was when Granddad was alive

The young man finally appeared from the backroom, lollygagging, eyeballing what he held in his hands. He gazed at her as if endeavoring to solve a mind-bending puzzle. Then he shook his head and pushed a piece of paper in front of her.

Lizzy picked up the note and studied the lazy scrawl on it as anger boiled up from somewhere deep in her gut.

❋ ❋ ❋

Sam contemplated the last sticky bite of pancake, then noticed the sudden stillness. His fork halted in midair, and he glanced into Gina's startled face and then on up into Lizzy's. She looked like she'd swallowed a grenade, and it was about to explode. What was she up to now? His pulse rate skyrocketed. He sighed and set his fork on his plate.

"I need to talk with Sam," Lizzy hissed through clenched teeth. Her seething gaze drilled him.

"Well, that's too bad, 'cause guess what? I was here first," Gina countered—typical Gina, totally oblivious to Lizzy's fury.

"Now!" Lizzy growled.

Unsure of how to handle the situation, Sam eyed Gina. She crossed her arms under her ample bosom and glared at Lizzy, a determined set to her jaw. It didn't appear that she was going anywhere.

"Fine. I don't care if the whole town hears what a self-centered, manipulative, lying jerk you are," Lizzy barked at him.

A river of molten anger rose in Sam's throat. What the hell was this all about? Somewhere during the last ten minutes Lizzy had evidently decided that he was near the bottom of the gene pool, and it was her job to let him and everyone else within earshot know about it.

"Well, I do," Mel interrupted in a stern voice. "These are my customers, and they're here to enjoy their breakfast in peace, not to listen to you two argue. Good grief. You'd think it was your fathers going at it the way you're carrying on."

Sam glanced at Mel. She had a nose for sniffing out trouble. Hopefully, she'd get Lizzy away from his table and calm her down. His eyes flicked Lizzy. Hers were fuming, and she seemed to be struggling to get enough air into her lungs. If someone didn't stop her, she'd be on top of him, fingers squeezing his throat, right here in front of Mel and the breakfast crowd.

Mel turned to Gina. "It's time for you to take off, dear. I'm sure you'll get a chance to bend Sam's ear the next time he's in town." Though Mel said it nicely, her voice had a firm edge to it that left no doubt it was an order, not a suggestion.

Gina opened her mouth to protest, then clamped it shut. She grabbed her purse and scooted out of her chair but managed to sear Lizzy with a scathing look before she wiggled off.

Lizzy plopped into the vacant seat. If she'd had daggers in her hands, she'd be slinging them at him. He wondered which would be worse, those daggers or the tongue-lashing he was about to receive.

"I'll just leave you two to settle this . . . quietly," Mel stipulated before she walked off.

"I've been over at the bank checking my account," Lizzy snapped.

So, what did that have to do with him? He raised an eyebrow. "And?"

"And there's a whole lot more money in there than there should be, that's what! And when I asked them where all that money came from, I found out it came from J.D. . . . and *you*."

She paused to suck in air, tears glistening in her eyes, lips quivering. "To think I'd nearly convinced myself that you didn't know about what happened back then. Ergh! Well, I don't want your money. I didn't then, and I don't now. I told J.D. that when he tried to buy me off. I told him when he tried to send me money. And I'm telling you now. I want you to get every single penny of your filthy money out of *my* bank account."

With that, Lizzy stood and marched from the diner, slamming through the door as she left. Sam stared after her, stunned, sorting through her words. She was obviously irate about the checks he'd given to Gus to deposit in her account, but he wasn't sure why.

He exhaled the air he'd been holding and told himself to calm down and think this thing through. What was it she'd said about J.D. buying her off? His mind flashed back to something Gus had said about Sam following in his father's footsteps and bolstering Lizzy's bank account. He hadn't paid it much mind at the time. Why would J.D. give Lizzy money—J.D. who'd sift through a mountain of hay for a lost quarter?

Well, whatever was festering under Lizzy's skin, he didn't see how there was much he could do about it now. After all, it was her money, not his. He'd give her some time to cool down, and with any luck, when he stopped by to work on her furnace, she'd be rational enough to listen to his new proposal. That is, if she let him into the house.

CHAPTER 19

By the time she arrived back at the farm, Lizzy was wallowing in guilt. Yes, she was angry. And yes, she had a right to be angry. But she probably shouldn't have confronted Sam in the midst of a roomful of gawking customers at Mel's. It was an embarrassing reminder that she was operating on the edge. Now she owed him an apology for humiliating him in front of his girlfriend and half the town. Still, it didn't come close to the apology he owed her—the one she'd never get.

The nerve of them: J.D. and Sam, two wily buzzards on a fence pole—always had been. That's why John had never fit in. John wouldn't stuff money down her throat to ease his conscience. Well, nothing, absolutely nothing, would ever make it right. Not their dirty money and not their lousy, insincere apologies. Nothing! If it was the last thing she did, she'd convince Sam to take his family's filthy money out of her account.

Still fuming, she hauled bags into the house. She'd managed to maintain enough self-control to stomp a trail through the mini-mart and collect a few groceries while her SUV was being filled at the gas tank. Halfway home, she'd realized that she hadn't picked up the paint or ordered firewood.

Oh well, maybe Super Sam would work his magic on her furnace, so she wouldn't need the firewood—if he made the effort. After the way she'd laid into him, he might be out of her hair for good. The paint? She'd pick it up the next time she was in town. Her sons wouldn't mind unpainted walls. She had the rest of her life to get them painted.

Or did she? J.D. had stuck his conniving self into that, too. Thanks to him, come April, she might be long gone from the farm, celebrating spring break with her sons in another location. But she couldn't think about that now. She had two months to make a decision. A lot could happen in two months.

Lizzy unpacked the groceries and added the supplies from the hardware store to a growing pile of leftover items and discarded junk in her old bedroom. As she worked, she sang several rock tunes from her teen years. Digging her memory for lyrics lured her thoughts from all that Craig money defiling her bank account.

At least, it did until everything was stowed away. She'd just plopped down into a rocker, Sid purring on her lap, when her gaze was drawn to the silent cuckoo clock. Another flare of anger ignited within her. At the very least, she should be able to rely on that wooden bird, shouldn't she?

Sid jumped from her lap with a reproachful meow when she rose to examine the clock. She lifted it from its home on the wall and carried it to the table.

Was the tiny bird still inside? She pried a door open with a fingernail and peeked inside. It was there all right, but there was something crammed around it—a piece of paper. Had John left a note for her here? Somehow, it made sense. She flexed her right hand to calm its trembling, then reached inside to pinch a corner of the paper between her thumb and index finger. Ever so slowly, she maneuvered it out of the tiny space.

She held it in her hand and stared at it, her heart dancing wildly. Did she really want to know what was written on it?

Which was irrelevant, she realized. She unfolded the brittle paper and carried it to the window to see it more clearly. John's scrawled letters covered the small piece of paper: *She didn't do it, Lizzy. All this time I blamed her, and now I find out she didn't even do it. Sometimes you miss what's right in front of your face. Sometimes you don't figure out who's the best bluffer until it's too late. I knew you'd come. We'll get through this together. John*

Lizzy's legs crumbled, and she sank to the floor, the note clutched in her hand. *We'll get through this together,* he'd written. "No, we won't," she murmured as she ran her fingers over the faded lines. "It's too late." Sparks of anger made her add, "Why couldn't you just spit it out, John? Why all of these vague innuendos?"

Of course, the answer was right there in front of her: he knew she'd come. Her heart ached for him, waiting for her, counting on her to be here.

She felt her control slowly crumble and madly searched for a distraction. Sam might arrive at any moment. In the shape she was in, instead of having a productive discussion with him, she'd bawl her eyes out on his shoulder again.

"No!" she snapped. "You're through making a fool of yourself in front of him."

Cooking usually freed the muddle from her mind. Maybe if she really thought this through, she'd find something to hang onto to calm herself.

Determined to regain control over her renegade emotions, Lizzy pushed herself up onto her feet. She dropped the note onto the table beside the cuckoo clock on her way to the kitchen. When she opened the cupboard, the bag of chocolate chips seemed to reach out and remind her of the many chocolate chip cookies she and John had devoured together.

She pulled the bag from the cupboard and gathered the necessary ingredients, anxious to get the dough into the oven, chocolaty fragrance permeating the kitchen. It would be like having a part of John here with her. John had always calmed her down and talked some sense into her when she was upset. She winced. Would the pain of missing him ever go away?

Mixing the dough for the cookies took little thought, which left her mind free to wander to the day she'd watched her grandparents being lowered into the cold, smelly ground—a day of pain and loss.

It was on that same day that J.D. had cornered her, intent on bribing her to keep her mouth shut about her pregnancy. "Get the hell out of here, and don't ever come back," he'd demanded, turning on her. Of course, she had left, and she had kept her mouth shut. But not because of him. It was the message he'd carried to her from Sam: "Tell Lizzy she'll bring disgrace to her grandparents' memory and to all of the Craigs if she stays." That had been her undoing.

"Take your money and shove it," she'd shrieked at J.D. before she'd stormed up onto the porch of the farmhouse.

He'd quirked a brow, a half-smile playing on his face, though it held no mirth. "You're definitely your father's daughter." With that, he'd turned and left. She'd stood there—alone and trembling, desolate, unsure of a future without her beloved grandparents beside her—and watched him drive off in his fancy Ford truck.

Lizzy still wondered what lay behind J.D.'s last parting remark. It was clearly meant to be an insult. As if the fact that he thought he could buy her off wasn't insult enough! She'd wanted to talk with John, but J.D. wouldn't let her near the ranch or John. It was probably for the best. Franny was right; John wasn't the same after he returned from Vietnam. It had been difficult to predict how he might react to J.D.'s latest dealings, so it was her policy to spare John as much of the truth as possible.

Of course, J.D. couldn't let it go. As long as she refused the money, he was the bad guy. And that must've chewed his craw to shreds because it was years before he finally gave up trying. She'd sent every single one of his checks back to him with the words "sent to wrong address" scribbled across the envelope.

Here, she'd thought she was finally free of him and his abuse. Yet the whole time she was throwing it in his face, he was having Gus deposit those checks into her bank account. The knowledge that J.D. was able to assuage his guilt infuriated her. She didn't want to think about that. She wanted to picture him on his deathbed, tormented by the horrible things he'd said to her on the afternoon of her grandparents' funeral.

It appeared that after J.D.'s death, Sam continued the flow of funds into her account, which had to mean that he was a part of J.D.'s shenanigans, too. The thought of it made her queasy. How could he behave the way he did towards her now if he was aware of everything that had transpired? The man was like his father—no integrity.

Lizzy had just stuck the first batch of cookies inside the oven when there was a knock on the door. The culinary distraction had definitely helped. Though she still longed to lay into Sam with fists and pointy-toed boots and force him to be admit he was the lowest of lowlifes, she'd determined that, in the end, she'd be free of J.D.'s machinations if she could convince Sam to take that money out of her account. Sure, she could remove it herself, but that would mean that she first had to accept it. There was no way that would happen.

Steeling herself, Lizzy opened the door to greet a precarious stack of paint cans held by a scowling Sam. She reached up to take hold of two cans, then stepped back so he could get into the house. Between the two of them, they managed to get all of the cans unloaded and neatly stacked on the floor. That was followed by an awkward standoff, the two of them eyeballing each other nervously. Lizzy tried to ascertain Sam's state of mind. Evidently, he was trying to ascertain, hers, too.

Quaking, her mouth so dry it was a struggle to get words out, she muttered, "Thank you. I completely forgot about the paint." She cleared her throat and forced herself to add, "And while I'm at it, I want to apologize for attacking you in the diner . . . and for being rude to your girlfriend."

Her nerves buzzing, she studied Sam. Flecks of anger sparked in his blue eyes, and he was working his jaw. What would he say?

He sighed exasperatedly and shook his head. "I never know what to expect from you, Lizzy. One minute you're at least civil. The next minute you're jumping down my throat about something." Then, as if it were an afterthought, he added, "And she's not. . . ."

The timer dinged, and they both turned towards the sound. Lizzy grabbed a potholder and pulled the cookie sheet from the oven. Rows of puffy, golden cookies emitted chocolaty steam into the space between them. Sam stared at the cookies, a peculiar expression on his face. Lizzy set the pan on the stove.

What could she say? Sam was right. Lately her behavior had been erratic, to say the least. That was one of the reasons she was here at the farm—to pull herself back together. She was as fed up with this emotional roller coaster as he. Just when she thought she'd finally reclaimed her sanity, something happened to push her over the edge again.

"I admit I've been a bit emotional," she agreed. "Look, can we sit down and talk?"

Sam rubbed his chin, his probing eyes studying her. Then he dropped into a chair and tossed his hat onto the seat next to him. Lizzy grabbed a plate from the cupboard and scooped half of the warm cookies onto it. She placed them in front of Sam and sat down across from him, wondering if he was still as fond of freshly baked cookies as he'd once been. Sam eyed the plate and selected a cookie. He leaned back and demolished it in two bites, his eyes still on Lizzy.

Was he waiting for her to speak? Well, she'd already played neighborly; it was time to get down to business. "I want you to take all of your family's money out of my bank account."

A puzzled frown creased his forehead. "And why's that?'

She cautioned herself to remain calm. If she got upset during this conversation, she'd come off as an irrational, hormonal female— actually, she probably would, anyway. "Because it's not *my* money."

"Seems to me it's in your account, so it must be your money." Sam picked up another cookie and bit off a chunk.

Agitation bubbled inside Lizzy, a roiling pressure she struggled to conceal. "It was never my money. I don't want anything to do with it. I'm not claiming it." She knew it sounded silly, but it was the principal of the thing. "All you have to do is walk into the bank and ask them to transfer it back into your account. I'll take care of the paperwork. Surely you can do that the next time you're in town?"

"Look, Lizzy. I don't know what was going on between you and my dad, and I have no idea why he filled your bank account with money. If you'd care to enlighten me, I'm all ears, but something tells me that's not gonna happen. So as far as I'm concerned, until you're ready to let me in on what's going on around here, that's between you and J.D.

"What I can tell you is this: for the last ten years, I've used your land to feed and water my cattle. Any money I put into your account was payment for those grazing rights. I'm not a freeloader. Therefore, I have no plans to take that money back. I'm sorry if you don't like it, but that's the way it is."

Relief oozed through Lizzy, relief that Sam wasn't a part of J.D.'s maneuverings and relief that Sam's money was compensation for his cattle wandering around on her land. Air spewed from her mouth in one long sigh as she sank back into the chair.

Sam's rationalization made sense; what had happened between her and J.D. was between them, not Sam's problem. For now, she'd have J.D.'s blood money transferred into a separate account and forget about it.

She eyed Sam, unsure of what to say. What, exactly, had she said to him in the diner? He munched on another cookie, eyeing her, too, clearly awaiting a response. "I'm sorry. I didn't realize that was the reason you put the money there. Let's just forget the whole thing."

His stare deepened. At last, he nodded. "Lizzy, in case you haven't noticed, you're a fish out of water here. How in the world are you gonna work this farm and take care of it on your own?"

He was up to something; she could feel it. "I'll manage," she answered warily.

"Are *you* going to patch the fences and plow the fields and rebuild the barn and sheds? Gus sold all of the farm equipment, so you don't even own a tractor. Just what do you know about farming, anyway?"

"I can always hire someone to help me," she argued.

He hesitated, his scrutiny of her increasing. "Have you ever thought about selling the farm?"

So that was it. He wanted her to sell her inheritance to him. Irritation crackled in her voice when she replied. "No, can't say that I have, Sam. Why? Are you looking to take over my farm in true Craig fashion—any way you can? It makes me wonder what you'd be willing to do to get it."

His frown deepened into a scowl. "I'd pay you well for it."

Lizzy's patience with civil banter had worn thin. "This is Stewart land, not Craig land, and I'm *not* selling it. It's been in my family for generations. My ancestors managed to hang onto it during the range wars by sheer will, and it'll not leave the family on my watch. Someday it'll belong to my sons." She paused to give him a hard look. "Besides, from what I hear, you have more than your fair share already, thanks to Pete Riley and a slew of others."

He was furious. Lizzy could see it in the fire in his eyes and the way he worked his jaw. "I saw you at the cemetery last night. It was too late to be way out there by yourself," he muttered tersely.

Where had that come from? What she did with her evenings was her business, not his. In fact, if she camped out in that cemetery, it would still be none of his business. "I'm forty-three years old, Sam. I think that's old enough to decide what I do and don't do," she retorted.

His right brow lifted. "Suit yourself." But he couldn't leave it at that. "It seems kind of morbid, though, to be hanging out at John's grave. He's gone, Lizzy."

Lizzy couldn't believe she was getting a lecture from this man who kept invading her privacy. This man who was eating her freshly baked chocolate chip cookies. He couldn't possibly have any understanding of why she visited John's grave.

Her pent-up emotions burst to the surface. She swallowed hard, determined to hold them at bay. "I know John's gone—no doubt about that. I'm just not sure why. So what's this about? Don't tell me you're worried about my emotional state?"

"Your emotional state? Hell, I have a pretty good read on that. I just don't get it. You're gone for a quarter century, and you didn't feel the need to visit John's grave even once during all that time, did you? So why is it that now you can't stay away from it? Where were you twenty-five years ago when John was alive and needed you? If you'd been with him then, he wouldn't be buried in that cemetery."

Shocked to her core, Lizzy could only stare at him. He looked as cool as a mountain spring, sitting there munching on another cookie, but she knew that underneath the calm façade, was a raging storm. He was angry because she wouldn't sell him her farm, and he was taking it out on her.

"And how about you, Sam. Where were you when your little brother needed you," she demanded as she rose and fled out the door, tears streaming down her cheeks, yet again.

As she ran from the house and Sam, the cold wind beating her face, a thought flashed through her mind: *what would Sam do to get his hands on her land?*

CHAPTER 20

Sam scrubbed his greasy hands at the kitchen sink. He'd tinkered with the furnace for nearly an hour, and there was still no sign of Lizzy. When he'd trekked to his truck to retrieve his toolbox and the parts he needed for her furnace, she was nowhere in sight.

She'd flat out turned him down on the sale of her farm, and his reaction to her nixing it bugged him more than the fact that she'd done it. He should be upset, already strategizing his next move. Instead, he would swear what he felt was relief. Whatever the hell that meant, he didn't even want to contemplate.

He'd have to sell some cattle or find another place to park them, but he supposed that in the long run, it would work out. April was two months off, and at the moment, he was just plain too worn out to worry about it. That last tiff with Lizzy had sent him tumbling over the edge, beyond fed up with the whole mess. As soon as he finished here, he was going to saddle up Ranger and take a badly needed break.

A stream of warm air flowed from a vent onto Sam's outstretched hand. At least, she now had heat, not that it made up for what he'd said to her. He should've kept his big mouth shut, but she'd egged him on, still angry over the money J.D. had slipped into her bank account. Then she wouldn't give up on her preposterous notion that John hadn't taken his own life. And she shouldn't be wandering around that isolated cemetery after dark, not with all of the peculiar things going on lately. He was set to tell her about the vehicle that had trailed her, but things had spiraled out of control, and she'd fled before he got to it.

He sighed and eyed the abandoned cookie dough and the half empty cookie sheet. Memories of a time long past assaulted him, a time when his mother had baked chocolate chip cookies with John and him. They were still his favorite, probably because they were tied to someone he loved, someone he'd lost too soon—just like John. He could see it: the two of them helping their mother gather the ingredients, then measure and mix them together, anxious for a bite of that first warm, chocolaty cookie. While they waited, she'd let them each eat one spoonful of the raw dough. He reached out and spooned a healthy dollop of the sticky dough onto his finger and stuck it into his mouth. It melted around his tongue, sugary sweet. Yep, it was as good as he remembered.

Swallowing the recollection, he grabbed a couple of cookies and wandered into the living room. All of the boxes were gone, so things must've found their way to where they belonged. The cat, stretched out on its side to soak up the fire's heat, didn't even look up when he stepped over to gaze at the photos on the mantel. He examined them closely, searching for a reason Eb and Lizzy had acted so strangely the previous day. Lizzy's sons did look like her, but there was something else about them, something familiar that he couldn't quite put his finger on. He wondered how old they were and thought it odd that Lizzy didn't talk about them. But then, she wasn't much inclined to converse with him about anything.

Sam moseyed around the room, munching on cookies and checking the heat flowing from the vents. He opened the bedroom door and stepped inside. Evidently, Lizzy had decided to risk frostbite and had moved into her grandparents' bedroom. Her sleeping bag was rolled out on the bed, and her belongings were scattered around the room.

A framed picture of John stood on the dresser, one he'd never seen before. A pang of sadness touched his heart as he picked it up to study it. John appeared to be maybe sixteen or seventeen in the photo. He was at the reservoir—blue sky, blue water, and blue eyes. Those eyes seemed almost sad.

Whoever had taken it had certainly captured John's spirit. It had to be Lizzy. Except for his mother, she was the only person who truly understood John.

Sam had never thought much about it, but it must've been hard on John to be so attached to his mother and then lose her at such a young age. Though Lizzy was younger than John, it was she who'd taken over the role of his mother. Back then, Sam had been so caught up in his own life and fulfilling his father's dreams that what was going on at the ranch was the last thing on his mind.

Besides, he and John were like labs and terriers—both Craigs but worlds apart in disposition. John had danced to the beat of his own drum, a beat Sam never got a handle on. And after John had returned from Vietnam, Sam had understood him even less. Towards the end, he'd looked at his little brother and seen a complete stranger.

Still, that was no excuse. John was his little brother, and he had promised his mother he'd take care of him—a promise he hadn't fulfilled. Pain swelled in his throat as he returned the photo to its spot on the dresser and wondered why Lizzy had put it in here instead of on the mantel with the other pictures.

The bedroom was thawing, too, which meant his job here was done. If he left, maybe Lizzy would return to the warm house. He suddenly remembered that she wasn't wearing a coat, and the temperature outside was well below freezing. Worry prodded him towards the kitchen door.

But the cuckoo clock on the oak table caught his eye. He paused to take a closer look and noticed the small piece of yellowed paper that lay beside it. Numerous creases indicated that it had been folded into a tiny bundle. The handwriting looked familiar. Curious, he picked it up and walked to the light from the window to get a clearer look.

Sure enough, those were John's scribbled words. It was written to Lizzy. Other than that, it made no sense. Who didn't do it? And what didn't they do? There was no indication when the note had been written. He glanced at the cuckoo clock. Was the note hidden there? If so, it must've been stuffed in there after Con and Dottie's death.

With all the crazy goings-on lately, he was all too familiar with the fingers of foreboding that jabbed him. Maybe Lizzy's preoccupation with John's death was warranted. Maybe there was something behind her suppositions, other than easing her own guilt. He gazed at the note in his hand, then considered the letter Franny had found. Did Lizzy know something about John's death that he and Eb didn't? If so, he was going to find out what it was, even if he had to pry it out of her.

He dropped the note onto the table, then strode through the kitchen, grabbing his hat and toolbox and one more cookie before he stepped outside.

Lizzy stood as still as a stubborn mule at the side of the house, gazing off into the bleak, frosted hills, arms crossed over her chest. Sam stuffed his toolbox inside the truck's cab and considered whether to approach her or not. No need to make matters worse, but he did owe her an apology . . . and he wanted to ask her about John's note. He slammed the door shut, hoping she'd respond. She didn't even glance his way.

He huffed and eyed his Dodge. "What the hell," he finally uttered. The damage was already done; he might as well finish it.

She spoke when he drew near, her voice ripe with sorrow, still staring into the distance. "Do you ever feel like these hills speak to you? I do. If I close out everything else and just feel what's all around me—the silence and the spicy fragrance of sagebrush and junipers, the wind and sun on my face—something speaks to me. John understood that."

She faced him, a wounded look to her. "There's not a day goes by that I don't wonder if I could've saved him if I'd stayed here. I did leave him when he needed me most. That's a truth I have to live with."

Sam's heart raced. He'd never put it to words, but sometimes he got this weird feeling that the land spoke to him, too. Things would pop into his head, and just like that, he'd have these amazingly insightful understandings. It was too weird to talk about.

"I'm sorry I said what I did, Lizzy. You're right. I wasn't there for him, either. I should've been," he admitted. "I just got it into my head that if you hadn't gone away and had stayed here instead, then you and John would've gotten married and, well . . . then everything would've turned out the way it was supposed to."

An incredulous look popped onto her face. She shook her head. "Marry John? Sam, John was like a brother to me. I'd never marry John!"

Sam's innards slammed against his chest. Had he heard right—never marry him? He'd have sworn that Lizzy and John were bound for a long, happily hitched life together. Just like that, his world twisted out of kilter. This was going to take some thought. "Did John feel the same way?" he probed.

She eyeballed him, that look still on her face, the one that questioned how Sam could've had such an inconceivable notion. "Of course. I mean, we didn't talk about it, but I know he did. Good grief! He had more girlfriends than you—if that's even possible.

"But that's beside the point, isn't it? I should've been here with him. Sometimes I wonder if I could've kept him alive. But we don't get a second chance, do we, Sam. If we did, maybe John wouldn't have been the one shot up in a war he thought was morally wrong. Maybe, we both let him down."

She was probably right. He'd felt the need to blame someone, and it was easier to blame her than wrestle with his own guilt. Still, after John had enlisted, there wasn't much he could do to keep him out of the army—short of helping him leave the country. Wouldn't J.D. have loved that!

"Don't you think I'd have liked to take my brother's place. He was too young to be there," he told her.

"Then why didn't you?" Lizzy asked, a thoroughly puzzled look on her face.

Sam was befuddled, too. "Why didn't I? What are you getting at?"

Her face went white, which was quite a feat in these temperatures. "You don't know, do you?" she whispered.

"Know what?"

Panic flashed in her eyes. He could almost see the wheels turning in that messed up head of hers. It seemed to Sam that there was a whole lot he didn't know. A sick feeling settled inside him. He rubbed his stomach to silence the queasiness.

"Spit it out, Lizzy!" he hissed.

"Sam, I thought you knew. I'm making such a mess of things. I'm so sorry. Can't we just leave it at that?" she begged.

"It's too late for that. If it's something that involves me, it's time I knew about it."

She studied him, probably working up the courage to tell him her big secret. His temper grew with each passing second, and he gave her a look meant to convey just that. She breathed deeply, then closed her eyes and rubbed her forehead.

When her eyes finally met his, the concern in them surprised him. "You were the one who got drafted; John was the one who went," she blurted.

Sam flinched, the wind knocked completely out of him. Whatever he'd expected to hear, it wasn't that. "What?" he sputtered.

"J.D. had plans for you, and they didn't involve getting shot up in some nasty war. He talked John into enlisting, so you wouldn't have to go."

Was she crazy? "That's impossible. I got a deferment," he argued.

Lizzy's tortured gaze slid beyond Sam to the icy peaks that bordered the skyline behind him. When she spoke, even her voice was distant. "Thanks to J.D. He called in some favors when he figured out you'd be drafted once you finished law school. On paper, I imagine it looks like you were needed to help run the ranch." She sighed deeply, and her eyes met his. "They wanted a warm body and didn't care which one of you it was. You got your deferment; John got to enlist."

His world twisted and turned. Sam balled his fists, fighting nausea. "And you thought I was in on it? How could you ever think I would let that happen?"

The compassion on Lizzy's face was unbearable. He had to get away from her, to think. He strode to his truck, climbed in, and tore out of the driveway, skidding on the icy mud. The accelerator pedal hit the floor, and he sped up the hill towards the ranch.

Eb would know if Lizzy's allegations were true. And if they were, Eb had some hefty explaining to do.

Sam wouldn't put it past his father. J.D. had *always* had big plans for Sam—political plans—and he'd had the connections to make it happen. If anyone could maneuver a switch like that, it would be his father.

But surely, he wouldn't sacrifice John for him?

Over and over in his mind, like a determined auctioneer, he heard the same words: "Please don't let it be true."

※ ※ ※

Lizzy felt like one of those mangled creatures Sid dragged onto the porch. She'd really blown it. If only she could crawl into a cave somewhere and hibernate the rest of winter.

Still, while she did feel like the lowest of life forms, some part of her felt lighter, as if one of the boulders that had been weighing her down had been lifted. In its place was a new slab—guilt. She was feeling downright loathsome about what she'd just done to Sam.

How in the world did Sam not know about the deal J.D. had cut on his behalf?

Leave it to J.D. He would've found a way, especially with Sam half a country away and focused on surviving law school.

When she opened the kitchen door, a wall of heat engulfed her. It was a little slice of heaven, one she didn't deserve. Thanks to Sam—whom she might never see again—she could now shed her long underwear.

The baking mess still cluttered the counter. It seemed like days since she'd mixed that cookie dough. Sam had eaten most of the cookies. The cinnamon roll she'd eaten with Franny lay like lava in her stomach.

"What the heck. Why mix food groups," she muttered to Sid, who was rubbing his body back and forth against her legs, before she grabbed the bowl of dough and carried it into the living room.

The rockers were handy, so she plopped down into one. As she drowned her troubles in the sweet, gooey dough, she considered her next step. She knew what she needed to do. The question was: could she muster enough courage to do it?

※ ※ ※

"So, it's true?" Sam demanded as he stood in the laundry room doorway and glared at Eb. He was so furious that he could feel himself sizzling.

Eb nodded, his tired old eyes brimming with sadness.

"You and J.D. didn't think I should have a say in it?" Sam snarled, the bitter taste of disgust so strong in his mouth that it nearly choked him.

It was the look on Eb's face that kept Sam under control. Eb looked completely wasted—face drooping like melted wax and body sagging against the washer. When Sam had stormed into the laundry room and confronted him with Lizzy's accusation, he'd watched a part of Eb wither away. That's when Sam knew it was true.

"It wasn't up to me. It was up to J.D. It was his doin's, not mine. I didn't put my nose in his business," Eb rationalized, his voice growing weaker with each word.

"Well, you kept the secret. That makes you a part of it. You knew I'd never let John go to Vietnam in my place. Dammit, Eb, how am I gonna live with this now? Can you help me with that 'cause I honestly don't know what to do to make this right? My conniving father is dead, so I can't even confront him about it." Sam was desperate. Guilt was chewing him up inside, and he knew it would only get worse.

"J.D. did what he thought was best. He didn't know John would get hurt. He thought it would help him grow up and take more responsibility."

Sam stared at Eb, astounded. Eb was actually trying to justify J.D.'s despicable actions. "Yeah, that was my dad all right," he stormed, "always manipulating things so he'd get what *he* wanted. It didn't matter if it was right or wrong. If J.D. wanted it, it happened."

He paused to suck air and scrutinize Eb's waxy face, then decided to go for it. "And it didn't stop with this sham, did it? I'm sick to death of all the lies. So what other little secrets have you and J.D. kept from me? Why was he funneling money into Lizzy's bank account? She claimed my father was buying her off. What's that all about?"

Eb wilted further. He laid his forearm across the washing machine for support, and his eyelids drifted shut.

"Well?" Sam prodded.

"You'll have to ask Lizzy about that," he mumbled weakly.

He was clearly hiding something. "You don't know why he was stuffing money into Lizzy's account every month?"

His lids lifted. "Nope. And now, if you'll let me by, I think I need to rest a bit."

Sam's mind was screaming at him to interrogate Eb until he got some satisfactory answers, but he swallowed the overwhelming urge. Eb was obviously not feeling up to it at the moment. With the way things had gone for Sam lately, Eb would drop dead from a heart attack, and Sam would have that on his conscience, too.

He stepped back to let Eb pass. Then, frustrated and furious with something over which he had no control, Sam charged to the barn to do the only thing he knew to do: saddle up Ranger and try to ride this thing out.

Then he planned to sit Lizzy down and finish that conversation he'd meant to have with her earlier. It was time he was let in on all the secrets lurking around these parts.

CHAPTER 21

Lizzy rang the doorbell again, then surveyed the empty yard. With luck, Eb would soon open the door. It'd taken her all morning to work up the nerve to tackle this venture. It couldn't fall apart now.

The altercation she'd had with Sam the previous day wasn't sitting well in her conscience. Plus, the aftereffects of drowning her guilt in a bowl of cookie dough had her stomach feeling like a couple of porcupines were quarreling inside it. Thanks to the heat blasting from the vents and a worrisome mind, her night had been mostly sleepless, so she'd felt wired before she'd even had a couple of cups of early morning caffeine.

In truth, she was still restless, apprehension pushing her to get this excursion over. Once she faced her fears, she'd enjoy a leisurely ride back to the ranch, the kind she and John had once enjoyed together.

The door remained closed. She rubbed her prickly stomach and surveyed the yard. Maybe Eb was in the barn.

Lizzy strode across the yard and through the barn door. A familiar face studied her from the tack room doorway—Chet, looking much older but just as dangerous. The rodents in her innards battled heatedly while she wrestled with the uneasiness Chet's presence had always produced. He tossed her one of his more charming smiles while his seedy glaze slid down her body. Lizzy clasped her hands together to keep them from wiping that lecherous smile off his face.

"Well! Well! If it ain't Lizzy Stewart, come back from the dead. Although, I got to admit you don't look the least bit dead. Hard to tell much, though, with all those clothes coverin' you up," he drawled, all too suggestively.

"Hi, Chet. Except for looking a whole lot older, I can see you haven't changed much. I honestly thought you might grow up one day, but I guess some things just stay the same, don't they?" she countered. There was something about Chet that had always brought out the worst in her.

His face sprouted a red glow, and anger sparked in his eyes. "You haven't changed much, either—same smart mouth and snotty attitude. I was thinkin' maybe you came here to say hello and renew our acquaintance, but that doesn't appear to be the case. So what are you doin' here?"

"Sam told me I could ride one of his horses, so I'm taking him up on the offer," she informed him, trying to keep her voice neutral. "If you just point me towards a horse and some tack, I'll do the rest."

Chet looked her over one last time before he grabbed a bridle from the tack room wall and sauntered off. When he returned, he was leading a sorrel quarter horse mare. He muttered, "Her name's Velvet," then dropped the reins and turned back to the tack room. A blanket and saddle draped his arms when he stepped back through the doorway. Without a word, he plopped them into her waiting arms. With that, he leaned against the doorway, his arms and legs crossed, and spit chewing tobacco into a tin can while he ogled her.

Lizzy told herself to ignore him and instead to concentrate on saddling the mare so she could get out of there. Luckily, it came back to her. The familiar barn odors—the sweet, musty smell of hay; the pungent odor of manure; and the tang of leather—would have been comforting had Chet not been scrutinizing her every movement.

She arranged the blanket on Velvet's back before she took a deep, steeling breath and probed, "I hear you spent quite a bit of time with John after I left."

"There a law against that?" he asked in a lazy drawl.

"No, I was just wondering if something might've been bothering him. Maybe he was afraid . . . or maybe he mentioned something to you that might've seemed . . . odd? Anything like that?"

The sharp ting of spit hitting the can preceded his response. "Why? You hankerin' to play detective? Well, here's your first clue: John was a nutcase, and you leavin' didn't help none."

Lizzy glared at him, anger burning in her nostrils.

His sleazy smile hinted at what was to come: "You know, if you're wantin' to play detective, I got a couple of things in mind that we. . . ."

"You wouldn't know a clue if it walked up and kneed you in the groin!" she snapped. "Well, here's a clue for you: you're not a kid anymore, so grow up. Isn't it about time your brain did your thinking for you, not that thing in your pants?"

That shut him up long enough for her to settle the saddle on Velvet and cinch it. When she turned back to him, he was still scrutinizing her, but the smile was gone. "Your mother—Rose—did she keep a diary?" Lizzy asked.

His eyes turned cold and wary. He spit a stream of muddy chew. "I don't see how that's any of your damn business," he uttered.

His reaction surprised her. "It seems to be a touchy subject."

"My mother's a touchy subject. Because she's *my* mother. But I guess you wouldn't know about that, would you?" He was furious, his eyes spitting fire. Lizzy had never seen him this angry.

"You get a letter from your long, lost love," he continued. "Then here you are snoopin' around and askin' nosy questions you have no business askin'. Makes me wonder what's in that letter."

Fear was building inside Lizzy. Still, she didn't give in to it. "You called the post office looking for my address, didn't you?'

"So what if I did. I was just tryin' to help Franny." His composure was returning. Soon, his trademark smile would be back in place.

Lizzy felt the tension inside her building. "Sure you were, Chet. Why did you want my address? Did you mail the letter to me?" she prodded.

A puzzled frown nearly hid his eyes. "What are you talkin' about? Franny sent that letter to you."

Well, that was that. At least, she now knew who had called the post office, though she couldn't help but wonder why—Chet had never been one to reach out a hand to help anyone but himself. "Did you leave that note on my front door?" she asked, though she couldn't think of a single reason he might want her gone.

His frown deepened. "Note? Seems Sam's right; you're completely off your rocker. I didn't leave no note for you anywhere," he spat.

She grabbed the reins and led the horse from the barn, then paused to adjust the stirrups. Chet followed and leaned casually against the barn, grimy can clutched in his hand.

It was time to haul her ass up into that saddle. Time slid back to when she was a child and had gazed up at Tonka's old sway back. As with Tonka, today the top of Velvet seemed insurmountable.

Her eyes slid to Chet—yep, he wasn't going to spare her the humiliation. She flashed him a hard smile before she reached a foot up and slid it into the stirrup. After several false starts and a good deal of unladylike grunting, she finally plopped into the saddle.

Sighing deeply, she arranged the reins and glanced at Chet one more time. He spit and tipped his hat to her. Lizzy felt a smile touch her lips when she nodded. After raising three sons, she had a better understanding of what Chet was all about. Still, it would've been nice if he'd matured past this adolescent phase. She nudged Velvet into a gentle trot and struggled to find her seat in the saddle as she bounced toward the sagebrush-covered hills.

Lizzy soon discovered that riding a horse was much like dancing: it was a part of who she was. Relieved to be rid of Chet, she trotted off across the open space.

It felt good to feel the familiar movement of a horse beneath her and to be a small, insignificant part of something much larger. The layer of shimmering frost had melted, leaving a world painted in subtle shades of brown and gray with a green juniper blotch or red boulder thrown in every so often to add a little interest. Overhead, puffy clouds floated like whipped cream dollops in an azure sea.

As if she sensed Lizzy's inner turmoil, Velvet set a leisurely pace, her hoof marks leaving imprints in the soft soil. Lizzy tried to relax and let her mind unwind, to rest up for what was to come.

* * *

Lizzy huddled a little deeper into her jacket and tugged her wool cap down around her ears. Though the weather had taken a warmer turn, it was still cold enough to cause discomfort, even with the layers of clothing she wore. The sun shone bright, but its tendrils of warmth were whisked away by the icy wind sweeping down from the north.

She inhaled a deep, piercing breath and gazed around her at the layers of gently rolling hills and the mysteriously shadowed gullies between them. Occasional rusty walls of rimrock dotted the steeper slopes, hard and jagged against the softer landscape. Off to the west were the Cascade Mountains, frosty staircases into the sky.

It'd been more than twenty-five years since she'd been on top of this hill and looked out over this vast land. The view was just as she remembered it.

Back then, she and John had spent hours here, studying every nook and cranny. He'd loved to sit up here—to be close to his mother and to dream about soaring out over the land like a bald eagle. It was the highest point around these parts. From the top of Velvet, she saw for miles and miles in every direction.

Would some of it belong to her son one day? As much as she despised succumbing to J.D.'s scheming, she had to admit that the pull of this land was strong.

A cloud of grief enveloped her. Was it like this on that February day so very long ago? Did John sit up here, look out over his land, and decide to become a part of it—to finally soar like an eagle? Or did someone do it for him?

She slid from Velvet, her lower half stiff and sore from the two hours she'd spent in the saddle. To get the blood flowing, she rubbed her seat and shook her legs.

The rim dropped down in front of her. She paused to find her courage, then stepped resolutely to the edge. Unable to look down, she stood transfixed, her heart beating wildly. She had to do this—just one fleeting glance down to where he had lain—and then she could take care of business.

Had John stood here like this, too, fear a palpable part of him?

Ever so slowly, Lizzy lowered her eyes to the ground below—

far below. This side of Eagles' Nest was a sheer slab of red rock, dropping straight down except for the few pillars and narrow ledges that scarred its surface. What would it be like to drop from here to that distant ground?

Suddenly dizzy, Lizzy swayed and stepped back, placing a hand on Velvet for support. She didn't want to think about it. Instead, she clutched her lurching stomach and dropped down onto her knees, trying to wipe the image of John's freefall from her mind.

The pock-marked rock lay just as she remembered it, nearly transparent layers of gold and black moss staining its crater-riddled surface. She and John had selected it and placed it there, a volcanic chunk that would go unnoticed yet would be easy to discern from the smoother, less blemished blocks surrounding it. Lizzy grabbed hold of it with both hands and rolled it forward. Shiny black bugs and many-legged creatures skittered frantically, much like her insides were doing at sight of the rusty, metal box still nestled in the soil after all of these years.

Once it had been shiny and black. John had always kept it wrapped in a plastic bag, and that was missing. Lizzy wondered about that as she reached out to pick it up.

John had been a dreamer—a thinker and a poet. J.D. had been a doer, one who didn't tolerate dreamers. Eagles' Nest was John's refuge. He'd sit up here for hours, contemplating life and its many mysteries, and he'd record those reflections in journals. Early on he'd learned to leave that part of himself here on this hill. Thus, the secreted box.

Lizzy shook it. It felt surprisingly light—too light. She ran her gloved fingers over the mottled surface, grabbed the handle on the lid, and yanked it. The lid didn't budge. She examined the seam more closely. Rust glued the lid in place.

Huffing with exasperation, she surveyed the rocks surrounding her and picked up a hefty one. Then she set the box on its side and pounded at the seam, the loud clanking noises shouting into the silent morning.

With a crunch, the lower part of the box caved in. Lizzy gave it one final pounding and set the rock aside to peer inside. An eerie, uneasy feeling slithered through her. Where were John's journals?

It didn't make sense. Even after he'd returned from war, he'd used his time here as a kind of therapy, recording his thoughts and feelings and searching for clarity. Why would he hide them elsewhere when Lizzy was the only other person who knew they were here? He wouldn't destroy them. She knew that as surely as she knew she'd find clues to the cause of John's death in his writings.

Something was wrong. She smelled it like she'd know if an irate mama skunk was on the prowl. She set the box back into the hole and pushed the rock back in place to hide it. Then she rose, grasped Velvet's reins, and strolled along the south rim, her mind concocting scenarios. Where were John's journals?

Movement below caught her attention, and she stopped to peruse the cemetery at the bottom of the hill. A horse stood at the entrance, which meant that someone must be visiting a grave. Evidently, she wasn't the only person around here who frequented cemeteries. She shaded her eyes with a hand, squinted, and scanned the gravestones, searching for this person whose—what was it Sam had called it, oh yeah—"morbid" habits were similar to hers.

The mass of marble towering over her grandparents' grave was easy to discern, a reminder that she needed to make plans to replace it. Her eyes traced a familiar path to the Craigs' mini-graveyard and settled on a spot of blue beside J.D.'s mausoleum.

Lizzy's heart hitched. Surely it wasn't Sam. He'd ridiculed her for visiting John's grave. But who else could it be? Eb wouldn't ride a horse way out here; he'd drive. She watched the man step around to John's grave and squat beside it. Eb's knees were too old to do that. It certainly looked like Sam.

He had to be really upset to visit this graveyard after chastising her for doing it. Guilt gnawed at her. Her whole adult life she'd held Sam accountable for a multitude of wrongdoings. In her mind, he was an evil partner in J.D.'s schemes and the preferential treatment J.D. had given him over John. She'd never considered that he might also be a victim of J.D.'s machinations.

Now—twice the previous day—she'd accused him of transgressions of which he had no knowledge. The scenarios she'd established in her mind were cracking and crumbling, and she was now sorting through the rubble to piece together something that made sense. Of course, she was only guessing at the truth.

The one thing she did know was that she had a severely mangled fence to mend, and since Sam was in the cemetery and couldn't escape without walking over her, she might as well take advantage of the opportunity to repair it now. With a resigned huff, she turned to Velvet and swore she heard her middle-aged body scream at the thought of another stint in that saddle.

Fifteen minutes later, she approached the iron gate and the bay gelding that was tethered there. Lizzy dismounted creakily, looped her reins around one of the iron posts, and shook at the kinks in her legs.

The gate was already open, so she didn't have to struggle with it. However, she did struggle with what to say to Sam. Nothing seemed appropriate, and she feared that the wrong words would slither through her lips and only make matters worse. If she wasn't careful, the whole thing would blow up in her face, and they just might end up killing each other. She supposed a cemetery was a fitting setting if that was to happen.

Sam was still a ways off, facing away from her, standing in the space between his mother's and his brother's graves. With each step she took, her heart pounded her chest harder. The trembling in her legs made negotiating around graves difficult. Distraught, she stopped, closed her eyes, and took deep breaths. The urge to run back to Velvet and escape tempted her, but she'd done too much running away. She needed to do this, for herself as well as for Sam. Resolved to follow through, she lifted her lids and stepped forward.

He turned, a dull, wounded look in his eyes. "I'm not in the mood for your tetchy attitude, Lizzy," he murmured.

"I know," was all she could think to say.

"You want me to leave then, so you can have your turn?"

He'd probably meant the words to be derisive. Instead, they seemed very sad. Her eyes sought John's beautiful headstone, and she inched toward it for support. "No. I was passing by and saw you here, and I figured this was as good a place as any to say I'm sorry."

"You're sorry for standing by and letting it happen? Or for keeping it a secret? Or for thinking that I'm the type of lowlife who'd send my brother to fight in my place? Or maybe you're sorry for telling me about it now, when I can't do anything about it except feel like one giant, smelly, disgusting pile of shit? Which is it, Lizzy?"

He looked so desolate standing there midst the remains of his ancestors, like a little lost boy. It reminded her of the Sam she'd known long ago, the one she'd adored and trusted. *The one who shattered your dreams,* she reminded herself.

"I'm sorry, but I *did* think you'd gone along with it. Every summer you'd come home from school. At first, you were the same old Sam. You'd tease me, play games with me, and do outrageous things with John and me.

"But gradually, you changed. It wasn't anything I could put my finger on. You just became more like . . . J.D. And as far as I was concerned, J.D. was the enemy."

The words rolled out, as if they'd been waiting patiently for the proper moment. She took a deep breath, and the ache of chilled air throbbed in her nostrils. "You weren't here, so you didn't see how he treated John. Each year it got worse. He was always holding you up in John's face. You were the perfect son, and John couldn't do anything right.

"John worshiped you. He would've done anything for you, and though he never would've admitted it, he wanted to please J.D. That's why he agreed to enlist in your place—that and the fact that it was a chance to get away from J.D."

A hawk soared in wide circles overhead, breaking her train of thought. Sam's eyes followed her gaze, and for several long moments, they both watched the hawk stalk its prey. When it swooped down, she turned back to Sam.

"John thought I agreed to it?" he asked.

"J.D. told him you did." She sighed and massaged the pressure building between her brows. "But he didn't believe much of what J.D. said. I think by then he'd almost given up on ever pleasing his dad, and he saw it as one last chance to do that. The point is, you didn't agree to it. You didn't even know about it. You can't do anything about something you don't know about.

"I'm sorry for the way you found out. It wasn't right. There's a whole lot in life that isn't right, things we have absolutely no control over. This is one of those things. It's too late to do anything about it, Sam, and you're just going to make yourself miserable if you don't accept that fact and let it go." Here she was—the pot—calling the kettle black, she surmised once she'd caught her breath.

Sam's troubled eyes turned to J.D.'s monolith, his jaw working as if words weren't enough. When he faced her, he looked bone weary. "It's not that easy, Lizzy."

As if she didn't know that? She warned herself to tread carefully. In the last few moments, a familiar ache had settled into her heart, one that had no business being there. "I know. Believe me, I do," she pleaded. "A lot of things happened while you were gone, things I'm realizing you know nothing about. John became a pawn in J.D.'s many games. I'm beginning to think you were as much a pawn as he was.

"It wasn't only the war that messed up John. When he left, things weren't going well. Then he returned, and nothing had changed . . . except him. He had all of that physical pain from his injuries, and he was an emotional mess. The alcohol helped him escape his demons, and believe me, the biggest and most persistent of those demons was his own father. If J.D. would've just left him alone, John might've had a chance."

Sam stepped closer, his eyes searching hers. "I watched him with you, Lizzy. He was different with you."

She reached out to touch John's headstone, to caress its cold solidity through her gloves. Sam was right; John was different with her. She'd never understood it. "You saw one very small part of the picture, Sam," she told him. "I tried to help him, to be there when he needed me. At least, I can tell myself that. But I was going to school, and I had responsibilities at the farm. I'd try to go to the ranch in the evenings and on weekends—to sit with him and give him some reprieve from J.D.'s constant haranguing.

"It was so hard for him to live that way, day after day. A few of his friends visited him . . . but not many. J.D. wouldn't let Junior come near the ranch, and John missed him. It got better when John could ride again. Then, at least, he could escape from J.D. There were times when it almost felt like old times, the two of us riding out to check on the cattle or to play hooky in one of our hiding places."

A harsh breeze bustling through from the north shivered through her body as the desolation of those months pressed to the forefront of her mind. "But dark shadows were always lurking nearby. Often, I'd show up and find him trying to chase them away with a whiskey bottle." She shook her head, a futile attempt to shake away the fear and frustration she'd felt during those times. "I didn't know how to help him. It broke my heart to watch him destroy himself. And then, of course, he had the accident to deal with. Maybe it was just too much for him." *Or maybe not,* she silently added.

Tears stung in Lizzy's eyes. She clenched her jaw, fighting them. It was preposterous that she'd never once shared these thoughts with another living soul, and here she was sharing them with Sam, of all people—in the middle of a graveyard.

Suddenly aware that he was standing close—too close—Lizzy retreated a couple of steps. Somehow, there'd been a shift in their relationship. Tiny needles of alarm and panic poked at her. It was time to end this little tête-à-tête. It was time to return to the farm. She'd told him what she'd come here to tell him. There was no need to hang around Sam any longer.

"And you left?" It wasn't accusatory—more like he was trying to understand.

Why did it always come back to this? Unable to look Sam in the eye, she studied the sagebrush-covered slope behind him and struggled again with the despair of that long ago day. "Yes, I left. I had plans to go away to college after I graduated. With my grandparents gone, there wasn't anything holding me here." *Except it was my home,* her mind screamed.

"Not even John?"

"Not even John." She hoped one little white lie would be okay.

Lizzy turned and stepped away before Sam could question her further. The conversation was growing sticky, and she had no desire to get caught up in an exchange of half-truths and innuendos. Of course, the full truth wasn't an option, either.

Then she halted to glance back. "I haven't thanked you for fixing my furnace. I really do appreciate you taking the time to get it going. How much do I owe you for the parts?"

She could see that the change of subject threw him off balance, the distress in his frown turning to puzzlement. "Nothing," he muttered. "I keep track of the money I put into the farm and subtract it from what I owe you. I'll add it to that." He started towards her. "I'll walk out with you."

Lizzy froze. Walk out with her? Of course; he didn't know she was on horseback. Surely he wouldn't feel obliged to ride back to the ranch with her? She'd planned to use that time to think—to piece together all of the numerous pieces of the puzzle that had become her life—and her mind never seemed to work right when Sam was around.

Shaking herself into action, she stepped briskly towards the gate, all the while clamoring for a way out of the predicament in which she now found herself. The tread of Sam's relentless footsteps from behind her only added to her fretfulness.

Lost in thought, she suddenly noticed that she no longer heard him. She turned. He was standing as still as the field of gravestones behind him, his eyes glued on the horses and a rather stunned look on his face. "You're riding," he murmured, more to himself than to her. "I thought you drove."

She doubted that he wanted an explanation. Still, she felt compelled to validate her actions. "The weather seemed so nice that I thought I'd take a ride. You did offer me a horse."

"I just didn't expect. . . ." He scowled at her. "It's fine. We need to have a chat, and the ride back is as good a time as any to do that."

CHAPTER 22

Sam was rode out. He'd spent the night in his saddle, wandering around the ranch while he sorted through the muddle in his mind. As if that wasn't bad enough, he'd just endured a brain-numbing session with Lizzy at the cemetery. It had left him drained and melancholy. He was operating on an empty stomach and a serious lack of sleep, and both he and Ranger were chomping at the bit to get back to the ranch.

He eyed Lizzy, who was riding beside him on Velvet. She seemed content to ride in silence. He wasn't. They had things to discuss.

It wasn't that his father's actions didn't make sense; they made too much sense. That knowledge had Sam whipping himself. He was downright furious that he'd let his father rule his life. He should've asked more questions. He should've confirmed every word J.D. muttered. He should've come home more often. He should've spent more time with John. His list of "should'ves" would fill a four-drawer file cabinet.

When it concerned his father, he'd had no illusions. He knew exactly what J.D. was capable of doing, and he'd gone along with it and done everything J.D. had told him to do—J.D.'s walking, talking marionette. Yeah, he'd played it safe, hadn't asked any questions, knowing he might not like the answers.

Lizzy had nailed it when she'd said that he and John were his father's pawns. At least, John had put up a fight, and in the end, had gotten J.D. where it must've hurt him most. Lizzy had been right about another thing, too: the war was only one of many strikes against John. No matter how hard John tried, he'd never met the expectations J.D. set for him.

Life on the ranch with his father would've been a living hell for John. Sam only had to put up with his dad in small doses. John had a future with J.D. to look forward to. Was it any wonder he'd chosen to follow in their mother's footsteps instead?

Something else kept tickling at the corner of Sam's mind, something Lizzy had said, but he couldn't quite latch onto it. He glanced over at her again. A pair of dark eyes and a red nose peeked from between her knit hat and the turned-up collar of her bulky coat. She seemed lost in thought, staring straight ahead, gently rocking with the horse's movements. Most likely, she'd snap at him if he disturbed her. Well, too bad. He had a couple of things to put out on the table.

"You doing okay?" she asked, startling Sam, her eyes still front and center.

Sam considered her question. Actually, he did feel better. The overwhelming torrents of guilt and anger no longer controlled him. Could be, his emotions were only numbed by fatigue, but he was surprisingly calm. "Yeah, I'm okay. I finally had it out with my dad. That was something that was way past due. Too bad he wasn't there to hear it." He paused to mull over what he'd said, then added, "It still felt pretty damn good, though."

She looked at him. "Surely you're not telling me that you were talking *with* J.D.? He is dead, you know?"

Warmth flooded his face. "Yeah, I know." At first, he'd just stood there, the fury and guilt waging a war inside him. "You know, I stared at that formidable black headstone of his, and all I could think of was how like my father it is . . . so hard and cold and imposing. Then the words just poured from my mouth. I'm not even sure where they came from. It was like I'd spent my whole life tucking them into a cage, and I'd finally found the key to unleash them." Yes, it had felt good to finally tell his father what he thought of him.

"I hope you shared a few choice words from me, too?" she queried.

Sam eyed her. "I don't think you need me doing your talking for you."

She stared at him long and hard, as if seeking something. Then she faced north again.

He searched for a way to turn the conversation. "You know, Lizzy, I don't think I've ever thanked you for what you did for John."

Her head swung around, eyes wary.

"Back when my mother was alive, John and I were pretty close. You might say the three of us—Mom, John, and I—led a charmed life." Sam had so few mementos of that life. Every spring when the lilacs bloomed, infusing the air with their heavy, cloying fragrance, he was transported back to the day he, John, and his mother had planted them as tiny bushes all around the ranch house. It was a secret they'd shared. J.D. had planted his rose garden, and the three of them had planted lilacs.

Sam shook his head to clear it. "Then one day, just like that, she was gone, choosing death over life with us. After that, everything changed. J.D. stayed home to rule the roost with his dictatorial thumb, and I came to have some understanding of why my mother felt the need to escape. I adjusted; John didn't. Not only did Mom desert him, so did I."

Though he'd loved his younger brother, he'd never put much effort into understanding him, especially after Lizzy entered the picture. "Then you came along, and I was off the hook. I walked away and told myself that it wasn't my problem—that you would take care of him. I don't know what John would've done without you."

Lizzy looked skeptical. "Why are you telling me all of this?"

Sam was convinced that the Lizzy of twenty-five years ago would've stayed with John as long as he needed her. No matter what she claimed, he knew she wouldn't have deserted John while he was in the shape he was in . . . unless she had no other choice.

"Why did you climb into Dottie's Buick, drive off, and leave your whole life behind you, Lizzy? What is it that you and Eb won't tell me? What happened around here twenty-five years ago that blew all of our lives to hell and gone?" With each question, his voice grew more desperate.

Lizzy turned as white as the snow on the mountains behind her. Sam noticed that her hands shook where they rested on the horn. "Do you think you can share a few private thoughts with me, and I'll spill my guts to you?" she demanded beseechingly. "I don't think so, Sam. So you finally feel the need to know what was going on here, huh? Well, you should've shown an interest then. It's over. And it's way past too late!"

Maybe for her, not him. "What was in the letter John sent you?"

She glared at him, her eyes desperate.

Anger reenergized him. "It's what brought you back here, isn't it? What was in it?"

"He wrote it to me, not you. Could be, there's a reason for that."

Other than a tangle with a frustrating female, this conversation was going nowhere. Maybe another approach would work. "I saw the note on the table, the one John wrote. If there's something going on here that concerns my family—be they alive or dead—I have a right to know about it."

"I'm sure you have many rights," Lizzy acknowledged sardonically. "They don't include harassing me. So lay off, Sam!"

Damn, she was infuriating . . . and stubborn. "Did you kill that cow?" he uttered through clenched teeth.

She looked like someone had goosed her, mouth hanging open, eyes popping. "Why would I kill your cow?" she challenged.

"Someone did. Her throat was slit."

He watched her swallow hard and reach up a gloved hand to cover her mouth. She looked more scared than guilty. "And it looked like someone was following you that night you went out to the cemetery. A car came to life when you drove off. It was too dark to get a good look at it, but it was right behind you."

Fear darkened her eyes into deep pools. Sam stared into them, probing for answers. His thoughts turned to the truck she'd claimed was parked outside the farmhouse and the warning attached to her front door. "Lizzy, if you know what's going on here, you need to tell me," he pleaded. "You could be in danger."

She slowly shook her head. "I don't know," she murmured, her voice weak and shaky. "I thought your cow died from natural causes or a coyote got it. And I don't know why anyone would follow me."

"Could it be tied to John's letter?" he demanded.

Like a frightened turtle, she pulled back into her shell. "I told you, I don't know!" she snapped.

With that, she turned her face away from him, but not before he'd seen a tear roll down her cheek. Sam gripped the pommel to keep from reaching out to her. There were moments when he got a glimpse of that old vulnerability he'd been so taken with years before. It was his undoing. Though he didn't want to acknowledge it, he was still drawn to her.

He huffed and settled back into his saddle, his thoughts sliding back to that night twenty-five years ago—the Fourth of July dance. If he'd had any grit, he would've run the other way. He hadn't. His eyes grazed Lizzy. Did she ever think about that night?

It was one of those idyllic High Desert summer nights. Cool evening shadows whisked away the searing daytime heat and allowed a velvety layer of darkness to nestle into place, wiggling into the niches and fringes that weren't illuminated by the twinkling strings of lights and stars that sparkled over the city park. The enticing beat and woeful strains of country western tunes filled the air around the portable dance floor, competing with the dizzying buzz of crickets and the persistent drone of frogs.

Sam lounged on the sidelines, chewing the fat with Chet and a couple of his old high school buddies. Then he spotted Lizzy walking toward the celebration with her grandparents. Against his will, his eyes lingered on her.

Gone was the braid that usually hung down her back. In its place were dark, shimmering waves that flowed around her shoulders with each step she took, shoulders left bare by a knockout red blouse that clung in all the right places. A pair of tan jeans hugged her long legs. He still remembered how their eyes had somehow melded. Later that night, when he'd played it back in his mind, he'd likened it to some romantic crap—like being sucked into a magical abyss where only the two of them existed.

It was Chet who'd given him a reality check. Leave it to his crude boyhood playmate to put Sam in his place. It'd gone something like: "Goddamn, Sam. You've got the hots for your brother's girlfriend. Can't say as I blame ya. I wish ya luck, buddy, 'cause you're gonna need it. Ain't no man around here who can get within two feet of that hot little body of hers. And believe me, most of us've tried. Course, maybe you'll get special treatment, you being soon-to-be family, huh?"

Chet's words had infuriated Sam. He'd stuck his clenched fists into his pockets to keep from slugging him and glared at Chet, who'd continued to ogle Lizzy while he poured a bottle of beer down his throat.

Through clenched teeth, Sam had managed to spit out, "I'd appreciate it if you didn't talk about my future sister-in-law like that." Then he'd stormed off and, because it seemed like the right thing to do, he'd headed towards the three Stewarts, who were now at the edge of the dance crowd. He should've kept right on walking.

Con and Dottie had two-stepped away, and somehow he'd ended up on the dance floor with Lizzy. He'd avoided her for two weeks; getting close to her now was courting trouble.

He closed his eyes and, like a disaster movie, it played through his mind: he and Lizzy two-stepping, a good foot of air between them. He makes it through that dance—nice and safe. The song ends, and knowing he shouldn't, he keeps hold of her hand and stands his ground. Her eyes drop to their joined hands and then up to meet his, and the two of them stand there, eyes locked in a silent search. The beat of the music finally breaks the spell.

When the band eases into a song with a slower beat, Sam's instincts scream that he's entering dangerous territory. He ignores them and instead pulls Lizzy into his arms. She ends up too close, and as the song progresses, she inches even nearer. By the time the band is halfway through their rendition of "For the Good Times," Sam and Lizzy sway as one to the music—the full length of her body pressed against his—and he's lost in the feel and smell of her.

Sam blinked the image from his mind and shook his head in frustration. Even today, every time he heard that damn song, his body went haywire.

He remembered closing his eyes and burying his face in Lizzy's hair. She'd turned to look up at him, and like a lovesick idiot, he'd leaned down until his lips were planted firmly on hers. She didn't fight the kiss. In fact, after an initial breath of surprise, she'd responded. Since Sam wasn't one to make out in public, he broke the kiss off before it developed further, though he'd pulled Lizzy even closer.

Then he'd glanced up, straight into the eyes of his younger brother.

John and Junior were partially hidden in the shadow of an

elm tree, and Sam probably wouldn't have even noticed them if John hadn't been watching him so intently. He still pictured the strange look on his brother's face. It wasn't anger; it embodied John's life—a whole lot of sadness and hopelessness.

Sam's heart had sunk to his feet; his stomach had hit his throat. Self-loathing threatened to consume him. His eyes had flicked to Lizzy. The urge to escape from her had been overwhelming. And that's exactly what he'd done. He'd left Lizzy standing on the dance floor and strode off into the darkness.

Except for that one brief glimpse at John's burial, that was the last time Sam had seen Lizzy Stewart. That is, until recently, when he'd walked into the farmhouse, and she'd wanted to chew him up and spit him out for hog feed.

Considering how he'd treated her that night at the dance, was it any wonder she was only barely civil to him? Still, twenty-five years seemed like a long time to hold a grudge over a couple of dances and what was mostly an innocent kiss.

Sam's gaze wandered over to Lizzy as he pondered how things would've turned out if he'd apologized and explained it all to Lizzy way back then.

Two days after the Fourth of July fiasco, his head pounding and his stomach threatening from a night out with his buddies, he'd climbed on a plane headed east. He hadn't returned to the ranch until he'd received the news of John's death several months later. It was then that he'd discovered that Lizzy was gone, too.

It'd been a quick trip home—J.D. had practically booted him out the door—just long enough to take in John's funeral and sneak away to the cemetery to say good-bye to his little brother before he caught his plane. Lizzy had been in her car at the cemetery that day. He'd wanted to talk with her, but when he'd started towards her, she'd driven off.

Like a bout of food poisoning, it hit him—an accident. Back at the cemetery, Lizzy had mentioned that John was in an accident. Sam rubbed at his apprehension. Was it why his father had pushed him off the ranch and onto that plane before he'd even had a chance to chat with anyone?

"What accident?" he asked Lizzy's undulating profile.

At first, he didn't think she'd heard him. Then he watched her body go rigid before she faced him, eyes questioning.

"You said something about John and an accident. What accident?" he prodded.

A myriad of emotions streaked across her face and settled into a pain-filled glower. "J.D. didn't tell you about that, either, huh? You know, for him being your father and all, he sure didn't keep you very well informed about what was going on back home. Weren't you curious enough to ask him . . . or Eb?" she snapped, facing north again.

She had a valid point. He'd already spent the night wrestling with that very question and was still making peace with the answer.

Undeterred, he pressed forward. "I'm asking you, Lizzy. What my dad did or didn't do doesn't make a whole lot of difference right now. As you pointed out, I can't go back and change it. I just want some answers."

"And what if those answers are a quarter of a century too late, Sam? What are you going to do about that? Are you going to be able to accept them and move on? It's true, you know. As much as we'd like to, we can't go back and change things. We do what seems right at the time; then we're stuck with it." She sighed deeply, her upper body lifting, and faced him. "Why can't you just let it rest in peace?"

She looked so sad and forlorn that Sam almost gave in to her appeal—almost. "I don't even know where I was twenty-five years ago," he told her. "I look back, and it's like looking at someone else's life. But what's really scary is that I look back to last month, and it feels the same way, like someone else has been living my life, and I'm a bystander. I really don't think anything you're gonna tell me will be any worse that that, do you?"

For a few too-brief seconds, Sam would've sworn he saw a glimmer of the Lizzy he'd once known. He had to catch himself from reaching out to her.

The glimmer faded, and she turned away. Sam had given up any hope of an answer when she faced him again. When she spoke, it was barely above a whisper. "It was towards the end of August, one of those sweltering days—you know, the kind where everything is parched and wilted and the ground is so hot you can see the sun's rays writhing.

"It was getting dark when the weather suddenly changed. You could feel the tension in the air. It'd been building all day to the point where you'd swear everything was going to explode. And it did, with thunder and lightning and drenching sheets of rain that poured down so fast the soil couldn't even begin to soak it up."

She stopped and gazed toward the northeast as if she was seeing that storm roll in again. Sam got the feeling she was struggling with something, so he bit his tongue and gave her the time she needed.

When she spoke, there were tears glistening in her eyes. "I begged them not to go. I told them it was too dangerous to drive in that rain at night. They said it couldn't wait. They left in Granddad's old pickup. I was so upset—worried about them—that I followed in the Buick."

Lizzy swiped at the tears trickling down her cheeks, sniffled, and continued. "It happened just as they were near the top of that last big hill before you get to the ranch. John was in his truck. He came over the hill. It was so dark you could barely see what was right in front of your headlights. He must've not seen Granddad."

That familiar sick feeling settled into Sam's gut. "John hit Con's truck? He was in the accident that killed your grandparents?"

Lizzy had a gloved knuckle clenched against her mouth as if it might help contain some of the pain etched on her face. She nodded.

Sam was confused. "I thought you were driving Con's truck?"

Her glistening eyes turned lethal. "So you believed J.D.'s lies, too."

"It's what he told me," he muttered—with this, too, he'd not questioned his father's fabricated version. The aftereffects of no sleep and an overload of upsetting disclosures had him drowning in half truths and Lizzy's new enlightenments. He grabbed a couple of snippets and plodded on. "Con and Dottie were killed . . . but John was okay?"

She nodded. "When John hit them, it knocked the pickup over. It rolled to the bottom of the hill and landed upside down. Granddad and Grandma were trapped inside. It was pitch dark and raining so hard that I couldn't see inside the pickup, even when I turned my headlights on it. The windows were shattered, and the cab roof was smashed. Grandma always carried a flashlight in her glove compartment, so I got that." A sob escaped before she added, "Then I saw . . . they hadn't made it. I went for help.

"That's when I saw John's truck. Except for the front of it, which was kind of crumpled, it wasn't even dented. John was lying down in the seat. He was breathing, and he had a pulse—not bleeding—so I left him. His truck blocked the road. I had to drive around it to get to the ranch."

Tears streamed down her cheeks. Sam felt like a jerk, but he was determined, once and for all, to get to the bottom of this whole mess. He hesitated only a second, then asked, "Had he been drinking?"

She swallowed, then nodded.

"And what happened to him?"

"J.D. hustled him back to the ranch before anyone could get a whiff of him. Sheriff Mulkins and an ambulance arrived. The ambulance took my grandparents. Mulkins went to the ranch to talk with John—probably didn't get anything out of him. Then he took me down to the courthouse and questioned me for several hours, most likely to make sure I'd keep my mouth shut about John. You know how close he and J.D. were—a two-man brotherhood."

Sam was stunned. How did he not know any of this? "They didn't press charges against him?"

She hesitated, rubbing her forehead, "I didn't say anything

about John's drinking. I couldn't do that to him. What good would it do? Granddad and Grandma were gone, and making John's life more miserable than it already was wouldn't bring them back. At my grandparents' funeral, Eb told me John was fine physically, and he didn't remember much about what happened that night. I wanted to talk with John—tell him it wasn't his fault—but J.D. wouldn't let me near him." She shrugged. "In the end, they just called it an unfortunate accident, which it was."

Sam's tired brain hit overload. As he tried to process what Lizzy told him, bits and pieces of information shot out at him, fragments that didn't fit into the appalling picture she'd painted. It turned into one big, confusing, muddled mess.

The attorney part of his mind scrambled to make sense of it. In the meantime, he stared at Lizzy. The look on her face begged for reassurance; he couldn't even give her that.

"So you didn't talk with John before you left?" he probed.

Her eyes searched his, begging for understanding, trying to communicate something. What it was, he hadn't a clue. Finally, she shook her head and turned away. Dammit! He wanted answers.

"Lizzy, this doesn't make sense. I know what those storms are like. You're telling me that Con and Dottie *and* John all decided to venture out for a joy ride on those dirt roads on a night like that? It'd be dangerous during the day, let alone at night. And you followed in Dottie's car? Why in the hell you'd do that is completely beyond my understanding.

"And then, you're telling me that without even talking with John, you took off to parts unknown, with no intention of returning? Yet you didn't tell the sheriff that the reason John plowed into your grandparents was because he was so snockered that he couldn't see what was right in front of him? Is that what you're telling me? Well, it's a crock of shit, and you know it. So what are you *not* telling me?"

By the time Sam finished his tirade, he was furious—furious at all of the secrets and unanswered questions and furious at all of the answers he wished he'd never been given. Lizzy refused to acknowledge him. He reached out and grabbed Velvet's reins to pull her to a stop. "Did you blame John for what happened to Con and Dottie? Is that why you left . . . and why you feel so guilty now?" he demanded.

Her head whipped around. "Of course not! None of it was John's fault. He was just trying to help me, and as always, he got caught in the middle. I can't believe you, of all people, have the nerve to ask me that!" she spit at him through clenched teeth. Sparks flew from her eyes, battling with the tears.

"What are you not telling me, Lizzy?" he reiterated.

He watched the life drain from her face. "Leave it alone, Sam," she pleaded. Jerking her reins from his hand, she kicked

Velvet into a gallop.

Frustration fueling his anger, Sam sat and watched her. Should he chase her down and demand the answers once and for all. Or should he let it go . . . for now?

❀ ❀ ❀

Lizzy wasn't sure which was worse—the anger that seethed through her veins and begged to be allowed to explode and obliterate everything it its path, or the hurt that gnawed and twisted inside her stomach and threatened to consume her.

As soon as she rode over a knoll and out of Sam's sight, she reined in Velvet to a walk and took deep breaths, struggling to gain control over her rampant emotions. The tears still flowed; she left them alone, figuring she was divesting herself of yet another bundle of the hurt and grief she'd carried around for far too long.

She glanced over her shoulder. There was no sign of Sam, so she wiggled in the saddle, searching for a position that would relieve some of the sore spots pestering her. As with the rest of her day, there were none.

Figuring she was only fifteen minutes from the ranch, Lizzy determined that she should be able to take care of Velvet and tuck her into her stall before Sam rode in. She didn't want to see him again. She wanted to regain control of her life—to be strong, a woman her sons could look up to and respect.

Sam's unrelenting presence prevented that from happening. Every time she was around him, she turned into either a blubbering idiot or a raving maniac. The constant ups and downs wore on her, and if it continued, she feared she really would end up crazy.

Why did he insist on riding back to the ranch with her? He was as anxious to divest himself of her as she was to be rid of him. Then he'd opened his big mouth to ask questions that weren't hers to answer. She hadn't told him that she was the one to blame for her grandparents' death. If not for her, they wouldn't have climbed in Granddad's pickup and driven off into that torrential downpour that dreadful night.

Of course, part of the blame was Sam's, too. She hadn't told him that, either.

It was just like J.D. to tell Sam a bunch of ugly lies. He wouldn't take the risk that Sam would return home and decide to stay. J.D. had his own plans for his favorite son, and living on a ranch out in the boonies wasn't a part of them. That was John's role in his carefully scripted drama.

Sometimes Lizzy wondered if that wasn't the reason John might've decided to end his life—merely to obliterate J.D.'s master plan. If so, she supposed that he was looking down on all of this and patting himself on the back because it truly was a job well done.

CHAPTER 23

Sam centered the stainless-steel tack over the strand of barbed wire and hammered it into the knotty, weathered juniper post. The warmer weather had held for several days, so he'd taken advantage of it to ride fence and mend the portions where the wire had worked loose. It had also gotten him away from the house and Eb, who was still silent and evasive and looking kind of peaked. Besides, he figured there was no chance of running into Lizzy way out here. Finally, he was getting some peace and quiet.

His growling stomach nagged at him again. He finally gave in to it and turned towards Ranger to retrieve his lunch and a thermos from his saddlebag. He dropped the hammer into the bag, then plopped down onto the hard, damp ground, leaning his stiff back against the post and stretching his long legs out to cross his ankles.

Though the sun's rays beat down from a cloudless sky, there was still a nip to the air. Sam filled the thermos lid with steaming coffee and took several sips, savoring the warmth that spread through him. He slid a ham and cheese sandwich from a plastic bag and bit a healthy chunk from it.

Sam figured he'd done himself a favor by riding fence himself instead of assigning a ranch hand to check it on wheels, which he usually did. The hours alone had given him the time to mull over the path his life had trod during the last couple of weeks. It hadn't been an easy task. After a lifetime of shoving his feelings aside and focusing his energy on getting the job done, forcing himself to examine those feelings had been like poking hot needles under his fingernails—he'd done that once by accident, so he had a good idea how it felt.

He shoved the last bite of sandwich into his mouth and washed it down with a gulp of coffee. Then he gazed out in wonder at the gently rolling hills that wandered aimlessly in every direction. This was his land—Craig land.

It hadn't always been. His ancestors had fought hard—and quite often illegally—to acquire it. A vision of Gina assaulted him, and he pushed it aside, guilt poking at him. Gina's family wasn't the only one.

He'd heard the stories, and they weren't pretty. His ancestors hadn't been above playing dirty to get what they wanted—mostly land. He supposed that J.D. had only followed in their footsteps. And the "coveting-thy-neighbor's-land" gene must be a keeper; Sam had certainly plotted to get his hands on Lizzy's.

Back during the Sheepshooters' War, his great-grandfather had nearly acquired that Stewart land—though stole it was closer to the truth. The story went that Con's grandfather had held onto it only through tenacity and a driving need to win his own private battle against men like J.D. Sam supposed that was where Lizzy got her feisty, stubborn qualities.

The Stewarts had been sheep folk, grazing their flocks on the slopes of the Cascades and Ochocos in the spring and summer and wintering them on their farm. Then the federal government had stuck its interfering fingers into something that was working tolerably. They'd closed down those mountain ranges to grazing.

The Stewarts, along with a slew of other sheep families, were forced to find other places to graze their sheep. Unfortunately, those places were land already being used to graze cattle. Sheep and cattle didn't mix well—sheep stripped the land clean and polluted the water to the point cattle wouldn't drink it—nor did cattlemen and sheep men. The result was an eleven-year battle and a lot of dead sheep.

Family legend had it that Sam's great-grandfather had fenced off land that didn't belong to him to keep sheep off it and had slaughtered his share of the wooly creatures. No doubt, he'd played a role in the burnings and beatings, too, but Sheepshooters were bound to silence about most of those wrongdoings. It was a stellar example of the local law intentionally turning a blind eye to illegal goings-on.

The end result was that the cattlemen won the battle, driving out a good many of the landowners who raised sheep and grabbing their vacated land to add to their own burgeoning acres. Sam's great-grandfather hadn't been one to let an opportunity pass; he'd gobbled up his share of land—land on which Sam was now gazing.

Sam pondered on all of that and wondered if anyone other than him ever thought back on those unlawful times and questioned his right to land that had been obtained so unfairly. The list of casualties was long. It included Mel's ancestors, and Junior's, even Eb's.

In 1906 the government decided to distribute grazing allotments. Legal jargon dictated exactly where animals could be grazed and limited the number on specific acreage. It also provided for determining who got to be where. The range wars ground to a halt, but the damage was already done. Many sheep folk had moved on to other occupations. Some, like the Stewarts, turned to raising cattle and dry land wheat.

Sam's meanderings drifted to what he might be doing right now if the sheep lovers had won that battle. For sure, there'd be a lot more sheep roaming around these parts—he couldn't remember the last time he'd seen one of the wooly beasts—and the bunchgrass would be nibbled to extinction, replaced with even more sagebrush and junipers. Hell, there wouldn't be anything left for an animal to graze on.

He huffed in resignation and poured himself another slosh of coffee. Whatever the outcome of those long ago skirmishes, it was history. This was his land now.

A deep sense of contentment settled into him with the realization that he was exactly where he wanted to be. Living on this land had been a part of his heritage for generations. It was in his blood. It had always been in his blood. And now he could feel it in his blood.

Sam knew J.D. had done his damnedest to separate him from the ranch. He'd sent him back east to school and had encouraged him to sign with a law firm as far from the ranch as possible. Then he'd isolated him from what was going on back here at the ranch.

But he also knew that he was as much at fault as his father. He didn't like seeing himself as a bad person or a weak person, but the truth was that by letting someone like J.D. control his life, he'd become both.

As he sat contemplating the idiosyncrasies of his life, Sam's attention was waylaid by the ominous gathering of dark clouds creeping onto the mountain slopes on the far western horizon. On another day, they might have gone unnoticed, but today they stood out, stark against the brilliant blue of the sky, a mighty strong hint that rain—or maybe even snow—was storming its way into Central Oregon.

Alarms blared in Sam's head. He hopped to his feet and stuffed the thermos and wrappings into his saddlebag. Once the straps were buckled snuggly, he raised the stirrup to tighten the cinch and settled himself into his saddle in preparation for a speedy trip home. He'd do pretty much anything to avoid being caught way out here where the only protection was open land and an occasional juniper.

❄ ❄ ❄

Lizzy tugged the lace curtain into place and stepped back to admire her handiwork. The delicate ecru lace blended nicely with the newly painted buttery yellow walls, providing that touch of elegance and hominess she desired.

There was something about lace that had always fascinated her. Perhaps it was the realization that, with patience and care, individual strands of thread can be woven into something of such timeless beauty. From watching her grandmother tat, she knew that one misstep could ruin an otherwise lovely piece. Then all of that work would be for naught.

She'd rescued the curtain that now draped that window. With a good dose of loving care and a few stitches here and there, she'd managed to reconnect the threads, mend the tattered lace, and restore them to a semblance of their former exquisiteness. A warm glow settled somewhere near her heart as her eyes caressed the newly decorated window. Yes, the results were definitely worth the painstaking effort it had taken to repair the damage.

Her gaze traveled the room, taking in the glistening oak furniture and the colorful braided rugs scattered across the newly waxed and polished hardwood floor. Since her last disconcerting encounter with Sam, she'd avoided him altogether and had instead focused her attention on making this house into a home, one that would make her grandparents proud. The labor and the resulting feelings of accomplishment were healing.

Now she was ready to move on and focus her attention on John's death, to start connecting those threads. There had been no more threats, no more dead cows, and no more strange vehicles hanging around the farm or following her. In fact, with Sam's absence, her life had become almost too quiet.

As her eyes scanned the room, they paused on Sid, stretched out on the floor soaking up the rays of sunlight streaming in through the west window. She smiled at the contented cat, then walked to the fireplace mantel to peruse the pictures of her three sons.

Lizzy picked up the photo of her three laughing little boys and relaxed into one of the rockers, relishing the photo. Where had all of the years gone? It seemed like only yesterday that they were digging in the sand and chasing waves. She could almost feel the gritty stickiness in their clothing and hair, smell the fresh salt air, and hear the seagulls squawking for more chunks of bread.

Her sons loved the beach, and she'd loved to spend time with them there, just the four of them, playing and exploring and lolling together on the warm sand, enjoying every single minute of their time together. Those had been such happy times. She'd been a part of something then. She'd felt needed and loved, just like when her grandparents had taken her in and made her a part of their family and when John had always been nearby.

What if all she needed to do was connect a few loose threads in her own life to bring all those wonderful feelings back? Was Eb right? Was she subconsciously heading in that direction? Her stomach fluttered at the thought of it.

She glanced at Sid, still stretched out and snoozing. "Right now, it's just you and me, Sid. But maybe someday it'll be different. Maybe I'll have a pack of grandchildren tearing around here. And they'll dress you up in their doll clothes and push you around in their doll buggies like I did. I'll make chocolate chip cookies for them and teach them how to play cards and be good bluffers. Maybe we'll even have some ponies, and we'll go out riding, just like John and I used to. And maybe Sam and Eb will be a part of it all."

Not if J.D. has his way, she reminded herself. She pushed the thought aside. "You just never know, do you? Maybe the best is yet to come."

Sid lifted his head and stared at Lizzy before he offered a supportive *meow*. Lizzy sighed deeply and rose, kissing her sons' image before she replaced it on the shelf. Then she noticed that Sid was no longer lounging in a pool of sunlight. In fact, the whole room was noticeably darker. She strode to the window and looked out at the wall of gray clouds steamrolling in.

A wave of dread plowed through her and landed deep in her gut. She knew a snowstorm when she saw one, and this one was going to be a doozy. If she looked really closely, she could already discern tiny snowflakes drifting in the air. How did she miss the drop in temperature and air pressure?

"Well, Sid, I hope you have your extra thick fur coat on because if we lose electricity, you're gonna need it. I'll bet we don't have more than five or six chunks of wood left out there. I should've had more delivered, huh?"

Sid licked the toes on his left hind paw. He didn't appear to be concerned about the impending storm, nor the lack of fuel.

"Just you wait. When you don't have a big roaring fire to curl up in front of, you'll be whistling a different tune." Lizzy was talking more to herself than Sid, mostly for comfort. "Well, I guess we better see what we can do to get ready for this thing."

She headed for the kitchen, Sid padding at her heels. When she opened the door, the cat darted outside.

"Don't be long. I don't want to have to come looking for you," she yelled after him. Sid was not an outdoor cat. Until the snow melted, he'd have to make do with his litter box.

The temperature had definitely dipped. The air was still. Minuscule puffs of ice floated around Lizzy. She loaded her arms with the five remaining pieces of firewood, carried them into the house, and laid them next to the fireplace. She'd planned to order more wood, but the weather had been so mild that it had completely slipped her mind.

Now she stared at the meager pile and said a silent prayer that the power would hold.

❋ ❋ ❋

By the time Sam made his way back to the ranch, the snow had settled in. It drifted around him—tiny white clouds falling silently to form a dazzling, plush carpet over the stark countryside. He was glad he'd hustled home. Light was fading fast. He hadn't dressed for frigid or wet weather when he'd left the house that morning and was now paying the price, shivering uncontrollably beneath the thick layer of ice crystals that coated his clothing and face. Before heading to the house, he brushed Ranger down and strapped a blanket over the horse's weary body. Then he led him into a stall and rewarded him for the exhausting trip with food and water.

Eb stood at the kitchen sink peeling potatoes when Sam stepped into the kitchen. He glanced up, relief evident on his face. "Good. You're back. I was worried you might get stuck out there. It sounds like this is gonna get a lot worse before it gets better."

The rich smell of roasting meat prodded a grumble from Sam's stomach. He tried to ignore it. There was too much to get done before the storm worsened to think about food. "Yeah, it doesn't look good," he agreed. "Luckily, I saw it coming and headed back around two or so."

Eb turned back to his spud peeling, and Sam ducked back into the mudroom to shuck his boots and outer layer of wet clothing. When he returned to the kitchen, Eb handed him a steaming mug of coffee. "That'll warm you up," he warned.

Sam took a hefty sip, and a ball of heat spread to his stomach, where it rested in a blazing glow. Yep, it'd definitely warm him up. It was one of Eb's special potions—coffee with at least a couple of shots of whiskey thrown in. "Thanks. I needed that," he murmured.

He leaned against the wall and nursed his brew while he watched Eb dice potatoes. "I'm gonna put some dry clothes on and go help the men get the horses settled into the barn. There's not much we can do for the cattle until morning. They should get along fine as long as this doesn't last several days."

"They took hay out earlier in the trucks and made sure the water troughs were full," Eb informed him. "Supper'll be ready in an hour."

A radiant buzz had Sam relaxed and mellow. Deciding he'd best forego the rest of Eb's concoction, he set it on the counter and headed to his bedroom to find some warmer clothing.

When he returned to the kitchen, Eb had the phone to his ear. "Here's Sam now. I'll talk with him about it, and someone'll go over and check on her. Don't you worry about it. We'll make sure she's all right. Okay . . . yeah . . . yeah. G'bye."

Sam's heart pounded in his chest. The only "she" person he could think of out here was Lizzy. Had something happened to her?

His mind played through the list of suspicious events related to her return, ratcheting his worry. He hadn't seen her in several days, but to be quite truthful, he'd done a lot of thinking about her. And all of that thinking had helped him to reach a decision: he either needed to stay a long ways from Lizzy Stewart . . . or closer than he wanted to contemplate.

Eb set the receiver back on the hook and faced Sam, concern etched on his face. "That was Franny Hawkins. Lizzy still doesn't have a phone, and Franny's worried about her. She was hopin' we could send someone to the farm to check on her. What d'ya think?"

The knot of worry in Sam's gut grew. If Lizzy had purchased more firewood, she should be fine. But if she didn't, she was in for a long, cold night. It was rare that the power lines didn't come down in a snowstorm like this one promised to be. Exasperated with the fact that he couldn't seem to mind his own business and stay out of hers, he uttered, "I'd better load my truck up with firewood and head over there. Hopefully, the worst of this will hold off a couple more hours. Do you have enough wood in here?"

Eb's worry lines vanished. "Yeah, there's plenty of wood. The generators are ready if the electricity goes. D'ya want to eat somethin' before you take off?"

Sam considered his grumbling stomach, then the steering wheel clenching, nearly blinded trip he had ahead of him. Driving through falling snow was a mesmerizing, other world experience. You just kind of floated along through the engulfing stillness, hoping you were somewhere close to where you should be. In the dark, it would be a hundred times worse.

"No, save my dinner. I'll eat when I get back. I want to get over there before this gets really bad."

Chet coughed, and they both flinched. He stood in the mudroom doorway, a menacing smile tweaking the corners of his lips. He was eyeballing Sam.

Sam was about to question him when Chet added his two cents to the conversation he'd evidently overheard. "Go ahead and eat your dinner. I'll take the wood over to her. Be worth it to see her face when she has to thank me for drivin' over in this storm just so's she can keep warm."

Though Lizzy might deserve to have Chet show up on her doorstep, Sam wasn't going to let that happen. Lizzy had been an irritation to Chet—he'd wanted her and thought he deserved her, but he couldn't get her. Sam suspected those feelings had been revived and were now driving Chet's offer.

"I need you to take care of the plowing equipment—get it hooked up and ready to go. If it snows like it's promising to, we'll need it first thing in the morning." It was a lame excuse, but Sam didn't have the time nor energy to invent a more credible one. From across the room, he heard Eb's sigh of relief.

Anger sparked in Chet's eyes, and a sneer marked his face. "Yes, sir, boss. I'll take care of that right away." He turned and stepped toward the door, then stopped and glared back long enough to add, "Oh, and be sure to give her a big kiss from me, too. Tell her I'm sorry I wasn't there to deliver it in person."

Sam heard the door slam and squelched the urge to follow Chet. Instead, he grabbed what remained of his hot toddy and downed it in one gulp.

He didn't want to think about kissing Lizzy. Now, thanks to Chet, that image would bounce around in his head the rest of the night.

CHAPTER 24

Lizzy studied the pile of items she'd collected during the last couple of weeks: the threatening message someone had tacked to her door, the page from the diary, the photo she'd found in Granddad's book, J.D.'s bribe, and the note John had stuffed around the bird in the cuckoo clock. She dropped John's letter onto the stack and carried them to the rocker.

Did they have any connection at all to John's death? If so, it would probably have to reach out and thump her on the nose for her to see it. She'd thought on it for days and had come up with nothing. For now, hopefully they would keep her mind off the snow accumulating in deceivingly innocent piles outside her windows.

John had mentioned a woman in the cuckoo clock note, a woman who hadn't done something he'd thought she had. The way he spoke of her made Lizzy think she was someone close to him.

Then there was the diary entry. It had been written on the day John's mother had taken her own life. With that flowery handwriting, it was surely written by a woman, a woman who wrote that she would finally get what she wanted thanks to something that had happened—thanks to Elizabeth Craig's death?

Who were these women? Lizzy wondered as she turned her attention to the fuzzy black-and-white photo that Mel claimed was Lizzy's father as a young boy. She wasn't convinced. The crooked smile on the boy's face belonged to John. Could she and John have shared a common ancestor several generations back?

The slam of a car door silenced her questions. Apprehension crept up her spin; a raging snowstorm would be the perfect setting for a murder—hers! "Who in the world is that?" she asked Sid, who was curled up in the other rocking chair.

The sound of her own voice gave her the courage to rise and tiptoe to the kitchen door, dropping her stash of prospective clues back into the desk as she passed by it. She pressed her ear against the rough wood, then jumped when a loud knock shook it. Drawing strength from the butcher knife she grabbed from the countertop, she inched the door open to peek outside.

There stood Sam, frosted with a light dusting of lacy snowflakes. Lizzy's heart did weird things. Why was he here? A hodgepodge of feelings coursed through her—trepidation, guilt, sorrow, and a tiny spark of something else. She didn't know what that something else was, and she didn't want to know.

"What are you doing here?" she asked.

"I brought you some firewood," he muttered through the flakes melting on his lips.

Well, that was a relief. Nonetheless, the idea that she was relying on Sam to provide her fuel for her fire didn't sit well. "I thought you weren't going to bring me any more firewood?"

"Franny was worried about you."

"Franny?"

"And Eb."

So it was their idea then, not his. He was only playing at being a hero. "They were worried, so you brought me firewood? How did you know I was out?" she probed, more because it was her turn than to get an answer.

He huffed. "Lizzy, I seem to spend a lot of time standing outside your door freezing my ass off while we discuss things that could be discussed just as well inside your house. How about if I stack the wood here beside the door, and then we finish this conversation?" Now he sounded like his old self—cranky and condescending.

Of course, he was right. Here she was, yet again, standing like a blathering idiot with the door open and all of her warm air trading places with the frigid outside air. No doubt about it, something about Sam caused her brain cells to malfunction.

Feeling her face blossom, she mumbled, "That's fine," before she closed the door and leaned her forehead against it. "Get a handle on yourself. You are not going to fall apart this time," she uttered tersely as she dropped the knife back onto the counter. Sam would only be here long enough to unload the wood. She could hold herself together that long.

She rubbed at her temples to relieve the rising pressure. Country etiquette dictated that if some generous soul braved a snowstorm to bring you provisions, you'd better be prepared to feed him. So he'd be here a bit longer; surely she could handle that, too?

She set to work. While Sam labored outside in the snow, Lizzy stirred the chicken soup that was bubbling on the back burner, then mixed together some baking powder biscuits and popped them into the oven.

With that done, she moved several armloads of firewood from the porch to add to the paltry pile beside the fireplace, noting that the wind was now whipping tiny chunks of ice into a frenzy. The world beyond the doorway was an agitating sea of white. Sam had backed his truck up to the steps and was engrossed in unloading the wood, puffy mounds of snow clinging to his hat and coat. He didn't even acknowledge Lizzy.

Fearing that the electricity would die at any moment, Lizzy chopped kindling and lit a fire. She blew on it until the flames leaped up to lick at the logs, savoring the heat after her brief stints outdoors. Sam had to be chilled to his bones. Though she was uneasy about his intrusion, she was also grateful for the wood. He was a real trooper to venture into a snowstorm to bring it to her. Whether it was at Franny's or Eb's insistence, or not, the fact that someone was concerned about her warmed her insides.

Lizzy heard movement at the front door and stepped to the kitchen. A snow-encrusted Sam dripped onto a rug she'd placed by the door. His gaze traveled over the kitchen.

"You don't waste any time, do you?" he said, clearly impressed with her handiwork.

"Not when I'm on a mission and have time on my hands," she informed him.

"It looks good. Smells good, too."

"That's because dinner's ready." She hesitated, then added. "Surely you can take a few minutes to eat before you head back?"

He seemed hesitant, too.

"It's the neighborly thing, you know?" she reminded him, only to wonder why she was trying to convince him to stay if she really wanted to get rid of him.

Evidently, he was still a fanatic about being neighborly. He pulled off his hat. Lizzy reached for it, and a shiver ran through her body from the chilly air clinging to him. "I'll take your hat and coat and put them by the fire. Maybe they'll dry off a bit."

The gloves and coat came off next. Sam handed them to Lizzy, and she carried them at arms length into the living room. When she returned, Sam was inspecting the soup in his stocking feet.

"You cook like this every night?" he asked skeptically, probably remembering her disastrous culinary experiments during her growing-up years.

"No, you just hit the right one." Lizzy grabbed a potholder and pulled the pan of golden-brown biscuits from the oven. Fragrant steam wafted out to roast her face. "You remember where the bathroom is, don't you? You can wash up in there."

While Sam cleaned himself up, Lizzy pulled dishes from the cupboards. She had just spooned a dollop of soup into a bowl for Sid when the lights flickered twice and the room went dark.

"Great!" she grumbled to no one in particular. The muted light from the fireplace drew her, and her eyes met Sam's through the dimness as he stepped from the bathroom. Tiny flurries raced across her nerves—something to do with the firelight and the snow, she was sure.

"I have some lamps ready," she informed him matter-of-factly before she set Sid's soup bowl near the leaping flames and snatched the box of matches off of the mantle. "Kitty! Kitty!" she called.

Sam walked towards her and reached for the matches. "I'll do that. You finish what you were doing."

Instead, Lizzy grabbed a finger lamp from the table. She lifted the chimney and held the lamp out to Sam. He struck a match and lit the wick, igniting a sphere of light that shone between them and illuminated his features. Though he'd most likely shaved that morning, his beard had grown out in thick, black bristles. Lizzy fought the urge to reach up and see if it was as prickly as it looked. Fearing she'd do just that, she replaced the chimney and clutched the lamp tightly to keep her hands where they belonged.

Sam stood as still as that silent cuckoo bird and stared at her, his eyes oozing a warm glow. He looked worn out. Tiny lines creased his forehead and the outer corners of his eyes, and beads of moisture glistened like dew against his dark hair. Her wayward hands didn't want to stay put; they wanted to touch him.

She suddenly realized that she was staring at him, too, and she stepped back, panic-stricken. What was happening to her? Her insides were doing funny things, and she was steaming inside her wool sweater.

"The other lamps are on the table," she muttered abruptly and forced her eyes from Sam's mesmeric gaze to the vibrant, licking flames. They landed on Sid's bowl, and her heart leaped in her chest. Where was Sid? It wasn't like him to miss a meal.

Pinpricks of unrest jabbed her as she searched into the darkened periphery, her eyes straining to see beyond the sphere of light. "Kitty! Kitty! Kitty!" she called.

That was odd; Sid always came when she called. When had she last seen him? Before Sam's arrival, he'd been lazing in the rocker.

The lamp clutched tightly in both of her hands, Lizzy rushed through the open door of her bedroom and circled the room, checking every nook and cranny. Then she fell onto her knees to search under the bed. There were no bright eyes shining at her.

The bathroom? He must be there, curled up in a ball and sleeping soundly, so soundly he didn't hear Sam wash up. Lizzy sprinted from the bedroom nearly slamming into Sam. She stepped by him and frantically searched each dark corner in the bathroom. Nothing!

Had Sid slipped outside while she was carrying wood into the house? She sank down onto the tub's rim, sorting through the implications in her panicked mind.

"What's wrong?" Sam asked from the shadows.

Lizzy heard the concern in his voice and glanced up. "It's Sid," she gasped, then thought to add, "my cat. He always comes when I call him."

Sam gave her a studied look. "Maybe he skittered past me when I came inside."

Goosebumps prickled on her arms, whether from the cool air or her fear she wasn't' sure. "Outside?" she whispered. "In the snowstorm?" How long could a cat survive in weather like this? Sid was an indoor cat. He wouldn't know how to stay warm in snow.

Instinct took over. She set the lamp on the floor and stood, then pushed past Sam. Her coat! She couldn't go out there without it. Her eyes grazed the down jacket drying by the fire. She snatched it and pulled it on over her sweater, zipping it shut as she raced for the kitchen door. One hand searched fleetingly for the flashlight she'd set on the counter while the other reached for the doorknob. Breathing a sigh of relief, her fingers closed around the flashlight. She pulled at the door. It slammed up against her, knocking her breath from her. She braced herself and edged around it.

A wall of frozen powder pummeled her. It was everywhere, hurling and churning, making the darkness even darker. From behind her, she felt Sam's firm grasp on her upper arm. He pressed resolutely against the door and pulled on her. Lizzy wedged herself between the door and the frame and refused to budge.

"Are you crazy," he muttered into her ear. "It's a cat, Lizzy. Cats know how to get by in weather like this."

Ice stung her left cheek; tears stung her eyes. She had to make a break for it before Sam talked some sense into her. "Not Sid," she cried. "He's old. Plus, he's never even been outside in a rainstorm."

"Don't do it," he warned.

"I have to. Sid's all I've got right now. I can't lose him." Lizzy jerked free of his grasp and lunged onto the porch, into the torrent of pelting ice.

She struggled to get her bearings. The flashlight was lost inside the sleeve of Sam's too-large jacket. She flipped the switch and worked her hand to the opening, not that it did much good.

The storm engulfed her—a roiling sea of white. Already, her ears and cheeks ached from the biting cold. As she inched her way forward, her frozen fingers searched for the rough texture of wood. Finally, she touched the porch railing through the snow piled on it. Using it as a guide, she cautiously shuffled forward and down the steps while she shrieked into the battering whiteness, "Kitty! Kitty! Kitty!"

Someone gripped her shoulder. Warm air tickled her ear. "Wait here. I'm going to get a jacket from my truck and turn on the headlights. Promise you won't move," Sam demanded.

Fighting the urge to grab onto him for comfort, she nodded. Then he was gone, and she grappled with the insanity of her actions. For her to battle a snowstorm to save Sid was one thing; for Sam to do it was quite another. But it was Sid, for Heaven's sake. He was family . . . and right now, her best friend.

She strained to hear anything other than the wind that whipped around her. "Kitty! Kitty! Kitty!" she shouted. Surely Sid would hear her and come running.

Of course, she wouldn't see him even if he was standing at her feet. Ever so slowly, she sank down onto her knees and swept her throbbing hand in an arc around her, praying it would touch a wet, furry body. It didn't. She tugged her hand up inside the sleeve to warm it. When she stood, she bumped into Sam's solid body.

"Dammit, Lizzy," he muttered. "What're you doing?"

She turned her face to meet his cheek stubble, her face so numb she barely felt the scratch. "Looking for Sid," she yelled.

"You're frozen," he said softly into her ear as he slid his hat down over her head.

Light now filtered through the whipping chunks of ice—Sam's headlights. Lizzy glanced down at the powerful flashlight he clutched in his hand. Maybe there was hope, after all. His right arm snaked around her to pull her close against his side.

"Where do you think he might be?" he asked.

Lizzy's thoughts had been on that. "If I were him, I'd crawl under the porch," she shouted. She gazed down to where her boots disappeared into the snow. Though she couldn't see it, she could feel how deep it was. She pulled his face close, so she wouldn't have to yell. "I'm going to get down and look under the porch. I'll use your flashlight. You hold onto the railing . . . and me."

Sam lifted the frozen fingers on her free hand to his mouth, cupped them in his own gloved hand, and blew on them, the whole time staring into Lizzy's eyes through a gauzy white curtain. Her heart did weird things again, and her body refused to move. He slid a glove over that hand and placed his flashlight in it. She handed him her smaller one. Then she steeled herself, dropped down onto her knees, and worked her way along the porch, feeling Sam's grip on the tail of her jacket.

She was more protected down here. As she pawed through the drifted snow with her gloved hand, she aimed the flashlight beam ahead and searched the underside of the porch. Rocks, bunchgrass, and sagebrush starts lay under sprinklings of snow, but there was nothing that resembled a cat. Her insides felt empty; her heart, crushed. If Sid wasn't huddled up under the other end of the porch, she had no idea where he'd be.

She pushed herself up onto her feet, and Sam bent down to

hear her report. "Let's check on the other side of the steps."

Sam tugged her close against him, sheltering her face from the cutting ice with his body as they plowed forward. "Please, Sid, be there," Lizzy whispered.

Battling the gusts of blowing snow, it seemed to take forever to reach something that was only a few yards away. Finally, she pulled her face from the comfort of Sam's chest and dropped down onto her knees again to search the underside of this side of the porch. Still, no Sid.

An overwhelming wave of loss washed over Lizzy. What would she do now? They were stranded at the house. If they ventured off, they'd be wandering blind.

She gazed into the chaos surrounding her, worry aching in her throat. She had to find Sid. If she lost him, she'd be alone on this desolate farm. Sid had been there with her, her one stable anchor through all the turmoil in her life during the last three years.

She had no choice; she had to try. It might be too late to save John and her grandparents, but surely she would rescue Sid in time.

Reaching up to Sam, her lips met his ice-cold ear. "Maybe he's in one of the sheds."

"I'll go look for him," he yelled. "You stay here. Or even better, go back in the house."

"No! It's my cat; I'll find him." With that, she yanked herself free and plunged into the furor.

Snow whirled around her, stinging her cheeks and blinding her. Everywhere she looked, it was the same. She shone the flashlight into the fray and trudged on, wishing the security of Sam's solid body was beside her. "Kitty! Kitty! Kitty!"

Lizzy plowed through the deepening snow for what seemed an eternity, calling out to Sid and trying to ignore the aching cold and fatigue that settled into her body. Luckily, Sam's jacket was long enough to protect the upper portion of her legs, but each step she took reminded her that she had on only one pair of thin socks inside her leather boots. Her feet throbbed. She wiggled her toes to persuade the blood to keep on circulating and squinted into the incessant motion of blowing snow. Surely she should've run into one of Granddad's sheds by now? She flicked off the flashlight and strained to see the beams from the truck's headlights. Nothing!

Desolate, she tucked her chin back into the jacket's neck and continued her search. "Kitty! Kitty! Kitty!"

Her voice sounded weak. How much longer could she wander around in this frozen madness, the frigid air sucking the energy out of her? Her legs felt like they had a couple of semis strapped to them. Maybe it was time to give up on the search and head back to the farmhouse.

Lizzy stopped and turned. Panic squeezed her throat. Where was the farmhouse? Frantic now, she stared in every direction, laboring to see through the white madness to what was beyond, fighting the urge to flee.

What should she do? She couldn't stand here and freeze to death, but if she kept on walking, she might end up moving away from the farmyard and into acres of empty land . . . and she would die without telling Sam or her son the truth—suddenly, she saw that as a colossal failure, dangling out there.

She shivered uncontrollably, the rattling of her teeth vibrating through her head, making her brain fuzzy. It would be easy to sink down into the snow and curl up into a ball, one like Sid curled himself into. No! She lifted a leg, only it didn't' lift. Fear roiled in her gut. "Kitty! Kitty! Kitty!" she cried feebly.

On her third call, an arm wrapped around her. Sam? Swirls of fog drifted inside her head. If she wasn't mistaken, he was unzipping her jacket. What the heck? Her words caught in her throat, rendering her speechless. A hand reached inside her jacket. Adrenaline surged through her veins. Her body went rigid, steeling itself for a fight.

Prepared to lash out, she felt it—the familiar contours of a feline body against her chest. She wilted. Frozen and aching from the intense cold, tears trickled warm threads down her frozen cheeks. She lifted an arm and cradled Sid, feeling his damp heat through her sweater.

Sam turned her towards him and took the flashlight from her hand to shine it on her face. His was covered with snow. Lizzy reached up her ungloved hand and made a feeble attempt to wipe it off. "Can you walk?" he asked.

Her teeth chattering, she nodded. Sam cradled her next to his body, pulling her along. Lizzy wondered where he got his strength. Her body refused to do what she told it to do. She closed her eyes to focus on holding on to Sid.

Then, just like that, the world stopped hurling ice at her and instead, decay and mildew odors tickled her nostrils. Confused, she lifted her eyelids and met Sam's worried gaze. She swiped futilely at the frozen ice on his face, then glanced around. Where were they?

"Don't ever do anything like that again!" Sam barked before he snatched the hat off her head and pushed it down onto his own. Only, he didn't look angry; he looked scared.

Lizzy stared at him, struggling to make sense of his words. She watched Sam unzip both of their jackets, then felt soft cloth against her face when he pulled her in next to him and wrapped his arms around her inside the down-filled coat. Sid was still—a damp lump between them. Lizzy settled her free hand into the warmth between Sid and Sam and relished the vibration of Sid's purring.

Sam's hands rubbed up and down her back. "Move your legs,"

he murmured.

She didn't want to move her legs. She wanted to nuzzle into Sam's warmth and sleep.

"Move them, or I'll pull your boots and jeans off and get them warmed up any way I can," he warned.

He wouldn't dare.

Sam's hands snaked around her waist to her bellybutton.

Lizzy forced a dead foot off the ground. Then another.

"Good girl. Keep them moving."

Easy for him to say. He didn't have those semis strapped to his feet.

His hands returned to her back, rubbing a stream of warmth into her. She focused on her feet, lifting first one and then the other, then wiggling her lazy toes. Slowly, an aching tingle filled her limbs as they came to life. She gritted her teeth against the pain. No longer dazed, something else caught her attention: Sam's hands were wandering farther south than was warranted. Her derriere was just fine, thank you!

Lizzy pushed back and scowled at him. "Having fun?"

His lips twitched. "You finally noticed, huh? Must mean you're gonna be okay."

He was right. That dazed, lethargic feeling was gone, and her body, though sluggish, was her own again. If it hadn't been for Sam, she'd be lying out in that snowstorm . . . dying.

"Thanks to you," she said. "I'm sorry. All I could think about was finding Sid before it was too late." She glanced down at the contented cat. "Where was he?"

"Huddled up outside, next to this shack. The door was closed or he would've stayed dry in here."

She owed Sam a lot. He could've left her to find her cat on her own. "Thank you," she whispered as she looked into his eyes, which were very bright and very close. "How did you find me?"

"I heard you calling your cat." He raised his eyebrows and quirked his mouth. "Good thing you're so stubborn. If you'd given up, I would've never found you."

She wasn't sure if it was a compliment or a putdown. Either way, it had saved her life. "Just goes to show that my faults are also my assets," she informed him with a smile.

He chuckled. "You think you can make it back to the house?"

Thoughts of leaving the cold, musty shed made Lizzy queasy. "What if we don't end up there?" she asked.

He studied her, concern settling into his eyes. "We will," he assured her.

"How can you be sure?" Her legs were shaking, from fear now.

"I tied one end of a rope to the bumper of my truck and the other end to me. All we have to do is follow it."

Why hadn't she thought of that before she tore out into a blizzard? She nodded hesitantly. "I'll be fine."

Sam released her arms and stepped back. Shivers raced along her spine with the loss of his body heat. He zipped the down jacket up over the top of Sid and pushed his hat down onto Lizzy's head. She pulled her arm inside the jacket to cradle the cat. Sam placed the flashlight in her other hand and curled an arm around her shoulder before he turned her towards the door and the icy assault that awaited them.

Protected by Sam's body, the trek back to the house took only a few minutes. Lizzy was amazed when she noticed the muted glow of headlights. She'd wandered around the farmyard for what had felt like hours and hadn't been far from her front door the whole time. Soon they'd be thawing out in front of the fireplace, their snowstorm foray only an unpleasant memory.

They fought their way up the steps and through the front door. Sam slammed it shut and leaned against it, gazing into her eyes with a look that heated Lizzy's body up faster than any fire would. His head was bare, his dark hair speckled with chunks of ice. He'd given her his hat and one of his gloves, and she'd taken his jacket. He unzipped it, scooped Sid from her arms to deposit him on the floor, and snagged the hat off her head. His movements were swift and crisp, like he had somewhere to be.

Her heart hammering away in her chest, Lizzy stood, riveted and watchful.

Sam reached his bare hand up and caressed her cheek, icy cold against the warmth that was now glowing there. He tugged at her shoulder with his gloved hand and drew her closer. Lizzy melted. All through her body, a weak tranquility settled in.

Both of Sam's hands cradled her face. Lizzy stared into his eyes, now fully aware of where he was headed. She knew she needed to call a halt to it but couldn't work up the strength to do so. When his lips touched hers—a mere whisper—her reaction caught her off guard and left her buzzing with an aching need.

Sam looked at her again, his thumb tracing her lower lip. Afraid her heart was going to burst from her chest, Lizzy inched closer. His lips landed on hers again, this time firm and demanding. Her traitorous lips opened to him, and she reveled in the feel and taste of him.

Sam's hands worked their way down her body, snaking inside the heavy jacket and drawing her up against his hard chest. The jacket fell to the floor. Lizzy's slipped her hands around the solid muscles in his upper arms, then slid them up to his neck, pulling him even closer. She slowly melded with him, losing herself and becoming one with him.

Then, through the haze, a sharp pain in her leg made her wince. And another. She drew back from Sam to peek down. Sid was climbing her leg, his sharp claws imbedded in her skin.

She glanced at Sam. He looked dazed and confused. Well, she was, too. Her whole body trembled with the need to continue what he'd started.

A replay of what had happened the last time she'd been swept away by Sam's hypnotic allure shot through her mind—another bone-chilling assault. It was she who'd lived with the consequences, not he. She jerked away from him, angry at herself. You'd think she had learned her lesson. Well, never again!

She reached down with trembling hands to grab hold of Sid— gently pulling his claws free from her leg—to hold him in her arms. They were even; she'd rescued Sid, and now Sid had rescued her.

But what about Sam? "Lizzy . . . I . . ." he began.

He looked like he'd just shot his best friend. So he was having second thoughts about what he'd just done, too—probably wondering what he was going to tell his beautiful young girlfriend.

"It's okay," she assured him. "I understand. You were caught up in the moment. As far as I'm concerned it didn't happen. And it won't happen again . . . please."

He still looked like he was in pain. If kissing her was that bad of an experience, why had he done it—again? It wasn't as if she'd forced him. Or had she?

"Thank you for finding Sid," she added, ready to move on to something less intimate. She was also ready for some alone time to calm what was going on inside her body . . . and to think. "I'm going to take him in by the fire."

Sam's eyelids closed, and he took a deep breath. When he lifted them, his eyes seemed more settled. He gathered the jacket and his hat off the floor and dressed himself as if planning another venture into the blizzard raging outside.

Lizzy eyed him, apprehension unsettling her. "You're not going out there again," she told him.

"I need to turn my truck lights off, or the battery'll be dead come morning." He slipped the glove off of her hand and onto his. "And I need to cool down," he announced as he grabbed the flashlight and disappeared out the door.

CHAPTER 25

Outside the cab of Sam's Dodge Ram truck, the storm raged, howling and hurling pellets of ice, a monotonous clinking against the windows. Inside it, he was dealing with his own raging storm as he debated the pros and cons of returning to the farmhouse. With a full tank of gas and warm clothing, he could most likely make it through the night right where he was. He'd have to run the engine every so often to keep the cab warm, but it sure as hell beat the frustration of being near Lizzy the rest of the night.

He'd really blown it with the kiss. If he could, he'd kick himself all the way back to the ranch—and then kick Chet. It was Chet who'd planted it in his mind, a persistent mental image that refused to budge. He'd nearly acted on it when they'd lit that lamp and she'd stood there gazing into his eyes as if waiting for him to do just that. Yep, he'd mentally slapped himself on the back for surviving that challenge unscathed.

But then her trembling body was plastered up against him in that shed, and he'd been worried sick that she might not make it. He'd nearly kissed her then, too.

He huffed, his insides knotted tighter than a trussed up calf. That wasn't the worst of it. Every second Lizzy was lost in that storm was pure hell. The need to find her and drag her back to the safety of the farmhouse had consumed him. With an evening like he'd been through, was it any wonder he'd completely lost his mind and pulled her into his arms for a kiss that had knocked his socks off, if not hers?

The click of a door handle halted Sam's mental self-flagellations. "Shit!" he uttered as a whoosh of ice-filled air flicked his face. With the click of a button, diffused light filled the cab, illuminating a snow-covered bundle with large dark eyes. Sam winced. He'd recognize those eyes anywhere.

It took both of her hands to pull the door closed. Then she leaned against it and unzipped her jacket down to her neck, and the two of them sat eyeballing each other. She chewed on her lower lip, shivering, her eyes fretful. "I was worried about you," she finally said in a shaky voice.

Sam was worn down. If he was one of Eb's cakes, Eb would stick a toothpick in him and declare him way past done. "I think I'd better spend the night in the truck," he told her before he turned the key in the ignition to get some heat pouring out of the vents.

Her eyes were full of questions. She removed her leather gloves and flexed her fingers in the flow of warm air. "Then I will, too," she murmured.

Over my dead body! Sam nearly blurted. She was *not* going to spend the night freezing her ass off in the cab of his truck. Unless, what she had in mind was to share body heat. He'd have no problem with that.

Irritated at his one-track mind, he growled, "Well, that kind of defeats my purpose."

"Oh," she whispered, her mouth hanging open. "I'm sorry." Her right hand closed around the door handle.

Sam reached across her to hold the door shut. He turned to look into her eyes but didn't expect them to be so close. Just like that, he was lost in those eyes, the urge to draw her close and kiss her a palpable part of him. His breath was ragged, but hers was, too, her lips parted and her eyes bottomless dark pools.

She'd asked him not to. Did he dare?

With one last effort, he pulled himself back to his side of the truck and leaned against the door, as far from her as he could get. "Lizzy, you and I, we're always at each other over something. I'm dog-tired. I don't have anything left to put into that tonight," he confessed.

"I'm sorry I've been so much bother," she mumbled forlornly. "But after all you've done for me tonight, I can't let you sit out here in this cold truck. Come inside. You can sleep by the fire."

"Cuddled up with you?" He shouldn't have said it, but dammit all! His mind wouldn't let it go.

She fidgeted with her zipper and frowned at him as if he'd confessed to killing that cow in her yard. "I'm not much of a cuddler," she murmured.

It was a curious thing to say. So far, he certainly had no complaints. "Why's that?"

"For one thing, I take my relationships more seriously than that." She hesitated, rubbing the bridge of her nose, as if in pain. "And for another, I'm the one who always ends up a doormat. It's not worth it."

"Not ever?" He was getting a sick feeling. Was she telling him something?

She sighed deeply. "I think so," she said quietly.

He felt like she'd stuck her hand in and wrenched out his heart. The wound was too raw to contemplate right now. He'd think about it later when he wasn't holed up within arm's reach of her. He swallowed at the burning in his throat and tried to sidetrack the emotional rush.

Noting that the snow on her had melted into tiny beads of water, Sam switched off the ignition. Then he turned to Lizzy. "Why'd you come back here?"

She blinked, surprised. "The truth?" she asked hesitantly.

Sam wondered if she meant it. "Yeah."

Lizzy's gaze turned to the unruly darkness outside the windows. She seemed to gather herself. Maybe he would finally get the full story.

"My life fell apart, just disintegrated into pieces until, other than my sons and Sid, there wasn't much left." She faced him then, her eyes sad, her fingers wringing. "First my husband discarded me as if I was one of his well-worn shirts that'd served its purpose. When he walked out the door, so did a job that I dearly loved and my coworkers, who were also my friends—oh, and the home I'd raised three boys in. Then my youngest son moved out.

"The final straw was when Dawn—she was a dear friend but more like the sister I never had—passed away from cancer. We'd been right there for each other—like they say, 'through thick and thin'—for more than twenty years. Just like that, she was gone."

"You must have other friends?" he offered, thinking Lizzy's ex must've been a dolt to not recognize how lucky he was to have her as his wife.

Lizzy shrugged, her eyes betraying the hurt she felt. "My ex has to be the good guy, which makes me the evil slut. He told a lot of whoppers and turned me into the home-wrecker, not him. He's charming and manipulative, well respected and with much more prestige and power than I have. He's also a sneak—managed to cheat his way through our marriage and keep it a secret. By the time he was through with me, my reputation was burnt toast. My 'friends' went out of their way to avoid me.

"Except for Sid, I was alone, wandering aimlessly around an empty apartment and putting all my effort into being miserable. No job, no husband, no kids, no close friends. I was wallowing in my grief—really embraced my role as a victim—and I couldn't climb out of the hole I'd buried myself in."

She paused and shook her head as if to shake the series of life-shattering events from her life. "Then I got John's letter, and I knew what I had to do. I ditched the apartment and most of what was in it. The rest I boxed up and put into storage. I did the same thing I did twenty-five years ago. I ran away from it all. Only, this time I came back here."

Lizzy's words sparked Sam's anger. He wanted that "dolt" to get what he deserved. "It seems to me you've let yourself be a victim,

Lizzy," he muttered. "Sounds like your ex took advantage of that."

She shrugged. "It is what it is." Her voice sounded so weary. "I've wasted enough of my life on him. My sons don't believe any of his lies; that's what matters. All I want right now is some peace in my life."

"Have you ever thought that you might have to go back and confront what's there to find that peace, that running away might not be the best thing for you?"

She studied him in the muted light for long moments, her dark eyes probing his. "I am back," she whispered.

She was talking in riddles. "Back for what? Did something happen to you here? Was it John? Is that why you left?" His legs felt cramped and restless. He stretched them out towards Lizzy. She watched him, an intrigued look on her face.

"John's a part of it," she finally admitted. "He claimed in his letter that both he and I were in danger. Although I do need to know if that's true and find out how he really died, I'm beginning to think that I latched onto that letter to justify my return.

"I think I'm here to confront something else, something I should've taken care of a long time ago. It scares me. I don't know if I can do it." She stopped, struggling for breath, as if she'd just sprinted a long leg on a relay team. Even in the murky light from the dome, Sam could see that her face was pasty white, her eyes frantic. "But I have to make it right, don't I?"

"Lizzy, will you just spit it out," he hissed, desperate for some closure. "I've had a rough day. I'm so wrung out that if you hung me over a chair to dry out, I'd sleep through the night right there. Just tell me what it is . . . please."

She stared at him, a "deer in the headlights" look to her. Then she snatched her gloves and was out of the truck and gone before Sam could reach out to stop her.

❋ ❋ ❋

Sam lay quietly, watching Lizzy sleep, a bittersweet ache resting heavy in his soul. Firelight danced across her features, highlighting first one and then another—a fluid shifting vision. The rise and fall of the heavy quilt she was wrapped in indicated that she was sleeping soundly. Even the cat was dead to this world, curled into the circle formed by Lizzy's body.

In her sleep, Lizzy was all peaceful softness, a softness that made him long to work his way across the floor and touch her. He couldn't discern a hint of the edginess that was a part of her when she was awake. Then, it was like some kind of force field clung to her, randomly throwing out sparks and bursts of energy. He didn't cope well with those sparks and usually ended up irritated and taking his irritation out on her.

Tonight had been different. Sure, there'd been tension between them, a restless, aching tension, unlike what he'd experienced during his previous dealings with her. It was the kind of tension that made him want to beat his head against a rock wall in frustration . . . or put his arms around her and draw her close.

There were also brief moments when he'd glimpsed the Lizzy that used to be. During one of those moments, she'd mentioned John's letter. Had John really believed that both his and Lizzy's lives were in danger? He doubted that it was true. He couldn't think of anyone who'd want to hurt John. Besides, the John he'd spent time with could've invented all kinds of wild stories and been thoroughly convinced they were true.

Still, his thoughts flashed on the note John had stuck in the cuckoo clock and the one on Lizzy's door. Then there was his slaughtered cow and the vehicle that appeared to be hanging around.

He hoped Lizzy wasn't in any real danger. She'd alluded to a need to confront someone about something that'd happened years ago. It's what had sent her scurrying back to the house tonight. Was it also the reason she'd driven off in Dottie's Buick in the middle of the night? But who around these parts would've harmed Lizzy? Chet's tarnished image flashed through his mind. Sam shoved it aside. He didn't want to think that Chet would stoop that low.

Instead, he eyed the dying embers in the fireplace and let his gaze wander up to the photographs on the mantel. Though nearly indiscernible in the shadows, he'd studied them enough to picture them in his mind. They were nice-looking boys, each of them with his distinct look. Something else about them nagged him. A funny warm feeling came over him every time he looked at them. He mulled it over and decided that they must remind him of Con or Dottie. Of course, they looked like Lizzy, too

He turned to look at her. When he'd returned to the house several hours ago, she was cocooned in a quilt on the couch, sleeping soundly. She'd left the kitchen door unlocked and a sleeping bag and pillow laid out on the floor beside the roaring fire. His heart had hitched at the sight of it.

He'd gazed longingly at Lizzy while he discarded his damp outer clothing and warmed his chilled body in front of the hot blaze. Then he'd stretched out on the sleeping bag and let the soothing affects of the mesmerizing flames lull him into a fretful slumber.

Sam wondered what time it was. Though he didn't want to disturb his warm bed, he pulled his left arm from it and held it out to the muted firelight. It was still a long stretch until morning, so he braced himself, unzipped the bag, and stood up. Prickly shivers raced through him. He grabbed several chunks of firewood and pushed them down into the hot coals. Soon flames licked their edges and warmed his outstretched hands.

Sam stood up, and his eyes met those of Lizzy's sons. The flash of recognition plagued him, yet again. What was it about them?

As if a bullet had pierced him, he understood. Struck numb, he studied the photos and tried to comprehend what it all meant. Then he picked one up to inspect it before he carried it with him into Lizzy's bedroom. Feeling his way clumsily in the dark, he made his way to her dresser and grabbed another photograph.

With the two pictures clutched in his hands, he returned to the living room and plopped into a rocker. And that's where he spent the remaining two hours before daylight peeked through the frost-covered windows. He spent them examining the two photographs and piecing together something that was finally making sense.

John was this boy's father.

❀ ❀ ❀

Lizzy sensed more than saw the subtle rays of sunlight filtering into her semi-consciousness. Her grogginess drew her back into sleep, but something prevented her from surrendering to its allure.

She wondered why it was so cold, then remembered the snowstorm . . . and Sam. It was odd that thoughts of him didn't elicit an onslaught of disturbing feelings. Not that they made her feel warm and fuzzy. They were just okay, which was a definite improvement.

Her heart rate picked up when she remembered the kiss. Heat rose in her cheeks. No doubt about it, the snowstorm had swept away her common sense. She'd almost confessed about the baby to him. Luckily, she'd escaped before her big mouth got the better of her. She and Sam were finally getting along. A disclosure like that would destroy their budding, tentative relationship.

Sid squirmed, and Lizzy reached a hand from beneath the quilt to settle the restless cat. If Sam had slept next to the fire, she didn't want Sid to awaken him. Stifling a yawn with her hand, she slowly lifted her eyelids, then pushed herself up onto an elbow to search across the room.

Sam sat in a rocker, staring at her, a storm brewing in his eyes. Uneasiness twisted inside Lizzy. Something was wrong.

Then she noticed what he held in his hands, and a rush of emotions consumed her. A lead ball landed in her stomach. She couldn't get enough air into her lungs, and she panicked. Was she going to pass out?

"Were you ever going to tell me?" he asked, his voice

wounded and broken.

All Lizzy could do was gape at him since everything had turned fuzzy and otherworldly.

"Well, were you?" he reiterated, more edge to his voice.

"Tell you what?" she finally managed to whisper while she stalled for time.

"Dammit, Lizzy! Quit the games. You know exactly what I'm talking about. You didn't plan to ever tell me about it, did you?"

His passion shocked her. She'd never seen Sam like this. It wasn't that he was shouting and out of control. It was more like he was barely containing his emotions. They seethed out of him and blasted across the room with her as their target.

She watched his eyes for signs that he was losing control and shook her head. "I don't know."

He turned more sad than angry. "He's my nephew. Don't you think I have the right to know that . . . and to know him? He's the only family I have left."

Lizzy blinked, confused. "Nephew?" she choked.

"Just quit it," he uttered tersely. "It's obvious when you look at these two pictures side-by-side. Your son is the spitting image of John. You know, every time I saw this picture, there was something about it that bothered me. This morning it suddenly hit me. So tell me, is it another one of those things everyone knew except me?"

Her mind racing, Lizzy sorted through the tangled mess, scrambling to make a decision, a decision that would alter the lives of everyone involved.

"You know, it's all finally making sense." He shoved a photo towards her. "He's the reason you left, isn't he? And the reason you didn't get out of your car at the cemetery. And then of course, you couldn't come back, could you?"

He paused to take a couple of deep breaths, then continued the barrage of questions. "What I don't understand is why you didn't just marry John. Was it my father? Is that why he tried to buy you off?"

Lizzy took in bits and pieces of Sam's tirade. She knew she had to answer him. She just didn't know which set of answers to give him—the truth or what would certainly pass as the truth.

"Dammit, Lizzy! I deserve some answers," he growled.

He was right. He did. So what was it going to be?

In the blink of an eye, she knew exactly what she had to do. It was time to put to rest the lies and secrets and misunderstandings that had been a destructive part of her life for far too long. Once she accepted that truth, a surge of clarity and relief flowed through her entire body. She was ready to see this through to the end, no matter the outcome.

Gathering Sid into her arms for moral support, she pushed

the quilt aside and sat up. Sam watched her every move, a determined set to his face. "You're right. You do deserve some answers, especially since they affect you . . . maybe more than you think."

She paused to pull herself together and to search for words that would explain a series of events that were easier left unspoken. How could she explain to Sam that he'd played a major role in those events when he appeared to have no knowledge of ever being a player?"

In the end, she decided it was best to lay it on the line and let it play itself out. She could sort it out later. "He's not John's son."

"We've already been there, so save your lies. Now I want the truth."

"It is the truth. He's not John's son." The rest of it stuck in her throat.

"Well, I can't wait to hear what you're gonna say next because he sure as hell looks like John. Are you gonna try to tell me that he's my father's son?"

The thought was repulsive. She shook it off and forged ahead. "Of course not! He's not John's son because he's . . . well . . . he's your son."

CHAPTER 26

Sam was numb from the frigid air surrounding him and the icy chill that had settled into his soul. The snowstorm had moved on—he wished he could say the same about the emotional storm raging inside him—leaving behind an endless white sea of frozen ice and livestock that needed food and water. That's what he was determined to focus on, that and staying warm enough to get the job done.

He would deal with the other later, when some of the rawness had worn off, and he could look at it with more clarity and less emotion. Right now, the deception was an eight-inch steel blade twisting in his gut. When he was ready, he knew where to get answers. He had a ranch to take care of first.

He hefted a hay bale with the forks clutched in his hands and threw it into his truck, his mind replaying his morning conversation with Lizzy.

"My son?" he'd uttered through clenched teeth, floored by her accusation.

"Yes." She'd looked determined, nodding her head and searching his face.

"And how do you explain the fact that the two of us—you and I—have never shared anything more intimate than a couple of kisses?" he'd challenged.

She'd hesitated, then argued, "Well, obviously we have. Although I wouldn't describe it as intimate."

"Then maybe you can tell me how you would describe it 'cause I sure as hell have no recollection of it," he'd hissed, squeezing the chair arms to keep from walking over there to shake some sense into her.

Her lips had twitched as if she were in pain. "I'd rather not talk about it. And now, it's time for you to leave."

He'd stormed out of the farmhouse, furious with her and her irrational allegations, leaving her to wallow in her lies. Against his better judgment, he'd climbed into his truck and plowed through the snow, arriving home safely by sheer determination and a whole lot of luck and innate sense of direction.

And still, it didn't make sense. Her absurd, concocted story was completely untrue—no doubt about that. But why accuse him? Why not just say the kid was John's and be done with it?

Sam heaved another bale into the truck, remembering how stunned he'd been when he'd seen those two photos side-by-side. If he hadn't known better, he'd have sworn they were of the same person. Of course, he and his brother shared many similar features, too. But that was irrelevant since the boy couldn't be his. He'd remember something like that.

He climbed up onto the truck bed to pile the bales into a neat stack, his mind refusing to let it go. Though Lizzy and the whole situation infuriated him, a warm glow had settled inside him with the knowledge that he had a nephew, one who shared some of his genes—he had family. There was now someone to take over the ranch when he was gone. It was even more reason for him to build it up and make it better. Since he didn't have a child of his own, it was certainly the next best thing. And God help anyone who tried to stand in the way of him getting to know his nephew, including Lizzy.

As Sam worked his way through the day, clearing roads and ensuring his livestock were well cared for, those same thoughts kept playing through his mind, over and over, like an old scratched forty-five. By the time evening rolled around, he finally felt comfortable enough with Lizzy's latest revelations and the role he hadn't played in them that he was ready to get to the bottom of the whole mess. He was ready to hunt down Eb.

He'd checked in with Eb when he'd arrived home that morning, drawing an outright speculative look. Eb had taken a second glance and vanished to the nether regions of the ranch house. No doubt about it; Eb knew something was up.

Thanks to the electricity that had flickered on mid afternoon, a whoosh of hot air blasted Sam's chilled body when he walked into the mudroom. He shucked his boots and damp outer garments and stepped into the kitchen. Eb wasn't in sight, but something that smelled inviting simmered on the stove. Sam turned the burner down beneath it and went in search of Eb. He found him in the living room stoking the fire in the massive fireplace.

Eb glanced his way but didn't meet his eyes. "You're back then. I've got supper on the stove," he mumbled, poking at the fire.

"I saw it. I turned the burner down. We need to talk. I'll be back down in a few minutes. Just want to take a hot shower and get into some dry clothes."

Eb stilled. Tension seemed to crackle around him.

When Sam returned to the living room, Eb sat in the overstuffed chair, a tumbler of amber liquid clasped in one hand, staring into the flames. Worry lines creased his troubled face. Sam poured himself a healthy shot of Scotch and settled into the recliner, facing Eb. Surprisingly calm, he sipped the alcohol and savored its fiery heat while he contemplated how to begin what was sure to be a difficult interrogation.

"I had an interesting conversation with Lizzy this morning," he probed.

A few more worry lines sprouted around Eb's eyes. "Hmmm."

"It seems she was pregnant with John's baby when she left here. You know anything about that?"

Eb took a healthy gulp from his glass and rolled it around in his mouth—stalling. "Johnny's baby? Lizzy told you that, did she?" he finally murmured.

Irritation spiked inside Sam. "Well, not exactly that. She told me some other preposterous story," he informed him. "Did you know about John's son, Eb?"

Their eyes locked. "Nope. I didn't know nothin' about that."

"You didn't know about it?" Sam demanded, surprised by Eb's denial.

"Nope." Eb shook his head and held Sam's eyes without flinching. He seemed determined.

Sam had never known Eb to lie. He might stretch the truth a bit or just keep silent, but Sam couldn't see him lying. Coming into this conversation, Sam had been so sure of himself. Now he was perplexed. He twirled the Scotch in his glass and watched the firelight flicker across its surface while he considered his options.

"Well, that's mighty interesting since one of her sons is the spitting image of John. And I'm having difficulty thinking that something like that went on around here without you knowing about it," he finally challenged.

Eb leaned forward. "Why don't you tell me Lizzy's story. Might be I know somethin' about that."

Sam didn't want to discuss Lizzy's story. Even the thought of it made him queasy. And the look on Eb's face and the tone in his voice were sparking alarms. Could Lizzy have spoken the truth? No! It was impossible. "I doubt you'd know about something that didn't happen," he stated adamantly.

"Suit yourself," Eb declared, his left eyebrow rising in query.

Sam recognized it as an offer and knew he had only a few seconds to make a choice: take him up on it, or not. A niggling voice told him to let it go. But if he walked away, he might never know the truth. It was clearly Sam's decision, and knowing Eb as he did, Sam doubted that he'd be given a second chance. He sipped at his Scotch, hoping to get a lethargic buzz before he put himself on the line.

"Lizzy claimed I'm the father. She implied that it wasn't her choice," Sam informed him. The words were so abhorrent to Sam that they came out through clenched jaws and were more of a hiss than an admission.

"And you don't believe her?" Eb asked.

"Hell, no! I would never do something like that, especially to Lizzy, and if I did, I'd certainly remember it," Sam assured Eb, as well as himself. But his voice hinted at the doubt that was creeping around inside him.

Eb's eyes searched Sam's for long moments before he sipped from his glass and spoke, his manner resigned. "I figured you didn't have any recollection of it. I couldn't see you leavin' if you did."

Sam shot forward in his chair, forearms braced on his thighs. "What are you talking about?"

"Lizzy told you the truth. I don't know any of the details of what happened, but I do know the baby was yours." With that, Eb shrank back into his chair as if he'd sprung a leak, and all of the air was rushing out of him.

That air seemed to swell inside Sam, the tension building to the point that he wondered if he'd explode into a million tiny pieces that Eb would then sweep up and discard. Maybe then, the whole mind-boggling incident would be gone from their lives. Eb wouldn't have to deal with it anymore, nor would Sam.

"Mine? How could it be?" he whispered, more to himself than to Eb.

Eb studied him from the sanctuary of his chair, sympathy splashed on his haggard face. "You need to talk this over with Lizzy."

There were so many emotions whirling around in Sam's pent-up body that even he couldn't sort them out. The one that burst to the surface was anger.

"Dammit, Eb. You tell me I somehow got her pregnant, and then you tell me to go talk with her about it. I'm sorry, but I'm drawing a complete blank here. There's one thing I do know, though, and that's that I'm not going to talk this over with Lizzy until I'm real clear on what the hell I did."

"You couldn't just leave it be, could you?"

The sadness in Eb's voice had no effect on Sam. "Leave it be? This is my alleged son we're discussing here, a son I've never even set eyes on. If it really did happen—and that's a big *if*—what the hell right did you and Lizzy have to keep him from me?"

Eb seemed to shrink even further. "It was J.D. We were told we weren't to say anything to anyone about it. He knew you had feelin's for Lizzy and was afraid you'd come back to the ranch if you knew about the baby."

"We? Who is we?"

"Johnny and me."

Fury and frustration seethed through Sam's veins. It seemed that everyone but him was aware of his transgressions. "John knew about this?"

"Yeah. He was there, too."

"There? Where? What are you talking about?" he barked.

"It's kind of a complicated story and not a very pretty one," Eb warned, giving Sam the option to opt out.

"Well, I think it's about time someone shared it with me, don't you? And I want to hear all of it, not the sugar-coated version!" he demanded, unable to mask the rage in his voice.

"You think you can handle it? Seems like you've been through a lot lately."

"I can handle it," Sam growled.

Eb seemed to pull inside himself. Where his mind wandered, Sam didn't know. But he did know one thing: Eb wasn't going to leave this room until Sam had the whole sordid story. At last, Eb downed the rest of whatever was in his glass and began to explain what had transpired on the one and only night of which Sam had no memory.

"It happened the night before you left, you know, to start your job at that law firm. I reckon it was a Sunday 'cause there'd been a Fourth of July dance the night before. I remember that 'cause Lizzy was here at the ranch keepin' Johnny company, and they were arguin' about somethin' that happened at that dance, somethin' that was not gonna sit well with J.D."

"I remember," Sam muttered, still not sure where Eb's recollections were headed. "Rose, Dad, Chet, and I had dinner at Mel's that night. You stayed home with John. After dinner, Chet and I were supposed to meet some guys at the Corral for some pool, but that part of the evening's pretty much a blur."

"Yeah. You got home around eleven, just about the time Lizzy was leavin' to go home. Evidently, you were so drunk that Chet dumped you in the driveway. Lizzy was tryin' to help you get to the house, but you'd set your mind on goin' to the barn. She tagged along to make sure you were okay.

"A little later, Johnny noticed her car was still here and went lookin' for her. He heard her cryin' and found her in the barn . . . but it was too late. She was upset. Wouldn't talk about it, but it was obvious what had happened. You were upstairs in your bed, passed out cold."

And just like that, Sam knew it was the truth. The knowledge knocked the wind completely out of him, to be replaced by waves of guilt and self-loathing. Eb kept on talking, but Sam heard it from a distance.

"We got Lizzy into the house so she could clean herself up. She'd calmed down some by then, and she made us promise we wouldn't say anything to anyone about what happened. She was scared to death that Con and Dottie would find out about it. Johnny drove her home in the Buick, and I followed him over, so's I could bring him back to the ranch. And that was that. Luckily, J.D. and Rose didn't get home until well after midnight."

He paused and sighed deeply. "If I hadn't been there, I'd have sworn it'd never happened. That is, until Lizzy turned up pregnant. Then, of course, all hell broke loose."

"There's more?" Sam inquired weakly, rubbing his forehead and praying there wasn't.

"Yeah, there's more. But I'm not sure you're up to hearin' it?"

"It can't be any worse than what I've just heard?" Sam implored. Along with all of the other emotions coursing through him, resignation had settled in. He'd get the telling of it over; then he'd attempt to deal with it.

Eb sighed resignedly. "A couple of months later, Dottie found out Lizzy was pregnant. There was a storm that evenin', a real bad one, bad enough that no one had any business bein' out in it. The rain was pourin' when J.D. got the phone call. Then he stomped up to Johnny's room. I could hear him yellin' all the way downstairs, so I heard what was goin' on. The call was from Con, and he was none too happy that his granddaughter was pregnant.

"Well, J.D. thought Johnny was the one who'd caused it, so he lit into him—chewed him up one side of the ranch and down another. Then he shut himself in his study. A few minutes passed, and then Johnny came runnin' down the stairs with his keys and tore out the door to his truck before I could stop him."

"The accident," Sam groaned. Having already hit an all time low, there wasn't much lower to go, so he just stared into the fire and listened.

"You know about that, huh? Seems that Con and Dottie decided to drive over to the ranch and hammer things out with J.D., even with the rain fallin' so's you couldn't see two feet in front of you. Lizzy got worried and followed them in the Buick, so she was there to see her grandparents killed. Johnny told me later that he was gonna talk Lizzy into sayin' the baby was his. He was gonna marry her. It probably would've worked out a whole lot better if the accident hadn't happened. Only, Lizzy would've never married Johnny."

"Why not?" Sam asked, surprised by Eb's assertion. Even in his agitated state, he couldn't see why Lizzy wouldn't find that an appealing solution to her predicament.

"Well, for one thing, J.D., most likely, wouldn't have allowed it." Eb rubbed his chin and eyed Sam closely. "And for another, though she had deep feelin's for Johnny, they weren't marryin' kinds of feelin's. She had her heart set on someone else."

That surprised Sam. If Lizzy had a boyfriend, perhaps the baby wasn't Sam's. Ironically, that thought didn't sit well with him. "There was someone else?" he murmured.

Eb smiled. "You're the daddy, Sam. There's no doubtin' that. Didn't you ever notice how Lizzy looked at you? She never showed a bit of interest in anyone else?"

"Shit!" Sam hissed. He rose to his feet and stepped to the fireplace to lean his forehead against the rough stone. The reality of this whole nightmare was incomprehensible.

"I'm right there with you on that. And I suppose you've figured out by now that Lizzy's the one that ended up at the bottom of the pile."

Yes, it was becoming clear to Sam. He had a lot to mull over, but one thing finally made sense—Lizzy. He turned to Eb, his drink clutched in his hand. "Why did she leave? Why didn't she stay at the farm and raise the baby there?"

"That's most likely J.D.'s doin's. He stopped by the farm to talk with her the afternoon of Con and Dottie's funeral. By that time, he'd figured out the truth of what'd happened, and he wasn't gonna chance you findin' out she was pregnant. I don't know what he said to her, but the next mornin' she was gone."

Eb's eyes glistened. It was evident that he'd struggled with Lizzy's departure. "You should've told me, you or John. You had no right to keep it from me."

Eb ran a gnarled knuckle under his left eye and sniffed. "Yeah, you're right. Someone should've told you. But it wasn't only J.D. Lizzy didn't want you to know either. She made Johnny and me promise we wouldn't breathe a word about what had happened to anyone, especially you. She had this notion in her head that you knew what you'd done and you were disgusted by it. That you were choosin' to turn your back on her. It seemed like she was more sad than mad at you."

Sam stared into the undulating flames. "Well, she's madder than an irritated rattler at me now." Of course, it was crystal clear to him now that she had every right to be.

"Oh, I don't know. I get the feelin' Lizzy's more interested in movin' on than holdin' grudges. Could be she just needs to hear you say you're sorry for what happened."

Sam's eyes darted up to meet Eb's. He ran his free hand through his hair and scratched his head in frustration. "How in the world do you apologize for something like this? I don't even know where to begin," he entreated, completely at a loss as to how to deal with the situation, let alone to begin to make amends, if it were even possible to do so.

"Maybe you just need to give her half a chance and see what happens," Eb suggested.

Was Eb right? The night before, other than that vexing tension between the two of them, Lizzy had seemed more like her old self. Sam sank back into his chair, rubbing at the bridge of his nose as he mulled things over. "I don't know. Right now things are so mixed up that I can't even sort out what's real and what's not. My whole life I've tried to do the right thing, to be honest and fair. Now here I am, closer to the end of my life than to the beginning, and I find out I'm everything I'd abhor in another person. And the hell of it is that I have been all along. What happened to John hurt like hell." He paused to gaze at Eb, his voice raw with emotion. "But what happened to Lizzy, I just don't know what to do with that."

The anguish and hopelessness that had settled into Sam was all encompassing. He wanted to fight it, to search for an escape from this deplorable person he'd become, but he couldn't muster up a glimmer of hope. Even placing some of the blame on J.D. didn't work this time. J.D. might have kept the truth from Sam, but what happened that night was his own doing—only his.

"You'll figure it out," Eb assured him. "It happened a long time ago, and Lizzy appears to have weathered it. You will, too. Just give it some time.

"And now I'm gonna go get supper on the table. I'll call you when it's ready."

The thought of food made him gag. "I'm not hungry. You go ahead and eat."

Eb's eyes searched Sam's. Deep worry lines etched his face.

"I need to be alone for a while," Sam murmured.

Eb pushed himself up out of the chair and seemed to waver momentarily before he caught his breath and shuffled off towards the kitchen.

Sam glanced at the half empty glass in his hand. He set it on an end table and settled deeper into his chair, clenching and unclenching his fists in an effort to release the emotional storm consuming him. If he managed to get himself through this, his life would never be the same again.

At least, it couldn't get any worse, could it?

CHAPTER 27

Gentle opalescent swells stretched out from the farmhouse porch as far as Lizzy could see, their icy surfaces glistening like rhinestones in the light cast by the nearly full moon, transforming the countryside into a thing of poignant beauty. She smiled, savoring the peaceful contentment that had clung to her throughout the day, and huddled deeper into her jacket, crossing her arms over her chest to warm her hands in her armpits.

At long last, her life had taken a turn for the better. Since the harrowing conversation with Sam that morning and her resulting meltdown, she was seeing through new eyes, eyes that were more clear and focused—less disturbed. He'd stomped out the door, and she'd sobbed uncontrollably for a half hour or so.

Then it was over. She'd sat on that sagging couch and felt as light as Grandma's meringue, finally free of the lies and guilt that had weighed on her. Gone were the self-loathing, the anger, and the fear that were a part of her every waking moment during the last twenty-five years.

She knew Sam didn't believe her; she didn't care. What he did with her revelation was up to him. She'd finally confronted him with the truth. That was what mattered. Now she no longer harbored the deep, dark secret, a constant reminder of the labels she'd allowed J.D. to nail to her so many years before.

Her thoughts slipped back to that wretched afternoon following her grandparents' funeral. J.D. was agitated when he'd arrived at the farmhouse, even more intimidating than usual in his expensive black suit and boots, his temper piercing her with cruel and hurtful accusations. He'd called her father a worthless nobody, then had laughed and told Lizzy that she was following in his footsteps. He'd blamed her for her grandparents' deaths, and he'd called her every demeaning name he could think of—slut, tramp, whore.

Shocked by his claims and grieving the loss of her grandparents, Lizzy had let him do it. She now realized that some part of her had taken it all in and believed J.D.'s horrid allegations.

Finally, she saw the truth: J.D. feared that she would contact

Sam. He'd lashed out in any way he could to keep her away from the ranch and Sam. If he'd only asked, she would've told him that she'd wasted enough time waiting around for Sam, that she had no intention of ever seeing or speaking to his precious son again.

The crunch of tires on ice and the soft purr of an engine drew Lizzy back to the frozen farmyard. Someone was driving by. Curious, she watched the glow of headlights light up the road and slowly turn into the farmyard. The night's serenity quickly fled, and her nerves pulsed with alarm. Blinded by the bright headlights, she measured the distance to the kitchen door and stood her ground.

The red jeep she'd noticed on her first visit to the ranch slid to a stop in front of her. She released her pent-up breath, a stream of fog shooting from her mouth. At least it wasn't Sam. But what was Eb doing out alone on a night like this? It was nearly midnight.

Lizzy shuffled cautiously down the icy steps and reached the vehicle just as Eb slid from it. He was bundled in so many layers of clothing that it was difficult to tell where the clothing ended and he began.

"You should be home in bed," Lizzy scolded as she grabbed onto his upper arm to support his tentative progress towards the farmhouse.

"So should you," he said in a shaky voice.

"I stepped outside for a few minutes to enjoy the view," she informed him, helping him up the steps. "Be careful; they're slick."

Lizzy tugged Eb into the warm house. His face was pale, his eyes anxious. He stood quietly, as if in a daze, so frail-looking that she nudged him into the living area and pushed him down into a rocker after pulling it closer to the fire.

"I'm going to make you a cup of hot tea. You sit here and thaw out," she told him before she rushed to the kitchen to heat some water.

"What is it, Eb?" she implored after they were both settled in front of the roaring fire and sipping their tea.

Eb gazed at her, his face a study in misery. "Sam," he murmured.

Lizzy fought a panicky feeling. Determined to keep fear from her voice, she probed, "Did something happen to him?"

"No, but he's havin' a difficult time."

Relief rushed through her, and concern. "He talked with you, huh? Did you tell him the truth?"

Eb sighed as if he carried the weight of this whole sorry mess on his bowed shoulders. "Yeah, I told him everything." His voice sounded so weary and forlorn.

"Did he believe you?" she asked hesitantly, apprehension making each breath a chore. She wasn't sure why it was important, but it was.

"Yeah, he believed me," he informed her, then added, "but he ain't dealin' with it too well. He just sits and stares into space. Wouldn't even eat supper. I'm worried about him. I'm not sure he'll get through this without some help from you. He doesn't remember anything about that night."

"I know," she told him. Then the reason for Eb's midnight mission punched her in the gut. "You want me to talk with him?" she gasped, leaning forward in alarm.

Eb nodded, his eyes pleading.

Lizzy sat for several moments, staring into her tea as if the leaves might materialize and tell her what to do. On the one hand, she reveled in the knowledge that she was finally released from Sam. On the other hand, though some dark part of her wanted Sam to suffer as much as she had, she was worried about him.

And she now realized that she, too, was responsible for what had happened. She'd known of J.D.'s propensity to lie when it worked to his advantage, yet she'd chosen to believe him instead of contacting Sam for more reliable answers. Perhaps, like Sam, she'd taken the easy route.

But how would Sam respond if she marched in tonight and insisted that they rehash this mess? If the events of early morning were any indication, not well.

❀ ❀ ❀

Lizzy's eyes didn't budge from the narrow, icy passage in front of her. If she concentrated hard enough, she could see the glazed road in the marginal light from her headlights. Even with her Explorer in four-wheel drive, she was sliding up and down the rolling hills that dotted the backcountry.

She squinted into the sea of ivory and rethought her decision to be behind the wheel, but she couldn't let Eb drive back to the ranch. Her eyes flicked to the passenger seat, a quick check. He still looked like a sudden sneeze would blow him over. He gazed straight ahead, his tired, old face shadowed with worry.

The last few hours had been wearing on him—actually, more like the last twenty-five years. Eb had carried the same secrets she had. For a quarter century he'd hauled around her burden. It had surely been a guilt-ridden task, especially after Sam returned to manage the ranch.

Lizzy sensed it—a tightening in her gut and a melancholic mood dive—before she realized they were climbing that last fateful hill before they reached the ranch. Memories of that long ago stormy night filtered through her mind. She supposed they'd always be here, ingrained in the soil and the bushes and the very air she breathed.

She felt Eb's eyes on her and turned a brief smile of reassurance his way. "Sam'll be okay," she assured him.

"I hope so," he murmured.

When they pulled up to the ranch house, all was quiet—a frosty winter postcard shimmering softly in the amber glow from yard lights. Anxious jitters unsettled Lizzy. What in the world was she going to say to Sam?

After supporting Eb into the kitchen, Lizzy took his coat and boots and in a soft but insistent voice shooed him off to bed. She watched his hunched form tackle the top step before her gaze slid to the living room. Was Sam still in there?

"Only one way to find out," she whispered, stretching her head high and steeling her shoulders, just as she had on that long ago day when Rose had answered the ranch house door and challenged her. That was the day she'd invited herself into the Craigs' life. Somehow, it seemed fitting that she finish what she'd started. Drawing a deep breath, she stepped forward.

Sam was a murky silhouette in the darkened room. He sat in what must be his chair, his long legs extended and eyes facing a spattering of dying coals. Lizzy walked to the pile of firewood beside the fireplace and grabbed several chunks and a sheet of newspaper. She knelt on the hearth and crumpled the paper onto the coals. Then she carefully piled the wood around the paper. Soon flames licked the paper and encircled the logs, melting the pitch that oozed from them.

Lizzy felt like she'd eaten a bowl of night crawlers, and now they were having a heyday, wiggling and twisting inside her, dividing and growing and consuming her strength. She swallowed at the ache in her throat, then stood and turned to study Sam.

Eb was right; Sam wasn't handling this well at all. He stared into the fire as if she wasn't standing in front of him shaking in her boots. His jaw was set, and his hands gripped the chair arms as if he were seated in a plummeting plane. Even his dark hair was disturbed, sections of it standing on end where his fingers had streaked through it.

Fearful that her legs would fold, she slid into the other chair. It felt oddly familiar. She told herself to relax and wait; when he was ready, they would talk. So they sat, each of them in their own chair, staring into the hypnotic flames.

The sudden crackling pop of exploding pitch startled Lizzy. Her eyes flicked to Sam. His remained on the fire.

"What are you doing here, Lizzy?" he asked, his voice husky with emotion.

"I'm here to help," she cautiously answered.

"I don't want your help. I have to work this out myself," he argued, though not very forcefully.

Well, too bad. She was here now and wouldn't leave until they'd reached some resolution. She stiffened her spine and forged onward. "This is something we have to work out together. It involves both of us. It's not just about you; it's about me, too . . . and our son."

He turned towards her, and his tormented eyes locked with hers. "Oh, God!" he breathed. "I'm so sorry, Lizzy. Will you ever be able to forgive me?" Then he buried his face in his hands.

Lizzy didn't hear sobs, but she knew that in his own way, he was crying. It wrenched her heart. She threw caution aside and pried herself out of the chair to cross the short distance and cradle the back of his head in her hands. Pulling him close against her chest, she ran her hands through his disheveled hair, wanting to comfort him and fighting the tears that pooled in her eyes. His trembling became a part of hers. Finally, his arms slid around her to pull her even closer. Drowning in an emotional whirlpool, time froze for Lizzy.

Gradually, she felt Sam relax and the tremors that had raked them both subside. His arms loosened; hers did, too.

As she stepped back, he grabbed her hands. "You don't hate me?" he murmured.

Lizzy met his probing gaze, and an encompassing serenity washed through her. The heat from the fire melted her even further. "I never, ever hated you, Sam," she informed him. "I wanted to so badly, but I couldn't. I still remember the first time I saw you. Grandma had given me a washtub full of peas, and I was sitting on the front porch shelling them. You were talking with Granddad. I couldn't take my eyes off of you. I was too young to even be thinking about such things, but I knew right then that one day I would marry you. I guess I convinced myself that was the way it was gonna be.

"Even after that . . . unfortunate night, when I felt so confused and betrayed, I still thought we would end up together. After that, I drove into town every day to check the post office box, certain each time that there'd be a letter waiting there from you, a letter telling me how much you loved me and how you couldn't live without me. Of course, there wasn't. I was hurt and humiliated and angry. I spent hours plotting how I was going to get revenge. But I didn't ever hate you . . . and I don't now." The truth inherent in that last statement shocked her.

"If I'd known about it, I would've been there with you," he insisted, his voice soft, full of supplication.

"I know that now," she acknowledged. "Actually, it helped when I figured out that you were totally oblivious to pretty much everything that went on around here while you were gone. The worst part was the wondering—how could you not know what happened that night . . . or know about the baby? All of those years of thinking you did know and . . . didn't care. I didn't understand how you could treat me like that. I thought you detested me."

He shook his head. "I don't remember any of it. When I think back, there's nothing. I remember eating dinner with Dad and Rose and Chet, and I remember walking with Chet to his truck afterward. But after that . . . I don't even remember when Chet dropped me off here at the house."

Lizzy did, as if it had happened only minutes ago. "Great friend he is. He shoved you out of the truck and drove off."

"And you were there?"

Lizzy pulled her hands free, her fingers tingling with the need to feel his touch again. Instead, she retreated to the safety of her chair. She sighed back into the plush softness, contemplating how to answer him. He surely had a right to know what had happened that night, and she was the only person who could tell him. It was just that it was so complicated, and it dredged up a slew of debilitating feelings that she avoided. In truth, because of those feelings, she'd never sorted through the ill-fated incident. Now she gazed into Sam's troubled eyes and knew she owed him an attempt.

"I was getting into the Buick when Chet drove up and pushed you out of his truck." She chose to skip the disgusting remark Chet had made before he'd gunned the motor and sped off. "You were swaying, and your words were kind of slurry. I grabbed onto you and was trying to get you to the house. Only you were set on going to the barn. Finally, you pulled free and headed off on your own."

Lizzy paused to think about what she'd just said. He had been surprisingly steady on his feet. In fact, he'd made it to the barn door before she decided it might be wise to keep an eye on him and had then run to catch up.

"And?"

She shook her wayward thoughts aside. How much should she tell him? No doubt, it was time for the truth—all of it. She closed her eyes briefly to muster up some fortitude. "I caught up with you in the tack room. You were determined to go for one last ride before you left the ranch. I insisted that you weren't riding anywhere in the shape you were in."

The memory flashed back, a bittersweet rush that left her breathless. He'd grabbed his saddle from its tree, staggering with the weight of it as he turned towards her. She'd caught him, the saddle clamped between their bodies and their eyes locked, his filled with a sad longing that drew her closer. The saddle had fueled their fire, both of them clinging to that solid barrier, too stubborn and determined to let go of it. It had seemed so natural when they finally did come together. Lizzy felt the raw emotion of it as if it were happening all over again. Her body shook, and stinging tears blurred her vision.

"Since you refused to give up your saddle, I tried to hold onto it and help you along, hoping you'd carry that saddle all the way back to the house and not realize where you were going. Truth is, we didn't make it out of the barn." She laughed softly and smiled, rubbing the pressure between her brows as she fought tears. "It was really kind of—I don't know—funny because you were so big and it was so awkward, and we kept falling down, and we were laughing about it. I guess we just fell down one time too many."

Curiosity replaced the anguish that had twisted his features. "Is that what happened? We fell down?"

"Yeah." Warmth blossomed in her cheeks with the memory of the languorous, yet impassioned, feel of his body settling over hers as their lips met, the saddle now discarded and forgotten. She faced the fire to escape his unsettling gaze. "Only that time you kissed me. You'd kissed me the night before, so I thought it would be okay. I was wrong."

"Why's that?"

Lizzy's heart reeled. She struggled to remain calm. "Well . . . you know, Sam," she floundered, turning to look at him, "I'm not even sure I understand what happened except that things got out of hand very quickly. And then it was over."

He leaned forward, his arms resting on his thighs and a puzzled frown etched on his face. "So that's how it happened?"

Lizzy was tentative. He seemed more relaxed, causing her to wonder what kinds of awful scenarios he'd concocted in his head. Her eyes searched the darkened corners of the room for words to help him understand. "You see, I'd never actually . . . had much experience before that night, so I didn't realize where things were heading until it was too late. I didn't know what you had in mind."

"Lizzy, I was drunk out of my mind. My body was doing all the thinking," he informed her in a weary voice.

She studied his face, her stomach churning, begging him to understand. "I know that now, but at the time, I didn't realize that. I remember feeling confused because in some ways, you acted drunk at times, but you didn't smell like alcohol, not like John did when he'd been drinking. When you kissed me, you seemed fine, and it felt right, like it was meant to be. But then . . . we didn't stop."

Overwhelmed with an intense surge of emotions, Lizzy closed her eyes and fought to silence her shaking limbs. She felt it again— the pain, the confusion, and the desire to scream. She'd closed her eyes and stuck her fist into her mouth to stay quiet, her teeth leaving bloody marks across her knuckles. She hadn't wanted Sam to get into trouble.

Then just like that, all had been still, as if Sam had evaporated into the warm summer air. Lizzy had opened her eyes and met his. What she saw in those eyes had driven icy spikes into her heart.

He'd glared at her as if she were an evil witch who'd cast a horrible spell over him. His face had said it all; he loathed the sight of her and was appalled by what had just transpired. He'd struggled to his feet and, just like at the dance the previous night, he'd strode away, this time staggering a bit.

Then ever so slowly, Lizzy had pushed herself into a dark corner and drawn her legs up under the full skirt of her soiled sundress to wrap her arms around her knees, sobs racking her body.

"Lizzy?"

Weakened by her memories, Lizzy glanced up.

"Did I force you?" He looked as sick as she felt.

She shrugged, then shook her head. "No, it wasn't like that. Afterward, I was so upset . . . and so alone. You didn't say anything to me, just looked at me like I was a filthy piece of trash. Then you got up and left me there. I didn't know what to do. I was so frightened and . . . ashamed." Tears trickled down her cheeks, and she fought to get those emotions from so many years ago under control. She was here to help Sam, not to make him feel worse.

Sam leaned forward, as if reaching out to her. He studied her, his face a mirror of the gut-wrenching emotions engulfing her. "Lizzy, there's no way I can ever make up to you for what I did. I know that. But you have to know that I'm not the kind of person who would intentionally do something like that. I'm not a heavy drinker— never have been. I don't know what happened that night. I don't remember drinking. Hell, I don't remember anything about that night!"

He rubbed his forehead, then eyed her, his hands folded as if in prayer. "I don't know if you'll ever be able to forgive me. I hope you will, but I'll understand if you don't. I do want you to know how sorry I am that I treated you so badly. Then I took off and left you to deal with the consequences. I'm sorry for that, too."

Yes, she had dealt with it all, the shame and humiliation that had only grown worse once she discovered that Sam had deserted her and left her pregnant. In desperation, she'd turned to her grandparents for help. That selfish mistake had cost them their lives. Lizzy had added their deaths to her already overburdened conscience and had faced the future disgraced and alone. J.D.'s visit to the farm following her grandparents' funeral had cemented the fact that she was a detestable person.

Now she faced Sam, those old feelings swirling around inside her and knew it was time to let it all go. He searched her face, his eyes pleading for understanding. Ever so slowly, she nodded. "I know you didn't mean for any of this to happen. I'm sorry, too. I'm sorry that things turned out as they did. And I'm sorry I didn't trust you enough to come to you instead of listening to J.D. He told me you didn't want to see me. That you said I was a disgrace to both of our families."

A pained expression crossed Sam's face.

"It's okay. I know you didn't say that. And I know you wouldn't intentionally hurt me."

He nodded. It was as if the engulfing torrent of emotions had drained right out of him. Now he looked battle-worn, the firelight playing on his weary features.

When he spoke, Lizzy felt his exhaustion. "I don't remember drinking much alcohol, but I must've. After we ate dinner, Mel brought us a bottle of champagne. I don't like the stuff, so I only drank a few sips. But I must've made up for it later. Strange though; the only thing I remember is walking to Chet's truck." Concern knitted his brows before he added, "So how are you doing with this now?"

It caught Lizzy unawares. It wasn't like Sam to ask about her feelings. Touched by it, tears stung her eyes. In case he misinterpreted their source, she quickly blurted, "I just want this to be over. Remember in your truck when I said that I wanted to get rid of the hurt and have some peace in my life? Well, I meant it. Finally, I don't feel all of that guilt and hurt dragging me down, tearing me apart. The past is gone, and I want to leave it there. I can't change it, and I won't let it control my future any longer."

"Do you really mean that, or are you just saying it to make me feel better?"

"It's over!" she asserted. "And besides, in retrospect, I now see that I was probably as much to blame as you for what happened that night. I was a young girl with a young girl's dreams. I didn't want it to happen, and I didn't particularly like it, but I suppose I had . . . wondered about it . . . and you. I mean, a part of me wanted to know." Her cheeks were blazing. "I could've stopped you; I didn't. I guess you'd call it blind trust. That's why I was so hurt when you left me there like that—then you didn't call me the next morning or even write to me—because I'd trusted you.

She sighed deeply and searched his troubled eyes before she smiled and added, "You know, something good did come out of all of this."

That got his attention. "What's that?"

She smiled again. "Well, actually two things. First, you have a son," she reminded him. "And I know I'm his mother, but he really is an exceptional young man."

"A son," he marveled, a wary smile touching his lips. "I've always wanted a son . . . and now I have one."

She nodded, savoring the look of wonder on his face. "And the other thing is that you don't have to move your cows off my land now."

He frowned.

"My sons will be here for a visit the first week of April," she informed him. The legal document Eb had given her barged into her thoughts. "That is, I hope they will."

He nodded in understanding and pushed himself up out of his chair. Lizzy watched, fascinated, as he stretched his arms, arching the kinks from his back. How many times had she watched their son go through those exact motions?

"I'm going to be a part of his life now. You do realize that?" he told her.

Lizzy's heart hitched. It seemed that each time she jumped over a hurdle, another one was there waiting for her. She had finally come to terms with her past. Hopefully, their son would, too.

CHAPTER 28

As he looked out over his land, peace and contentment flowed through Sam, a warm glow that seeped into the nooks and crannies of his mind and body. It was something he'd missed for a long time, though he hadn't been aware of its absence until it was again a living, breathing part of him. Fearing that it might be transitory, he sideswiped analyzing these new feelings in any depth.

It wasn't that his life had been bad. It'd just been . . . well, flat. He'd been living one day at a time, doing what needed to be done to get through each day, his focus on the ranch—his responsibility. The days had blurred together into seasons and the seasons into years, and he'd lost track of those years since they were all pretty much the same.

Now he had something by which he could delineate his life; he had a son. The path he'd taken to attain that son was paved with guilt and shame—the pain and suffering of others. Forgiveness wasn't an easy thing for him to accept, but to heal, he had to come to terms with his life for what it was, then move on.

He knew any self-inflicted punishment he chose to bestow upon himself now wouldn't change what had happened. Still, knowing it was one thing, and letting go of it was another. He'd reached the conclusion that guilt was a mighty tenacious creature.

Of course, the upturn in his life had much to do with Lizzy. He wasn't sure how he was going to handle that fact. For now, she was giving him the distance he'd requested—time to sort it all out and settle into it. Hopefully, when the time was right, things would fall into place.

In the meantime, he derived a certain amount of pleasure from the knowledge that Lizzy Stewart lived a few hills over, and soon their son would visit his mother.

As the sun's rays blossomed over the eastern horizon, Sam lolled in his saddle at the top of the hill, feasted his eyes on the majestic sunrise, and dreamed about that day and what it might foretell.

❀ ❀ ❀

It promised to be one of those days when spring, though still waking and not quite ready to join in the festivities, peeked around the corner and reached out a warm hand to touch the spirits of those in its path. Lizzy had awakened with the knowledge of it, a glowing wave coursing through her veins and arousing her senses to the promises that lay ahead. The anticipation of a glorious sunrise had drawn her to the cemetery, and to John. It was a morning that was sculpted for him, the sun sneaking into the day, its presence betrayed by the rosy flush that brightened the eastern sky.

Lizzy zipped her jacket against the early morning chill and filled a tin can with water from the bottle she'd brought with her. Then she pulled out a handful of sunny daffodils from a bucket and dropped them into the can. She'd cut the flowers from the shimmering sea of yellow that had magically appeared in the dreary farmyard several days before. A plentiful bunch was already nesting with her grandparents, their cloying fragrance muted by the soft breeze that whispered amongst the gravestones.

Kneeling beside John's grave, she trailed fingertips through the dew on his ivory headstone, surprised by the stone's coldness, and wondered if it would ever be warmed by the sun's rays. Her fingers wandered over to his mother's memorial to trace the familiar letters of her own name—*Elizabeth*. Someday, maybe someone would do the same in her memory.

"I brought you some daffodils," she whispered to John. "They've taken over Grandma's yard. I thought they might cheer you up. Not that you need cheered up, do you? Honestly, I don't know, John. I want to think of you as being at peace, but I just don't know."

She dropped onto her seat, crossed her legs in front of her, and pondered her words. Had John really decided to end his life? While she didn't want to believe it was true, in the past few weeks nothing had materialized that would indicate otherwise. Sure, there were some unsettling hints that all was not right: John's letter, the diary page, the missing journals, the notes from the cuckoo clock and her front door, the vehicle that had followed her, and the slaughtered cow. The problem was that they might be tied to John's death, or they could be a result of her return to the farm. Then again, their malevolence might be only a product of her overactive imagination.

Whatever the case, she was beating her head against a concrete wall. She'd questioned everyone who'd been close to John— except Junior, of course. Nothing. She'd even spent a day at the county library perusing newspaper accounts of his death, only to confirm what Eb had told her.

The last person to see John had been Chet. He'd watched

John trot from the ranch on the back of Lilac, the horse John had raised from a young filly. His bulging saddlebags were strapped on behind his saddle—Lizzy wondered about that—so no one at the ranch had worried when he didn't show up for dinner. The next morning, Eb noticed Lilac nibbling on the dead lawn and ran to investigate. The saddle and saddlebags were still strapped to Lilac's back. Her bridle was gone. A search party was organized. Of course, Eb knew where to look, so he was the one who'd found the missing bridle at the top of the rimrock and John's body at the bottom. They figured he'd died not long after he'd left the ranch.

Lizzy's thoughts turned to the mess the buzzards had made of that cow's carcass, and her stomach heaved. "Poor Eb," she breathed.

So John had been headed to Eagles' Nest that morning. She eyed his gravestone. "But what was in your saddlebags?" she murmured. A lunch and a thermos of coffee? A Book? Maybe something to spread on the cold, wet ground? Lilac had returned with empty saddlebags.

"Did you meet someone up there? Were you running from someone—hiding something? Or was it just you, all alone, seeking peace in the wrong place?"

Lizzy sighed deeply. Maybe it was time to let it go? A few more weeks, and her sons would be here for a visit. By then, she needed resolution.

"I wish you were sitting here beside me, so you could explain it to me. Whatever happened, I'd try to understand. I would've come back. You know that, don't you?" Lizzy listened for an answer she knew would never come.

Her eyes flicked J.D.'s grandiose burial ground and the wasted space that separated it from John's. If his burial plot was any indication, John's last days had not been good. Had John been buried any closer to the fence, he'd be outside the Craig family plot—not that he would care. Still, if Rose, who had no Craig blood running through her veins, rested in prime acreage, John surely deserved some, too.

"I might have to leave the farm soon," she muttered, her thoughts turning to another of J.D.'s plots—the document designed to keep Sam's son from him. In the end, J.D.'s plan had failed. There was some joy in that.

"I came here to tell you about Sam. He knows about everything now. The sad thing is that he didn't know about any of it. I really blew it, John. If I hadn't been such a coward, I would've talked with Sam. Then I would've stayed here, and maybe you'd still be alive. We all let J.D. control our lives, didn't we—you, me, and Sam?"

Sensing Sam's presence, Lizzy's heart began a restless patter. She glanced around, then searched up at Eagles' Nest. Sometimes lately, she'd been aware that Sam was nearby, but except for a few fleeting chance conversations, she'd seen little of him during the past few weeks. It was probably a good thing; she was struggling with a familiar aching need to be near him. It scared the heck out of her.

Her mind traveled back to that harrowing night at the ranch. She and Sam had ended up in the kitchen, eating peanut butter and jelly sandwiches and discussing their son. He'd looked her intently in the eyes and requested time to deal with all the information and quandaries that had been thrown at him lately.

A soft, invasive sound interrupted Lizzy's ponderings. "Anyway, that's how things are right now," she whispered hurriedly before she turned to see who was encroaching on her solitude.

A woman stood by the Craig entrance, her brassy hair piled high against the sunrise and a huge bouquet of vibrant flowers cradled in her arms. Lizzy froze, awestruck, wondering what in the world *she* was doing here.

"Mornin', Lizzy," the woman greeted her. "You're certainly an early riser. I'm usually the only one out here this time of morning."

All Lizzy could do was gape—her mouth hanging open, speechless—while she watched Mel step to J.D.'s atrocious tomb. Mel replaced a bunch of dried flowers with a garish array of brilliant blossoms, a flamboyant display when compared to her own humble handful of daffodils. Why anyone would bring J.D. Craig even one scrawny weed was beyond her understanding.

"Do you come here often?" Lizzy inquired tentatively, curious as to why Mel would make regular visits all the way from town to such an isolated cemetery.

"I try to make it once a week. It's hard to get away, so I come early." She smiled and shrugged. "But come spring, J.D. has to have his flowers. I wouldn't put it past him to pop right up out of his grave and demand an accounting if I stopped bringing them."

Lizzy pulled herself to her feet and faced Mel, curiosity overcoming the manners instilled within her. "Mel, I'm sorry, but you've lost me. Why do you bring J.D. flowers?"

Mel's carefully penciled eyebrows rose an inch or so while her determined chin dropped. Her eyes challenged further prying. Lizzy steeled herself and didn't flinch, eyeballing Mel over Elizabeth Craig's grave.

Like an over inflated balloon, air rushed from Mel's mouth before she spoke. "As you well know, sometimes things aren't exactly what they appear to be."

Mel gave her an inquisitive look, and Lizzy hesitantly nodded in understanding. Funny; John had mentioned that exact same quandary in his letter?

"Well, I guess you might say that's the way it was with J.D. and me. Although we might've appeared to be just friends, our relationship was a bit more . . . complicated."

"You were lovers?" Lizzy blurted derisively before she caught herself. The idea of Mel sharing an intimate relationship with J.D. was bizarre and disgusting. J.D. didn't deserve Mel—no way. Her eyes flitted to the grave at her feet. And where did John's mother fit into this threesome?

Mel frowned, then shrugged it off. "Yes, we were lovers, but it was much more than that. I know how much you disliked J.D., and I know you have your reasons. But there was more to J.D. than what you saw. He had his reasons for what he did. You might not agree with them, but he did what he did because he thought he had to."

"J.D. had to control everything and everyone. He didn't care who he took down in the process," Lizzy snapped, glaring at the black monument he'd erected in his memory. Bitter bile burned in her throat at the mere thought of all he'd done.

"Yes, he did like to be the one in control. I guess that's one of the things I admired about him, the way he'd take control of a situation," Mel admitted, reaching out to stroke the massive black stone. Her thoughts appeared to drift elsewhere. Finally, she turned to Lizzy and added, "But I do see how it played against you . . . with John and Sam and the baby. And then there was that thing with your father."

Mel's words silenced Lizzy. Evidently, Mel was privy to the whole menagerie of dirty little secrets and lies and a whole lot more—like one that concerned her father. Nervous flutters came to life inside Lizzy. "What about my father?" she murmured.

"You don't know?" Mel asked, clearly stunned.

Lizzy hesitated, dread urging her to leave it be. She cautiously shook her head.

"Hmmm. I thought Con or Dottie or Skip, or even Eb, would've told you."

Lizzy shook her head again, fearful that if she opened her mouth, she'd tell Mel to keep it to herself.

Mel seemed to mull it over, her lips twisting erratically, before she finally spoke. "We all grew up together—Skip and J.D. and Elizabeth, and me . . . and Rose and Eb, too. Skip and J.D. spent a lot of time together, living next to each other and all. They didn't get along all that well, both of them being so headstrong and full of themselves."

Mel paused, her eyes focused past Lizzy, no doubt lost in another time. Lizzy waited.

"Your father wasn't as bad as people made him out to be. He just had a lot of spirit, and he liked to have a good time. It was fine when he was younger, but as he got older, it didn't sit well with J.D. I think J.D. just got tired of picking up the pieces for Skip, and he didn't like being mixed up in the messes that seemed to follow Skip wherever he went. And there was Elizabeth—Sam and John's mother and, no doubt, your namesake."

With that, Mel's eyes dropped to the coral gravestone. Lizzy reached out to touch it, whether to reassure John's mother or herself she didn't know.

"Elizabeth was the only person who really had a handle on Skip. The two of them were close and growing closer the older they got. I've often thought that if they'd stayed together, Skip would've been okay."

So that was why she and John's mother shared a name. Lizzy had always wondered about that. If her father had loved Elizabeth enough to name his daughter after her, why didn't he marry her?

Remorse blossomed on Mel's face. "The problem was J.D. He wanted Elizabeth, not because he loved her, but because Skip had her—and because Elizabeth was the kind of woman he wanted for his wife. Her family had money and prestige. Elizabeth was beautiful and sophisticated, with style and grace and the fancy clothes to go with it all."

"What about you?" Lizzy asked, aware of the pain Mel must have felt.

"Me?" Mel chuckled softly. "As far as J.D. was concerned, I wasn't marrying material. Don't look so worried. I made peace with that fact a long time ago. J.D. knew I'd always be there, whether he married me or not. No matter what, I loved him. When it comes right down to it, that's what love's all about. The fact is I saw a lot more of him that his wife did.

"Anyway, J.D. wanted Elizabeth, and he could see that things weren't going to work out that way with Skip around. I don't know the whole story of what happened, but just like that, Skip took off. We all knew J.D.'d played a part in his going. J.D. should've been upset about Skip leaving. Instead, he strutted around like a cock in the henhouse for weeks after that. And as usual, he got what he wanted—Elizabeth." Mel paused, than added, "Only, once he got her, he didn't want her."

Lizzy's heart went out to the woman who lay at her feet and shared her name. She understood what her life had been like living with a man who viewed her as an object, not a person. Appraising the large gap between Elizabeth's grave and her husband's, she said a silent prayer of thanks that John's mother had been spared J.D.'s direct presence in death, at least.

Mel chuckled, interrupting Lizzy's ruminations. "Leave it to Skip to have the last laugh, though. When it comes to smarts, J.D. wasn't even in the same ballpark as your dad."

"What do you mean?"

"Your dad . . . Skip. He's buried right over there on the other side of that fence," Mel informed her, nodding in that general direction.

Stunned, Lizzy stared at Mel, struggling to put meaning to Mel's words. Then she spun around and circled John's grave to reach the fence. A rather plain gravestone lay as close to the iron posts as it could be placed. She could barely make out the inscription on its weather-mottled surface: *John Conner Stewart, born 9-15-29, died 2-15-74.*

"I didn't know my father's name was John," she murmured to no one in particular, her heart beating erratically.

Mel must have heard her. "Yeah. It was John Conner, same as your grandfather's. When he was just a little tike, they started calling him Skip because he never slowed down and was always bouncing around, like a skipping stone. Somehow, it stuck."

Something else bothered her about her father's inscription. She glanced down at John's grave to confirm her suspicion, then felt the blood drain from her brain. Grabbing onto the fence for support, she murmured. "Mel, John and my father died within a few days of each other. Don't you think that's odd?"

Mel hustled over to have a look. "What are you talking about?" she asked, checking both of the dates herself. Then, except for the bright blotches of scarlet she'd brushed onto her cheeks and slathered on her lips, Mel's face turned a sickly, ashen hue.

"What is it," Lizzy demanded.

Mel shook her head as if to rid herself of an unpleasant thought. "Oh . . . nothing. It must be a coincidence. I wasn't sure exactly when your father was buried. I do remember when J.D. noticed the headstone. He was fit-to-be-tied when he saw Skip was buried there. J.D. tried to get him moved, but it was Skip's space fair and square, so they wouldn't move him. Me, I thought Skip had a right to be buried next to his son and the woman he loved."

So her father did continue to love Elizabeth.

Like a streak of lightning, Mel's words struck Lizzy and stunned her. If her father had a son, then she must have a brother. Like a crazy hummingbird, her eyes darted around, searching for his grave.

Then realization hit her, and she fought the waves of nausea reaching up to strangle her. "John is my brother!" she gasped to anyone alive enough to hear, knowing in her heart she was right. "He was named after Granddad . . . after my father; not J.D."

With that knowledge, her world flew apart. She gazed down in wonder at the puzzle that lay before her, each jagged piece fitted snuggly into its rightful place. She thought of the photo she'd found in Granddad's book and the familiar sensation she'd felt that day in the barnyard when she'd first looked into John's eyes. Then there was Sam's son; was it any wonder he looked so much like John?

Lightheaded and gasping for air, she sank down onto her knees and buried her face in her hands.

Why did her father do it—he'd dropped her off and told her to take care of John but had neglected to inform her that John was her brother? If she'd known the truth, she would never have left John with J.D., an abusive man who wasn't even his father. She should've taken him away with her. She should've saved him—her own brother.

And why hadn't she seen it? It all made so much sense, yet she'd remained oblivious. Day after day, she'd watched it unfold—Sam, the perfect son, and John, the son who could do nothing to please the man who *wasn't* his father. John, the son who resembled his real father.

She rubbed at the throbbing in her temples and looked up. "J.D. knew?" she muttered to a watchful Mel.

Mel nodded. "Oh, yeah. He knew. Not at first but later. Although, why we all didn't figure it out sooner is beyond me. John was nothing like J.D. and a whole lot like Skip.

"In the months before John's death, Skip was spotted around town. Then the day before John's funeral, one of those big wreaths arrived at the funeral parlor with the word "SON" plastered across it. It was from Skip. J.D. threw a royal fit and threw what was left of the flowers into the garbage. He realized what Skip was telling him. He knew it was true."

Mel eyed John's grave and shook her head. "Even though the hole was already dug, J.D. wanted to bury John somewhere else. It was Eb who put his foot down and insisted John be buried here. I'd never seen Eb like that before, and I haven't since. He actually threatened J.D. Told him he'd tell Sam about the baby if John wasn't buried right here beside his mother."

She sighed. "And that's about that. So yes, John is your half brother. Skip and John had been seen together, so I thought it was what John wrote you about in that letter. I'm surprised you didn't figure it out."

"So am I," Lizzy agreed, reliving the strange feelings of *déjà vu* she and John had shared. Hadn't John even mentioned it in his letter? And Eb had known, too. It seemed that Eb was the caretaker of many secrets.

So John and her father had spoken. Then they had died only days apart. It seemed like a strange coincidence, one that sent unsettling twitters through Lizzy.

Thoughts of the letter ignited another question: "You knew about the letter?"

Mel chewed at the red on her lips and eyed Lizzy speculatively. "Nelda Johnson brought me the letter—you went to high school with her. Well, she works at the drug store now, and she found it on the floor in the makeup aisle and thought I'd know what to do with it. I almost threw it away. Then I figured it was from John, so it was probably something you needed to read. But I had another reason, too"

"Oh?"

"I wanted you to come back. I've been worried about Sam. Each year, he gets more gloomy—seems to pull into himself, like a grouchy old snapping turtle. Then Gina Riley suddenly zeroed in on him, and I was afraid of how that might end. She's got the looks and cunning to snag him and will do pretty much whatever it takes to get what she wants. Sam's been so lonely. He deserves a little happiness. I was hoping . . . well . . . never mind." Her cheeks blossomed.

Lizzy's cheeks blossomed, too. She sideswiped Mel's hopes to get some answers. "Why didn't you put your return address on the envelope?" she asked, perturbed that she still didn't know how the letter had gotten from Gus Woolridge's office to Clark's Drug Store.

"It wasn't from me. I was just the go-between. I suppose I could've given it to Sam or Eb. Anyway, I dropped it in the mailbox like it was; didn't mess with it at all."

A vision of Sam popped into Lizzy's head. How would he handle another new twist in his life? "Sam doesn't know about John?" she inquired, already knowing Mel's answer.

"I don't think so. After John was buried, J.D. never spoke of it again. He pretty much wiped John from his mind. That's why he didn't' notice Skip's grave until a long time after it'd been put there. He wouldn't even visit the cemetery until he realized he was dying and had me bring him out here to take a look at his own plot."

"Sam deserves to know the truth," Lizzy told her.

Mel sighed, her wrinkled face taking on a few more weary creases. "I suppose he does. As much as I don't want to do it, I'll take care of it when the right time comes along," she assured Lizzy. "And now I need to get back to town. Breakfast can't happen around there without me there to supervise it."

On impulse, Lizzy threw her arms around Mel and hugged her. "Thanks, Mel."

"Oh, anytime. If you want the dirt on anyone around here, I'm the one to come to. It's quite a responsibility, you know, carrying around everyone's secrets and deciding when it's time for them to be revealed." She laughed sardonically before adding, "Maybe I should write a book, huh? Clear my mind and conscience."

"Maybe you should, but I don't think anyone would believe any of it," Lizzy teased.

Mel chuckled and walked away into the brilliant, blinding orb that blazed above the eastern horizon, leaving J.D. and the rest of the Craigs—oh, and Rose—to enjoy the remainder of the morning in peace. Lizzy watched her slender form pass through the gate before she reached down to pull several of the daffodils from the cluster she'd given John. She touched his headstone and whispered, "Brother."

Then she laid several daffodils at the base of Elizabeth's elegant gravestone before she carried the remaining few to her father's humble resting place. Using the gloves and bottle of water, she scrubbed the dirt and grime from the weathered granite.

When it was relatively clean, she sat back on her heels, smiled, and whispered, "Way to go, Dad. You got him good."

CHAPTER 29

Sam gazed across the table at Mel, mulling over what she'd just told him. A worried frown pressed deeper creases into the wrinkles etched into her forehead, and she chewed what remained of a rather gaudy shade of lipstick off her lower lip.

Searching for clarity, his eyes traveled the room to where Junior and Franny were having a heated discussion. Franny looked like she wanted to throw her stack of dripping flapjacks at her scowling husband. Sam would've paid to see that.

He glanced down at his empty mug. When Mel had offered to buy him a cup of coffee, he'd had in mind that they would discuss something less thought-provoking, like the weather or how the fish were biting in the reservoir—maybe even the fact that Gina had finally moved on and now had her claws firmly embedded in Chet.

Thoughts of Gina drew his focus to a corner booth where she sipped tea and nibbled on a pile of fruit. One of the young hotshots from Gus Woolridge's law office sat across from her. She glanced Sam's way, and her sunny smile turned into a thunderhead. Then again, maybe she hadn't moved on.

"Are you okay?" Mel asked.

Sam eyed her and slowly nodded, hoping he really was all right. At the moment, he was surprisingly calm, almost numb. Could be it would hit him later.

Mel's news explained a lot of things Sam had often questioned, like why John was so different from him and why, when their mother died, John had been so much more devastated than Sam. The honest-to-God truth was that she had treated Sam different than she had treated John. Sam had known it and accepted it. Now he knew why: Sam was J.D.'s son, and she had barely tolerated J.D.

He set his jaw and ground his molars together with memories of his father's long absences. When his mother was alive, Sam had rarely seen his father, and he'd never seen his parents display affection towards each other. Actually, he'd suspected that his mother went out of her way to avoid being in the same room with J.D. Through it all, she'd maintained her composure and had been a loving, spirited woman.

When she'd chosen to end her life one cold winter day, Sam had been blindsided. He still didn't understand it. There had been no signs that it was coming—no depression nor sadness, no angry rages, no drugs nor alcohol. Nothing. Perhaps he was finally getting a glimpse inside his mother's secret life, the one that had pushed her over that edge.

Sam's not-so-pleasant reminiscences left a bitter taste in his mouth. He tried to swallow it away, to rid himself of the memories. He didn't want to confront the realities of his parents' dysfunctional marriage. To live through it the first time was bad enough. Thank goodness Eb had always been there for John and Sam—good old steadfast, dependable Eb.

"I'm fine," Sam assured Mel, silently wincing at the bitterness in his voice. "You knocked the wind out of me for a few minutes there, but I'll deal with it. So you and Dad had a thing then? Is that something hidden between the lines here?" he asked, knowing full well what her answer would be.

A scarlet blush swept into Mel's face. She nodded slowly and murmured, "Yeah, me and J.D. were together all along—since high school. I know it must hurt to know your dad was spending his time with me instead of you boys and your mother, but that's the way it was."

Hell, yes, it hurt! He glanced around the noisy diner and thought of his mother and her infidelities. She was probably thrilled that Mel kept her husband occupied. J.D. hadn't been a pleasant person. How had Mel tolerated him all of those years?

"If you could put up with him, you were welcome to him. It left less of him for us to enjoy," Sam uttered, doing little to hide his disgust.

"You've been through a lot lately, haven't you, Sam?" Mel's eyes were full of concern. It was almost Sam's undoing.

To still the agitation building inside him, he shifted his focus to Junior and Franny, who where still going at it. It didn't help. "My whole life has been turned upside down," he blurted, pausing to gulp the cold dregs in his mug. "What you've just told me amounts to sprinkles on the cake when you compare it to finding out that I let my little brother get shot up in a war in my place. Not only that, but I've laid claim to part of the blame for Con and Dottie's death and my brother's suicide. And on top of that, I treated Lizzy—a person I cared deeply about—like shit and then let someone else raise my son, a son I just recently learned about."

His spark of anger turned quickly into a fiery blaze. "Of course, you knew about all of that, didn't you, Mel? And you never once considered telling me any of it over a cup of coffee, did you?"

At least Mel had the courtesy to turn as rosy as the patches of rouge she'd swabbed onto her cheeks. She gripped her coffee mug, the bright pointed tips of her fingernails tapping a cadence on the creamy pottery. "Oh, I thought about it many times," she admitted. "But I couldn't. There were other people's lives involved in a decision like that. It wasn't mine to make."

Sam rubbed the ache in his forehead and fought to gain control over his unbridled emotions. Blaming Mel for something that wasn't her fault wouldn't appease his anger, nor his frustration. He sighed in resignation and contemplated the many lies and secrets and the tangled web they'd woven around everyone involved.

"Does Lizzy know about this?" he asked, worry snaking into his conscience.

A breath of relief rushed from him when Mel nodded. "Yeah, we were at the cemetery at the same time last week, and it all came out. She wanted you to know. I told her I'd tell you. She's turned into quite a woman."

Sam felt Mel's feline eyes probing. He'd tried his damnedest not to give too serious thought to the matter, knowing it would only complicate an already complicated situation. He hadn't determined how he and Lizzy were now related, but a romance with his brother's sister had a somewhat decadent ring to it.

Rather than look Mel in the eye and spill his guts, Sam studied his hands. "Yes, she did turn out to be quite a woman," he agreed evasively. "Con and Dottie would be proud of her."

"That's it?" Mel muttered.

Warmth suffused Sam's cheeks. He closed his eyes, struggling with the feelings that had become increasingly difficult to ignore. The hell with it! He lifted his lids and met Mel's speculative stare. "You think it's possible to pick up a relationship where you left it, even if you left it there a while back—a long while back?"

"Are we talking about Lizzy here?" Mel asked.

He nodded, then sighed in frustration. "I can't seem to get past the idea that I'd like to see more of her . . . in a romantic way."

"Have you told her?"

Mel's words sent Sam's heart racing. "Hell, no! I think she had an interest in me back then, but I've seen no signs that she does now. If anything, she has a passing tolerance for me."

Still, he'd carried this pestering infatuation around with him for a quarter century. The clock was ticking. If he was going to find closure—whatever the outcome—he needed to make a move soon. He didn't want her to slip away again.

"Well, how're you gonna know if you don't climb out on that brittle limb and mention it to her?" Mel pressed. Her fingernails tapping rhythmically on the table, she gave him a perceptive look. "Sam, I've watched you for more years than I want to count, trying out every woman for miles around and dropping them as soon as they flexed their talons. If you've finally found someone who holds your interest, don't let her slip through your fingers just because of that arrogant Craig pride you inherited from your daddy. You might not get another chance."

Sam pondered Mel's words, then sighed. "Maybe you're right. Maybe it is time I let her know how I feel. What I'm doing now sure isn't working." As soon as the words were out of his mouth, he wanted to retrieve them. No way was he going to bare his soul to Lizzy. Just the thought of it had him as spooked as a skittish gelding.

Still, he hadn't met a gelding that couldn't be tamed. If they could manage their fear, shouldn't he—a grown man—be able to manage his?

How would Lizzy react if he were to finally disclose his true feelings towards her? Maybe it was time to find out.

❀ ❀ ❀

Lizzy was on a mission, and nothing was going to stop her. For weeks, she'd thrown things into the spare bedroom. Today she was mucking it out.

Even if she decided to take heed of J.D.'s threat and meet her sons elsewhere during spring break, she wanted the room to be ready for them. The thought of being J.D.'s guinea pig stuck in her craw, and she wouldn't surrender to it unless she had no other choice. She had two weeks to get this last room scrubbed and painted and to set up the beds she'd ordered. She also had two weeks to decide how she'd handle J.D. this time.

As she sifted through the stacks of junk, she sorted things into piles. Every window and door in the house was wide open to let in fresh spring air, yet a fire blazed in the fireplace, a disposal for armloads of discarded paper. Perusing each piece of paper was a time-consuming ordeal, but she was afraid she might burn something important—maybe another message from John. She and Sid lounged on several of Grandma's old patchwork quilts, Sid watching every move Lizzy made.

Lizzy glanced up and grabbed the first thing she saw—the crumpled bag the postman had handed her on her first trip into town. She scrutinized it and shook her head at how much it had terrified her only weeks ago. She'd feared there might be a letter from Sam inside it, a letter written twenty-five years ago that would confirm the lies J.D. had told her. Or a letter in which Sam declared his love for her. Now she knew there was no letter from Sam; he hadn't written one.

She dumped the bag's contents onto the floor and scanned it. It was mostly junk mail—ads and postcards and solicitations—with a few bills, cards, and magazines mixed into the mishmash, dusty and discolored from sitting in the post office backroom for too many years.

From the top of the pile, Lizzy selected a bill from the Mobile gas station. It was for twenty-one dollars. "Things sure have changed, Sid," she proclaimed, eyeing the vigilant cat. "Back then, you could fill your car up for five bucks. We couldn't make it to town on five dollars worth of gas now."

Lizzy threw the bill into the discard pile and selected an envelope addressed to her, then ripped it open and pulled out a card that screamed of the seventies. "Wow! Talk about a blast from the past. Can you believe we actually chose to invite these colors into our lives? What were we thinking?" she shrieked, holding the card out so Sid could marvel at it, too.

On the front, weaving through giant burnt orange mushrooms with harvest gold polka dots—an avocado green frog roosting on it—was a brief note expressing sympathy. The message continued inside and was signed: *Our most sincere condolences, Rose and Chet.* Lizzy tossed it onto the keep pile. If nothing else, it would remind her to never make that color *faux pas* again.

Then she noticed another envelope with her name printed on it. Yellowed with age, this one was postmarked December 23, 1973. There was no return address. Lizzy held it up to the light streaming in through the window. It appeared that a folded sheet of paper was inside.

"What do you suppose this is?" she murmured more to herself than to the cat. Something about the letter unsettled her, maybe the unfamiliar handwriting.

She broke the seal and slid the paper from the envelope, unfolded it, and read: *Dear Lizzy, I hope you will read this letter and understand. I also hope you will forgive me for what I am sharing with you. I am sorry I wasn't a better father and that I couldn't give you the home you deserved. After your mother died things fell apart and I couldn't look after you. And now I have cancer and I am dying. Soon I will join Elizabeth the woman you were named for. And John will be with us. He seems to be following in my footsteps. Now that you're not here to watch over him something needs to be done. I worry about what his friend will do to him and how he will suffer. I can't leave him here with J.D. Don't worry. I will take care of it.*

Lizzy stopped reading, and the letter drifted to her lap. Numbed by her father's words, she fought for air, gagging on the deluge of feelings pouring up out of her body. *And John will be with us,* he'd written. Was her father saying that he planned to kill John, his own son? Was that why the dates of their deaths were only days apart? The thought sent chilling shivers through her.

Drawing a deep breath, Lizzy picked up the letter and read on: *You have your own life to live now so please do not feel guilty. Remember that I always loved you even when I left you at the farm. I knew your grandparents would give you a better home than I could and you would get to know your brother and you would watch out for each other. Please forgive me. With love, Your father.*

The damning evidence clasped in her trembling hands, Lizzy stared at it and wondered what in the world she should do with it. On the one hand, it might exonerate her. On the other hand, it placed a huge burden on her already bruised shoulders, a burden she didn't want.

How long she sat like that—a myriad of feelings and questions raging inside her—she wasn't sure. Sensing a change in Sid's demeanor, she squinted at the cat and noticed that he was eyeing something behind her. Her heart leaped to her throat—the kitchen door was wide open.

"It's just me, Lizzy," Sam's husky voice murmured from behind her. "The door was open, so I came on in."

Lizzy's stomach refused to settle. She quickly refolded the letter and stuffed it and the envelope inside the pocket of her jeans as she rose to her feet to face Sam.

"It's been awhile," she greeted him, plastering a stiff smile on her face and telling herself to relax.

He nodded in acknowledgment, his eyes probing hers. "I was driving home from town and thought I'd stop." He looked nervous, which unsettled Lizzy even more. "I had a chat with Mel this morning, and I wanted to talk with you about it."

"And?" she probed, concerned that he might be having difficulty with the news that John was only his half brother.

He rubbed his bristly jaw, his eyes tortured. He wasn't handling the news well at all. "She suggested that I discuss my feelings with you," he explained. "It's about our relationship."

It tore her apart, seeing him like this. "I'm sorry, Sam. You've been through so much lately. Then to find out about John."

"John?" He looked confused. "Oh . . . well, actually there's something else I'd like to. . . ."

It was the way Sam said John's name that put the sting in her eyes. She closed them, willing herself to remain calm.

"What's wrong?" Sam asked, wary concern in his voice.

"Oh," she spluttered, angry with herself for tearing up. "Just when I think it's over, it's not. Here I am, sick to death of all of the secrets and the problems they've caused, and now I'm trying to keep another one from you."

"Dammit, Lizzy. Just tell me what it is."

He looked as weary of it all as she. "Why don't we sit on the porch," she suggested.

When they were both sitting in the metal lawn chairs she'd dragged from the attic, Lizzy dug the letter from her pocket and handed it to Sam. He eyed it curiously before he unfolded it and began to read. Lizzy sat quietly and watched the play of emotions on his face, wishing she had a window to his thoughts.

Finally, he shook his head, most likely in disbelief. "Well, it's certainly open to interpretation. Do you think he's saying that he plans to kill John?" he asked incredulously.

She shrugged. "That was my first impression," she admitted, disappointed that Sam hadn't read something else between the lines. "I knew my father was many things, but I never would've dreamed that he was crazy. And he would've had to be, wouldn't he, to intentionally hurt his son?"

"I would think so." He continued to study the letter, a bewildered look on his face, as if hoping to find some answers to his questions encrypted on it. "If that's what this letter's about, maybe John found out about it? Maybe it's what John's talking about in the letter he wrote to you?"

Lizzy hadn't considered that. "It could be. I'm certain John discovered I'm his sister. John and my father died a few days apart. Maybe he planned to kill John and then kill himself. It doesn't explain the note from the clock, though. And then there's the reference to John's friend. He has to be talking about Junior."

Sam nodded, obviously deep in thought as he stared at the golden countryside. The tang of pollinating sagebrush wafted in the breeze that was feathering his hair. Lizzy fought the urge to reach up and play with his ruffled locks.

"So what do we do now?" she posed, turning the decision over to him.

He studied her, and she let him. He was the legal expert here, not her. "I don't know, but before you go off half-cocked and do something you'll regret later, you need to take some time to think this through. It might be that doing nothing is best."

"Even if it's a lie?" Though she might agree with Sam, deceit had already taken a serious toll on both of their lives.

"Lizzy, everyone involved in this lie is dead. You and I know the truth. No one else would care."

"How about Eb? He'd want to know," she argued.

Sam massaged his temple. "I can tell him."

Lizzy was tempted to let it go. "I don't know, Sam. I promised myself there'd be no more secrets." She said it more out of a desire to convince herself than to sway him, then cringed at the memory of J.D.'s document, still secreted in her desk.

"Maybe there are times when a secret is better off left alone. Have you thought about how this might affect you . . . and your sons?

That thought had crossed her mind, but she'd chased it away, feeling guilty for her selfishness. However, what he'd said might apply to J.D.'s document. Maybe Lizzy had the only copy. What if it disappeared?

She shoved that thought aside to consider Sam's question. "It doesn't seem like the right thing to do . . . for John."

"What would he get out of it? He's dead. You do know that, don't you?"

Blaming it on a tough few weeks, she let his remark slide. "Maybe I should give it to the sheriff and let him decide what to do. John's name might be cleared."

"Do you think he cares?" Sam demanded.

Clearly, Sam was weary of this conversation. She was, too. But she was still torn. "Well, maybe I care," she murmured.

He sighed in exasperation and examined her closely. "So is this something that's gonna haunt you? Whatever your decision, you need to be able to live with it."

"Why does it have to be my decision?" she entreated, annoyed that Sam wouldn't make it, so she could be done with it.

"I think that's pretty obvious, don't you?"

She wanted to scream, *No! I've already made my share of decisions!* Instead, she said, "I suppose so, but I need some time to think about it. If I decide to give it to the sheriff, I promise I'll talk with you first."

Sam folded the letter and handed it to Lizzy. "Okay. I'll tell Eb. Then I'll leave it up to you to let me know what you decide." He stared at her with troubled eyes for several long unsettling moments. Finally, he huffed and said, "I need to get back to the ranch. Are you gonna be okay?"

"Yeah, although, I was feeling a whole lot better before I found this," she said, indicating the letter as she rose to her feet. "I'll adjust to this, too . . . I guess."

He pushed himself up out of the chair and closed his eyes, massaging his forehead. When he looked at her, Lizzy got the feeling a battle was waging inside him. She watched him in silence, a familiar tune from a long ago dance floating around in her head and nervous flutters bubbling up from somewhere inside her.

With a sigh, Sam dropped his baseball cap on his head, pulled it snugly into place, and murmured, "Enjoy your day," before he took the steps two at a time and strode towards his truck.

Lizzy watched him back out of the farmyard, then breathed a sigh of relief and squared her shoulders. She still had a bedroom to clean and paint, and nothing—absolutely nothing—was going to stop her. *No more getting sidetracked*, she told herself as she stuck the letter back into the envelope and tucked it into Granddad's desk.

She returned to the bedroom and surveyed the pile of mail left to sort through. "No time like now," she muttered.

Then her eyes landed on Rose's sympathy card. She stared at it, stunned, her stomach churning. How had she missed it?

With shaky fingers, she picked up the envelope to carry it to Granddad's desk. The top was rolled back, and she rifled through its contents until she found the page from the diary. She laid the two pieces of paper—the diary page and Rose's envelope—side-by-side, took a deep breath to calm her catapulting nerves and examined the handwriting. Though she was no handwriting expert, it certainly appeared that they both could've been written by the same person.

CHAPTER 30

The sun stretched languorously from the east across the dewy morning, blinding Lizzy with its brilliance. To the west, fondant-iced mountain peaks—Jefferson, Three Sisters, Three Finger Jack, Washington, and a spattering of others—dazzled against the vibrant blue sky. It promised to be another beautiful spring day. Once this mission was completed, the day would be pure indulgence.

Her father's letter was burning a hole in her pocket. She'd mulled it over long and hard. Although it implied that her father's intent was to harm John, it didn't come right and state it. She'd stossed and turned most of the night deliberating on whether she should involve the law. In the end, she'd decided to not give it to the sheriff. He'd just say the letter didn't prove anything except that her father was as flaky as everyone thought him to be.

However, she did plan to share it with one person: that "friend" her father had mentioned in his letter. She knew with an unshakable certainty that he was referring to someone who seemed plagued by John's death more than she—Junior. Was John really suffering at Junior's hands? Junior couldn't find it in his heart to forgive Lizzy for leaving John. But Lizzy got the feeling Junior couldn't forgive himself for John's death, either. He reeked of secrets. Lizzy aimed to find out why.

She shivered and felt the prickle of goose bumps on her arms. Junior scared her. She didn't trust him—never had.

Pulling her gaze from the peaceful morning, she faced her Explorer and what was sure to be a difficult confrontation. More often than not, she left the SUV unlocked, so she wasn't surprised to find it so this morning. She tugged the door open and slid into the driver's seat, plotting her visit with Junior in her head as she turned to set her purse on the passenger seat.

Her stomach heaved. The world twirled. Her tingly body seemed to float. She grabbed onto the steering wheel to ground herself, her eyes glued to the disgusting display on her passenger seat, struggling to make sense of it.

It appeared to be a stuffed lamb. Once soft and plump—a

258   SUZANNE GRANT

child's cuddle toy—it was now a mangled, slashed mess. Scarlet-stained stuffing puffed from numerous gashes to form a nest around its mutilated body. A note lay next to it, much like the one that had been tacked to her front door weeks ago. Only, the message written on this note was more sinister: *THIS IS YOUR LAST WARNING. LEAVE OR YOU DIE!*

Lizzy slammed the door locks into place, and her eyes shot to the farmyard, searching for signs of danger, the peaceful setting now desolate and sinister. Someone had been here again, someone who now threatened to kill her. Why would anyone want her dead? It had to be tied to John's death.

Suddenly, it was even more imperative that she have that chat with Junior, only not alone. She dropped her purse on the floor mat and studied the polyester carnage on her passenger seat, images of Sam's bloody cow popping into her mind. At least, this time it wasn't the real thing. Then she turned on the engine, backed out of the driveway, and headed south. Hopefully, she could convince Sam to join her on her trip to Hawkins Hardware.

As she drove, Junior held her thoughts hostage. He'd been wild and reckless, a hothead with a surly attitude, when she'd left here—and yes, he was still a hothead with a surly attitude. She'd always wondered why John—sweet, introspective, dreamy John—hung around with Junior. But John had his wild side, too, especially after he returned from Vietnam.

Franny had said that Junior changed drastically after John's death. Why? Did he know something important that he'd kept a secret all of these years, something that was now being threatened by Lizzy's return? If so, how far would he go to protect himself?

Lost in her speculations, a flash of metal in her rearview mirror startled her. She squinted at the reflection. A vehicle was not far behind her, moving progressively closer at a fast clip. It looked like a pickup truck—Sam's? She let up on the gas and pulled as far to the right as possible to give the truck passing room. It slowed and hung back just far enough that Lizzy couldn't make out the license plate number through the dust cloud the Explorer kicked up.

Fingers of foreboding tickled her spine. She slowed even more and leaned forward, her eyes inches from the rearview mirror, as if it might bring the driver into focus. The truck slowed, too. Beams of sunlight reflected from its windshield, blocking her view of the cab's interior.

Lizzy rounded a corner and glanced back. Her heart leaped and landed in her throat. It wasn't Sam. This truck was silver, much like the one she'd spotted outside the farmhouse window weeks ago.

She swallowed at her panic as she rapidly considered her options. If she stopped and waited for the truck to pass, she'd be an easy target with no protection. Yet if she sped up and outdistanced the other vehicle—a big "if" on this rough road—she'd be left wondering if she really was being followed. So she continued as she was, hoping if she kept her eyes glued to the mirror, she'd get a clear view of the driver or the license plate.

The fork to the ranch lay just ahead. Lizzy eyed it, her heart racing. Would the silver truck follow her or would it continue on south?

❋ ❋ ❋

Across the table from Sam, Eb spread strawberry jelly on a slice of toast. "So what do you think Lizzy'll do?" he asked Sam.

"She wants to involve the law. I'm hoping she'll change her mind." Sam shrugged. "But I never could predict what Lizzy'd do. Maybe that's what's so appealing about her."

Eb threw him a thoughtful look and was opening his mouth to speak when noises from the mudroom waylaid him. Their eyes shot toward the sounds. Lizzy burst into the kitchen, prompting him to rethink what he'd just said.

There was a whole lot more appealing about Lizzy than her predisposition to be unpredictable. His blood stirred, and he told himself to get a grip. There was fire in her eyes this morning; she was up to something, and he didn't need any more intrigue in his life right now.

"Mornin'," she hissed, jaw set, brows creased in a brooding frown.

"Mornin', Lizzy," Eb responded. Sam nodded, wondering what had her so stirred up. He hoped she wasn't here to further complicate his life.

As if the clock were ticking and she was low on time, Lizzy marched to a cupboard, grabbed a coffee mug, and filled it with brew. She faced them and chugged a healthy gulp before she leaned back against the counter. Then she breathed a stream of air and chewed on her lower lip, lost in thought. "You know of anyone around here who drives a silver truck, more light than dark?" she finally asked.

"Not that I know of," Eb answered, looking to Sam for confirmation. "You know of anyone, Sam?"

"Nope," Sam agreed, uneasiness settling inside him. "You still being bothered by one?"

"Oh, I'm not sure. I told you about that silver truck outside the farm window a while back. Well, on the way over here, there was a silver truck behind me. When I slowed down, it did, too, and it stayed back just far enough that I couldn't see the license plate. When I turned towards the ranch, it stayed on the main road, so it's probably only my imagination. I just thought I'd ask."

Sam's mind rewound to the night he'd snooped on Lizzy from the top of the hill. He'd had the feeling she was being followed that night, too, and he'd bet his new Resistol hat that it was a truck.

"Has anything else happened?" As soon as he said it, he knew he wasn't going to like the answer. Lizzy's face turned an ominous ashen color, and panic flashed in her eyes.

She sighed and murmured, "I have something to show you . . . outside," before she marched back out through the mudroom door, coffee mug still clutched in her white-knuckled fingers.

Sam and Eb eyeballed each other and pushed themselves up out of their chairs. Eb looked as worried as Sam. Sam hurried after Lizzy, his pulse revving. Eb's shuffling footsteps trailed him.

Lizzy pulled the door open on her SUV and stood back to allow Sam access to its interior. Sam steeled himself and gazed inside. He flinched, then leaned in for a closer look.

At first glance, it'd looked like a dead animal of some kind, but it was only a stuffed toy staged for impact. Someone had designed this to scare Lizzy into leaving the farm. Must've figured that the last note and the real slaughtered cow hadn't worked, so they'd make another last ditch effort before. . . .

Sam didn't want to go there. This grotesque mess reeked of desperation. Why would someone want Lizzy away from the farm enough to threaten her with death? Could she possibly be right about John? Maybe someone did murder him. Rubbing at the agitation he'd awakened in his gut, he stepped back to let Eb have a look.

Lizzy's eyes brimmed with questions. "It's time to call in Matt Grover, the county sheriff," he told her. "I've tried to write this all off as circumstance up until now, but this is intentional. Evidently, you're a threat to someone, and they want you gone. Any idea who it might be, or why?"

She shook her head, chewing on her trembling lower lip. "The only thing I can think of is John. I've been asking a lot of questions about his death, and I spent a day at the library looking through old newspaper clippings. Maybe someone doesn't want me snooping."

Something sparked in her eyes. She turned towards Eb, then paused, concern settling into her features. Sam's eyes followed hers, and he nearly reached out to Eb. He'd aged twenty years in the last five minutes. His face was pasty and slack, his body hunched and frail-looking. He looked like he could crumble at any moment.

"Are you okay?" Lizzy whispered.

Eb nodded, though hesitantly. "It just knocked the oomph out of me—not a pretty sight," he whispered. "I'll be fine. It's you I'm worried about."

"Me, too, but don't make yourself ill worrying about me . . . please. I'm going to get to the bottom of this. Which brings up something I've been wondering about: John's saddlebags?"

Eb frowned. "His saddlebags?"

"Yeah. The news articles I read claimed he left the ranch with bulging saddlebags, but when Lilac returned to the ranch, they were empty. So what happened to whatever was in those saddlebags? Did you see anything up at Eagles' Nest when you found him—a lunch, binoculars, books, a blanket . . . anything?"

The creases in Eb's face deepened. "No, there was nothing, not on top or down below."

"And another thing," Lizzy asserted, "John kept his journals on top of that hill, hidden inside a metal box under a large rock. He'd spend hours up there writing in them, but he never removed them from there, not ever. I looked for them, but they're not there now. Did you ever see them around the house, Eb?"

The uneasiness that had sprouted inside Sam blossomed further with each word Lizzy spoke. Eb looked emaciated. He shook his head and stared blankly at the house.

Lizzy narrowed her eyes, studying Eb. She seemed to hesitate, then added, "That diary page in Granddad's desk that you read, was that Rose's handwriting? Is that why it upset you?"

Eb wilted further and fell back against the truck. His eyes roamed everywhere except to Lizzy. Finally, he nodded. Sam had no idea what Lizzy was talking about, but Eb certainly did, and he wasn't liking that last question.

"Do you know why it was there?" she prodded.

"No." Eb rasped, his gaze snapping over to meet Lizzy's. "Rose always kept a diary. I'd forgotten about that until I saw that page. I don't know what happened to her diaries. After she died, Chet took care of her stuff. Maybe he could tell you."

Lizzy studied him closely, then sighed. Sam felt tension seeping from her.

"Sam told me about Skip's letter," Eb uttered.

A pained look crossed Lizzy's face. She pulled the letter from her jacket pocket and handed it to Eb.

With trembling hands, Eb slid his reading glasses out of his shirt pocket and perched them on the end of his nose, his weary eyes peeking over the tops of the frames. He slipped the letter from the envelope and his eyes scanned its lines. Lizzy sipped her coffee, her eyes glued to Eb. Sam watched them both. He had a terrible feeling about where this day was headed.

At last, Eb removed the eyeglasses and looked up, his eyes sad. "Well, it seems Skip might've been shy a few screws, all right. I knew Johnny spent some time with him before he died, but it's hard to imagine Skip hurtin' Johnny. I just don't see it happenin'. Skip was always more about havin' fun than harmin' others, and if he was plannin' to kill someone, it'd more likely be J.D. Have you decided what you're gonna do with this?"

She shrugged. "I'm not sure yet. That's why I'm here." Her focus shifted to Sam. "I know you wanted me to let it go, Sam, but I can't. I have to do what I can to make things right, especially after this," she said, indicating the cab of the truck with a sweep of her hand. "In the end, this letter's most likely nothing more than a plea for forgiveness and understanding. My dad doesn't come right out and say he planned to kill John. He probably meant that John would be here at the ranch, near him and Elizabeth. But there is someone who needs to read this letter—Junior—and the sooner we can get to town and take care of it, the better."

"Junior?" Sam blurted. Of all the people he *didn't* want to spend time with, Junior was at the top of his list.

"Uh-huh. I know he's the friend my dad mentions in his letter. I need to know what was going on between John and Junior."

Sam studied her. Why was he a part of this? It was no skin off his back if she destroyed that letter without telling another soul about it. He doubted that it was even remotely related to the current threats on Lizzy's life, and to his way of thinking, pawing through this pile of shit after all of this time was going to be one huge pain in the butt, mostly hers.

"Right now?" he stalled, grasping for a few seconds to sort through the potential fallout if Lizzy took this thing public. "Are you sure you want to open all of this up again?"

Their eyes locked. She nodded determinedly. "Yes, and I want to get it over with now, before I talk with the sheriff about all of the other creepy things going on around here."

"And I need to come with you?" he probed.

"I don't want to go alone. Junior scares me," she whispered, her eyes desperate.

Sam massaged his forehead. Did he really want to confront Junior about something that had happened eons ago? If he said no, she'd do it alone. And what if Junior was actually linked to all of the other stuff that had been happening? Lizzy's life could be endangered.

Eb broke the spell. "You sure you want to open up this can of worms, Lizzy?"

"Oh, yes," Lizzy, asserted. "I have to do it for John. Are you coming, Sam?"

Sam took a deep breath and shook his head to clear it. He had no choice; he had to tail after her. "Oh, what the hell," he muttered as he dug his keys from the pocket of his Wranglers. "I just hope you know what you're getting us into. I'll drive my truck. We can stop by and talk with the sheriff after our powwow with Junior."

He headed towards his Dodge Ram, then stopped to glance back at Lizzy, hoping this day ended better than it had begun.

CHAPTER 31

Lizzy knew Sam was upset. He wanted her to bury her father's letter and forget about it. And maybe she would, after she confronted Junior. Maybe then she could put the letter behind her and move on to figuring out who was threatening her and the truth behind John's death. Then again, maybe Junior was behind the whole sordid mess.

She glanced at Sam and felt her pulse quicken, then frowned at the gnawing urge to reach out and touch him. She'd loved the Sam of twenty-five years ago with an unwavering ardor that could only be described as foolhardy. Was she now attracted to the ghost of that Sam, or was something else going on here? Who was this man sitting next to her?

The desire to know if there was anything left of the Sam she'd once loved and adored was overpowering. She wished he'd share what was going on inside his head. Hers was warning her to flee from these newly awakened feelings while she still could, that she was heading for a whole lot more heartache. *No, never again,* she told herself firmly.

Sam focused on the road, as if unaware that she sat here beside him. Lizzy turned back to the vast sea of golden yellow that brightened the countryside. The sagebrush had blossomed, its pollen permeating the air, wreaking havoc on sensitive sinuses. Thankfully, the antihistamines she'd purchased at the drug store were doing their job.

When Sam pulled out onto the rut-free smoothness of the highway, Lizzy took a deep breath and plunged in. "Why are you so afraid of this letter? What do you think it's going to do to you?"

His eyes flicked to hers and locked momentarily. "I'm not afraid of what it'll do to me; I'm afraid of what it'll do to you."

It caught her off guard, a bittersweet torrent of joy and fear gushing through her. Warmth crept up into her face. "That's very flattering, but I can do my own worrying."

"I know that. I just don't want you to get hurt again. If Skip had something to do with John's death, it's a mute point now, and making it public will affect both you and your sons. He's your father, you know . . . and yours sons' grandfather. Do you want them to have to deal with something that's of no consequence today?"

Sam was right—if the contents of the letter really were of no consequence. "What if my father is somehow related to the threats and other weird things that are going on?" she argued.

He huffed. "There is that," he muttered. "Junior's an asshole, but maybe he'll have some answers. And we need to get some before someone decides to act on those threats." He glanced at her, his gaze intense, "Like I said, I don't want you hurt."

A warm ache settled in Lizzy's chest. She turned back to the blur of gray and gold rushing by outside the window, reflecting on how nice it felt to have Sam express interest in her well-being.

They had traveled through town and parked before Sam spoke again. "Junior's truck is here, not Franny's car," he murmured.

Lizzy stared at the front door, her heart pounding so hard she thought it might beat a hole through her chest. "I don't know what's going on with him, but something keeps telling me it's related to John's death. Franny said he changed drastically after that—cleaned up his act. He's always been a jerk—no change there. But he's hateful now, especially towards me. Except for me, Junior was John's best friend. If he knows anything about John's death, I'm hoping what's in this letter might drag the truth out of him. He needs to find some peace . . . for Franny's sake, if not his."

Sam frowned at her as if she had a few loose screws. "You sure we're talking about the same man? Seems to me, Junior enjoys being prickly."

"Uh-huh. That's why you're here with me. Just trust me on this . . . please," she implored, weary of her many failed attempts to explain complicated circumstances.

He studied her, then nodded.

Lizzy stared at the hardware store. It loomed large and red, the closed sign dangling in the window. "This isn't gonna be fun. He'll probably chew my ear off before I say anything."

Sam eyed her skeptically. "He'll be so busy chewing mine off that he won't get to yours. There's no love lost between Junior and me. Lord knows what John told him about me."

So both she and Sam headed Junior's list of dislikes. She'd hoped Sam would be her buffer. Resolved to put this behind her, she muttered, "Let's get this over with."

They met at the front door. Sam pounded on the glass until Junior materialized from the back of the store. He didn't look happy. In fact, he appeared to be slinking back into the shadows. Sam kept on banging until, after a few muttered words that Lizzy was glad she couldn't hear, Junior stomped to the door and cracked it open to give them a contemptuous look.

"I knew the two of you would hook up. You know what they

say about birds of a feather," he barked.

"Sure do, Junior," Sam replied smoothly, pushing the door open, so he and Lizzy could slip past Junior, into the store, "but since we're not flocking, I really don't see how it's relevant right now. Lizzy has something she wants to discuss with you. Then we'll get out of your hair."

Junior's glance at Lizzy reminded her of a rabid dog. "And it couldn't wait another fifteen minutes?" he snarled before he slammed the door shut.

Irritated, Lizzy gritted her teeth and rolled her eyes as she strode towards the back of the store. "Come on, Junior. Let's get this done before Franny gets here."

"Franny's already here," came a female voice from in front of them.

Lizzy's stomach clenched. Franny didn't need to be a part of this, especially if it got ugly. A few more steps and there sat Franny in a pool of light behind the counter, a wounded puppy look to her.

"Mornin', Franny," Sam greeted her from behind Lizzy.

"Good mornin', Sam. Lizzy. What's going on?"

Guilt grabbed Lizzy. She wanted answers, but she didn't want Franny to be hurt in the process. "It's just a letter I found," she informed her. "I thought Junior should read it."

"And I shouldn't?"

Lizzy was frazzled. It didn't seem appropriate to ask Franny to leave her own store, but she didn't know what secrets Junior might be harboring. She didn't want to be the one to tip the scales on what appeared to be an already rocky marriage.

"So . . . it's okay if I stay, then?" Franny prodded.

Lizzy looked to Sam for assistance. "I don't see why not," he mumbled.

Leave it be, Lizzy told herself as she faced Junior. He hung in the shadows, brows furled and eyes glaring over the rims of his glasses. If he spoke, Lizzy suspected it would be to growl.

She slid the letter from her pocket, unfolded it, and held it up to the light. "I found it in a bag of my grandparents' mail," she informed them. "It was written by my father." She took a deep breath and began to read, *"Dear Lizzy. . . ."*

By the time Lizzy finished reading the letter, her voice was shaky and weak, as was she. It was one thing to read it silently and quite another to voice its contents aloud. She stuffed the letter back into the envelope and into her pocket, and her eyes drifted shut. Sorrow swelled inside her; she tamped it down. Tears threatened; she swallowed them. She had to gain control over her rampant emotions and question Junior about her father's accusation.

Sounds of agony startled her, and her eyes popped open.

Junior was on his knees. He rocked back and forth, a heart-wrenching series of moans streaming from behind the hands covering his face.

Something awful was happening to him. Lizzy took a step towards him but was brought up short by an iron grip on her shoulder. Before she could berate Sam for being so callous, Franny walked forward and gathered Junior into her arms. Lizzy watched in silence as the two of them set a cadence, swinging back and forth like the pendulum on a giant clock. Lizzy was shocked. Was Junior traumatized by something her father had written or by something else related to John's death?

Ever so slowly, Junior wound down. The plaintive sounds subsided, and the rocking slowed to a halt. Franny stepped back and pulled Junior's hands from his face to examine it. Tears glistened in her concerned eyes.

Junior rocked back onto his seat and gazed at his wife, his face twisted in misery. "I'm so sorry, Fran," he whispered.

"Sorry?" she probed, a puzzled frown creasing her forehead.

Junior's eyes closed. "I thought it was me . . . that I did it?"

"What are you talking about?"

"John. I thought it was my fault," he lamented.

Franny's frown deepened. "Your fault? I don't understand."

Lizzy didn't understand either. She hadn't expected this. She'd gone out of her way to avoid Junior's annoying accusations when all along, he was convinced that he'd caused John's death? Sam's restraining hand still rested on her shoulder, but she'd been quiet long enough. "What did you do to John, Junior?" she asked.

Junior flinched, as if he'd forgotten she and Sam were still in the room. His beseeching eyes spun to meet Lizzy's, but he only stared at her in silence.

"Was it drugs," she demanded, wincing when Sam's grip tightened.

Blood drained from Junior's face, leaving it pale and gaunt. His eyes grew wary. "You knew?" he breathed.

"Of course, I knew," she informed him, irritation spurring her on. "I also knew that J.D. warned you to stay away from John—you and your drugs and booze. What happened, Junior?"

He took his time answering her, probably to conjure an excuse for something totally inexcusable. "I should've left him alone. I don't know why I didn't, but I couldn't," he whined.

Clearly upset and confused, Franny released his hands and stepped back from him. When she spoke, it was with disbelief. "You were giving John drugs? Why would you do that? I thought he was your friend?"

"He was my friend. That's why I shared my drugs with him. It was somethin' we did together."

Franny's face turned as vivid as Junior's was ashen. It was as if her auburn locks were ignited by the fury simmering within her. When she spoke, she was fuming. "Together? Friends listen to your problems. They are there for you when you need them. They go to lousy movies with you and tell you the truth when you're a mess. Friends do lots of things for you, but they *don't* give you drugs!"

"I know that now. But back then it seemed like the right thing to do."

"Right thing to do? I don't believe this, Junior! You knew John was trying to get better, and you gave him something that would only make him worse."

Junior eyeballed Franny, obviously grasping for a way out of the mess he was in. "I thought it might help. He missed Lizzy so much." The whiny quality in his voice had kicked up a couple of notches. Lizzy wanted to grab him by the collar and shake him.

"Don't blame Lizzy. It was your doin's, not hers." Franny enunciated each word as if it would take that to get through to him.

It took Junior awhile to respond. For the first time during the whole verbal exchange, he actually seemed to think about what he'd done. "I know. It was just somethin' John and I did. When he came back from Vietnam, he was different. The drugs helped him cope."

Franny's fire seemed to fizzle. When she spoke again, it was more with resignation than challenge. "Were you giving him drugs the whole time?"

"No, I had to be careful. J.D. caught us and threatened to kill me if he ever saw me around John or the ranch again. Then just like that, John didn't want to drink or have anything to do with drugs."

Lizzy felt Sam's growing restlessness behind her. If he gripped her shoulder much tighter, he'd leave bruises. His impatience finally won out. "Why did you think you'd caused John's death, Junior?" he demanded.

Junior turned to stare at Sam, fear lurking in his eyes. He'd lost his glasses during his emotional display, and Lizzy wondered if he could see Sam clearly enough to comprehend the anger emanating from the body behind her. She could feel it, pulsating streams of energy forcing their way into her consciousness, whipping her own nerves into a frenzy. She struggled to control them.

The vise tightened on her shoulder—she winced—as they waited for Junior to respond, three sets of eyes glued to his panic-stricken face.

"It was the day he died," he finally began in a quiet, shaky voice. "We were up at Eagles' Nest—you know, on top of that hill out by the cemetery. John always wanted to go up there. We'd agreed to meet up there that mornin'." That said, he stopped.

Lizzy grabbed her heart to muffle its pounding, certain that everyone in the room could hear it. Sam's voice barked from behind her. "Cut to the chase, Junior!"

Junior gaped at Sam. He expelled a long gust of air, then murmured, "Like I said, John refused to have anything to do with drugs or alcohol. He said he had to stay alert, that he'd discovered somethin', and he thought someone was gonna try to kill him because of it." His eyes darted to Lizzy. "He said Lizzy was gonna help him figure out what to do, that she'd be back here soon."

Guilt and sadness waged a war for superiority inside Lizzy. She stuck her fist in her mouth to keep from shrieking. John had counted on her; she'd let him down.

Sam must've sensed her turmoil; his hands now gently massaged her shoulders. "Keep going," he muttered to Junior.

"I'd scored some good stuff, so I was feelin' mellow, just layin' there on a tarp John'd brought, lettin' the drugs do their thing. John was writin' in one of those journals he kept buried up there. He'd brought a thermos of hot cocoa and some sandwiches. We ate. Then I don't remember much of anything until several hours later." He stopped and gazed at Franny, a pained expression on his face. "That's when I found him."

Lizzy couldn't stand much more. No matter what had happened to John, the guilt would always be a part of her. Even if she'd been unable to stop his death, she should've been there to protect him from Junior and J.D. . . . and her father.

"What happened?" she heard Sam ask in a husky voice.

Junior gazed at Sam with lifeless eyes. "He was at the bottom of the cliff. I figured I must've done it—maybe I went berserk or we were horsin' around and he fell off. There was no one else around, so it had to be me . . . didn't it?"

He sighed and shook himself, as if shaking aside that last thought. "But that letter—sounds like Skip was up there, too. John had been talkin' with him, you know. Skip must've done it."

A shudder passed through Lizzy's body. She focused on Sam's massaging hands, hoping they'd stifle the sobs threatening to erupt. Whatever the truth, it was now lost forever, buried six feet under in an insignificant cemetery that was surely a haven for legions of long lost secrets.

As far as Lizzy was concerned, it was up to Junior to make peace with his ghosts. Right now, she needed a few answers. Then she wanted to get away from him.

"What happened to the journals?" she asked.

Junior got a surprised look on his face, which quickly morphed into puzzlement. He shook his head. "I don't know," he breathed. "When I woke up, they weren't there."

"And the tarp and thermos?" she prodded. "Lilac returned to the ranch with empty saddlebags. Was she gone when you woke up?"

"No, I took off her bridle and sent her home—dropped the bridle on the ground. I was sleepin' on the tarp, so I folded it up and took it with me. Threw it into the garbage behind the store the first chance I got. The thermos? I don't remember seeing it."

"How about now?" Sam asked. "Have you been writing threatening notes to Lizzy and following her, trying to keep her quiet about John's death?"

Junior looked stunned and truly puzzled. "No," he uttered, shaking his head firmly.

"You sure," Sam demanded.

"Yeah, I'm sure," he snapped, glaring at Sam. Evidently, Junior had hung on to his prickly attitude.

Well, that's that, Lizzy told herself. Junior had kept his secret a long time. She wondered if, like her when she'd confessed hers to Sam, Junior's tortured conscience would finally get some reprieve. Some deep down, spiteful part of her hoped not.

Lizzy glanced at Franny's stricken face and met a pair of eyes riddled with pain and confusion. Feeling her heart go out to her friend, Lizzy murmured, "I'm sorry."

"It's okay," Franny assured her. "It's not your fault. At least, it explains why he's been such an ass to live with. And now, I think it might be best if you leave. We need to try to sort this out."

"Are you sure. You can stay at the farm with me, you know?"

"Yeah, I know. And I appreciate it. But I want to make sure I understand what happened before I decide what I'm gonna do. You two go along, and don't worry about me. I'm a big girl."

Lizzy didn't argue. Perhaps Junior did possess a few positive attributes. Since Franny seemed to care about him, there must be something about Junior that was worth loving. Just because Lizzy hadn't seen it, didn't mean it wasn't there.

She gave Franny a big hug and stepped back. "If you need anything, you know where to find me. I have a phone now," she reminded her.

"Thank you," Franny lipped.

Lizzy glanced at Junior one last time. He was a motionless blob of misery, sitting on the floor crossed-legged with his long limbs sticking out everywhere. His world had been one plagued by guilt. She wondered what it would be now that he had someone new to pass the blame onto.

Sam's troubled eyes met hers. She passed by him, reaching a hand around his upper arm and settling it into the crook of his elbow. Surely, since he'd held onto her throughout that unraveling conversation, she could hold onto him on their walk out the door.

As she walked, she contemplated her dilemma. She was no further ahead than when she'd started; she still didn't know what had happened to John, and she didn't know who wanted her well away from the farm. Time was running short. She needed to make some decisions that would affect the rest of her life.

CHAPTER 32

Sam watched a jackrabbit hop erratically along the dirt road in front of them. Its long ears stood erect like TV antennas and alarm shone in eyes that darted frantically back at the truck on its tail. For some reason, it reminded him of their recent encounter with Junior. Perhaps it was the panic that emerges when one is trapped, cornered with little wiggle room. Yet Junior had tried to wiggle his way out of the role he'd played in John's death, using every excuse he could think of to exempt himself from actions that were downright disgusting.

Yes, they were disgusting, but no more disgusting than his own actions. Did that mean they were both disreputable, or were they entitled to a few lapses in judgment?

Spotting a hole in the wall of sagebrush that lined each side of the dusty road, the rabbit made one final leap and disappeared into a golden puff of pollen. Sam wished he could divest himself of his problems that easily.

His eyes flicked to the passenger seat and Lizzy. She'd been silent since they left town, staring out the front window. Sam figured her mind was on what had taken place back at the hardware store. It'd upset her. He'd felt it in the shoulder he grasped and had seen it in her bearing—her hands clenched at her sides and her body becoming more rigid with the mounting tension.

"So how many are there?"

Caught up in his mind's meanderings, her words startled him. She still faced forward, but he swore she'd said something. "What?" he asked, confused.

"I asked you how many there are."

"How many what?"

She turned towards him, her lips trying to smile. "Wrinkles. I assume you were counting my wrinkles. You've had your eyes on me more than the road."

His face grew warm—she'd noticed. "You don't have wrinkles. Well, maybe just some tiny little crinkles beside your eyes and mouth. But you're still attractive."

Now it was Lizzy who blushed. "Attractive?"

Sam had been grasping at straws. "Attractive" was the word that had popped into his mind. "What the hell! You know you're beautiful," he muttered.

"I've never felt beautiful."

At a loss for words, Sam eyeballed her. She looked serious. It was absurd. He scrutinized her high cheekbones, her alluring dark eyes, and her sensual mouth and wondered how she could not recognize her own beauty. It caused a major commotion inside him.

"Well, you are," he blurted, returning his eyes to the road.

An uncomfortable silence followed. "I take it back. There was that one time," she barely whispered.

If Sam hadn't had his radar zeroed in on her, he would've missed it. A pang of jealousy prodded him to ask, "When was that?"

He watched her eyes slide over to him, guarded, her cheeks two pink blossoms. "It was nothing."

"I doubt that."

"You probably wouldn't remember," she parried.

"I have a pretty good memory."

"Really?"

It was his turn to be embarrassed. Clearly, she was referring to their ill-fated sexual encounter. "That's the one, and only, thing I have no memory of, Lizzy. And you're trying to change the subject."

She shot him a look that said she didn't want to go there. "It was that night—you might not remember it—the Fourth of July. There was a dance in town."

His heart raced. How could he forget? "I remember it."

"Well, we were dancing—you and I—and for once, I didn't feel like the awkward, gangly misfit who even my own father didn't want. For those few minutes, I felt like I was the luckiest and the most beautiful girl on the dance floor." She paused to sigh. When she resumed, her voice had an edge to it. "Then you walked off and left me standing there. I was hurt and humiliated."

Sam's eyes darted between the road and Lizzy, struggling through a patch of deep road ruts. "I'm sorry," he said, guilt nibbling on him.

She frowned.

"Lizzy, I thought you were going to marry John. I'd just kissed you, for God's sake, and I looked up, and there he was, standing right there and looking me in the eye. I had to get away from you."

Surprise flickered in her eyes. "Well, you might've told me that. Here, all of these years, I've been thinking I'm just possibly the worst kisser in the universe."

Something in her voice said she wasn't kidding. Unsure of how to reply, he searched for words to help her understand. There were none. "I didn't stop to think. I saw John, and I just took off. I'm sorry I treated you so badly," he finally muttered.

Their eyes met briefly. She shrugged. "It was a long time ago," she murmured, but her eyes said a whole lot more: she was still very much in touch with those feelings of hurt and humiliation.

They rode in silence for awhile, and Sam's thoughts returned to a quandary that had been nagging him for several weeks and was now blaring at the forefront of his conscience, thanks to Junior. Since it seemed to be a day to tackle difficult issues, he decided to take this one on, too. His blood pounding in his temples, he did just that. "Lizzy, do you think it's possible to do some very bad things and still be a good person?"

Her eyes met his, probing. "As in all of the bad things you've done?"

"Yeah."

"Do you think you're a bad person?"

He shook his head, pulling words together that made sense. "I think I'm responsible for a lot of things I'm not proud of, things I wish hadn't happened. I hurt you. I hurt my brother. I'm sure there are many others I've hurt somewhere along the line."

A vision of Gina popped into his mind. He swallowed the lump of remorse and continued. "Hell, if my father had had a heart, I probably would've even hurt him. I just wonder if there's any absolution, or if I'm doomed to be a lowlife."

"I think you're the only person who can answer that."

His eyes shot to her. "What do you mean?"

"Well, look at Junior. What he did was so terrible that he's been plagued by it since John's death, yet just like that, he's feeling absolved of the despicable things he did. It doesn't change the fact that he did them—he did. He's just released himself from them."

"Junior's as guilty now as he was then!" His resolute response surprised even him.

He felt her probing gaze, but he focused on his driving, slowing to let a mama quail and her chicks scurry across the road.

"Probably," she finally murmured. "But the point is that he doesn't see himself that way anymore. He can accept the fact that he harmed his friend, but he can't accept the fact that he might've caused his death." He heard her deep sigh. "So I guess what I'm saying is that I think it depends on how much leeway you're willing to give yourself. It seems to me that you don't allow yourself much of a margin for error."

Sam thought about what she'd said. She was probably right. He was raised to always strive to do the right thing. It was what made a man honorable. Yes, he'd tried to do the right thing, but in the process, he'd done a whole lot of wrong things. Would he ever be able to accept his own flawed character? He hoped so.

Right now, he needed to know one last thing. His heart raced at the thought of it. "So how much margin do you allow me, Lizzy? Do you think you'll ever be able to get past what I did?" He paused, working up the courage to continue. "Is there still a chance for us to take up where we left off?"

He wanted her to say there would always be a chance for them, that if they were destined to be together, they would be. He wanted her to say of course, she could put the reprehensible things he'd done aside and still care for him. He wanted to hear a lot of things.

What he heard was, "I don't know," delivered in a soft, bleak voice.

He didn't know if it was cause for hope of not. His eyes flitted to her, but she was gazing out the window.

Dismayed, Sam focused on the rolling golden clouds that blanketed the countryside as far as he could see. This time of year, Oregon's High Desert held a special beauty, shimmering in the warm spring sun and exuding the pungent fragrance of juniper and sagebrush. But soon the tiny blossoms would wither away into nothing, and the hot summer rays would suck the life out of what was left. The countryside would return to its somber self. He wondered if that was his fate, too. It was a disquieting thought, one that he'd rather not contemplate.

The stillness stretched between them, long moments of silent tension that were finally broken when Lizzy murmured, "Remember when you asked me to give you some time, Sam? Well, I'm asking for that now. I don't know what's going to happen, and I don't want to make promises I can't keep. I'm just beginning to figure out who I am and where I am and to come to terms with who and where I've been. And my future? I only hope and pray that it brings me peace and happiness."

Sam's heart quickened. Lately, those same feelings had bombarded him. Something warm settled inside him with the knowledge that he and Lizzy shared this.

"You know," she continued, "I've been thinking a lot about our lives lately, and it made me think of Grandma's tatted lace. You remember how she'd sit for hours with those little bobbins of thread and her tatting shuttle, her fingers in constant motion and her attention focused on those plain little strands of thread? Then she'd hold up this beautiful piece of lace, those individual threads interlaced and perfectly knotted.

"Well, it made me think of all of us—John, Eb, my grandparents, you, me. At one time, our lives were beautifully intertwined and knotted in just the right places—or so it seemed, anyway. But then a thread broke or a knot loosened, and it all began to unravel. Somehow, our lives became frayed and tattered remnants of something that was once so precious and lovely."

Their eyes met. Hers glistened with emotion. "Is this making any sense?" she asked.

Fearful that if he spoke, his voice would betray the flood of feelings engulfing him, Sam nodded. A pheasant shot up out of a patch of bunchgrass, its colorful feathers shimmering against the blue sky, and he tried to focus on it.

After a few moments, Lizzy continued. "Well, Grandma's lace curtains are yellowed with age, and the threads are broken in places. They need a lot of tender, loving care. Since I know how much time and effort she put into them and how beautiful they can be, I decided to try to salvage them. What I found out is mending something that intricate and complicated isn't easy. It can be done, but it takes a lot of time and patience.

"That's what I'm asking from you—that time and patience. There are still a lot of tangled knots and loose threads that we need to deal with before we'll know how our lives might fit together. And I need to tie one of those knots soon: I need to know if my sons will be safe here."

Ripples of alarm sprang to life inside him. "Are you thinking about leaving?"

"If I can't figure out what those threats are all about, I'll have to. They have to be related to John's death, so I need to find out what really happened to him. I thought Junior might be behind what's been going on, but now I don't think so. And my dad? I doubt it. In his letter, John claimed I was in danger, too, and my father didn't mention anything about that in his letter."

Her obsession with John was driving him crazy. "You know, Lizzy, there is the possibility that you'll never know what happened to John, that it's out of your reach."

"Then what's with all of the weird things going on, and the notes?" she argued. "Even Junior said that John had to stay alert because he thought someone wanted to kill him. And what happened to the missing journals and the thermos? Maybe he wrote something incriminating in those journals that someone found out about. Junior said he didn't remember anything that happened after they ate lunch. Maybe someone put something in that hot cocoa or their sandwiches to make John go crazy and fall of that cliff."

Lizzy was right, of course. There were too many things that just didn't add up. He needed time to think it through. It'd been so long since he'd pieced suppositions, clues, and evidence together that he could almost hear the rusty cogs in his brain creaking with the effort.

"I don't want my sons here if it'll endanger them," Lizzy

added, her voice shaky. "Once I know what happened to John, I'll know if it's safe for them to be here."

Their eyes locked, hers moist and pleading for understanding. "He was my brother, and I let him down. Don't you understand that?"

Feeling the sting in his eyes, Sam nodded. "I do understand." After all, John was his brother, too. Lizzy wasn't the only one who'd failed him.

Sam's arm was draped over the armrest that divided the front seats. Lizzy reached out and grasped his hand in her own. Giving it a soft squeeze, she whispered, "Thank you."

Sam watched the embers in her eyes shift, softening into a warm, penetrating glow. Then he turned back to the dusty, pot-hole-riddled road and contemplated what he'd seen in Lizzy's beautiful brown eyes.

CHAPTER 33

Sheriff Grover didn't look old enough to order a beer at the Corral. Lizzy's eyes kept drifting to him, hoping he might age some, so she could relax, confident that the law had her back. Instead, those hopeful glances only made her more nervous. He couldn't be a day over nineteen.

Sam appeared to have no qualms about his age—more specifically, his lack of it. The two of them were throwing legal jargon around like they were soul mates, which only increased Lizzy's apprehension. Compared to Sam's deep, mellow voice, the sheriff sounded like a prepubescent teen.

Lizzy watched him slip a camera from his shirt pocket and click photos of the faux carnage in her passenger seat. He'd already questioned her about it. She'd told him what she knew—nothing. Then she'd given him the note that had been tacked to her front door and told him about the slaughtered cow she'd found in her yard and the silver truck that seemed to be lurking in the neighborhood.

With trepidation, she'd handed John's letter to him—the kid couldn't have even been born twenty-five years ago—and attempted to explain its significance. He'd frowned appropriately while he eyeballed her as if she were in the throes of dementia.

There were times when she wondered if she might be—either that or she was caught up in some bizarre dream world. That morning had not started off well, with the unsettling mess in her front seat and the silver truck on her tail. It hadn't ended well, either. After that harrowing encounter with Junior, followed by the difficult conversation with Sam on the way back to the ranch, she felt like the only soufflé she'd ever baked—deflated and droopy. She had hit overload and retreated to where she could observe what was going on, but from a distance.

Her eyes scanned the ranch yard and were drawn to the barn. Chet and Eb stood in the shade outside the door. They appeared to be in a heated discussion about something. Eb leaned toward Chet like a loose fence post—gnarled and twisted—his mouth moving miles per minute. He didn't look happy. Chet slouched against the barn, spitting crud into a tin can and shooting verbiage at Eb every so often. He didn't look happy, either. Their intense voices drifted across the yard, but Lizzy couldn't make out what they were saying.

She turned back to Sam and Sheriff Grover. The sheriff was flicking gritty-looking fingerprint dust on the passenger door. As if it were magnetic, it clung to everything it touched. She sighed and turned away, certain much of it was in her car to stay.

Her thoughts turned to the conversation she'd had with Junior less than two hours ago. She hadn't told the sheriff that Junior was up on that hill with John the day he died. She was counting on Junior to do that. If he did, he'd surely mention her father's letter. Then she'd have to turn that over to the sheriff, too. For now, it was nesting safely in her pocket.

The scuff of Eb's shuffling footsteps drew her to him. He dabbed at his sweaty face with a red handkerchief, his mouth working—obviously, still agitated. A cardboard box dangled from his left hand.

"You feeling okay?" she asked him. "Maybe you should go inside and rest awhile."

"I'm fine," he muttered, parking himself beside her and eyeing Sheriff Grover's fingerprinting adventure.

Lizzy eyed it, too, and was sorry she did. Her dashboard was now covered with sooty swatches, as was the leather passenger seat. "Chet giving you a hard time?" she probed.

"What makes you think that?" he snapped.

Startled, Lizzy studied him. He wouldn't meet her eyes. "It didn't look like a friendly discussion," she argued.

He shrugged and walked the box around the vehicle to Sheriff Grover.

Lizzy watched the sheriff transfer the perforated sheep and stuffing into the box. The note went into an envelope. Then the three men approached her.

"You get anything?" she asked, mostly because she felt the need to say something. Obviously, her fingerprints were all over her Explorer.

"I'll have to get your prints and compare them before I'll know," the sheriff chirped. "Anyone else been in your car recently?"

"Just Eb," she told him. "And I cleaned it well before I moved here—scoured it—so there shouldn't be any other prints in there."

"That's good." He set to work on the driver's side, scattering fingerprint dust like an over enthusiastic tooth fairy, every so often pausing to adhere a print to a sheet of clear film.

Finally, he closed the lid on the powder container and turned to them. "Any idea what this is about," he asked.

Lizzy shrugged. "Like I said before, the only thing I can think of is John's death," she told him. "Why would anyone care whether I stay at the farm or leave unless they're worried I'll discover something about his death that they want kept secret? But why butcher a cow and tear up a stuffed sheep? Why not just leave the notes?"

"What did you say?" Sam demanded.

She stared at him. Was he in a foul mood too, like Eb? "I said, 'Why not just leave the notes?'"

"No, before that, about the cow and sheep. Maybe that's what this is all about."

"I'm not following you, Sam," Sheriff Grover muttered.

Sam seemed to pull his thoughts together before he voiced them. "I'm wondering if this might be tied to the Sheepshooters' War in some way. You've heard of it, right?"

A puzzled frown crept onto Sheriff Grover's baby face. Scarlet patches blossomed on his smooth cheeks. He hesitantly shook his head.

"It was back in the late 1800's, up until about 1907, in this part of Oregon and farther east. The cattle ranchers waged quite a battle against the sheepherders to keep them off grazing land they'd claimed for their cattle. It got pretty bloody, and a lot of sheep were slaughtered by cattlemen before the feds established grazing allotments and things finally quieted down," Sam informed him.

"And you think that's tied to what's going on with Lizzy?" the sheriff questioned.

Lizzy questioned it, too. She and John had nothing to do with those long ago goings-on. According to Granddad, his father had lost a good share of Stewart sheep to the raiders. After things had settled down, the Stewarts had turned to farming and raising cattle to hold onto their land, land on which she now resided.

"I don't know, Matt. It's the only thing that makes sense to me," Sam argued. "That slaughtered cow was mine, not Lizzy's, so maybe someone's trying to get back at me for something."

"I thought the notes were meant for Lizzy?" Clearly, Sheriff Grover wasn't buying Sam's speculations.

"They were. Maybe someone wants her away from here, so she doesn't get caught up in what's going on. That sheep was only a stuffed animal, not the real thing. Back when the Sheepshooters were on the warpath, Lizzy's ancestors were sheep people. Mine were cattle ranchers, and they were very much involved in all the dirty goings-on around here. The law looked the other way, and those who were involved were duty-bound to keep their mouths shut, no matter what happened.

"In the end, things didn't turn out well for some of the sheep men. Many of them lost their sheep and their land. My ancestors saw an opportune moment and grabbed that land."

Lizzy tried to follow Sam's reasoning, but she couldn't pull her focus from Eb. He seemed to be shrinking into himself, his shoulders hunched, head hanging. Color drained from his face leaving it ashen and waxy. Lately, he appeared to be struggling with some kind of serious health problem—his heart maybe?

"I'm telling you this, because there are some around these parts who haven't forgotten that fact—their family land is now part of the Craig Ranch," Sam explained. "What do you think, Eb? You think someone might still hold a grudge about that?"

Eb flinched. Then his eyes locked with Sam's. Lizzy got the feeling there was underlying meaning in Sam's question, but she had no idea what it was.

The two of them stared at each other for endless tense moments before Eb finally mumbled, "Beats me. I haven't heard no rumblin's."

The sheriff still wasn't buying it. "So you're saying someone wants to get even with you for something that happened a hundred years ago?"

Sam shrugged. "I'm just saying it's a possibility. It's worth checking into. Off the top of my head, I can't name all the folks around here who were sheep people and those who raised cattle. The historical society or the county records should have that information. I'll try to come up with a list of farms that were added to the ranch." His eyes flicked Eb before he added, "I need to think on this awhile. I'll give you a call when I have something."

Sheriff Grover eyed Sam dubiously and nodded. "We better go dig up that cow," he muttered. "You got a shovel?"

Sam's worried gaze turned to Lizzy, his eyes questioning.

"I'm gonna take off," she told him.

"I'll stop by and take a look around the farmyard when I'm done here," the sheriff informed her. "Park out on the road."

"Keep your eyes and ears open, and give me a call if anything seems unusual. And keep your doors and windows locked, all of them," Sam added. Then he strode off, Sheriff Grover's gangly form trailing in his boot prints.

You ready to head to the house?" Lizzy asked Eb, hoping he would lie down and rest once he was inside.

Eb sighed and nodded before he gave her a strange look and murmured, "Be careful, Lizzy."

Lizzy watched him shuffle toward the ranch house. He looked bone weary, his feet dragging in the dust as if each step was a monumental undertaking.

This was the second time Eb had warned her to be careful. Was he just worried about her? Or was he harboring another secret, one that might save her life?

CHAPTER 34

The phone rang, again. Lizzy raced for it. She'd already missed one phone call while she stood watch on the porch waiting for the mysterious silver truck to reappear. Earlier, she'd glimpsed it from the side yard, a mere streak as it zoomed by the farmhouse on its way south in the direction of the ranch, a cloud of fine dust settling in its wake.

"This is Lizzy," she gasped, slamming the receiver against her ear.

"Hi, Lizzy. It's Franny," came a surprisingly chipper voice from the other end of the line.

"I'm so glad you called. How are you doing?" Franny had been through a lot with her husband's revelations the previous day. Maybe she was taking Lizzy up on her offer to come stay at the farm for awhile.

"Oh, I'm fine. You know me. Once I get a handle on things and calm down to a simmer, I usually get over it. What happened between John and Junior took place a long time ago. Junior was young and brainless back then, and you and I know how John latched onto anything that'd help him get through the day.

"Junior's let John's death fester inside him way too long. He's talking with Matt Grover, the county sheriff, about it as we speak." A deep sigh filtered through the phone line. "Maybe he'll be tolerable to live with now that he doesn't have that secret eating him up inside. Hey, maybe I'll be the one sharing my risqué stories."

Lizzy wished she had Franny's resilience. She found it difficult to forgive Junior . . . and herself. She sighed, too. "I'm glad, Franny. Just remember that I'm here for you if you need me."

"Oh, I know that. But I didn't call to talk about myself. It's something Junior said last night. I thought you might like to know about it."

"Sure," Lizzy replied, wondering what else Junior might have concealed these many years.

"He just mentioned it in passing. I didn't think much about it at the time, but darned if it didn't pester me all night. He said he can't get past the idea that there was someone else up there with John and him that day."

A familiar queasiness settled inside Lizzy. Her hand dropped, the receiver trembling in it, while she struggled to control her skyrocketing emotions. She took a deep breath and returned the receiver to her ear. "Did he think it was my father?"

"Actually, he thinks it was a woman," Franny told her. "Don't you think that's odd? Why would a woman be up there with the two of them? Junior said maybe it was the ghost of John's mother, come back to get her son. He said it's more like a dream than real, so it was probably only his imagination. And it could be, Lizzy, but I thought maybe. . . ."

Franny's voice faded as Lizzy's mind scrambled for answers. A woman! If Junior's memories were true, it was someone other than her father. Perhaps someone who'd written that "it" was done?

Lizzy lifted the desk lid and rifled through a stack of papers until she found the diary page to read: *It's done. Now I will live my dream.* Her mind shot back to the day Eb had read those lines—lines his sister Rose had carefully scribed in fancy handwriting—and then retreated hastily to his Jeep, his face sickly pale. Had John hidden the diary page there for her to find, an entry that was written on the day of his mother's death? If so, there would be a reason he wanted her to read it.

Franny's voice was a mumbled garble from the other end of the line.

Was there a connection between Elizabeth Craig's death and Rose? And John's death? Was it Rose who was at Eagles' Nest with John and Junior that February day? If so, why? Lizzy's mind scrambled for answers that didn't materialize.

"Lizzy, are you there?"

Lizzy blinked herself back to Franny's frantic voice. "I'm here, Franny. Just thinking. Thank you for letting me know about this. I'm not sure what it means."

"Okay. Well, gotta go. You take care now."

"You, too, Franny. Bye."

Her mind swirling with unanswered questions, Lizzy clicked off the phone with her thumb and stared into space. If not Rose, then who else could've been up on that hill with John and Junior. Mel was a lady with many secrets, and she admitted to a long-time affair with J.D. Could it have been her?"

The phone jangled in her hand, and she jumped, then clamped the receiver to her ear. "This is Lizzy," she squeaked.

"The answer to your question is with John and his mother. Be there." The voice was low—soft and muffled, as if it floated through a sea of cotton. It was followed by a resounding click and a persistent buzz.

❀ ❀ ❀

The black gelding tossed its head and snorted, fighting the pull of the rope Sam gripped tightly. Sam swiped at the sweat tickling his cheek with his shirtsleeve, then anchored his weight against the animal and kept a firm hold with his gloved hand. The horse was certainly a spirited young thing. It was all Sam could do to hold onto him while he cantered in the confines of the circle Sam had set for him.

Unexpectedly, the horse halted and faced Sam, ears alert, only to shy away and tug at the rope. Sam heard it, too; a rider was approaching. Swearing under his breath, Sam dug his heels into the loose soil and leaned back. "Easy now, Thunder. It's nothing to get spooked over," he murmured soothingly.

The rhythm of hoof beats grew louder. Someone was sure in an all-fired hurry, and it wasn't helping him calm the jittery gelding. Sam glanced around, then did a double take. What in the hell was Gina doing out here at the ranch racing around on one of his horses?

He watched her slide the horse to a stop on the other side of the fence, raising a gritty fog of dust with her entrance. Sam eyed the lather on the mare's coat in disgust and clenched his teeth with anger, struggling to keep from tearing into her about her abusive behavior. That would have to wait. He turned back to the gelding and inched slowly up the rope, drawing closer to the horse while it eyeballed him with nostrils flared and wild eyes.

"Sam, you have to come!" Gina gasped from behind him.

Irritated, he glanced around. Gina's eyes were as wild as the gelding's. She stood at the fence, her hands gripping the top rail and her breathing an audible struggle. What was she up to now?

"It's Chet," she wheezed. "He's riding up to the top of that hill by the cemetery."

Sam couldn't see how that warranted the exhibition Gina was making. He turned to the gelding and stepped towards him, noting that he'd lost some of the fire in his eyes.

"He's meeting Lizzy Stewart up there."

Trepidation snaked up from Sam's gut to claw at his throat. He faced Gina. "What?" he barked.

Gina still breathed hard. Rivulets of perspiration trailed down onto her cheeks. Her eyes flitted around the yard like a honeybee seeking nectar. "I came out to go riding with him. I've done it before, so I thought it'd be okay. But he told me to come back to the ranch. Said he didn't want me along." She paused to suck in air. "I'm worried, Sam. Chet was really mad about something."

"What did he say?" Sam demanded, his own breathing irregular now.

"He just said he was meeting her up there, that they had something that needed settled."

"Dammit, Chet," Sam uttered as he reached for Thunder. Chet had always had a "thing" for Lizzy. Was that what he'd meant? Or was it something even worse than that? Fear twisted his insides into tight coils. His heart pounded with the need to find Lizzy. He slipped the halter from the horse's head and set him loose. Then he jogged to the fence, vaulted over it, and raced to his truck.

Gina climbed into the passenger seat just as he turned the key in the ignition. "Get out!" he growled, his patience gone.

"No! I'm going with you," she snapped as she pulled the door shut. "You're not gonna hurt him." Her chin was a stubborn line.

Sam couldn't afford the time to fight her. He gunned the motor and tore out of the ranch yard, hurling shards of gravel and a dust storm into the early afternoon heat. His mind was focused on one goal: he had to reach Lizzy before it was too late.

❀ ❀ ❀

Surely John's spirit watched over her, Lizzy surmised as she leaned down to touch his sun-warmed headstone, seeking comfort and reassurance. She trickled her trembling fingers through the dust that dappled its surface, her mind on the events of the last couple of days.

She'd had high hopes that Junior might have the answers she sought. Then she could leave John's death in the past and move on.

But reality continued to dog her. She was even more confused now. First, a phone call from Franny and then one that had summoned her here. Her eyes darted around the cemetery, searching for the face behind the voice. Where was her caller?

Lizzy had sat in her SUV for over an hour, doors locked, scanning the countryside for signs of life. Finally, she'd worked up the courage to leave the safety of the vehicle and enter the cemetery, her nerves twitching at each minute movement and sound.

She knew it was foolish to come here alone, but she hadn't been able to reach Sheriff Grover or anyone at the ranch by phone. Fearing she'd lose what might be her only opportunity to discover the truth, she'd finally ventured out here on her own. Now she felt like one of those little ducks in the carnival shooting gallery.

A movement startled her. She flinched as a shadow passed on the ground near her feet, then looked up to see an eagle soaring overhead. Was it an omen?

She grabbed her gyrating stomach and forced herself to take deep breaths and concentrate on the matter at hand. How had John died? Was it by his own hand? Did he reach a point where the only future he could envision was to join his mother at the bottom of a cliff? Lizzy wanted to believe that wasn't true, but she also knew how lost he'd become, relying on drugs and alcohol to make his existence tolerable.

Still, Junior claimed that John had refused the drugs and alcohol because he'd feared for his life. That corroborated what John claimed in his letter. So were those claims the result of a true set of circumstances or only the imaginings of a sick man? What could John have discovered that would have caused him to write that letter? And why didn't he go to the sheriff for help?

Shivers of foreboding crept up Lizzy's spine. Today the usually comforting cemetery felt sinister. She turned in a slow circle to study every inch of her surroundings, searching for a reason to be here. There was none.

Her thoughts turned to her father. He'd finally made contact with John and told him the truth: he was his father, not J.D. And what if John had discovered that his own father planned to kill him? Would John then fear for his life, or would he take advantage of the opportunity to escape from that miserable life? Maybe he'd thought Skip would hunt her down and kill her, too?

John had died three days before her father. If her father was in his last days with cancer, surely he wouldn't have the strength to climb up to Eagles' Nest and then overtake someone as big and strong as John had been. Besides, Junior thought it was a woman up on that hill, not her father.

Now Junior was a piece of the puzzle, too. For twenty-five years Junior had been convinced that he'd caused John's fall off that rimrock. Maybe he did.

And there was Rose, with her flowery, hand-written diary entry. The caller had said the answer was with John and his mother. Lizzy's eyes traveled to Rose's incongruous grave and then to John's and his mother's. Elizabeth and her sons had planted lilacs while J.D. planted rosebushes. John had claimed that his mother hated roses, yet they adorned her gravestone.

Mel was having an affair with J.D. Maybe Rose was, too. Unlike Mel, maybe Rose wasn't content to be J.D.'s mistress. Maybe she wanted to be his wife.

Lizzy knew she needed to talk with Eb. He had loved John like a son, but he'd also loved his sister. Was that the reason he'd looked so sickly lately—because he was torn between two people he'd loved? Surely he wouldn't protect his sister's memory over the truth of John's death? Lizzy wanted to think not, but she couldn't get past the look on his face when he'd read that page from Rose's diary.

"What happened that long ago February day?" Lizzy wondered aloud. She glanced up towards Eagles' Nest as if it might provide an answer. Instead, her eyes reached the top and were momentarily transfixed by a bright beam of light. It appeared to be the reflection from a metal object. Lizzy squinted to examine the area directly above her, her heart beating a rapid tattoo in her chest. Was someone up there?

Except for the glare, nothing seemed amiss, so she turned back to John's grave, then froze in place when a gunshot blasted the silence, and a bullet whizzed by her head.

CHAPTER 35

For Lizzy, time froze. Except for her frantically pumping heart, her body turned to stone, as still and silent as the gravestones that surrounded her. She ordered her limbs to move; they refused.

A second shot hit John's headstone, inches from her leg. Shards of rock peppered the air. Lizzy's darting eyes searched. They locked on J.D.'s black monolith.

The third bullet grazed her right shoulder—a sharp sting. She watched a crimson rivulet creep down her arm, fascinated by the absence of a screaming pain.

Another bullet zinged by on her left. She flinched, and her body surged to life. With the shot of adrenalin, she took two propelling steps and dove behind the formidable black shield—J.D.'s gravestone. Craving its protection, she pressed her back into its solid surface. Warmth oozed into her chilled body.

A fifth bullet sparked dust near her left foot. Lizzy gathered her knees close. She buried her head into them, and wrapped her arms tightly around her trembling legs. The taste of fear was so pungent she gagged on it.

Another gunshot boomed. Lizzy braced herself and cringed with the abrasive snap when it blasted the stone directly behind her. She mentally checked for wounds, then thanked J.D. for his narcissistic tendencies.

A whining ping above her head sprinkled fragments of black granite over her.

Then all was quiet—too quiet. She almost preferred the zooming bullets to the quandary of not knowing. Her body trembled uncontrollably. Her upper arm now radiated fiery pain. Slowly, she expelled her breath and turned to examine the wound. The bullet had cut a furrow through the skin and into the underlying tissue. Blood oozed from it, but it was the least of her worries. She needed to focus on getting out of here. For all she knew, the shooter was headed down the hill with a loaded rifle aimed at her.

Lizzy surveyed the graveyard. The iron gate into the Craig family plot dangled open. To reach her Explorer, she had to get through it. Her eyes traced a route to the cemetery entrance and safety. Which would be more prudent: a beeline sprint to the front gate or the slower option of weaving back and forth amongst the gravestones, hoping she didn't trip and fall?

She mentally steeled herself, then pushed herself onto her knees and cautiously peeked around the edge of the massive stone. Bunchgrass rippled in the breeze and, except for an occasional juniper tree or chunk of red rock, a sea of gold-frosted sagebrush spread out from the cemetery to the top of the hill. Lizzy examined every inch of that slope, her eyes seeking even the slightest defect. It was as it should be—not even the glare of a gun barrel—she finally concluded, trembling at the thought of leaving her fortress.

As she gathered herself onto the balls of her feet, she breathed a silent prayer: "Lord, I hope you're with me on this one, because I don't think I can do it if you're not here to move my feet and watch my back. And if you have a little courage to spare, I sure could use it."

Like a splash of ice-cold water on a sizzling hot day, realization blasted her. She glanced at John's final resting place in sudden understanding. This was what he'd lived with: hour after hour, day after day of this mind-blowing terror. Like her, he didn't know what he was walking into or running from or what lay in wait for him. Was it any wonder he'd come home a changed person, tainted by fear and the incongruent realities of war?

"I'm sorry," she whispered. Sorry for so much: for being so wrapped up in her own life that she hadn't tried to see into his. For lacking the courage to stay and see things through to the end. For not being here when he needed her. Most of all, for not believing in him.

John hadn't taken his own life. She knew that with a clarity that was unwavering. She should've known it all along. He would've fought as hard as she would now fight to remain alive.

"So let's do it," she uttered as she took a deep breath, pushed herself up, and lunged forward in a race for the iron gate.

Rounding the gate, her eyes zeroed in on her red Explorer—her homing device, a magnet drawing her forward as time perpetually slowed its pace. Over gravestones and errant sagebrush and tumbleweeds and across slabs of cement, she sprinted until her heart pounded at her ribs and her lungs begged for air, all the time waiting for a bullet to explode in her back.

She zipped through the cemetery gate, dug keys from her pocket, and glanced into the SUV. Then she climbed inside and slammed the locks into place. In her shaky right hand, the keys rattled against the dash and refused to cooperate. Supporting the key with her left hand, she finally pushed it into the ignition and turned it. Relief seeped through her when the vehicle hummed to life. She backed out onto the road and gunned the motor in her flight toward town, the booming of her heart a deafening roar.

Whether on horseback or on foot, descending the hill wouldn't be an easy task. Once it was behind her, it should be a clear road into town and Sheriff Grover. However, she wasn't out of danger yet. She might be a moving target now, but from the top of that hill, she was still a target. So she kept half an eye on the road in front of her while most of her focus was on the hill to her left.

She had rounded the corner and was ready to breathe a sigh of relief and head down the straight stretch toward the farm and town when she noticed a truck. It sat well off the main road at the very foot of the hill. Sam's truck.

A zillion thoughts raced through Lizzy's mind, a rolling turmoil of havoc and indecision. Ahead of her lay safety. But what was Sam's truck doing out here? Was Sam trying to kill her, and if so, why? And if not, then why was he here? And that would mean there was someone else here, someone who had been shooting at her. And Sam?

Enticed by the path that lay before her, Lizzy pressed the accelerator to the floor, then slammed her foot onto the brake. Again, she perceived the situation with a lucidity that mystified her. Sam wouldn't harm her. If he was here, then he was in danger, too. A lot could happen in the time it would take her to get to town . . . or to the ranch.

She rested her damp forehead on the steering wheel, panic-stricken at what she was contemplating. What could she possibly do on her own?

In answer, her mind reeled back to her first night on the farm. She pictured Sam standing in front of her with a gun clutched in his hand. It hadn't been a rifle; it'd been a shotgun, a shotgun he surely stored in his truck. With it, she'd at least have a fighting chance.

Lizzy edged the Explorer off the dirt road, into the battered countryside, and plowed through the sagebrush. Branches scraped the vehicle's sides, and large rocks sent her bouncing, but she slowly ate up the distance and was soon pulling up next to the truck. Yes, it definitely was Sam's.

Her gaze scoured her surroundings and found nothing suspicious. She dropped her eyelids momentarily, gathering courage, then stepped from the relative safety of the vehicle and approached the truck. It was empty, the windows down. She pulled herself up and peeked into the interior. Except for a denim jacket and a liter of bottled water, the seat was bare. No guns were in sight. She opened the door and picked up the jacket. It was too small to be Sam's. Her hands deftly checked the pockets but came up empty.

Fighting panic, she drew the seat forward. A canvas gun case hung from the headrests. One pocket was open—empty. She unzipped the other and pulled out a shotgun. It felt warm and heavy in her hands and came with a false sense of security. She cocked it open and found two empty chambers. "Now what?" she whispered.

Dropping the gun onto the seat, she climbed into the cab and slipped open the glove compartment. It was crammed with papers and manuals, a flashlight, and a small first aid kit—no shotgun shells. Lizzy grabbed the first aid kit and stuffed it inside her shirt. She ran a shaky hand beneath the seat and touched a square box.

"Bingo," she breathed as she dropped the box onto her lap and opened it to find six red shells. After dropping two of them into the chambers, she slammed the gun shut, crammed the rest of the shells into her jean pockets, and slid from the truck.

If she took time to think about what she was about to do, Lizzy knew she'd haul her butt back into her SUV and hightail it out of here. "So don't think about it," she muttered resolutely. "Just get your butt up that hill, and make sure Sam's okay."

Since her red Explorer would be easily spotted by anyone who glanced down the hill, Lizzy figured that taking the added time to sneak up the slope would be ridiculous. Still, she walked around to the far side and ascended where there were a few more junipers and the sagebrush grew thicker. Though the bleeding had slowed to a trickle, her right shoulder throbbed, so she shifted the shotgun to her left hand before setting off.

The sun beat down from a cloudless sky and sucked the air dry. Lizzy longed for the water bottle she'd left in the truck. Golden puffs of pollen floated around her, and insects buzzed their appreciation of the abundance of tiny pungent blossoms. An occasional birdcall and a jet's purr far above were the only other noises that broke the encompassing silence.

Lizzy kept one eye glued upward—expecting at any moment to find herself staring into a rifle barrel—and the other eye scouring her path, ever watchful for a cranky rattlesnake that had slithered out to soak up the sun after a cold, sleepy winter.

She'd never ascended the hill on foot and grew frustrated with what an arduous and slow-going task it was. Her thighs screamed for a break, and her hair and blouse were damp with perspiration, but she continued to push forward.

When the crest was finally within reach, Lizzy crouched into the sagebrush, switched the shotgun to her right hand, and slowly crept her way to the top. She peeked out over the flattened area before her and studied each square inch of it. It was as it had always been, as it had been years before when she and John had sat up here and shared now defunct dreams and as it had been several weeks ago when she'd wanted to recapture some of that lost hope.

Her mouth parched and insides vibrating like an over-revved

motor, Lizzy braced herself and stepped into the open. Surrounding her in every direction was a sweeping vista. Warily, she made her way around the periphery to look down onto the cemetery. Yes, J.D.'s massive black stone was a perfect target from this vantage point. The irony of it brought a bitter smile to her lips: what she detested in J.D. was, quite possibly, what had saved her life.

She continued on until she found the shell casings scattered in the dirt beside a large pockmarked rock. The dirt was unsettled around the rock, indicating that it had been dropped there recently. She paused to consider whether she should pick up the casings or leave them, then continued on around the rim.

John's Eagles' Nest lay directly ahead of her, its rock face marred by an incongruous amalgamation of protrusions as well as by the death of both John and his mother. It would have been easy to sidestep it and proceed on her way. Instead, she ignored her queasiness and stepped forward to peer over its edge.

What she saw immobilized her and left her gasping, too stunned to cry out. In front of her, the earth stopped and abruptly dropped off, leaving a sheer surface that extended down seventy feet or so. Lying face up on an outcropping about twenty feet below was Sam. His body curled into the cliff, legs splayed outward and one arm tucked under his head, as if he were sleeping peacefully in his own bed. The gash on his forehead told another story. Blood oozed from it to paint a ruby trail down his cheek. From this distance, Lizzy couldn't tell if he was breathing.

"Sam," Lizzy's voice rasped into the silence. Instinctively, she stepped to the very edge of the drop-off to watch for a response. There was none. Pain seared her heart as she madly searched for a route to him.

Before she actually heard the soft tread of feet, she sensed a presence and stiffened. Her hand shifted on the shotgun, the index finger finding its place on the trigger.

"He can't hear you, you know—dead." The voice behind her was vaguely familiar.

Unable to turn around on the cliff's edge, part of Lizzy's mind raced to identify the voice while the other half wondered if there was a rifle pointed at her back. Reeling with the pain of Sam's death and fear for her own safety, she scrambled to assess her situation and come up with a plan of action, one that would utilize the shotgun that shook in her iron grip. She was balanced at the edge of a precipice. One misstep and she would join Sam. She cautiously lifted a foot, prepared to step back.

"Stay right where you are!"

It was an order Lizzy didn't ignore.

"What's wrong? Cat got your tongue? Last time we met, you

sure had enough to say. Well, guess what? You won't be ordering me around today, will you? Now put that gun down on the ground."

Lizzy imagined that voice rambling on at length, its snooty, whiny tone grating on the nerves of others. She'd heard it only once before but could easily picture the perfect face and body that went with it. What she couldn't grasp was why Sam's girlfriend wanted to kill her.

"And why should I do that?" Lizzy asked, stalling for time.

"Geez, are you stupid or what? Who do you think was shooting at you—Sam? Now put the gun down before I put a bullet in your back. Or maybe I should just shoot you in the leg. That'd send you over the edge, wouldn't it? The two of you together forever. Ain't that just romantic?" She ended with a scornful laugh.

"Oh, I doubt you'd do that. There'd be no way to explain it, *Gina*," Lizzy said, surprised at the grit in her voice. She kept a death grip on the shotgun, unwilling to give it up unless she had no other choice.

"So you know my name, huh? Well, aren't you just so smart? But you know what? I won't have to explain nothin' to no one. That's what. Nobody but Sam knows I'm here, and he's not gonna tell no one nothin', is he? Now get rid of the gun!"

She ignored the command. If Gina wanted to shoot her, she'd have done so already. Lizzy's nerves were stretched as taut as the strings on a finely tuned violin, yet she had to stay perfectly still. She eyeballed the ground far below, then ordered her limbs not to shake and threw out some bait: "What makes you think Sam's dead?"

Gina bit. "What do you mean? Course, he's dead. Just look at him. Don't he look dead to you?"

Yes, Lizzy's heart cried. *He definitely looks dead*. What she said was, "Dead men don't move, do they?" and silently implored Gina to come closer and take a look. She didn't.

"He's moving? That can't be. I saw him hit the rocks, and there's all that blood. He was supposed to go all the way to the bottom, like his brother and mother. No one will question it, you know. They saw the two of you fighting in the diner. Word around town is Sam wants you to leave." She paused, then added. "You're just trying to rattle me, aren't you? He's dead; I know he is."

Lizzy forced her mind from that thought. If she didn't get out of this mess soon, she'd be dead, too. She suspected that Gina was a talker—loved to hear the sound of her own voice. Maybe she could take advantage of that and sidetrack her. "Why did you do it? I thought Sam was your boyfriend," she probed, her eyes never leaving Sam's still body.

"He was until you showed up and ruined it for me, you and your high-and-mighty attitude. Just like that, he wouldn't have nothin' to do with me. Well, that's okay 'cause guess what? It's not him I was after anyway. Geez, the guy didn't even know how to kick back and have fun. Way too serious about everything. Wasn't even interested in getting it on, if you can imagine that. Still, I'd rather have him than Chet. But sometimes you gotta take what you can get."

"Why does it have to be Sam or Chet? Why settle for someone you don't even like?" Things were starting to spin around Lizzy, and her arm pulsed pain, the shotgun too heavy in her hand.

Gina sniggered contemptuously. "What do you think? The ranch, dearie. Look at all that land out there. Part of it belongs to me. J.D. stole it from my dad, but I'm gonna get it back, it and the land the Craigs stole from my family a hundred years ago. I promised my dad, and I don't make promises I don't keep.

"I don't give a shit which one of them I have to marry to get it. Don't plan to keep him around long, anyway. Sam would've made it less complicated, but thanks to you, it didn't look like Sam was gonna be coming back to me. So he had to go. That's how I got him up here, you know? Hoped I'd be able to kill two birds with one stone, and it's working out so far."

"What do you mean, that's how you got him up here?" Gina's story didn't make sense. Lizzy was starting to question the woman's sanity. The searing sun beat down from a cloudless sky as she searched for a way out of her dilemma. There was none. A stiff breeze would catapult her to the bottom of the cliff.

Gina laughed again, high and maniacal. "I told him you were up here, that's what. Told him Chet was gonna meet you here. Everybody knows Chet's always had the hots for you—lord knows why. But Sam believed it. Did everything just like I planned. Even carried his rifle up here.

"Then he saw you down at the cemetery and got all excited, so I hit him on the head with a rock. Geez, the man weighs a ton. I thought I'd never get him dragged over here to the cliff. And now you're up here, too, right where you're supposed to be, and this is gonna work out a whole lot better than shooting you would've. They might've had a hard time believing that Sam shot you."

"Why did you shoot at me? I didn't know you were up here."

She chuckled. "Because you have to go, too. That's why I called you."

"You called me? Do you know that happened to John and his mother?"

"Yeah. They fell off that cliff. Everybody knows that."

"But you said. . . ."

Gina laughed contemptuously. "I sure did, dearie. Chet told me how you've been bugging everyone, asking questions. I figured that's all it'd take to get you here. And guess what? I was right. Only you were supposed to come up here like I told you to, not go to the cemetery."

Lizzy tensed. Unless she came up with a plan quickly, she'd die without ever knowing the truth. "Why do you want to kill me?"

"If you'd stayed away, I wouldn't have to. I've been watching you, you know? I tried to warn you off. Even butchered that damn cow—bloody, gory, mess, but Sam deserved it for ditching me for you—so you'd get scared and leave. I can't have you bringing your boy back here to complicate things. You see, I figure you're the only one who knows he's Sam's kid—Sam didn't. With you gone, no one will know he's a Craig."

Lizzy's heart beat wildly. It hadn't been her imagination. Gina had been driving that silver truck. "What are you talking about?"

"The truth, that's what. I work in Gus Woolridge's law office. He might not be there anymore, but all his files are. They popped up when we were looking for your address. And J.D. Craig kept a file there stuffed full of his nasty secrets, some of them dealing with you and your little boy. Only guess what? It's not there anymore, 'cause I'm the one that found it. And now I've got it. No one else was much interested in it, but when I saw what it was, I took me a closer look and knew it was my chance to get back what's owed me and make good on my promise to my dad.

"It's just too bad I lost that letter Franny brought to the office. I was gonna burn it. It's what made you come back here, ain't it? Chet told me you got it. You see, J.D. willed the ranch to Sam; he doesn't mention anyone else, only Sam. But Sam, he willed the ranch to his kids first, and if he doesn't have any kids, it goes to Eb and Chet. With you gone, there won't be any children to contest the will. Sam's gone now, and Eb ain't far behind, so the ranch'll belong to Chet. And guess what? Chet's gonna belong to me, so. . . ."

"Chet's not gonna belong to nobody," announced a wheezing male voice from behind Lizzy.

Alarm rushed through Lizzy and left her feeling hopeless and resigned—empty. Gina had spoken as if she and Chet were in this together. She tried to think through Gina's bizarre plan, but it was too much for her jumbled mind to process. Her injured arm was numb from holding onto the shotgun, but she refused to let it go.

She glanced down at Sam, swayed forward slightly, and swore she saw his hand move. A ray of hope shot through her. If he was alive, she had to save him.

"Chet, thank God you're here," Gina purred. "I've arranged it so you can finally own the ranch. All we have to do is get rid of her and we're set. Everything you deserve is gonna be yours—all that land the Craigs took from your family—and I'm gonna get my land back, too."

"Where's Sam? I heard gunshots and saw his truck at the bottom of the hill . . . and that's his rifle. What the hell's goin' on?"

Chet sounded perturbed.

Lizzy's heart skipped. Sam's hand *was* moving, the fingers clenching as if in pain. It was difficult to concentrate on what was going on behind her when all she could think about was getting to him. She pushed that thought aside; if Gina and Chet knew he was still alive, they'd kill him.

Lizzy tried to sense where Chet might be. While Gina was distracted, maybe she could move away from the edge without it being noticed. Then she might even be able to turn around. Ever so slightly, she turned her head to glance back. Gina stood a few feet behind her, the rifle at her shoulder. It was aimed at Lizzy, but her eyes were on Chet, who was standing several feet from her. Lizzy slowly inched her feet back.

"Sam's taken care of. You don't have to worry about him. It's just her," Gina told him, jabbing the gun barrel at Lizzy. "I'd think you'd be thrilled to get rid of her. You said she treats you like shit."

Chet's confused eyes studied Lizzy. "Get rid of her? I'm not gonna do that. Now where's Sam?" he demanded

So Chet wasn't in on it! Maybe there was a chance she and Sam would live through this, after all. That is, if Gina didn't convince Chet to go along with her plans.

"What do you mean? Course, you are," Gina screeched. "You have a right to that ranch. A good portion of that land belonged to your family before the Craigs stole it—you told me so. And you've worked that ranch as long as Sam has. With Sam and her gone, it'll be ours."

"Dammit, Gina. Put that gun down and tell me where Sam is?" Chet spat, alarm rising in his voice.

"We gotta get rid of her first. She had Sam's kid, but no one else knows that. With her gone, we won't have to worry about no kid messing things up for us."

Shock blossomed on Chet's face. He scrutinized Lizzy long and hard before he turned back to Gina. "Put the gun down, Gina."

"No, not until you push her over the edge." Gina was growing alarmed, too, her voice a high-pitched whine.

Lizzy felt their eyes on her. She stood perfectly still, gazing down at Sam, praying Gina wouldn't notice the distance she'd put between herself and the edge of the cliff.

"I'm not gonna be a part of no killin', so put the gun down and tell me where the hell Sam is!" Chet barked.

Gina hesitated several seconds, than uttered irritably, "He's down there."

Chet appeared at Lizzy's side and peered down at Sam. "Oh, God, Gina! What did you do?" he gasped, glancing back at her.

"I did it for us," Gina begged, her voice desperate. "You don't have to be a part of it. Just grab that shotgun. I'll push her over. Everything's gonna be okay. I deserve that ranch. J.D. stole my dad's farm. He forced my dad to sign our land over to him. It was the only way to get money for my mom's cancer treatments. All we have to do is get rid of her, and everything will be like it's supposed to be."

"No! No more killin'!" Chet cried as he backed away from the rim.

"Why not? Your mother did her share of killing for that land. Now it's time for you to man-up."

Without forethought, Lizzy twirled and gaped at Gina.

"Don't talk about my mother like that!" Chet demanded, his voice full of pain.

"It's true. I've got a diary full of all the awful things she did," Gina told him.

"Who did she kill?" Lizzy whispered, not sure if she wanted to hear the answer. Gina had an odd look in her eyes. Just how sane was she?

"Elizabeth Craig." Gina's voice was a harsh whisper. "Elizabeth and John."

Tears trickled down Lizzy's cheeks. Whether tears of relief or sadness, she wasn't sure. Perhaps, a bit of both.

"Shut up, Gina. You know that's a damn lie," Chet warned.

"It's not," Gina snapped. "And I've got her writing to prove it, inside a diary covered with little pink rosebuds. Sound familiar? I found it in J.D.'s files. He must've found it after Rose died and kept it for himself."

Chet's face shattered. Lizzy felt as ill as he looked. "Why?" was all she could muster.

"Why what, kill them?" Gina challenged. "Because J.D. treated her like shit, that's why. She loved him. She thought he loved her. Finally, she opened her eyes and figured out that he was only using her."

"He planted her that rose garden. He shouldn't have done that if he didn't love her," Chet gasped, his words seeking understanding for the woman who had deceived even him.

Through her anguish, Lizzy stared at them, trying to make sense of it all. "Tell me what Rose did," she begged.

Chet glared at Gina, torment written on his face. Gina seemed oblivious to what her words were doing to him. She basked in her moment of glory, a peacock preening with the knowledge that only she held.

"Elizabeth brought a lunch with her when she rode up here that day. Rose had drugged her tea. Then Rose came up and pushed Elizabeth over the edge.

"But even with Elizabeth gone, J.D. wouldn't marry her. Like all men, he kept saying he would, but he didn't. It made Rose bitter.

Just like me, she decided she was gonna get her family land back. She wanted it for you, Chet. She thought if Sam and John were out of the picture, she'd have J.D. all to herself, and she could persuade him to leave the ranch to her or Eb. But first she had to get rid of Sam and John."

A choking sound from Chet drew Gina's attention. She broke eye contact to turn to him, a faraway look to her "That's why she drugged Sam. Put something in his champagne when you were all eating dinner in town one night. Once he was passed out in your truck, she was gonna sneak away from J.D. and kill him—make it look like a robbery. But he didn't stay in your truck. Went into the Corral with you. She was furious. Sam left the next day, so she didn't get another chance at him."

So Rose was the source of what happened that night, a night that ripped all of their lives apart. A dazed numbness settled inside Lizzy. She wanted to sink down and cry for all that had been lost because of Rose's bitterness and greed. But that was a luxury that would have to wait. Right now, she needed to know one final thing: "What about John?"

Gina's wild eyes shot back to Lizzy. Was it pity Lizzy saw lurking in their depths? At last, Lizzy got the answers she'd been seeking.

"Rose figured that if she let him be, John would destroy himself. Then her diary went missing. She knew it was John who took it, but she didn't want to do anything about it until she got it back. She watched him like a hawk. Followed him to the farm and saw where he was hiding it. She took the diary and told him to keep quiet about his mom's death, or she'd say that Eb did it.

"Course, she knew he'd blab to someone about it, so guess what? He had to die, too. She knew John spent a lot of time on top of this hill, so she spiked his thermos one morning and followed him up here. Junior was here with him. They were out like lights. That's when she got rid of John, same way she got rid of his mama. She figured if they didn't believe John jumped, then Junior'd get blamed. Only Junior kept his big mouth shut—hard to believe him keeping quiet about something, huh? No one even knew he was up here."

"Oh, God," Lizzy whispered as she sank to the ground, Gina and her rifle forgotten. Finally, after all of these years, she knew the truth. Could she have saved John? Probably not. At least, no more so than he could have saved himself. Rose had been controlled by hate, greed, and anger, the same emotions that now controlled Gina.

Gina! Lizzy's head jerked up. Gina stood over her, the rifle pointed at Lizzy's head. Chet was behind Gina. He looked like he needed to curl up in a safe corner and cry. Lizzy suppressed the desire to reach out and comfort him.

In any other situation, she would've commiserated with Gina, too. After all, they were both victims of J.D.'s evil. But it was ludicrous to feel sympathy for someone who had allowed her pain to develop into a maniacal need for vengeance. Surely, Gina could've pushed forward with her life, made something of herself, as Lizzy planned to do if she made it through this alive.

"Isn't that just so sad," Gina quipped, glancing back at Chet. "Well, guess what? If your mom did what she had to so you could have the ranch, then you need to have the balls to finish it. We can do this, Chet. We can finally have what's rightfully ours. The only people who're gonna know about it are you and me and. . . ."

"You're not gonna kill Lizzy, Gina. I won't let you," Chet stated resolutely.

Gina's eyes narrowed. "Oh, I get it. You think now that Sam's dead, you can finally have her for yourself. Is that it?"

"Sam's not dead," Lizzy declared. If she didn't get help soon, he would be.

Chet eyed Lizzy skeptically, then approached the rim and looked down.

Gina stamped her foot and shrieked. "Quit it! Just quit it! Sam is, too, dead, and you're gonna join him. So just shut your big mouth before I. . . ."

Chet's voice silenced her. "He is alive," he said incredulously. "Sam, can you hear me? It's Chet."

A weak, raspy voice reached Lizzy's ears. "Yeah, I can hear you."

"No!" Gina screamed. She stomped around Lizzy to have a look, then aimed the rifle barrel at Sam.

Joy bubbled inside Lizzy; Sam was alive and able to speak. It was as if a herd of stampeding mustangs flew off her chest. Gina was not going to ruin it. She extended the shotgun barrel sideways, rammed it back against Gina's heels, and knocked her feet from under her. Gina landed flat on her back with a thud beside Lizzy. The rifle fired, the explosion pounding through Lizzy's ear.

Before Gina could get her bearings, Chet grabbed the gun from her hands and pointed it at her. "Get over there," he ordered, indicating that she was to move away from the edge of the cliff.

Tears painted streaks of black mascara down Gina's pale cheeks. "I did it for you," she sobbed as she slid her butt backward on the rocky ground, her eyes glued to the gun that was aimed at her.

"That's far enough." Chet grasped his buckle and pulled the belt from his jeans. He turned to Lizzy. "You wearin' a belt?"

Poking at the ringing in her ears, Lizzy shook her head.

"Hold that shotgun on her 'til I get her tied up then."

Lizzy aimed the shotgun at Gina. Then Chet reached down, unclasped Gina's buckle, and with one tug, pulled her belt free. Lizzy watched him secure Gina's hands and feet with the two belts.

Gina moved on to out-and-out bawling, but it didn't appear to bother Chet in the least. When he was done, he stepped back and glared at Gina. "You know, you might want to say a prayer that Sam don't die. Right now, all you have to worry about is attempted murder." Then he joined Lizzy at the rim, and they both gazed down at Sam. His eyes were closed, and he wasn't moving.

"You still with us, Sam?" Chet yelled.

Pain marred Sam's features. Lizzy held her breath, silently begging him to hold on. It seemed like an eternity before his lips finally moved, his voice faint. "Yeah, everything okay up there? Is Lizzy okay?"

"I'm here, Sam," she choked, tears stinging her eyes. "We're going to get help. Are you all right?" What was she thinking? Of course, he wasn't all right.

Sam opened his eyes and looked into hers. "I've been better. Not gonna complain, though. I'm alive."

Yes, Lizzy's heart cried. *He is alive. Thank you, God, for letting him live.* When she'd thought him dead, it was as if her own heart had stopped.

She wondered when it had happened—the night of the snowstorm? Or the following night when he'd been so upset over her confession? Or was it the previous morning, when Sam had gone into town with her to confront Junior?

No. It was long before that. She'd loved Sam Craig since that first day, the day she'd sat on the front porch shelling peas and gazed into his mesmerizing blue eyes.

Now those eyes were filled with debilitating pain. Sam couldn't move, and she couldn't get to him. She closed her eyes and prayed that help would arrive before it was too late. She and Sam had a lot of wasted time to make up.

CHAPTER 36

Lizzy studied the hand she cradled in hers, its work-toughened features a testament to the strength and character of its owner. She skimmed her thumb over the crisp dark hairs that coated its surface—watching them spring back into place—and on down the length of one long finger. Though the hand was scarred and calloused, the nails were surprisingly well kept, clean and neatly trimmed.

It was this hand that had given her the first ray of hope that Sam might still be alive. When it had moved that fraction of an inch while he lay on the ledge, Lizzy's heart had soared. Now she held onto it, unwilling to let go of something she'd let slip away from her so many years ago. She'd clung to it during the flight to the hospital. There was no way she would let go of it now, at least not until she was absolutely certain Sam would make it through this alive.

Her thoughts slid back several hours to that gut-wrenching place where Sam's life dangled precariously on a rocky cliff. She saw herself arguing with Chet, adamant that she was staying with Sam. Chet was ghostly pale, reeling from the accusations Gina had thrown at him in such a heartless manner. After what he'd just learned about his mother, he didn't want another death on his conscience, and he seemed sincerely concerned about Sam's wellbeing.

He wanted Lizzy to be the one to ride down the hill and race to the ranch for help. Lizzy refused. She had to be with Sam, to force him to hold on by sheer will, if nothing else. Besides, Chet was a more skilled rider than she. He'd get help more quickly.

Gina made it difficult to think—trussed up, howling like a starving coyote—and Chet eyeballed Lizzy like she was plotting climbing routes down to Sam and would be playing Mazama lady as soon as he was out of sight. Lizzy wasted precious minutes arguing with him. Then in frustration, she ordered him to get his ornery ass down the hill and bring some help.

In truth she worried about Chet. She and Sam owed much to him. If it hadn't been for him, they might both be lying dead at the bottom of a cliff below the spot John had once dubbed Eagles' Nest.

But they weren't, thanks to Chet. He'd climbed on his horse

and raced down that hill. When he was gone, Lizzy ignored Gina's caterwauling while she searched for a way to reach Sam. Finally, she gave up and lay flat on the ground, her head and torso suspended over the edge and eyes riveted on Sam's every move as she talked nonstop drivel for over an hour.

She cautioned him to lie still, fearful that one wrong move would send him plummeting to the bottom. He lay there, clearly in too much pain to speak, his eyes never once leaving hers and telling her more than words ever would. It was the longest two hours of her life.

By the time the buzz of a helicopter vibrated across the vast, open space, Gina had succumbed to either a reality check or hoarseness. Lizzy murmured a prayer of thanks before she stood and hooded her teary eyes to search the western sky.

It came in fast, like a thirsty mosquito, and hovered over the cliff—its propellers churning up a storm of dust and bits of grass and sagebrush—and then slowly descended onto the flat hilltop a few feet from where Gina sat, a panic-stricken expression on her once flawless face. Three men emerged from it, their arms loaded with ropes and equipment. Two of them glided down ropes to where Sam lay.

Lizzy was so caught up in watching their movements that she didn't realize Chet was standing beside her until he shouted. "Sheriff's on his way. Why don't you go with Sam? Looks like you need to get that arm looked at."

Her arm? She stared at it in awe, thinking how strange it was that it had happened a lifetime ago, yet the blood still encrusted it. She glanced up at Chet then and saw the concern in his eyes, eyes she'd once seen as only threatening. *People deal with life in strange ways,* she thought. It would be interesting to get to know Chet for the person he really was, one who hid beneath a veneer marked by snide and callous remarks.

"Thank you," she yelled as she turned away, only to look back and add, "I'm sorry."

He nodded as if he knew all the many things for which she was offering her regrets. There wasn't time to go into detail. At that moment, two men climbed up over the rim with a stretcher in tow. Sam lay on that stretcher, strapped onto the board like the papooses Lizzy had often seen when she was a young girl.

After extricating him from the many ropes that secured him, the men rushed Sam into the chopper. Fearful of being left behind, Lizzy stuck to them like pine pitch and was lifted up through the door to sit beside Sam on the endless trip to Bend and medical help. She found his hand tucked between a couple of straps and wiggled her fingers around it to clasp it tightly in her own while the men worked around Sam, probing his body and asking him questions.

Now, here she sat—floating in the aftershock and trying to come to terms with all that had happened—still holding that hand. She dropped her eyelids and thanked God that she and Sam had made it through alive.

"How's your shoulder feelin'?" Eb asked from the chair beside her.

Lizzy glanced up, shrugged her good shoulder, and mumbled. "Okay." It was throbbing from the stitches now holding the wound together, but she wouldn't admit it. Sam was lying here with several broken ribs, a dislocated shoulder, a broken leg, a lump on his head the size of a beefeater tomato, and only God knew what else, so she wasn't going to whine over thirteen measly stitches.

She turned to check Sam. He didn't appear to feel any pain. Whatever they'd slipped into his IV had him sleeping like a newborn kitten, his features relaxed into a dreamy, peaceful expression.

"Once those drugs wear off, it's gonna be nigh on impossible to keep him down. He's gonna want to get back to the ranch," Eb informed her.

Eb was right, of course. Lizzy merely nodded, too tired to think that far ahead. It was a good thing Eb was here to handle things. He'd arrived at the hospital a few minutes before Sam had been brought to his room. After a briefing of the day's events, Eb had left Chet to deal with Sheriff Grover and the ranch and had driven to the hospital in Bend alone.

The minute he'd walked through the door, Lizzy had thrown herself into his arms and soaked his shirt with tears. Thanks to him, she'd been able to sit with Sam while Eb took care of the paperwork.

"I'm gonna head back to the ranch first thing in the mornin'. That way, he won't have a way to get there," Eb added. "It's gonna be up to you to keep him in this here bed. Think you can do that?"

Lizzy doubted that she could stop Sam from doing anything he set his mind to, but she didn't want Eb to worry. "I'll do my best," she mumbled, without much conviction.

Eb studied her closely. "You gonna be all right? I'll stay if you want me to."

It would've been so easy to say yes, but she knew there was a whole lot of unpleasantness to sort out back home. And Eb's sister, Rose, was at the center of what needed to be sorted out. Chet had filled Eb in on what had happened both today and in the past. When Eb told Lizzy about that chat, he'd given her a fairly significant look, a look that spoke of how bad he felt about it all.

"No, you get back to the ranch," she assured him. "They'll need you there. I'll take care of Sam. Even if I have to hogtie him—fortunately, I do still remember how to do that—he'll stay in bed."

She must've sounded more convincing because Eb nodded.

"Okay. But I want you to give me a call if you need somethin'. We'll get your car here as soon as we can. Just don't let Sam know you have it. I'm sure Chet and Mel and probably a whole lot more folks are gonna be itchin' to come check things out for themselves, so there'll be no problem gettin' things to you."

Lizzy didn't want to think about how dirty and disheveled she was, with her bloody blouse torn in places and bits of grass and sagebrush still clinging to her hair. Eb had brought her purse to her, so she should be able to get what she needed from the gift shop or a nearby store.

"Thank you, Eb. I'll be fine. If someone could just drop by my house and give Sid—my cat—some food and water, that would be a great help."

"Will do. I'm countin' on you to call me if there's any changes here," Eb reminded her.

She nodded and pulled her mind from the changes Eb was talking about while she studied his troubled eyes.

"I should've told you, Lizzy. The minute I had my suspicions, I should've told you," he confessed.

Lizzy squeezed his hand. "It's okay. I understand why you didn't. Rose was your sister. Besides, you weren't certain," she assured him, then added, "were you?"

"No. That was definitely Rose's writin' on the diary page, but I could only guess at what she was writin' about. I knew she and J.D. were carryin' on at times, but J.D. carried on with a lot of women. I had no idea Rose took it that serious. And I knew she thought Chet deserved some of the land for himself."

He gazed at Lizzy—eyes ablaze—and slowly shook his head. "She did that to Elizabeth and Johnny. And I don't even get the satisfaction of meetin' up with her in heaven and givin' her my two cents worth. She ain't gonna be there. Good thing that stroke took her. She didn't have the wherewithal to destroy her diary. If she'd done that, we'd never have found out the truth."

"Probably not," Lizzy agreed, wondering if J.D. had read Rose's diary and let the truth slide. Junior had said that John was writing in a journal that day he died—probably recording his own tidbits about Rose and her nasty deeds. Most likely, Rose had taken John's journals with her that day to destroy them.

Eb was in such pain. It tore at Lizzy's heart. "If there's one thing I've learned, Eb, it's that you can't change what's done. It's over. Let it go."

The murmur of voices passing by in the hall filtered into the darkened room. Eb nodded wearily. "At least, Chet wasn't involved. I was worried sick about that. Worried somethin' might happen to you. He told me he didn't have nothin' to do with what was goin' on, but I didn't believe him. I should've had more faith in him."

"Chet deserves a medal," Lizzy acknowledged. "If not for him, Sam and I would probably both be dead. It's a good thing Gina *did* shoot at me or he wouldn't have ridden up the hill to investigate. After today, I'm gonna spend some time getting to know Chet."

"Yeah, it can't have been easy for him, playin' second fiddle to Sam and Johnny and now learnin' about his mom." Eb sighed, his brows creasing into a frown. "I need to get back. Be there for him."

"Well, if you're gonna take off in a few hours, you'd better curl up in that comfy chair and get some shut-eye," she told him, wishing he had his own bed to curl up on. "I'll watch Sam."

"I suppose you're right. Don't want to fall asleep drivin' home." He leaned his head against the chair back and stretched his legs out to cross them at the ankles. "I gotta say, though, that floor looks a sight more comfortable than this chair."

Lizzy smiled and grabbed a blanket from the foot of Sam's bed to hand to Eb. "Here. Maybe this'll make it a little more cozy."

Eb chuckled and took the blanket. "You sure do know the way to a man's heart, Lizzy," he crooned as he wrapped the blanket around his shoulders.

Then he gave her a meaningful look and added, "I hope this time you'll stick around and see it through."

Lizzy thought back to the document Eb had given her, the one J.D. had signed when he was dying. Gina hadn't mentioned it. In fact, she'd claimed that Sam willed his ranch to his children, which would surely make J.D.'s deathbed threat meaningless. Besides, if Lizzy had the only copy, then she had the power to make it disappear.

Eb's eyes took on an intensity that surprised Lizzy. "You belong at the farm, Lizzy, you and your boys. You should've been there all along. I'm sorry I didn't step in sooner and make things right. But that's water under the bridge. You've got a second chance. Don't walk away from it. You know, he does love you."

Yes, she did know. Or, at least, she thought she did. Right now, it felt far too complicated. All she wanted to think about was getting Sam through this. Then she'd move on to whatever might come next. She smiled and nodded to reassure Eb, then clasped Sam's hand more tightly in her own.

What would she do if he didn't love her?

❋ ❋ ❋

Sam fought his way through the haze that engulfed him. The pull of the dazed, drug-induced state was overpowering, drawing him back into its tranquil warmth. But he didn't want that. He had to do something. He knew he did. He just couldn't remember what it was.

His body was one big raging blob of pain, so much pain that it seemed dulled by the intensity. It hurt to breathe. It hurt to move even a fraction of an inch. It even hurt to think. He knew that if he let himself drift, the pain would retreat again, that awful pain that had been his constant companion since he'd awakened on the cliff ledge and stared at death.

An image of Lizzy drifted around in his head, and he mentally grabbed it and forced the fog to clear, struggling to remember. Back at the hill, it'd been Lizzy's voice he'd heard through the pain. Her voice had forced him into consciousness. He'd sensed that she was in danger, and that had helped him to focus on what was taking place above him rather than on his intense pain. Most of what they'd said up there had filtered down to him, so he'd been able to piece together what was happening.

It had fueled his fury and left him frustrated. Perched precariously on the outcropping, one slight movement could've sent him tumbling to the bottom of the rock wall. He'd been saved by some kind of divine providence. By all rights, he should be dead.

The decision to take off with Gina had been a foolhardy one. When she'd told him of Chet's intention, he'd charged ahead at breakneck speed like a lovesick idiot, his thoughts silenced by fear and anger. In fact, he hadn't stopped to consider what he was doing until he'd glimpsed Lizzy at the cemetery below him. Then it was too late. Gina had pushed him off that cliff and had then used his rifle in her attempt to kill Lizzy, a rifle he'd hauled up that hill.

What he couldn't quite grasp is what Lizzy was doing up there. If she'd escaped from the cemetery, why hadn't she driven to the ranch for help? She knew there was someone at the top of that hill with a loaded rifle, someone who had tried to kill her. So why had she stopped and climbed to the top? And she'd had a gun, too. Where did she get that?

Maybe she'd seen Sam's truck on her race to the ranch. Had she thought he was shooting at her and then been so irate that she'd climbed up there to confront him? That thought left Sam with another kind of pain, one that couldn't be squelched by drugs.

It prodded him to fight through the murkiness and lift his eyelids. It felt like nighttime. Muted light filtered into the room from somewhere. He was reasonably certain he was in a hospital room. Though he remembered bits and pieces of what had taken place after the helicopter dropped down onto the hilltop, those memories were mottled by pain and blackness. In his mind, Lizzy had been with him, but for all he knew, that was only wishful thinking.

Sam struggled to think coherently and focus on his surroundings. Someone's loud snoring reverberated nearby, nearly drowning the subdued distant murmur of hospital life.

Then there was something softer, almost more a feeling than

a sound—deep rhythmic breaths of sleep. In fact, he swore something was brushing against his hand. He curled it and encountered resistance. Something soft and pliable was nestled in it. Sam rubbed his thumb over the smooth surface and along the slender fingers, and his heart beat faster.

There was a rustling movement. He moved his head several inches, clenching his jaw against a blast of pain, and looked into Lizzy's drowsy eyes. She rubbed the back of one hand across her forehead and smiled dreamily. He stared, reveling in her beauty, and noted the blood and dirt spots on her face and the grass entangled in her dark hair. She appeared to be okay.

"I would never intentionally hurt you," he finally managed to mumble, his voice deep and raspy.

"I know that." It was barely a whisper.

Their eyes melded. He searched for words. "Then why did you climb up the hill?"

"I thought you were in trouble."

Relief flowed through him, and the first thing that popped into his mind came out of his mouth. "That was stupid."

He sensed her retreat. "So was going up there with Gina," she murmured. "Did you really think I'd meet Chet up there?"

"I didn't stop to think about it."

"Well, neither did I."

He didn't have the strength for a battle. He just wanted her back, wanted her to understand. "I thought Gina was going to kill you."

Tears gleamed in her eyes. "And I thought you were dead."

"Lucky thing Chet came along when he did," he whispered in a search for neutral ground, rubbing his thumb along her knuckles. "Are you okay?"

She nodded and seemed to relax. "Did you hear everything?"

"Pretty much."

She hesitated, her eyes unsure. "Then you know what happened to your mother . . . and John?"

"Yeah." He knew all right, and it had left deep-down clumps of sadness and loss inside him. "Guess we were both right, huh?"

A puzzled frown creased her forehead.

"All those goings-on were tied to the Sheepshooters' War and to John's death . . . and my mom's," he explained. "Both Rose and Gina wanted their land back."

"Yeah, and Rose wanted to kill you, too." She hesitated, then added, "She drugged you that night."

Her eyes probed his. "Yeah, but it still doesn't excuse what I did." He watched for a response. There was none, so he changed the subject. "How's Eb holding up?"

"He's doing okay. As soon as he found out what had

happened, he rushed here." Her eyes skittered sideways, and she smiled. "That's his snores you're hearing. He's heading back to the ranch in the morning. He says you're not to worry; he and Chet will take care of things."

Sam made a feeble attempt to smile. "Seems like I'm gonna owe Chet a lot by the time I get through this. I'll probably never hear the end of it. Might have to give him a chunk of land to get him to shut up. How's he handling this?"

Lizzy shrugged, then winced. "I hope he can get past the guilt he's feeling . . . and make peace with the fact that his mother's a murderer. He called earlier to check on you and told me Gina's being held in the county jail. She turned Rose's diary and J.D.'s files over to Sheriff Grover. You know her gift for gab. Chet said they couldn't shut her up; she confessed to everything. When I get back to the farm, I'll turn over the page from Rose's diary—John hid it in Granddad's desk—and the note from the clock."

"So did you get all of your questions answered?" he asked.

She frowned. "Questions?"

"Yeah, from the letter, the one John sent you," he clarified.

"Yes . . . well, mostly. I was never sure if there was something to it or if it was just John's imagination. Everything he wrote was true. I'm not sure I was in danger, but he was. And things were certainly not as they appeared to be. Beneath the surface, there was a whole lot of other stuff going on. In the note from the clock, John must've been writing about your mother."

She paused as if to think something through, then added, "And I think I'm finally convinced that I didn't cause John's death. Not that it helps much; I still miss him."

Something tore at Sam's insides. "So do I," he rasped. His strength was running low. While he could still talk, he needed to know. "Are you going to leave now that you know what happened to John?"

She smiled. "No. You're stuck with me."

"Can't think of anyone I'd rather be stuck with," he murmured, overwhelmed with relief and the need to pull her closer. Instead, he relaxed into the comfort of the bed.

She must've sensed his fatigue. "And now you've talked enough. Eb put me in charge of you, and I'm going to use my authority to decree that it's time for you to rest."

"Okay, but first I need to do something," he informed her.

"Do something? If you think you're getting out of this bed, well you just. . . ."

"Come here . . . please," he implored as he pulled his trembling hand from her grasp and slowly cupped it around the back of her neck.

Panic flashed in her eyes. Sam ignored it and mustered up the strength to pull her face close and whisper, "It's time we finished what we started on that dance floor." He drew her lips down to meet his.

As kisses go, it probably looked pretty pathetic, but it sure as hell felt like fireworks to him. She was tentative at first, just like that first time. Then ever so slowly, she relaxed into it and soon responded with a fervor that took him to places he had no business going in the shape he was in.

When she ran her hand through his hair, it gave him a jolt of pain and shot him back to reality. He winced, and she pulled back and stared at him with faraway eyes, concern wrinkling her forehead.

He smiled through the pain and whispered," Did I ever tell you that you're, just possibly, the best kisser in the Universe?"

"I wish you'd told me that twenty-five years ago," she said, her eyes still dazed and unfocused.

"So do I, but I couldn't. I thought you were going to marry John. I couldn't do that to him."

She nodded and whispered, "I know."

"I won't give up so easily this time," he assured her.

Her eyes took on their usual intensity. "I want to believe that."

"I promise." He knew he should stop there, but he couldn't. "How about you?"

She just stared at him, eyes uneasy. Finally she sighed and a smile lit up her face. "I love you, Sam," she murmured, her voice soft as a summer breeze. "I think I always have. I love you. That's just the way it is."

All he could do was ogle her with what he knew was a stupid-looking grin plastered across his bandaged and bruised face. His heart pattered painfully in his chest. "Well, that's good," he managed to croak.

"Why's that?"

She looked unsure, like she was ready to grab her words back. There was no way that was going to happen. He'd waited too long for this. "'Cause I love you, too," he declared. "And I'm damn tired of trying to ignore it. As soon as I'm feeling up to it, I'm gonna show you just how much I love you. So be forewarned; I plan to make up for a whole lot of lost time."

For endless moments, they gazed at each other, trying to establish some faith and familiarity in their new relationship.

"Hmmm. You're gonna make me wait, huh?" Lizzy finally asked, a twinkle in her eyes.

"At least, until morning," he teased. "At the moment, I'm a bit incapacitated, and something tells me I'm gonna need my strength." He didn't add that he was confident it would be well worth the wait.

"So your feeling a bit weak, are you?" she inquired, her voice dripping with sincerity. She drew closer to Sam, close enough that he felt her breath caress his cheek when she whispered, "Poor Sam. Maybe I can help." Her lips dropped down onto his.

Sam managed to say a silent, hasty prayer—*Lord, heal my wounded body . . . quickly*—while he still had the strength to do so.

CHAPTER 37

Lizzy stood inside the doorway, savoring every second of her new life, a precious gift she'd never again take for granted. Sam lay quietly in his hospital bed. He stared out the window at the brilliant blue sky and the mountains in the distance. With the early spring, the Cascade Range already looked like an array of giant ice cream sundaes, hot fudge and marshmallow topping flowing down their slopes—a small part of her perfect world.

It was amazing how one's life could change from a barren waste to this newfound opulence in only eight weeks. She supposed that was why it was so important to hang in there and roll with the punches during daunting times, to cling to the knowledge that no matter how bad things get, they will eventually get better. She shuddered with memories of the many times she'd nearly lost hope. When one is scavenging on the bottom, hope often seems an unreachable luxury.

Both good and bad had made the two of them who they were today. She wouldn't have wanted Sam any other way. She studied his battered body, and something tugged at her heart. Of course, she wanted him in good health, too.

Life's many lessons had transformed her. When she'd finally confronted her demons and let go of what she couldn't control, she'd discovered something far better. Contentment had settled into her very soul. She'd sought peace and had finally found it.

Sam turned towards her. Lizzy sensed the raw pain he was struggling to mask. The love he'd declared the previous night blazed in his eyes. She smiled, knowing her eyes were bright with the wonder of loving him, too.

The need to touch him drew her closer. She leaned down to gently kiss his lips, and a radiating glow spread through her body. "You're awake. I wish I could say you look better. Can I do something to help?"

He attempted a smile and barely shook his bead. "Yesterday I didn't think it could get any worse; I was wrong. I don't want the morphine, and the stuff they're giving me isn't helping much. Today should be the worst of it," he murmured, his voice soft and gravely.

His eyes drifted shut.

Lizzy wished she could harbor some of his pain for him. The Tylenol she'd taken for her shoulder had calmed it to a tolerable ache.

She debated whether she should continue with what she'd come here to do or just sit down beside him and let him rest quietly. She decided to let him choose. "I have a surprise for you. Are you feeling up to it?" Nervous twitters unsettled her.

His eyes fluttered open. "Surprise?"

"Uh-huh."

"It wouldn't by any chance be a new head . . . and a new body?"

"Uh-uh," she said, shaking her head. "I like your old head and body way too much to trade them in for something newer. Besides, I haven't had the chance to get to know them well yet," she teased as she leaned down to kiss him again. "No, this is better than that."

"Nothing could be better than that," he muttered.

"This is." She hesitated, contemplating how to prepare him. "We made the national news—you and I. I guess that's what happens when your father is J.D. Craig, deceitful, conniving, wily rancher extraordinaire."

He frowned. "That's my surprise?"

Lizzy laughed. "No. That's the reason for your surprise." She decided that it would be easier to just show him and turned to leave. "Wait right here."

"Where do you think I'm gonna go?"

A familiar glint was in his eyes when she turned back. Warmth flushed in Lizzy's cheeks. "Uh . . . I'm kind of nervous about this. I'll be right back."

Sam smiled disarmingly. "Did I tell you yet today that I love you?"

His words caused utter turmoil inside Lizzy. Her heart beating wildly, she lowered her lips to meet his, then felt his shaky hand on the back of her neck prolonging the kiss. He was weak, and his hand dropped away too soon. "Yes, you did tell me," she whispered. "Several times, as a matter of fact. But I'll never get tired of hearing it. And I'll never get tired of saying it to you, either. I do love you."

For long moments, Lizzy was lost in Sam's beautiful blue eyes, floating in a sea of happiness and enticing possibilities. At last, she sighed contentedly and said. "And now for your surprise." Then she turned and walked from the room.

She stood in the hall and gazed lovingly at the young man who had waited patiently for his summons, at his wavy dark hair and his anxious blue eyes. His tall, muscular frame leaned against the wall, legs crossed in front of him. Her heart swelled as she reached out a hand to him.

"You sure about this?" he asked doubtfully, his eyes mirroring the same apprehension she was feeling.

"Of course; you're his son."

Though she hadn't told him specifically who his father was when he was younger, she'd always been honest with him. When he'd telephoned her at the hospital early that morning, beset with worry over what he'd heard on the news, she'd asked him to come. Digesting the vital facts of his parentage hadn't been easy for him, but once he'd asked his questions and had some time to mull over the answers, he'd asked to meet Sam.

Now he walked towards her and closed his hand around hers. Lizzy took a deep breath, hoping she was doing the right thing. "Ready?"

He set his jaw and nodded, the same determined look on his face that she'd so often seen on Sam's. They stepped through the door together and approached the bed.

Sam looked straight at them. She watched his eyes catch fire and burn with a fiery passion. He tried to sit up but only grimaced in pain and sank back onto the bed. Tears glistened in his eyes.

"This is your surprise," she proclaimed proudly, her voice husky with emotion. "Sam Craig, meet your son, John."

With that, Sam reached out to shake his son's hand. Lizzy stood silently, watching the exchange, a warm glow permeating every part of her being.

If you enjoyed *Tattered Lace*, you might also find *Blue Bucket*, of interest. Set in the antique capital of Oregon—Aurora—it is a lighthearted mystery with a cast of quirky characters, numerous twists and turns, and a touch of romance:

One stormy spring morning Kit O'Maley takes a swan dive to the pavement to avoid a speeding car in the Hazelnut Grove Primary School parking lot. She bandages her injuries and stoically faces another day of teaching, but it soon becomes apparent that the frightening incident is only a prelude of what is to follow. Later that morning, an unexpected invitation arrives that sends her carefully controlled life spiraling out of control and into the antique capital of Oregon—Aurora. Soon Kit is ensconced in a historic home, the scene of a recent murder, and she's struggling to distinguish trash from treasures in her newly acquired antique shop. Nosy neighbors seem to have their own agendas, and her money-hungry kinfolk aren't feeling that family love. And everywhere she turns, she confronted by whispers from the past—a cache of gold nuggets, Oregon's lost Blue Bucket. To top it off, she must uncover a murderer before she becomes the next victim.

Suzanne Grant, who spent her growing-up years in Central Oregon, is enamored of her state's beauty, its people, and its historical mysteries. Prevalent in her writing is her fascination with the ways in which the past reaches out to impact who we are today. She enjoys weaving mystery-driven tales that transport readers into unique times and places.